JENNI CALDER was born in Chicago, educated in t
and has lived in or near Edinburgh since 1971
time teaching and freelance writing, includin;
worked at the National Museums of Scotland fr(
as education officer, Head of Publications, script editor for the Museum of
Scotland, and latterly as Head of Museum of Scotland International. In the
latter capacity her main interest was in emigration and the Scottish diaspora.
She has written and lectured widely on Scottish, English and American
literary and historical subjects, and writes fiction and poetry as Jenni Daiches.
She has two daughters, a son and a dog.

Sir Walter Scott's

WAVERLEY

Newly adapted for the modern reader by
Jenni Calder

Luath Press Limited
EDINBURGH
www.luath.co.uk

First published 2014

Reprinted 2017, 2018

ISBN: 978-1-910021-25-5

The publishers acknowledge the support of

ALBA | CHRUTHACHAIL

towards the publication of this volume.

The paper used in this book is recyclable. It is made from
low chlorine pulps produced in a low energy, low emissions manner
from renewable forests.

Printed and bound by
Bell & Bain Ltd., Glasgow

Typeset in 9.5 point Sabon by
3btype.com

contents

acknowledgements

With grateful thanks to Craig Galbraith, who read the newly adapted text for continuity and checked for errors, and to all those who encouraged the enterprise.

introduction

Waverley was Walter Scott's first novel, and gave its name to all his fiction that followed – the Waverley Novels. It was published anonymously in July 1814, but Scott was already well-known and much-read as the author of narrative poems which celebrated Scottish history, myth and landscape. The novel's full title was *Waverley or, 'Tis Sixty Years Since* which at once signalled to his readers that this was fiction set in the past, and in 1814 this was a new and adventurous notion. Although it was many years before he admitted authorship of the Waverley Novels, acquaintances and attentive readers were not slow to identify him.

In his own time Scott was enormously popular, translated into many languages and read all over the world. His influence on 19th century fiction was without parallel. More recently, although his achievements are acknowledged, he has not been much read. There is considerable academic interest, in Scotland and overseas, but there is a perception that his narratives are too entangled and his prose too dense and idiosyncratic for the modern reader. But Scott is a wonderful story teller, creating unforgettable characters and vividly illuminating the past. His intention was to capture for his readers in the first decades of the century a Scotland that was fast disappearing, if not already disappeared. He is equally precise and evocative in describing the interior of a crumbling Highland cottage and the furnishings of a grand castle, the movement of Highland cattle thieves through mountain passes and the clash of troops on a Lowland battlefield. He wants us to know how people dressed, how they spoke, the songs they sang, the weapons they carried, the food they ate.

Waverley is set at the time of the Jacobite Rising of 1745–46. Its full title signals the novel's perspective – Scott is looking back to the past and attempting to picture and explain it for the benefit of the present. The 'sixty years' is a reminder that Scott began the novel in 1805, the year in which his first long poem *The Lay of the Last Minstrel* was published, then set it aside. Years later, he rediscovered the manuscript and finished the novel. He is telling a story that is intrinsically dramatic, but it is important for his purpose that the past is explained as well as dramatised. To help achieve this, he uses the device of a young English hero of romantic inclinations, ignorant of Scotland, naïve about politics, and highly susceptible to environment and events. For reasons which Scott is at great pains to elucidate – it's worth remembering that he was a lawyer as well as a natural story teller – Edward Waverley is caught up in the Rising, and narrowly escapes the drastic consequences of its failure. In the course of describing his adventures, Scott provides an account of the Rising, its background, and genesis, as well as incident and outcome, which is both compelling and balanced.

Edward Waverley's innocence and ignorance invite a vivid portrayal of Highland life and landscape, and of the clan system, which, by the time Scott was writing, had largely disintegrated. He was writing for readers, even Scottish readers, for whom Scotland beyond the Highland Line was an almost unknown, wild country inhabited by wild people. He conveys that wildness, but also the many positive qualities – loyalty, hospitality, cultural richness. His portrayal of

Fergus MacIvor, the handsome, courageous and ambitious chieftain, his beautiful, sophisticated and equally ambitious sister Flora, his steadfast foster brother Evan Dhu, and sly, impetuous henchman Callum Beg, are strikingly memorable. The Baron of Bradwardine is a finely observed blend of the noble and the ridiculous, and his compliant daughter Rose turns out to have more spirit than first appears. Scott's subtle and dynamic portrayal of Charles Edward Stuart conveys a real understanding of what drew so many to his cause. Waverley himself is engaging and compassionate, and learns from his exposure to the harsh realities of war and politics.

Along the way are many comic characters and episodes, which leaven the narrative without undermining its historic force. Scott's use of both Gaelic and Scots adds to the novel's richness and contributes to our appreciation of time and place. He is an intensely visual writer, in his recreation of landscape and the figures that move over it, in his description of Edinburgh, in his careful depiction of the Jacobite troops mustering in the shadow of Arthur's Seat, and wrapping themselves in their plaids on the eve of the battle of Prestonpans with the campfires of the *sidier roy* (redcoats) glowing through the fog.

Scott saw himself as an interpreter of the past, and in his fiction often turns aside to provide explanations and background material. Again, we often see the lawyer's mind at work. It may be paradoxical, but two hundred years after *Waverley*'s first publication some of this explanation seems less necessary. Most of the time, the narrative itself provides what we need to know. For this reason, in undertaking the adaptation of *Waverley*, I have pruned some of Scott's lengthier filling in of background. Where further explanation is helpful, I have added footnotes. I have also trimmed Scott's prose – his delight in language can sometimes lead to an over-enthusiasm which can impede the modern reader. His love of diversion into interesting and entertaining byways can slow the impetus of the plot. His writing is full of literary allusions and quotations, often in Latin, which would have resonated with his contemporaries but much less so with today's readers: many of these have been removed. Except in cases of direct quotation I have not referenced those that remain. I have modernised spelling and slimmed down the original's profusion of punctuation. A glossary of Scots, Gaelic and unusual words is provided at the back. Words and phrases explained in the text are not included.

Waverley was the start of the career of an extraordinary novelist who brought Scotland's contentious and difficult past within the horizons of millions of readers, most of whom had little awareness of the small northern nation's distinctive history. It was followed by many more novels that dramatised and illuminated Scottish events, people, places, character and culture. In his own words, 'What makes Scotland Scotland need not be lost' – and he did his utmost to ensure that this was indeed the case. Generations have enjoyed Scott's fiction as tales of adventure, romance and conflict, and as invitations to enter a vividly illuminated and illuminating past. To read *Waverley* is to start out on an enticing journey.

Jenni Calder
September 2014

volume I

chapter one

Introductory

The title of this work has not been chosen without grave deliberation. I have assumed for my hero, WAVERLEY, an uncontaminated name, bearing with its sound little of good or evil, excepting what the reader shall be hereafter pleased to affix to it. But my supplemental title was a matter of more difficult election, since that may be held as pledging the author to some special mode of laying his scene, drawing his characters and managing his adventures. By fixing the date of my story Sixty Years before this present 1st November 1805, I would have my readers understand that they will meet in the following pages neither a romance of chivalry nor a tale of modern manners.

The object of my tale is more a description of men than of manners. The force of narrative is upon the characters and passions of the actors, those passions common to men in all stages of society, and which have alike agitated the human heart, whether it throbbed under the steel corslet of the fifteenth century, the brocaded coat of the eighteenth, or the blue frock and white dimity waistcoat of the present day. Upon these passions it is no doubt true that the state of manners and laws casts a necessary colouring; but the deep ruling impulse is the same. The proud peer, who can now only ruin his neighbour according to law, is the genuine descendant of the baron who wrapped the castle of his competitor in flames, and knocked him on the head as he endeavoured to escape from the conflagration. Some favourable opportunities of contrast have been afforded me by the state of society in the northern part of the island at the period of my history, and may serve at once to illustrate the moral lessons which I would willingly consider as the most important part of my plan, although I am sensible how short these will fall of their aim if I shall be found unable to mix them with amusement – a task not quite so easy in this critical generation as it was 'Sixty Years Since'.

chapter two

Waverley Honour. A Retrospect

It is sixty years since Edward Waverley took leave of his family to join the regiment of dragoons in which he had lately obtained a commission. It was a melancholy day at Waverley Honour when the young officer parted with Sir Everard, the affectionate old uncle to whose title and estate he was presumptive heir. A difference in political opinions had early separated the baronet from his younger brother, Richard Waverley, the father of our hero. Sir Everard had inherited from his sires the whole train of tory or high-church predilections and prejudices which had distinguished the house of Waverley since the great civil war. Richard, who was ten years younger, beheld himself born to the fortune of a second brother, and saw early that to succeed in the race of life it was necessary he should carry as little weight as possible.

Yet reason would have probably been unable to remove hereditary prejudice, could Richard have anticipated that Sir Everard would have remained a bachelor at seventy-two. The prospect of succession might in that case have led him to endure the greater part of his life as 'Master Richard at the Hall, the baronet's brother,' in hopes that ere its conclusion he should be distinguished as Sir Richard Waverley of Waverley Honour, successor to a princely estate, and to extended political connections. But when Sir Everard was in the prime of life, and certain to be an acceptable suitor in almost any family, and when, indeed, his speedy marriage was a report which regularly amused the neighbourhood, his brother saw no road to independence save that of relying upon his own exertions and adopting a political creed more consonant both to reason and his own interest than the hereditary faith of Sir Everard in high church and the house of Stuart. He therefore entered life as an avowed whig, and friend of the Hanover succession.[1]

The tory nobility had for some time been gradually reconciling themselves to the new dynasty. But the wealthy country gentlemen of England, a rank which retained a great proportion of unyielding prejudice, stood aloof in haughty opposition. The accession of a near relation of one of these inflexible opponents was considered as a means of bringing over more converts, and therefore Richard Waverley met with a share of ministerial favour more than proportioned to his talents or political importance. His success became rapid. Sir Everard learned that Richard Waverley, Esquire, had been returned for the ministerial borough of Barterfaith, that he had taken a distinguished part in the debate upon the Excise Bill in the support of government, and that he had been honoured with a seat at one of those boards where the pleasure of serving the country is combined with other important gratifications.[2]

The baronet, although the mildest of human beings, was not without sensitive points in his character; his brother's conduct had wounded these deeply. He examined the tree of his genealogy which, emblazoned with many a mark of heroic achievement, hung upon the wainscot of his hall. Had Lawyer Clippurse, for whom his groom was dispatched, arrived but an hour earlier he might have

---

[1] George, Elector of Hanover, a Protestant, succeeded to the throne in 1714. The 1701 Act of Settlement's exclusion of Catholics from the throne brought an end to the reign of the Stuarts, who went into exile. There were several attempts to restore the Stuarts to the throne, most notably in 1715 and 1745, the year in which *Waverley* begins.

[2] The Excise Bill introduced in 1733 which proposed an excise duty on wine and tobacco. It was defeated.

had the benefit of drawing a new settlement of the lordship and manor of Waverley Honour on a representative of the family associated with regicide. But an hour of cool reflection is a great matter. Lawyer Clippurse found his patron involved in a deep study, which he was too respectful to disturb otherwise than by producing his paper and leathern ink-case. Even this slight manoeuvre was embarrassing to Sir Everard, who felt it as a reproach to his indecision. He looked at the attorney with some desire to issue his fiat, when the sun, emerging from behind a cloud, poured at once its chequered light through the stained window of the gloomy cabinet in which they were seated. The baronet's eye, as he raised it to the splendour, fell right upon the central scutcheon, impressed with the same device his ancestor was said to have borne in the field of Hastings; three ermines passant, argent, in a field azure, with an appropriate motto, *sans tache*.[1] 'May our name rather perish,' thought Sir Everard, 'than that ancient and loyal symbol should be blended with the dishonoured insignia of a traitorous roundhead.'

All this was the effect of a sun-beam just sufficient to light Lawyer Clippurse to mend his pen.[2] The pen was mended in vain. The attorney was dismissed, with directions to hold himself in readiness on the first summons.

The apparition of Lawyer Clippurse at the hall occasioned much speculation in that portion of the world of which Waverley Honour formed the centre. But the more judicious politicians of this microcosm augured yet worse consequences to Richard Waverley from a movement which shortly followed. This was no less than an excursion of the baronet in his coach and six to make a visit to a noble peer on the confines of the shire, of untainted descent, steady tory principles, and the happy father of six unmarried and accomplished daughters. Sir Everard's reception in this family was sufficiently favourable, but of the six young ladies his taste unfortunately determined him in favour of Lady Emily, the youngest, who received his attentions with an embarrassment which showed at once that she durst not decline them and that they afforded her anything but pleasure. Sir Everard could not but perceive something uncommon in the restrained emotions at the advances he hazarded, but assured by the prudent countess that they were the natural effects of a retired education, the sacrifice might have been completed had it not been for the courage of an elder sister, who revealed to the wealthy suitor that Lady Emily's affections were fixed upon a young soldier of fortune. Sir Everard manifested great emotion on receiving this intelligence. Honour and generosity were hereditary attributes of the house of Waverley. With a grace worthy the hero of a romance, Sir Everard withdrew his claim to the hand of Lady Emily. He had even the address to extort from her father a consent to her union with the object of her choice. The officer immediately after this transaction rose in the army with a rapidity far surpassing the usual pace of unpatronized professional merit.

The shock which Sir Everard encountered upon this occasion had its effect upon his future life. His resolution of marriage had been adopted in a fit of

---

[1] In heraldry, three silver ermines walking towards the right with right forepaw raised, against a bright blue background. The French motto means 'without stain'.

[2] Sharpen his quill pen.

indignation. The labour of courtship did not quite suit the dignified indolence of his habits. He had but just escaped marrying a woman who could never love him and his pride could not be greatly flattered by the termination of his amour, even if his heart had not suffered. The memory of his unsuccessful amour was with Sir Everard, at once proud and sensitive, a beacon against expressing himself in fruitless exertion for the time to come. He continued to live at Waverley Honour in the style of an old English gentleman of ancient descent and opulent fortune. His sister, Miss Rachael Waverley, presided at his table, and they became by degrees an old bachelor and an ancient maiden lady, the gentlest and kindest of the votaries of celibacy.

The vehemence of Sir Everard's resentment against his brother was but short-lived, yet he continued to maintain the coldness between them. Accident at length occasioned a renewal of their intercourse. Richard had married a young woman of rank, by whose family interest and private fortune he hoped to advance his career. In her right he became possessor of a manor of some value a few miles from Waverley Honour.

Little Edward, the hero of our tale then in his fifth year, was their only child. It chanced that he with his keeper had strayed one morning to a mile's distance from the avenue of Brerewood Lodge, his father's seat. Their attention was attracted by a carved and gilded carriage drawn by six stately black horses. It was waiting for the owner, who was at a little distance inspecting a half-built farm-house. I know not in what manner he associated a shield emblazoned with three ermines with the idea of personal property, but he no sooner beheld this family emblem than he stoutly determined in vindicating his right to the splendid vehicle on which it was displayed. The baronet arrived while the boy's maid was in vain endeavouring to make him desist from his determination to appropriate the coach and six. The rencontre was at a happy moment for Edward, as his uncle had just been eyeing wistfully the chubby boys of the stout yeoman whose mansion was building by his direction. In the rosy cherub before him, bearing his eye and his name and vindicating a hereditary title to his family and patronage, Providence seemed to have granted him the very object best calculated to fill up the void in his hopes and affections. The child and his attendant were sent home in the carriage with such a message as opened to Richard Waverley a door of reconciliation with his elder brother. Their intercourse, however, continued to be rather formal than partaking of brotherly cordiality, yet it was sufficient to the wishes of both parties. Sir Everard obtained in the frequent society of his little nephew something on which his pride might found the continuation of his lineage, and on which his gentle affections could at the same time fully exercise themselves. Richard Waverley beheld in the growing attachment between the uncle and nephew the means of securing his son's succession to the estate.

Thus, by a sort of tacit compromise, little Edward was permitted to pass the greater part of the year at the Hall.

chapter three

Education

The education of Edward Waverley was somewhat desultory. In infancy his health suffered by the air of London. As soon, therefore, as official duties called his father to town, his usual residence for eight months in the year, Edward was transferred to Waverley Honour, and experienced a change of lessons as well as of residence. This might have been remedied had his father placed him under the superintendence of a permanent tutor. But he considered that one of his choosing would probably have been unacceptable at Waverley Honour, and that Sir Everard's selection would have burdened him with a disagreeable inmate, if not a political spy, in his family. He therefore prevailed upon his private secretary, a young man of taste and accomplishment, to bestow an hour or two on Edward's education while at Brerewood Lodge, and left his uncle answerable for his improvement in literature while at the Hall.

Sir Everard's chaplain, Mr Pembroke, was not only an excellent classical scholar, but reasonably skilled in science and master of most modern languages. He was, however, old and indulgent, and the youth was permitted, in great measure, to learn what he pleased and when he pleased. The looseness of rule would have been ruinous to a boy of slow understanding, and equally dangerous to a youth whose animal spirits were more powerful than his feelings. But the character of Edward Waverley was remote from these. His powers of apprehension were so quick as almost to resemble intuition, and the chief care of his preceptor was to prevent him from acquiring his knowledge in a slight and inadequate manner. And here the instructor had to combat another propensity too often united with brilliance of fancy and vivacity of talent, that indolence of disposition which renounces study so soon as curiosity is gratified and novelty is at an end. Edward would throw himself with spirit upon any classical author which his preceptor proposed, and if it interested him he finished the volume. But it was in vain to attempt fixing his attention on critical distinctions, beauty of expression, or combinations of syntax. Alas, while he was thus permitted to read only for his own amusement, he foresaw not that he was losing the opportunity of gaining the art of concentrating the powers of his own mind for earnest investigation, an art far more essential than even that learning which is the primary object of study.

To our young hero the indulgence of his tutors was attended with evil consequences, which long continued to influence his character and utility. Edward's power of imagination and love of literature inflamed this peculiar evil. The library at Waverley Honour contained a miscellaneous and extensive collection of volumes assembled during the course of two hundred years by a family inclined to furnish their shelves with the literature of the day without much discrimination. Through this ample realm Edward was permitted to roam. Sir Everard had never been himself a student, and held that idleness is incompatible with reading, and that the mere tracing the alphabetical characters with the eye is in itself meritorious, without considering what ideas they may convey. With a desire of amusement therefore, which better discipline might have converted into a thirst for knowledge, young Waverley drove through the sea of books like a vessel without a pilot or a rudder. Edward read no volume a moment after it ceased to excite his interest, and the habit of seeking only this sort of gratification rendered it daily more difficult of attainment, till the passion for reading produced a sort of satiety.

Ere he attained this indifference, however, he had read and stored in a memory of uncommon tenacity much curious though ill-arranged information. And yet, knowing much that is known but to few, Edward Waverley might justly be considered as ignorant, since he knew little of what adds dignity to man and qualifies him to support an elevated situation in society.

The occasional attention of his parents might have prevented the dissipation of mind incidental to such a desultory course of reading. But Mrs Richard Waverley died in the seventh year after the reconciliation of the brothers, and Waverley himself was too much interested in his own plans of wealth and ambition to notice more respecting Edward than that he was of a very bookish turn, and probably destined to be a bishop. If he could have discovered and analysed his son's waking dreams, he would have formed a very different conclusion.

chapter four

Castle-Building

Edward was in his sixteenth year when his habits of abstraction and love of solitude became so marked as to excite Sir Everard's affectionate apprehension. He tried to counterbalance these propensities by engaging his nephew in field-sports, but although Edward eagerly carried the gun for one season, when practice had given him some dexterity the pastime ceased to afford him amusement. Society and example might have had their usual effect, but the neighbourhood was thinly inhabited, and the home-bred young squires were not of a class to form Edward's usual companions, far less to excite him to emulate them in those pastimes which composed the serious business of their lives. Sir Everard had resigned his seat in parliament, and as his age increased and the number of his contemporaries diminished, gradually withdrew himself from society, so that when Edward mingled with well-educated young men of his own rank he felt inferior, not so much from deficiency of information as from the want of the skill to command that which he possessed. An increasing sensibility added to this dislike of society. The idea of having committed the slightest solecism, whether real or imaginary, was agony to him; for perhaps even guilt itself does not impose so keen a sense of shame as a sensitive youth feels from having neglected etiquette or excited ridicule. It is not surprising that Edward Waverley supposed that he was unfitted for society, merely because he had not yet acquired the habit of living in it with ease and comfort.

The hours he spent with his uncle and aunt were exhausted in listening to the oft-repeated tale of narrative old age. Yet even there his imagination was frequently excited. Family tradition and genealogical history, themselves insignificant, serve to perpetuate a great deal of what is rare and valuable in ancient manners and to record many curious facts. Our hero would steal away to indulge the fancies they excited. In the corner of the large and sombre library he would exercise for hours that internal sorcery by which past or imaginary events are presented.

As living in this ideal world became daily more delectable, interruption was disagreeable in proportion. The extensive domain that surrounded the Hall, usually termed Waverley Chase, had originally been forest and still retained its pristine and savage character. It was traversed by broad avenues, in many places half-grown up with brushwood. With his gun and his spaniel, and with a book in his pocket, he used to pursue one of these long avenues which after an ascending sweep of four miles gradually narrowed into a rude and contracted path through the cliff and wooded pass, and opened suddenly upon a deep, dark lake. There stood in former times a solitary tower upon a rock almost surrounded by water, which had acquired the name of the Strength of Waverley because in perilous times it had often been the refuge of the family. There in the wars of York and Lancaster, the last adherents of the Red Rose carried on a harassing and predatory warfare till the stronghold was reduced by the celebrated Richard of Gloucester.[1] Through these scenes it was that Edward, like a child amongst his toys, culled from the splendid yet useless imagery with which his imagination was stored visions as brilliant and as fading as those of an evening sky.

chapter five

Choice of a Profession

So far was Edward Waverley from expecting sympathy with his own feelings that he dreaded nothing more than the detection of the sentiments dictated by his musings. He neither had nor wished to have a confidant with whom to communicate his reveries, and so sensible was he of the ridicule attached to them that had he to choose between any punishment short of ignomy and the

---

[1]   The Wars of the Roses, 1455–85, in which the houses of York and Lancaster contended for the English throne. Lancastrian Richard, Duke of Gloucester, became King Richard III in 1483.

necessity of giving a composed account of the ideal world in which he lived the better part of his days, he would not have hesitated to choose the former infliction. This secrecy became doubly precious as he felt the influence of awakening passions. Female forms of exquisite grace and beauty began to mingle in his mental adventures, nor was he long without comparing the creatures of his imagination with the females of actual life. The list of the beauties who displayed their finery at the parish church was neither numerous nor select. By far the most passable was Miss Cecilia Stubbs, daughter of Squire Stubbs at the Grange, who more than once crossed Edward in his favourite walks through Waverley Chase. Ere the charms of Miss Cecilia Stubbs had erected her into a positive goddess, Mrs Rachael Waverley gained some intimation which determined her to prevent the approaching apotheosis. Even the most unsuspicious of the female sex have an instinctive sharpness of perception in such matters. Mrs Rachael applied herself not to combat but to elude the approaching danger, and suggested to her brother that the heir of his house should see something more of the world than was consistent with constant residence at Waverley Honour. Sir Everard would not at first listen to a proposal which went to separate his nephew from him. Edward was a little bookish, he admitted, but youth was the season for learning, and no doubt when his rage for letters was abated his nephew would take to field-sports and country business.

Aunt Rachael's anxiety, however, lent her address to carry her point. Every representative of their house had visited foreign parts or served his country in the army before he settled for life at Waverley Honour. A proposal was made to Mr Richard Waverley that his son should travel, under the direction of his present tutor. He saw no objection to this, but on mentioning it casually at the table of the minister, the great man looked grave. Sir Everard's politics, the minister observed, would render it highly improper that a young gentleman of such hopeful prospects should travel on the continent with a tutor doubtless of his uncle's choosing. What might Mr Edward Waverley's society be at Paris, what at Rome, where all manner of snares were spread by the Pretender and his sons?[1] If Mr Richard Waverley's son adopted the army, a troop, he believed, might be reckoned upon in one of the dragoon regiments. A hint thus conveyed was not to be neglected with impunity, and Richard Waverley deemed he could not avoid accepting the commission thus offered him for his son. Two letters announced this determination to the baronet and his nephew. Edward was now (the intermediate steps of cornet and lieutenant being overleapt with great agility) Captain Waverley of the Gardiner's regiment of dragoons, which he must join at their quarters at Dundee in Scotland, in the course of a month.[2]

Sir Everard received this intimation with a mixture of feelings. At the period of the Hanoverian accession he had withdrawn from parliament, and his conduct in the memorable year 1715 had not been altogether unsuspected. There were

---

[1]   The Pretender and his sons: the exiled James VIII and III was called by the Hanoverians the Pretender, from French *pretender*, to claim. James's sons were Charles Edward, the 'Young Pretender', and Henry, who became a cardinal.

[2]   James Gardiner, who was killed at the battle of Prestonpans, 1745, was in 1743 based in East Lothian. Scott described him as 'this gallant and excellent man'.

reports of private musters of tenants and horses in Waverley Chase by moonlight, and cases of carbines and pistols addressed to the baronet. But there was no overt act to be founded on, and government, contented with suppressing the insurrection of 1715, felt it neither prudent nor safe to push their vengeance farther than against those who actually took up arms. It was well known that Sir Everard supplied with money several of the distressed Northumbrians and Scotchmen who were imprisoned in Newgate and the Marshalsea, and it was his solicitor and counsel who conducted the defence of some of these unfortunate gentlemen at their trial.[1] It was generally supposed, that had ministers possessed any real proof of Sir Everard's accession to the rebellion, he would not have ventured thus to brave the existing government.

Since that time Sir Everard's Jacobitism had been gradually decaying, like a fire which burns out for lack of fuel. His tory principles were kept up by some occasional exercise at elections, but those respecting hereditary right were fallen into a sort of abeyance. Yet it jarred severely that his nephew should go into the army under the Brunswick dynasty. But he concluded that when war was at hand, although it were shame to be on any side but one, it was worse shame to be idle than to be on the worst side. As for Aunt Rachael, her scheme had not exactly terminated according to her wishes, but she submitted to circumstances, and her mortification was greatly consoled by the prospect of beholding her nephew blaze in complete uniform.

chapter six

The Adieus of Waverley

It was upon a Sunday evening that Sir Everard entered the library, where he narrowly missed surprising our young hero as he went through the guards of the broadsword with the ancient brand of old Sir Hildebrand, which usually hung over the chimney in the library beneath a picture of the knight and his horse. Sir Everard entered, and after a glance at the picture and another at his nephew, began a little speech.

'My dear Edward, it is God's will, and also the will of your father, that you should leave us to take up the profession of arms. I have made such arrangements that will enable you to take the field as the probable heir of the house of Waverley, and sir, in the field of battle you will remember what name you bear. And Edward, my dear boy, remember also that you are the last of that race, and the only hope of its revival depends upon you. Therefore, as far as duty and honour will permit, avoid unnecessary danger and keep no company with rakes, gamblers and whigs, of whom there are but too many in the service into which you are going. Your

---

[1]   Newgate and the Marshalsea were prisons in London, the former on the site of the Old Bailey, the latter in Southwark.

colonel, as I am informed, is an excellent man for a presbyterian, but you will remember your duty to God, the Church of England and the – (this breach ought to have been supplied with the word king, but as unfortunately the word conveyed a double and embarrassing sense, the knight filled up the blank otherwise) – the church of England, and all constituted authorities.' Then he carried his nephew to the stables to see the horses he destined for his campaign. Two were black, superb chargers both. The other three were stout active hacks, designed for the road or for his domestics, of whom two were to attend him from the Hall. 'You will depart with but a small retinue,' quoth the baronet, 'compared to Sir Hildebrand when he mustered before the gate of the Hall a larger body of horse than your whole regiment consists of.' Sir Everard had brightened the chain of attachment between the recruits and their young captain, not only by a copious repast of beef and ale by way of parting feast, but by such a pecuniary donation to each individual as tended rather to improve the conviviality than the discipline of their march.

After inspecting the cavalry, Sir Everard again conducted his nephew to the library, where he produced a letter sealed with the Waverley coat-of-arms. It was addressed, 'For Cosmo Comyne Bradwardine, Esq. of Bradwardine, at his principal mansion of Tully Veolan, in Perthshire, North Britain. These – By the hand of Captain Edward Waverley, nephew of Sir Everard Waverley of Waverley Honour, Bart.' The gentleman to whom this ceremonious greeting was addressed had been in arms for the exiled family of Stuart in the year 1715, and was made prisoner at Preston, Lancashire.[1] He was a man of a very ancient family and somewhat embarrassed fortune, a scholar according to the scholarship of Scotchmen, that is his learning was more diffuse than accurate. Sir Everard accomplished the final deliverance of Cosmo Comyne Bradwardine from certain very awkward consequences of a plea before the king at Westminster. The baron of Bradwardine posted down to pay his respects at Waverley Honour. A congenial passion for field-sports and a coincidence in political opinions cemented his friendship with Sir Everard; and having spent several weeks at Waverley Honour he departed with many expressions of regard, warmly pressing the baronet to return his visit and partake of the diversion of grouse-shooting upon his moors in Perthshire.

Sir Everard's habits of indolence interfered with his wish to pay a visit to Perthshire, but there was still maintained a yearly intercourse of a hamper or cask or two between Waverley Honour and Tully Veolan, the English exports consisting of mighty cheeses and mightier ale, pheasants and venison, and the Scottish returns being grouse, white hares, pickled salmon and usquebaugh, all which were meant and received as pledges of constant friendship between these two important houses. It followed as a matter of course that the heir-apparent of Waverley Honour could not with propriety visit Scotland without being furnished with credentials to the Baron of Bradwardine.

When this matter was settled, Mr Pembroke expressed his wish to take a private leave of his dear pupil. It had pleased Heaven, he said, to place Scotland in a more deplorable state of darkness than even this unhappy kingdom of England.

---

[1] At Preston, Lancashire in November 1715 a Jacobite army was besieged and defeated by government forces.

Here, at least, the church of England yet afforded a glimmering light. There was a hierarchy, there was a liturgy. But in Scotland it was utter darkness, and excepting a sorrowful, scattered and persecuted remnant, the pulpits were abandoned to presbyterians and to sectaries of every description. It should be his duty to fortify his dear pupil to resist such pernicious doctrines in church and state as must necessarily be forced at times upon his unwilling ears. Here he produced two immense folded packets, which appeared each to contain a whole ream of closely-written manuscript. They had been the labour of the worthy man's whole life, and never were labour and zeal more absurdly wasted. His destined proselyte, seeing nothing very inviting in the titles of the tracts and appalled by the bulk of the manuscript, quietly consigned them to a corner of his travelling trunk.

Aunt Rachael's farewell was brief and affectionate. She cautioned her dear Edward, whom she probably deemed somewhat susceptible, against the fascination of Scottish beauty. She allowed that the northern part of the island contained some ancient families, but they were all whigs and presbyterians except the Highlanders, and respecting them there could be no great delicacy among the ladies where the gentlemen's usual attire was, to say the least, very singular and not at all decorous. She concluded her farewell with a moving benediction, and gave the young officer a valuable diamond ring and a purse of broad gold pieces.

chapter seven

A Horse-Quarter in Scotland

The next morning Edward Waverley departed from the Hall amid the blessings and tears of all the domestics and the inhabitants of the village. He proceeded on horseback to Edinburgh, and from thence to Dundee, a sea-port on the eastern coast of Angus-shire where his regiment was quartered.

He now entered upon a new world, where, for a time, all was beautiful because all was new. Colonel Gardiner, the commanding officer of the regiment, was himself a study for the romantic and inquisitive youth. In person he was tall, handsome and active, though somewhat advanced in life. In his early years he had been a very gay young man, and strange stories were circulated about his sudden conversion from doubt, if not infidelity, to a serious turn of mind. It may be easily imagined that the officers of a regiment commanded by so respectable a person composed a society more sedate than a military mess always exhibits, and that Waverley escaped some temptations to which he might otherwise have been exposed.

Meanwhile his military education proceeded. Already a good horseman, he received instructions in field duty; but when his first ardour was passed his progress fell short of what he wished and expected. The duty of an officer, accompanied with so much pomp and circumstance, is in its essence a very dry study depending chiefly upon arithmetical combinations requiring much attention and a cool head to bring them into action. Our hero was liable to fits of absence, in which his blunders excited some mirth and called down some reproof. This circumstance impressed him with a painful sense of inferiority. He asked himself in vain why his eye could not judge of distance or space so well as those of his companions, why his head was not always successful in disentangling the various movements necessary to execute a particular evolution, and why his memory did not always retain technical phrases and minute points of field discipline. Waverley was naturally modest, and therefore did not fall into the egregious mistake of supposing such rules of military duty beneath his notice or conceiving himself to be born a general because he made an indifferent subaltern. The truth was that the vague and unsatisfactory course of reading which he had pursued had given him that wavering habit of mind which is most averse to study and riveted attention. Time in the meanwhile hung heavy on his hands. The gentry of the neighbourhood showed little hospitality to the military guests and the people of the town, chiefly engaged in mercantile pursuits, were not such as Waverley chose to associate with. The arrival of summer, and a curiosity to know something more of Scotland than he could see in a ride from his quarters, determined him to request leave of absence for a few weeks. He resolved first to visit his uncle's ancient friend. He travelled on horseback with a single attendant, and passed his first night at a miserable inn where the landlady had neither shoes nor stockings, and the landlord was disposed to be rude to his guest because he had not bespoke the pleasure of his society to supper. The next day, traversing an open and unenclosed country, Edward gradually approached the Highlands of Perthshire, which at first had appeared a blue outline in the horizon but now swelled into huge gigantic masses which frowned defiance over the more level country that lay beneath them. Near the bottom of this stupendous barrier, but still in the Lowland country, dwelt Cosmo Comyne Bradwardine of Bradwardine, and there had dwelt his ancestors since the days of the gracious King Duncan.[1]

chapter eight

A Scottish Manor House Sixty Years Since

It was about noon when Captain Waverley entered the straggling hamlet of Tully Veolan, close to which was situated the mansion of the proprietor. The

---

[1]   Duncan I, king of Scots 1034–1040, murdered by Macbeth.

houses seemed miserable in the extreme, especially to an eye accustomed to the smiling neatness of English cottages. They stood on each side of a straggling un-paved street where children, almost in a primitive state of nakedness, lay sprawling as if to be crushed by the hoofs of the first passing horse. Occasionally, when such a consummation seemed inevitable, a watchful old granddame rushed out of one of these miserable cells, dashed into the middle of the path, and snatching up her own charge, saluted him with a sound cuff and transported him back to his dungeon, the little white-headed varlet screaming a shrilly treble to the growling remon-strance of the enraged matron. Another part of this concert was sustained by the incessant yelping of a score of idle curs, which followed, snarling and snapping at the horses' heels.

As Waverley moved on, here and there an old man bent as much by toil as years, his eyes bleared with age and smoke, tottered to the door of the hut to gaze on the stranger and the horses, and then assembled with his neighbours to discuss whence the stranger came and where he might be going. Three or four village girls, returning from the well or brook with pitchers and pails upon their heads, formed more pleasing objects, with their thin short-gowns and single petticoats, bare arms, legs and feet, uncovered heads and braided hair. Nor could a lover of the picturesque have challenged either the elegance of their costume or the symmetry of their shape, although a mere Englishman might have wished for clothes less scanty, the feet and legs somewhat protected from the weather, the head and complexion shrouded from the sun, or perhaps might even have thought the whole person and dress considerably improved by a plentiful application of spring water with soap. The whole scene was depressing, for it argued a stagna-tion of industry and perhaps of intellect. Even curiosity, the busiest passion of the idle, seemed of a listless cast in the village of Tully Veolan. The curs alone showed any activity. The villagers stood and gazed at the handsome young officer and his attendant, but without those eager looks that indicate the earnestness with which those who live in monotonous ease at home look out for amusement abroad. Yet the physiognomy of the people was far from exhibiting stupidity. Their features were rough but remarkably intelligent, and from the young women an artist might have chosen more than one whose features and form resembled those of Minerva.[1] The children also, whose skins were burned black and whose hair was bleached white, had a look of life and interest. It seemed as if poverty and indolence, its too frequent companion, were combining to depress the natural genius of a hardy and intelligent peasantry.

Such thoughts crossed Waverley's mind as he paced his horse slowly through the rugged and flinty street of Tully Veolan, interrupted only in his meditations by the occasional cabrioles which his charger exhibited at the assaults of the canine Cossacks.[2] The village was more than half a mile long, the cottages irregularly divided by yards of different sizes which were stored with gigantic plants of kale encircled with groves of nettles, and here and there a huge hemlock or the na-tional thistle. The dry stone walls were intersected by narrow lanes leading to the

---

[1]   Roman goddess of wisdom and handicrafts.
[2]   Tribal cavalrymen from southeastern Russia.

common field, where the joint labour of the villagers cultivated alternate ridges and patches of rye, oats, barley and pease, each of such minute extent that at a little distance the variety of the surface resembled a tailor's book of patterns. In a few instances there appeared behind the cottages miserable wigwams compiled of earth, loose stones and turf, where the wealthy might perhaps shelter a starved cow or sorely galled horse. But almost every hut was fenced in front by a huge black stack of turf on one side of the door, while on the other the family dunghill ascended in noble emulation.

About a bow-shot from the end of the village appeared the parks of Tully Veolan, square fields surrounded and divided by stone walls five feet in height. In the centre of the exterior barrier was the upper gate of the avenue opening under an archway, battlemented on the top and adorned with two large weather-beaten mutilated masses of upright stone, which had once represented two ramp-ant bears, the supporters of the family of Bradwardine. The avenue was straight, running between a double row of ancient horse-chestnuts, planted alternately with sycamores which rose to such huge height and flourished so luxuriantly that their boughs completely over-arched the road beneath. Beyond these venerable ranks were two walls overgrown with ivy, honeysuckle, and other climbing plants. The avenue seemed little trodden, clothed with grass of a deep and rich verdure excepting where a foot-path tracked the way from the upper to the lower gate. This nether portal opened in front of a wall battlemented on the top, over which were seen the high steep roofs and narrow gables of the mansion, with ascending lines cut into steps and corners decorated with small turrets. One of the folding leaves of the lower gate was open, and as the sun shone full into the courtyard behind a long line of brilliancy was flung from the aperture up the dark and sombre avenue.

The solitude and repose of the whole scene seemed almost monastic and Waverley, who had given his horse to his servant on entering the first gate, walked slowly down the avenue, enjoying the cooling shade and so much pleased with the placid ideas of seclusion excited by this quiet scene that he forgot the misery of the hamlet he had left behind him. The opening into the paved courtyard corresponded with the rest of the scene. The house, which seemed to consist of two or three high, steep-roofed buildings projecting from each other at right angles, formed one side of the inclosure. It had been built at a period when castles were no longer necessary, and when the Scottish architects had not yet acquired the art of designing a domestic residence. The windows were very small. The roof had projections called bartizans and displayed at each angle a small turret, rather resembling a pepper-box than a Gothic watch-tower. Neither did the front indicate absolute security from danger. There were loop-holes for musquetry and iron stanchions on the lower windows, probably to repel any roving band of gypsies or resist a predatory visit from the caterans of the neighbouring Highlands. Stables and other offices occupied another side of the square. The former were low vaults, with narrow slits instead of windows. Above these dungeon-looking stables were granaries, called girnels, and other offices, to which there was access by outside stairs. Two battlemented walls, one of which faced the avenue and the other divided the court from the garden, completed the inclosure. In one corner was a pigeon-house, of great size and rotundity.

Another corner of the court displayed a fountain, where a huge bear carved in stone predominated over a large stone basin into which he disgorged water. This work of art was the wonder of the country for ten miles round. All sorts of bears, small and large, were carved over the windows, upon the ends of gables, terminated the spouts, and supported the turrets, with the ancient family motto 'Bewar the Bar' cut under each. The court was spacious and well paved. Everything around appeared solitary, and would have been silent but for the splashing of the fountain, and the whole scene maintained the monastic illusion which the fancy of Waverley had conjured up.

chapter nine

More of the Manor House and its Environs

After having satisfied his curiosity by gazing around, Waverley applied himself to the massive knocker of the hall-door, the architrave of which bore the date 1594. But no answer was returned, though the peal resounded and was echoed from the court-yard walls, startling the pigeons in clouds from the rotunda which they occupied and alarming anew even the village curs, which had retired to sleep upon their respective dunghills. Tired of the din which he created and the unprofitable responses which it excited, Waverley turned to a little oaken wicker-door, well clenched with iron nails, which opened in the court-yard wall. It admitted him into the garden which presented a pleasing scene. The southern side of the house, clothed with fruit trees and having many evergreens trained upon its walls, extended its irregular front along a terrace bordered with flowers and choice shrubs. This elevation descended by flights of steps into the garden proper, and was fenced along the top by a stone parapet with a heavy balustrade ornamented with huge grotesque figures of animals seated upon their haunches, among which the favourite bear was repeatedly introduced. Placed in the middle of the terrace a huge animal of the same species supported on his head and fore paws a sun-dial of large circumference.

The garden exhibited a profusion of flowers and evergreens. It was laid out in terraces which descended from the western wall to a large brook, which had a tranquil appearance where it served as a boundary to the garden but near the extremity leaped in tumult over a dam, and there forming a cascade was overlooked by a summer-house with a gilded bear on the top. The brook, assuming its natural rapid and fierce character, escaped down a deep and wooded dell from which arose a massive but ruinous tower, the former habitation of the Barons of Bradwardine. The park displayed a narrow meadow, or *haugh* as it was called, which formed a small washing-green, the bank behind it covered by ancient trees.

Waverley began to despair of gaining entrance into this seemingly enchanted mansion when a man advanced up one of the garden alleys towards the terrace. Trusting this might be a gardener or some domestic belonging to the house, Edward descended the steps to meet him, but as the figure approached he was struck by the oddity of his appearance and gestures. Sometimes he held his hands clasped over his head, sometimes he swung them like a pendulum, and anon he flapped them repeatedly across his breast. His gait was as singular as his gestures, for at times he hopped with great perseverance on the right foot, then on the left, and then putting his feet close together he hopped upon both at once. His dress, antiquated and extravagant, consisted in a grey jerkin with scarlet cuffs and slashed sleeves showing a scarlet lining, with a pair of scarlet stockings and a scarlet bonnet proudly surmounted by a turkey feather. It was apparently neither idiocy nor insanity which gave that wild, unsettled expression to a face which naturally was rather handsome, but something that resembled a compound of both, where the simplicity of the fool was mixed with the extravagance of a crazed imagination. He sang with great earnestness, and not without some taste, a fragment of an old Scotch ditty:

> *False love, and hast thou played me thus*
> *In summer among the flowers?*
> *I will repay thee back again*
> *In winter among the showers.*[1]

Here lifting up his eyes he beheld Waverley, and instantly doffed his cap with many grotesque signals of surprise and respect. Edward, though with little hope of receiving answer, requested to know whether Mr Bradwardine were at home. The questioned party replied:

> *The Knight's to the mountain*
> *His bugle to wind*
> *The Lady's to greenwood*
> *Her garland to bind.*[2]

This conveyed no information and Edward, repeating his queries, received a rapid answer in which, from the haste and the peculiarity of the dialect, the word 'butler' was alone intelligible. Waverley then requested to see the butler, upon which the fellow, with a knowing look, made a signal to Edward to follow and began to caper down the alley up which he had made his approaches. 'A strange guide this,' thought Edward, 'but wiser men have been led by fools.' By this time he had reached the bottom of the alley, where on a little parterre of flowers he found

---

[1] Traditional, collected in David Herd's *Ancient and Modern Scottish Songs*, 1776, vol. ii.
[2] Probably by Scott.

an old man at work without his coat, whose appearance hovered between that of an upper servant and gardener, his red nose and ruffled shirt belonging to the former profession, his hale and sunburnt visage, with his green apron, to the latter.

The major domo, for such he was, laid down his spade, slipped on his coat in haste, and, with a wrathful look at Edward's guide, probably excited by his having introduced a stranger while he was engaged in this laborious and, as he might suppose it, degrading office, requested to know the gentleman's commands. Being informed that he wished to pay his respects to his master, that his name was Waverley, the old man's countenance assumed a great deal of respectful importance. He could take it upon his conscience to say his honour would have exceeding pleasure in seeing him. Would not Mr Waverley choose some refreshment after his journey? His honour was with the folk who were getting doon the dark hag. The two gardener lads had been ordered to attend him, and he had been just amusing himself in the meantime with dressing Miss Rose's flower-bed that he might be near to receive his honour's orders. He commanded Edward's fantastic conductor, by the name of Davie Gellatly, to go look for his honour and tell him there was a gentleman from the south had arrived at the Ha'. 'Can this poor fellow deliver?' asked Edward. 'With all fidelity, sir, to any one whom he respects. I would hardly trust him with a long message by word of mouth – though he is more knave than fool.'

Mr Gellatly seemed to confirm the butler's last observation by twisting his features at him, when he was looking another way, into the resemblance of the grotesque face on the bole of a german tobacco pipe, after which he danced off to discharge his errand. 'He's an *innocent*, sir,' said the butler; 'there is one such in almost every laird's house in the country, but ours is brought far ben. He used to work a day's turn well enough, but he helped Miss Rose when she was flemit with the Laird of Killancureit's new English bull, and since that time we call him Davie Do-little, for he has done nothing but dance up and down without doing a single turn, unless trimming the laird's fishing-wand or may be catching a dish of trouts at an orra time. But here comes Miss Rose, who will be especial glad to see one of the house of Waverley at her father's mansion of Tully Veolan.

chapter ten

Rose Bradwardine and her Father

Miss Bradwardine was but seventeen, a very pretty girl of the Scotch cast of beauty, with a profusion of hair of paley gold, and skin like the snow of her own mountains in whiteness. Her features had a lively expression, her complexion was so pure as to seem transparent, and the slightest cause sent her whole blood at once to her face and neck. Her form was remarkably elegant, and her motions easy and unembarrassed. She came from another part of the garden to receive Captain Waverley with a manner that hovered between bashfulness and courtesy.

Edward learned from her that the *dark hag*, which had somewhat puzzled him, had nothing to do either with a black cat or a broomstick, but was simply a portion of oak copse which was to be felled that day. She offered to show the stranger the way to the spot, but they were prevented by the appearance of the Baron of Bradwardine in person, clearing the ground at a prodigious rate with long strides which reminded Waverley of the seven-league-boots of the nursery fable.[1] He was a tall, thin, athletic figure, old indeed and grey-haired, but with every muscle rendered as tough as whip-cord by constant exercise. He was dressed carelessly, more like a Frenchman than an Englishman, while from his hard features and rigidity of stature he bore some resemblance to a Swiss officer of the guards.[2] His language and habits were as heterogeneous as his external appearance.

Owing to his natural disposition to study, or perhaps to a Scottish fashion of giving young men of rank a legal education, he had been bred with a view to the bar. But the politics of his family precluding the hope of his rising in that profession, Mr Bradwardine travelled for several years and made five campaigns in foreign service. After 1715 he had lived in retirement, conversing almost entirely with those of his own principles. The prejudices of ancient birth and jacobite politics, greatly strengthened by habits of solitary authority, though exercised only within the bounds of his half-cultivated estate, were there indisputable and undisputed. For, 'the lands of Bradwardine had been erected into a free barony by a charter from David the First, which implied that the Baron of Bradwardine might imprison, try, and execute his vassals and tenants at his pleasure'.[3] The present possessor of this authority was more pleased in talking about prerogative than in exercising it. Still, the conscious pride of possessing it gave additional importance to his language and deportment.

At his first address to Waverley it would seem that the hearty pleasure he felt to behold the nephew of his friend had somewhat discomposed the upright dignity of the Baron's demeanour, for the tears stood in the old gentleman's eyes when, having first shaken Edward heartily by the hand, he embraced him and kissed him on both sides of the face. The hardness of his grip and the quantity of Scotch snuff which his *accolade* communicated, called corresponding drops of moisture to the eyes of his guest. 'It makes me young again to see you here, Mr Waverley! A worthy scion of the old stock of Waverley Honour, and you have the look of the old line, not so portly yet as my old friend Sir Everard. And so you have mounted the cockade?[2] Right, right; though I could have wished the

---

[1] Fairy tale boots which allow the wearer to cover seven leagues in a single step.

[2] Swiss mercenaries were employed by the kings of France and were particularly noted as disciplined and steadfast.

[3] A free barony was an estate granted by the Crown along with jurisdiction covering civil disputes and all but the most serious crimes. David I of Scotland reigned 1124–1153.

[4] A knot of ribbon worn on an army officer's hat, black for the Hanoverians, white for the Jacobites.

colour different. But no more of that, I am old, and times are changed. And how does the worthy knight baronet and the fair Mrs Rachael? Ah, ye laugh, young man, but she was the fair Mrs Rachael in the year of grace seventeen hundred and sixteen, but time passes, that is most certain. Ye are most heartily welcome to my poor house of Tully Veolan! Hie to the house, Rose, and see that Alexander Saunderson looks out the old Chateau Margoux, which I sent from Bordeaux to Dundee in the year 1713.'[1]

Rose tripped off demurely enough till she turned the first corner, and then ran that she might gain leisure to put her own dress in order and produce all her little finery, an occupation for which the approaching dinner-hour left but little time. 'We cannot rival the luxuries of your English table, Captain Waverley, but I trust you will applaud my Bordeaux. Right glad I am that ye are here to drink the best my cellar can make forthcoming.' This speech continued from the lower alley up to the door of the house, where four or five servants in old-fashioned liveries, headed by Alexander Saunderson the butler, who now bore no token of the sable stains of the garden, received them. With much ceremony and real kindness the Baron conducted his guest into the great dining parlour hung round with pictures of his ancestry, where a table was set forth for six persons. A bell announced the arrival of other guests.

These, as the Baron assured his young friend, were very estimable persons. 'There was the young Laird of Balmawhapple, given much to field-sports but a very principled young gentleman. Then there was the Laird of Killancureit, who had devoted his leisure *until* tillage and agriculture, and boasted himself to be possessed of a bull of matchless merit. He is but of yeoman extraction, but this gentleman has good blood in his veins by the mother and grandmother and he is well liked and knows his own place. And God forbid, Captain Waverley, that we of irreproachable lineage should exult over him, when it may be that in the eighth, ninth, or tenth generation, his progeny may rank with the old gentry of the country. Rank and ancestry, sir, should be the last words in the mouths of us men of unblemished race. There is besides a clergyman of the true episcopal church of Scotland. He was a confessor in her cause after the year 1715 when a whiggish mob destroyed his meeting-house and plundered his dwelling-place of four silver spoons, his mart and his meal-ark, and two barrels, one of single and one of double ale, besides three bottles of brandy. My baron-baillie and doer, Mr Duncan Macwheeble, is the fourth of our list.

---

[1] Claret, wine of Bordeaux, France.

chapter eleven

The Banquet

The entertainment was ample and the guests did great honour to it. The Baron eat like a famished soldier, the Laird of Balmawhapple like a sportsman, Killancureit like a farmer, Waverley himself like a traveller, and Baillie Macwheeble eat like all four together, though either out of more respect or in order to show his sense that he was in the presence of his patron, he sat upon the edge of his chair, placed at three feet distance from the table and achieved a communication with his plate by projecting his person towards it in a line which obliqued from the bottom of his spine, so that the person who sat opposite to him could only see the foretop of his periwig.

This stooping position might have been inconvenient to another, but long habit made it, whether seated or walking, perfectly easy to the worthy Baillie. In the latter posture, it occasioned an unseemly projection of the person toward those who happened to walk behind, but those being at all times his inferiors he cared very little what inference of contempt they might derive from the circumstance. When he waddled across the court to and from his old grey pony, he somewhat resembled a turnspit walking upon its hind legs.[1]

The clergyman was an interesting old man, with much the air of a sufferer for conscience sake. When the Baron was out of hearing, the Baillie used sometimes gently to rally Mr Rubrick, upbraiding him with the nicety of his scruples. Indeed, he himself, though at heart a keen partisan of the exiled family, had kept pretty fair with all the different turns of state in his time.

When the dinner was removed, the baron announced the health of the king, politely leaving to the consciences of his guests to drink to the sovereign *de facto* or *de jure*, as their politics inclined.[2] Miss Bradwardine, who had done the honours with natural grace and simplicity, retired and was soon followed by the clergyman. Among the rest of the party the wine flowed freely round, although Waverley, with some difficulty, obtained the privilege of sometimes neglecting his glass. At length, the Baron made a private signal to Mr Saunders Saunderson, who left the room with a nod and soon after returned, his grave countenance mantling with a mysterious smile, and placed before his master a small oaken casket mounted with brass ornaments of curious form. The Baron unlocked the casket, raised the lid and produced a golden goblet moulded into the shape of a rampant bear, which the owner regarded with a look of mingled reverence and delight. 'It represents the chosen crest of our family, a bear, and *rampant*, because a good herald will depict every animal in its noblest posture. Now, we hold this most honourable achievement by the concession of arms of Frederick Red-beard, emperor of Germany, to my predecessor Godmund Bradwardine, being the crest

---

[1]   A small dog on a treadmill which turned a roasting spit.

[2]   Latin, in fact or by right, ie toasting either George II, the actual monarch, or James Stuart, believed to be king by right.

of a gigantic Dane whom he slew in the lists in the Holy Land.[1] The cup, Captain Waverley, was wrought by command of Saint Duthac, abbot of Aberbrothock, for another baron of the house of Bradwardine, who had valiantly defended the patrimony of that monastery.[2] It is properly termed the Blessed Bear of Bradwardine and has always been esteemed a solemn heirloom of our house, nor is it ever used but upon seasons of high festival, and such I hold to be the arrival of the heir of Sir Everard under my roof. I devote this draught to the health and prosperity of the highly-to-be-honoured house of Waverley.' During this harangue he carefully decanted a cobwebbed bottle of claret into the goblet, and at the conclusion devoutly quaffed off the contents of the Blessed Bear of Bradwardine.

Edward, with horror and alarm, beheld the animal making his rounds, and thought with great anxiety upon the motto 'Beware the bear', but foresaw that a refusal on his part to pledge their courtesy would be extremely ill received. Resolving, therefore, to submit to this last piece of tyranny and then to quit the table, he did justice to the company in the contents of the Blessed Bear, and felt less inconveniency from the draught than he could possibly have expected. The others began to show symptoms of innovation. The frost of etiquette and pride of birth began to give way and the formal appellatives with which the three dignitaries had addressed each other were now abbreviated into Tully, Bally and Killie. When a few rounds had passed, the two latter craved permission to ask the grace cup. This was at length produced, and Waverley concluded the orgies of Bacchus were terminated.[3] He was never more mistaken in his life. As the guests had left their horses at the small inn of the village, the Baron could not, in politeness, avoid walking with them up the avenue, and Waverley attended the party. But when they arrived at Luckie Macleary's, the Lairds of Balmawhapple and Killancureit declared their determination to acknowledge the hospitality of Tully Veolan, by partaking what they called *doch and dorroch*, a stirrup-cup, to the honour of the Baron's roof-tree.[4]

The Baillie, knowing by experience that the day's joviality hitherto sustained at the expense of his patron might terminate partly at his own, had mounted his pony and, between gaiety of heart and alarm for being hooked into a reckoning, spurred him into a hobbling canter. The others entered the change-house, leading Edward in unresisting submission. Widow Macleary seemed to have expected this visit, for it was the usual consummation of merrybouts, not only at Tully Veolan but at most other gentlemen's houses in Scotland. The guests acquitted themselves of their gratitude to their entertainer's hospitality, did honour to the place which afforded harbour to their horses, and indemnified themselves for the previous restraints imposed by private hospitality in the general licence of a tavern.

Accordingly, in full expectation of these distinguished guests, Luckie Macleary

---

1   Frederick Red-beard or Barbarossa was Friedrich I, *c*.1132–1190, King of Germany and Holy Roman Emperor.

2   St Duthus or Duthac, *c*.1000–1065. The abbey of Aberbrothock (Arbroath) was in fact not founded until 1178 but later there was a chapel in the abbey dedicated to St Duthac.

3   Latin name for Dionysus, Greek God of wine.

4   The main roof beam of a house. A toast to the roof-tree was a toast to the security of the home.

had swept her house for the first time this fortnight, set forth her deal table newly washed, propped its lame leg with a fragment of turf, and arranged four or five stools of huge and clumsy form in full hope of custom and profit. When they were seated under the sooty rafters, thickly tapestried with cobwebs, she appeared with a huge pewter measuring-pot, containing at least three English quarts, familiarly denominated *a Tappit Hen*, and which reamed with excellent claret just drawn from the cask.

It was soon plain that what crumbs of reason the Bear had not devoured were to be picked up by the Hen; but the confusion which began to prevail favoured Edward's resolution to evade the circling glass. The Laird of Balmawhapple demanded a bumper 'to the little gentleman in black velvet who did such service in 1702, and may the white horse break his neck over a mound of his making'.[1] Edward was not at that moment clear-headed enough to remember that King William's death was said to be owing to his horse stumbling on a mole-hill, yet felt inclined to take umbrage at a toast which seemed to have an uncivil reference to the government that he served. But ere he could interfere, the Baron had taken up the quarrel. 'Sir, whatever my sentiments, I shall not endure your saying anything that may impinge upon the honourable feelings of a gentleman under my roof. Sir, do ye not respect the military oath by which every officer is bound to the standards under which he is enrolled? But you are ignorant, sir, alike of ancient history and modern courtesy.'

'Not so ignorant as ye would pronounce me,' roared Balmawhapple. 'I ken well...'

Here the Baron and Waverley spoke both at once, the former calling out, 'Be silent, sir! Ye not only show your ignorance, but disgrace your native country before a stranger and an Englishman,' and Waverley entreating Mr Bradwardine to permit him to reply to an affront which seemed levelled at him personally. But the Baron was exalted by wine, wrath and scorn.

'I crave you to be hushed, Captain Waverley. In my domain, and under this roof, I am *in loco parentis* to you, and bound to see you scathless. And for you, Mr Falconer of Balmawhapple, let me see no more aberrations from the path of good manners.' 'And I tell you, Mr Cosmo Comyne Bradwardine of Bradwardine,' retorted the sportsman, 'that I'll make a moor-cock of the man that refuses my toast, whether it be a crop-eared English Whig or ane who deserts his own friends to claw favour with the rats of Hanover.'[2] In an instant both rapiers were brandished. Edward rushed forward to interfere, but the prostrate bulk of Killan-cureit, over which he stumbled, intercepted his passage. If readier aid than Waverley's had not interposed, there would certainly have been bloodshed. But the well-known clash of swords aroused Luckie Macleary as she sat beyond the earthen partition of the cottage engaged in summing up the reckoning. She boldly rushed in with the shrill expostulation, 'Wad their honours slay each other there,

---

[1]   The gentleman in black velvet is a reference to the animal whose mole hill caused William III's horse to stumble and throw its rider, which resulted in William's death. The white horse is the emblem of the House of Hanover.

[2]   Crop-eared English whig probably refers to the cropped haircut of the Puritans (Round-heads) but possibly also to the cropping of ears as a punishment.

and bring discredit on an honest widow-woman's house, when there was a' the lealand in the country to fight upon', a remonstrance which she seconded by flinging her plaid over the weapons of the combatants. The servants rushed in, and being tolerably sober separated the incensed opponents with the assistance of Edward and Killancureit. The latter led off Balmawhapple, cursing and vowing revenge, and with difficulty got him to horse. Our hero, with the assistance of Saunders Saunderson, escorted the Baron to his own dwelling, but could not prevail upon him to retire to bed until he had made a long and learned apology for the events of the evening, of which there was not a word intelligible.

chapter twelve

Repentance, and a Reconciliation

Waverley slept soundly, and then awakened to a painful recollection of the scene of the preceding evening. He had received a personal affront – he, a gentleman, a soldier and a Waverley. True, the person who offered it was not at the time possessed of the moderate share of sense which nature had allotted him. True, in resenting this insult he might take the life of a young man and render his family miserable, or he might lose his own, no pleasant alternative even to the bravest.

Yet he had received a personal insult, he was of the house of Waverley, and he bore a commission. He descended to breakfast with the intention of taking leave of the family and writing to one of his brother officers to meet him at the inn mid-way between Tully Veolan and the town where they were quartered, in order that he might convey such a message to Balmawhapple as the circumstances seemed to demand. He found Miss Bradwardine presiding over the tea and coffee, the table loaded with warm loaves, cakes, biscuits, together with eggs, reindeer ham, mutton and beef ditto, smoked salmon, marmalade, and all the other delicacies which induced Johnson himself to extol the luxury of a Scotch breakfast.[1] A mess of oatmeal porridge, flanked by a silver jug, which held an equal mixture of cream and buttermilk, was placed for the Baron's share of this repast, but Rose observed that he had walked out early in the morning.

Waverley sat down almost in silence and with an air of abstraction. He answered at random one or two observations which Miss Bradwardine ventured to make, so that feeling herself almost repulsed she left him to his mental amusement of cursing Ursa Major as the cause of all the mischief which had already happened and was likely to ensue. He started, as looking towards the window he beheld the Baron and young Balmawhapple pass arm in arm, apparently in deep conversation.

---

[1] In 1773 Dr Samuel Johnson with James Boswell made an expedition to the Highlands and Islands. Though critical of much that he encountered he was at times impressed by the quality of hospitality they experienced.

At this moment Mr Saunderson appeared with a message from his master, requesting to speak with Captain Waverley. With a heart which beat a little quicker, Edward obeyed the summons. He found the two gentlemen standing together, an air of complacent dignity on the brow of the Baron, while something like shame blanked the bold visage of Balmawhapple. The former slipped his arm through that of the latter, and thus seeming to walk with him while in reality he led him, advanced to meet Waverley. 'Captain Waverley, my esteemed friend has craved of my age and experience to be his interlocutor in expressing the regret with which he calls to remembrance certain passages last night. He craves you, sir, to drown in oblivion the memory of such solecisms, and to receive the hand which he offers you in amity.'

Edward immediately and with natural politeness accepted the hand which Balmawhapple, or rather the Baron, extended towards him. 'It was impossible,' he said, 'to remember what a gentleman expressed his wish he had not uttered, and he willingly imputed what had passed to the exuberant festivity of the day.'

'Handsomely said,' answered the Baron, 'for if a man be intoxicated, an incident which on festive occasions may take place in the life of a man of honour, and if the same gentleman, being sober, recants the contumelies spoken in his liquor, the words cease to be his own. And now let us proceed to breakfast, and think no more of this daft business.'

Edward, after so satisfactory an explanation, did much greater honour to the delicacies of Miss Bradwardine's breakfast-table than his commencement had promised. Balmawhapple, on the other hand, seemed dejected and Waverley now observed that his arm was in a sling. To a question from Miss Bradwardine he muttered something about his horse having fallen and, seeming desirous to escape, he arose as soon as breakfast was over, mounted his horse and returned to his own home.

Waverley now announced his purpose of leaving Tully Veolan, but the unaffected mortifcation with which the good-natured old gentleman heard the proposal deprived him of the courage to persist in it. He gained Waverley's consent to lengthen his visit for a few days, and then invited his guest to a morning's ride. 'I would willingly show you some sport, and we may meet with a roe who will serve to show how my dogs run.'

The stamping of horses was now heard in the court, and Davie's voice singing to two greyhounds. The Baron, in a pair of jack-boots of large dimension, now invited our hero to follow him as he stalked clattering down the staircase, tapping each huge balustrade as he passed with the butt of his massive horse whip.

chapter thirteen

A More Rational Day than the Last

The Baron was mounted on an active and well-managed horse. His light-coloured embroidered coat and superbly barred waistcoat, his brigadier wig surmounted by a small gold-laced cocked hat completed his costume. In this guise he ambled forth over hill and valley, till they found Davie Gellatly leading two tall greyhounds and presiding over half a dozen curs and about as many bare-legged boys.

These *gillie-wet-foots,* as they were called, were destined to beat the bushes, which they performed with so much success that after half an hour a roe was started, coursed and killed. After this ceremony, the Baron conducted his guest homeward by a pleasant and circuitous route commanding an extensive prospect of different villages and houses, to each of which Mr Bradwardine attached some anecdote of history or genealogy.

The ride seemed agreeable to both gentlemen because they found amusement in each other's conversation, although their characters and habits of thinking were in many respects totally opposite. Edward was warm in his feelings, wild and romantic in his ideas, with a strong disposition towards poetry. Mr Bradwardine was the reverse of all this and piqued himself upon stalking through life with the same upright gravity which distinguished his evening promenade upon the terrace of Tully Veolan. As for literature, he sometimes could not refrain from expressing contempt at poem-making.

Yet they met upon history as on a neutral ground in which each claimed an interest. The Baron, indeed, only cumbered his memory with matters of fact, the hard outlines which history delineates. Edward loved to round the sketch with the colouring of a vivid imagination, which gives light and life to the actors in the drama of past ages. Yet with tastes so opposite, they contributed greatly to each other's amusement. Mr Bradwardine's narratives and powerful memory supplied to Waverley fresh subjects for his fancy and opened to him a new mine of incident and character. And he repaid the pleasure by an earnest attention, valuable to all story-tellers, more especially to the Baron, who felt his self-respect flattered by it. Besides, Mr Bradwardine loved to talk of the scenes of his youth spent in camps and foreign lands, and had many interesting particulars to tell of the generals under whom he had served and the actions he had witnessed. Both parties returned to Tully Veolan in great good humour. There was no other guest except Mr Rubrick, whose information and discourse, as a clergyman and a scholar, harmonized very well with that of the Baron and his guest.

Shortly after dinner, the Baron proposed a visit to Rose's apartment. Waverley was accordingly conducted through one or two long awkward passages at the end of which Mr Bradwardine began to ascend by two steps at once a narrow winding stair, leaving Mr Rubrick and Waverley to follow at leisure.

After having climbed this perpendicular cork-screw until almost giddy, they entered Rose's parlour. It was a small but pleasant apartment, opening to the south and hung with tapestry, adorned with pictures of her mother in the dress of a shepherdess and of the Baron in his tenth year, in a blue coat, embroidered waistcoat, laced hat and bag-wig with a bow in his hand. Edward could not help smiling at the odd resemblance between the round, red-cheeked visage in the portrait and the gaunt, bearded, swarthy features which fatigues of war and advanced age had bestowed on the original.

Miss Rose now appeared from the interior room of her apartment to welcome them. The little labours in which she had been employed showed a natural taste, which required only cultivation. Her father had taught her French and Italian, and a few of the authors in those languages ornamented her shelves. He had endeavoured also to be her preceptor in music, but she had made no proficiency further than to be able to accompany her voice with the harpsichord, but she sang with great taste and feeling, and with a respect to the sense of what she uttered that might be an example to ladies of much superior musical talent. Her singing gave more pleasure than could have been extracted by a much finer voice and more brilliant execution unguided by the same delicacy of feeling.

A projecting gallery before the windows of her parlour was crowded with flowers of different kinds, which she had taken under her special protection. This balcony commanded a most beautiful prospect. The formal garden lay below, while the view extended beyond down a wooded glen where the river was sometimes visible, sometimes hidden in copse. Here and there rocks rose from the dell with massive or spiry fronts, and a noble though ruined tower frowned from a promontory over the river. To the left were two or three cottages, part of the village. The glen was terminated by Loch Veolan, into which the brook discharged itself and which now glistened in the westering sun. The country seemed open and varied, and the scene was bounded by distant hills which formed the southern boundary of the strath. The view of the old tower introduced some family anecdotes and tales of Scottish chivalry, which the Baron told with great enthusiasm, and Rose was called upon to sing.

chapter fourteen

A Discovery – Waverley Becomes Domesticated at Tully Veolan

The next morning Edward arose betimes, and in a walk around the house came suddenly upon a small court in front of the dog-kennel, where his friend Davie was employed about his four-footed charge. Instantly he began to sing part of an old ballad.

> *Young men will love thee more fair and more fast;*
>   Heard ye so merry the little bird sing?
> *Old men's love the longest will last,*
>   And the throstle-cock's head is under his wing.
>
> *The young man's wrath is like light straw on fire;*
>   Heard ye so merry the little bird sing?
> *But the red-hot steel is the old man's ire.*
>   And the throstle-cock's head is under his wing.[1]

Waverley could not avoid observing that Davie laid a satirical emphasis on these lines. He therefore approached and endeavoured to elicit from him what the innuendo might mean, but Davie had no mind to explain and had wit enough to make his folly cloak his knavery. Edward could collect nothing from him excepting that the Laird of Balmawhapple had gone home 'wi' his boots full o' bluid'. In the garden, however, he met the old butler. By a series of queries Edward discovered, with a painful feeling of surprise and shame, that Balmawhapple's apology had been the consequence of a rencontre with the Baron in which the younger combatant had been disarmed and wounded in the sword arm.

Greatly mortified at this information, Waverley sought out his friendly host and anxiously expostulated with him upon the injustice he had done him in anticipating his meeting with Mr Falconer. The Baron urged that the quarrel was common to them and that Balmawhapple could not, by the code of honour, *evite* giving satisfaction to both, which he had done in his case by an honourable meeting, and in that of Edward by such a *palinode* as rendered the use of the sword unnecessary. With this explanation Waverley was silenced, if not satisfied.

It is probable that a young man accustomed to more cheerful society would have tired of the conversation of the Baron, but Edward found agreeable variety in that of Miss Bradwardine, who listened with eagerness to his remarks upon literature and showed great taste in her answers. The sweetness of her disposition had made her submit with complacency and even pleasure to the course of reading prescribed by her father. Rose was the very apple of her father's eye. Her

---

[1]   Probably by Scott.

constant liveliness, her attention to all those little observances most gratifying to those who would never think of exacting them, her beauty and her generosity, would have justified the affection of the most doting father.

His anxiety on her behalf did not, however, seem to extend itself in labouring to establish her in life, either by a large dowry or a wealthy marriage. By an old settlement, almost all the landed estates of the Baron went after his death to a distant relation, and it was supposed that Miss Bradwardine would remain but slenderly provided for, as the good gentleman's cash matters had been too long under the exclusive charge of Baillie Macwheeble to admit of any great expectations from his personal succession. The Baillie loved his patron and his patron's daughter (though at an incomparable distance). He thought it possible to set aside the settlement on the male line, and had actually procured an opinion to that effect from an eminent Scottish counsel, but the Baron would not listen to such a proposal. He had a perverse pleasure in boasting that the barony of Bradwardine was a male fief, the first charter having been given at that early period when women were not deemed capable to hold a feudal grant because a woman could not serve the feudal lord in war, on account of decorum, nor assist him with advice, because of her limited intellect, nor keep his counsel, owing to the infirmity of her disposition. He would triumphantly ask, how would it become a female, and that female a Bradwardine, to be seen employed in pulling off the king's boots after an engagement, which was the feudal service by which he held the barony of Bradwardine. 'No,' he said, 'Heaven forbid that I should do ought that might contravene the destination of my forefathers or impinge upon the right of my kinsman, Malcolm Bradwardine of Inch Grabbit, an honourable though decayed branch of my own family.'

The Baillie durst not press his own opinion any farther, but contented himself with deploring to Saunderson the laird's self-willedness, and with laying plans for uniting Rose with the young Laird of Balmawhapple, who had a fine estate and was a faultless young gentleman, being sober as a saint – and who, in brief, had no imperfection but that of keeping light company – 'o' whilk follies, Mr Saunderson, he'll mend, he'll mend'.

'Like sour ale in the summer,' added Davie Gellatly, who happened to be nearer the conclave than they were aware of.

Miss Bradwardine, with all the simplicity and curiosity of a recluse, attached herself to the opportunities of increasing her store of literature which Edward's visit afforded her. He sent for books from his quarters, and English poets and belles lettres opened to her new sources of delight. Her music, even her flowers, were neglected. These new pleasures became gradually enhanced by sharing them with one of kindred taste. Edward's readiness to comment, to recite, to explain difficult passages, rendered his assistance invaluable, and the romance of his spirit delighted a character too inexperienced to observe its deficiencies. Upon subjects which interested him he possessed that flow of natural eloquence supposed as powerful as fashion, fame or fortune in winning a female's heart. There was therefore an increasing danger in this constant intercourse to poor Rose's peace of mind, which was the more imminent as her father was too much abstracted in his studies and wrapped up in his own dignity to dream of his daughter's incurring it. The daughters of the house of Bradwardine were, in his opinion, placed high above the clouds of passion which might obfuscate the intellects of meaner females. They were governed by other feelings and amenable to other rules than those of idle affection. He shut his eyes so resolutely to the natural consequences of Edward's intimacy with Miss Bradwardine that the whole neighbourhood concluded that he had opened them to the advantages of a match between his daughter and the wealthy young Englishman, and pronounced him much less a fool than he had generally shown himself.

If the Baron had really meditated such an alliance, the indifference of Waverley would have been an insuperable bar to his project. Rose had not precisely the sort of beauty or merit which captivates a romantic imagination. She was too confiding, too kind. Was it possible to bow and to adore before the timid yet playful little girl who now asked Edward to mend her pen and now how to spell a very long word? These incidents have their fascination, but not when a youth is looking for some object whose affection may dignify him in his own eyes, rather than stooping to one who looks up to him for such distinction. It seems probable that their very intimacy prevented his feeling for Rose other sentiments than those of a brother for an amiable and accomplished sister, while the sentiments of poor Rose were gradually assuming a shade of warmer affection.

Edward had applied for and received permission to extend his leave of absence. But the letter of his commanding-officer contained a friendly recommendation to him not to spend his time exclusively with persons who were not well affected to a government which they declined to acknowledge by taking the oath of allegiance. Waverley was sensible that Mr Bradwardine had acted with most scrupulous delicacy in never entering upon any discussion that had the most remote tendency to bias his mind in political opinions. Sensible, therefore, that there was no risk of his being perverted from his allegiance, Edward felt as if he should do his uncle's old friend injustice in removing from a house where he gave and received pleasure, merely to gratify a prejudiced suspicion. He therefore wrote a very general answer, assuring his commanding-officer that his loyalty was not in any danger of contamination, and continued an honoured guest of the house of Tully Veolan.

chapter fifteen

A Creagh, and its Consequences

When Edward had been a guest at Tully Veolan nearly six weeks he descried signs of unusual perturbation in the family. He repaired to the fore-court, where he beheld Baillie Macwheeble cantering his white pony down the avenue with all the speed it could muster. He had arrived upon a hasty summons, and was followed by more than a score of peasants from the village, who had great difficulty in keeping pace with him.

The Baillie summoned forth Mr Saunderson, who appeared with a countenance in which dismay was mingled with solemnity, and they immediately entered into close conference. Passing towards the garden, Waverley beheld the Baron measuring and re-measuring with swift and tremendous strides the length of the terrace, his countenance clouded with offended pride and indignation, and the whole of his demeanour indicating that any enquiry concerning the cause of his discomposure would give pain if not offence. Waverley therefore glided into the house without addressing him, and took his way to the breakfast parlour, where he found Rose who seemed vexed and thoughtful. 'Your breakfast will be a disturbed one, Captain Waverley. A party of caterans have come down upon us last night, and driven off all our milk cows.'

'Caterans?'

'Yes, robbers from the neighbouring Highlands. We used to be quite free from them while we paid *blackmail* to Fergus MacIvor, but my father thought it unworthy of his rank to pay it any longer so this disaster has happened.[1] It is not the value of the cattle that vexes me, but my father is so much hurt at the affront, and is so bold and hot, that I fear he will try to recover them by the strong hand. If he is not hurt himself he will hurt some of these wild people, and there will be no peace between them and us perhaps for our lifetime, and we cannot defend ourselves as in old times for the government have taken all our arms, and my dear father is so rash – O what will become of us!' Here poor Rose lost heart altogether, and burst into a flood of tears.

The Baron entered at this moment and rebuked her with more asperity than Waverley had ever heard him use. 'Was it not a shame,' he said, 'that she should exhibit herself before any gentleman in such a light, like the daughter of a Cheshire yeoman! Captain Waverley, I must request your favourable construction of her grief, which ought to proceed solely from seeing her father's estate exposed to depredation from common thieves, while we are not allowed to keep a half score of muskets, whether for defence or rescue.'

Baillie Macwheeble entered and by his report of arms and ammunition confirmed this statement, informing the Baron in a melancholy voice that though the people would certainly obey his honour's orders, yet there was no chance of their following the *gear* to any *guid* purpose, as there were only his honour's body servants who had swords and pistols, and the depredators were twelve Highlanders completely armed after the manner of their country. He assumed a posture of silent dejection, shaking his head slowly with the motion of a pendulum, and then remained stationary, his body stooping at a more acute angle than usual and the latter part of his person projected in proportion.

There was an awful pause, after which all the company began to give separate

---

[1]   It was customary to pay protection money to prevent raids and the theft of cattle.

and inconsistent counsel. Saunderson proposed they should send someone to compound with the caterans, who would readily give up their prey for a dollar a head. The Baillie opined that this transaction would amount to *theft-boot* or composition of felony, and recommended that some canny hand should be sent up to the glens to make the best bargain he could, so that the Laird might not be seen in such a transaction.[2] Edward proposed to send off to the nearest garrison for a party of soldiers and a magistrate's warrant. And Rose, as far as she dared, endeavoured to insinuate a course of paying the arrears of tribute money to Fergus MacIvor Vich Ian Vohr, who, they all knew, could easily procure restoration of the cattle.

None of these proposals met the Baron's approbation. The idea of composition was ignominious, that of Waverley only showed that he did not understand the state of the country and of the political parties which divided it, and standing matters as they did with Vich Ian Vohr, the Baron would make no concession to him. In fact, his voice was still for war, and he proposed to send expresses to Balmawhapple, Killancureit, Tulliellum and other lairds, who were exposed to similar depredations, inviting them to join in the pursuit.

The Baillie, who by no means relished these warlike councils, here pulled forth an immense watch the colour and nearly the size of a pewter warming-pan, and observed that it was now past noon and that the caterans had been seen in the pass of Bally Brough soon after sunrise, so that before the allied forces could assemble, they would be far beyond the reach of the most active pursuit and sheltered in those pathless deserts where it was neither advisable to follow nor indeed possible to trace them.

The proposition was undeniable. The council therefore broke up without coming to any conclusion, only it was determined that the Baillie should send his own three milk cows down to the Mains for the use of the Baron's family and brew small ale as a substitute in his own. To this arrangement the Baillie readily assented, both from habitual deference to the family and a consciousness that his courtesy would, in some mode or other, be repaid tenfold.

The Baron having retired, Waverley seized the opportunity to ask whether this Fergus with the unprounceable name were the chief thief-taker of the district?

'Thief-taker!' answered Rose, laughing. 'He is a gentleman of great honour and consequence, the chieftain of a branch of a powerful Highland clan, and is much respected, both for his own power and that of his *kith*, *kin* and *allies*.'

'What has he to do with the thieves then? Is he a magistrate, or in the commission of peace?'

'The commission of war rather, if there be such a thing,' said Rose, 'for he is a very unquiet neighbour to his un-friends, and keeps a greater *following* on foot than many that have thrice his estate. As to his connection with the thieves, that I cannot well explain. But the boldest of them will never steal a hoof from any one that pays blackmail to Vich Ian Vohr.'

'And what is blackmail?'

---

2 Theft-boot was a collusion between the victim of robbery and the thief in which stolen goods were returned on condition of an agreement not to prosecute.

'A sort of protection money that gentlemen and heritors lying near the Highlands, pay to some Highland chief, that he may neither do them harm himself nor suffer it to be done to them by others. And then if your cattle are stole, you have only to send him word and he will recover them. Or he will drive away cows from some distant place where he has a quarrel and give them to you to make up your loss.'

'And is this sort of Highland Jonathan Wild admitted into society and called a gentleman?'[1]

'So much so that the quarrel between my father and Fergus MacIvor began at a country meeting where he wanted to take precedence of all the Lowland gentlemen present, only my father would not suffer it. And then he upbraided my father that he paid him tribute, and my father was in a towering passion for Baillie Macwheeble had contrived to keep this blackmail a secret from him. And they would have fought, but Fergus MacIvor said, very gallantly, he would never raise his hand against a grey head that was so much respected as my father's. O I wish they had continued friends!'

'And did you ever see this Mr MacIvor, if that be his name?'

'No, that is not his name. The Lowlanders call him by the name of his estate, Glennaquoich, and the Highlanders call him Vich Ian Vohr, the Son of John the Great, and we upon the braes here call him by both names.'

'I am afraid I shall never bring my English tongue to call him by either one or the other.'

'But he is a very polite, handsome man,' continued Rose, 'and his sister Flora is one of the most beautiful and accomplished young ladies in this country. She was bred in a convent in France, and was a great friend of mine before this unhappy dispute. Dear Captain Waverley, try your influence with my father to make matters up. I am sure this is but the beginning of our troubles, for Tully Veolan has never been safe when we have been at feud with the Highlanders. When I was a girl of about ten, there was a skirmish fought between a party of twenty of them and my father and his servants, behind the Mains. The bullets broke several panes in the north windows, they were so near. Three of the Highlanders were killed, and they brought them in wrapped in their plaids, and laid them on the stone floor of the hall. And next morning their wives and daughters came crying the coronach and carried away the dead with the pipes playing before them. I could not sleep for six weeks without starting and thinking I heard these terrible cries, and saw the bodies lying on the steps, all stiff and swathed up in their bloody tartans. But since that time there came a party from the garrison at Stirling, with a warrant from the Lord Justice Clerk, and took away all our arms. And now, how are we to protect ourselves if they come down in any strength?'

Waverley could not help starting at a story which bore so much resemblance to one of his own daydreams. Here was a girl, scarce seventeen, the gentlest of her sex, who had witnessed with her own eyes such a scene as he had used to conjure up in his imagination. He felt at once the impulse of curiosity and that slight sense of danger which only serves to heighten its interest.

---

[1] Jonathan Wild was a notorious thief hanged in London in 1725.

The circumstances concerning the state of the country seemed extraordinary. He had often heard of Highland thieves, but had no idea of the systematic mode in which their depredations were conducted, and that the practice was connived at and even encouraged by many of the Highland chieftains, who not only found these *creaghs* useful for the purpose of training individuals of their clans to the practice of arms, but also of maintaining a wholesome terror among their Lowland neighbours.

It seemed like a dream to Waverley that these deeds of violence should be familiar to men's minds and currently talked of as happening daily in the immediate neighbourhood, without his having crossed the seas and while he was yet in the otherwise well-ordered island of Great Britain.

chapter sixteen

An Unexpected Ally Appears

The Baron returned at the dinner hour, and had in great measure recovered his composure and good humour. He not only confirmed the stories which Edward had heard from Rose and Baillie Macwheeble, but added many anecdotes concerning the state of the Highlands. The chiefs he pronounced to be in general gentlemen of great honour and high pedigree, whose word was accounted as law by all those of their own sept or clan. But he went on to state so many curious particulars concerning their manners and customs that Edward's curiosity became highly interested and he enquired whether it were possible to make with safety an excursion into the neighbouring Highlands, whose dusky barrier of mountains had already excited his wish to penetrate beyond them. The Baron assured his guest that nothing would be more easy, providing this quarrel were first made up, since he could himself give him letters to many of the distinguished chiefs, who would receive him with the utmost courtesy.

The door suddenly opened and, ushered by Saunders Saunderson, a Highlander fully armed and equipped entered the apartment. Had it not been that neither Mr Bradwardine nor Rose exhibited any emotion, Edward would certainly have thought the intrusion hostile. As it was, he started at the sight of what he had not yet seen, a mountaineer in his full national costume. He was a stout dark man of low stature, the ample folds of whose plaid added to the appearance of strength which his person exhibited. The short kilt showed his sinewy and clean-made limbs, the goat-skin purse flanked by a dirk and pistol hung before him. His bonnet had a short feather which indicated his claim to be treated as a Duinhé-Wassell, or sort of gentleman. A broadsword dangled by his side, a target hung upon his shoulder and a long Spanish fowling-piece occupied one of his hands. With the other hand he pulled off his bonnet and the Baron, who knew well the proper mode of address, immediately said, with an air of dignity much, as Edward thought, in the manner of a prince receiving an embassy, 'Welcome, Evan Dhu Maccombich, what news from Fergus MacIvor Vich Ian Vohr?'

'Fergus MacIvor Vich Ian Vohr,' said the ambassador in good English, 'greets you well, Baron of Bradwardine and Tully Veolan, and is sorry there has been a thick cloud interposed between you and him, which has kept you from considering the friendship that has been between your houses of old, and he prays that the cloud may pass away, and that things may be as they have been heretofore between the clan Ivor and the house of Bradwardine. And he expects you will also say you are sorry for the cloud, and no man shall hereafter ask whether it descended from the hill to the valley or rose from the valley to the hill, and woe to him who would lose his friend for the stormy cloud of a spring morning.'

To this the Baron of Bradwardine answered with suitable dignity that he knew the chief of Clan Ivor to be a well-wisher to the *King* and he was sorry there should have been a cloud between him and any gentleman of such sound principles, 'for when folks are banding together, feeble is he who hath no brother'.

This appearing to be fully satisfactory, that the peace might be duly solemnized the Baron ordered a stoup of usquebaugh, and drank to the health and prosperity of MacIvor of Glennaquoich, upon which the Celtic ambassador, to requite his politeness, downed a mighty bumper of the same generous liquor, seasoned with his good wishes to the house of Bradwardine.

Having thus ratified the preliminaries of the treaty the envoy retired to adjust with Mr Macwheeble some subordinate articles. These probably referred to the discontinuance of the subsidy, and apparently the Baillie found means to satisfy their ally without suffering his master to suppose that his dignity was compromised. After the plenipotentiaries had drunk a bottle of brandy in single drams, which seemed to have no more effect upon such seasoned vessels than if it had been poured upon the two bears at the top of the avenue, Evan Dhu Maccombich declared his intention to set off immediately in pursuit of the cattle, which he pronounced to be 'no far off'.

Our hero was much struck with the ingenuity of Evan Dhu, who on his part was obviously flattered with the attention of Waverley and his curiosity about the customs and scenery of the Highlands. Without much ceremony he invited Edward to accompany him on a short walk of ten or fifteen miles into the mountains, and see the place where the cattle were conveyed to, adding, 'If it be as I suppose you never saw such a place in your life, nor ever will, unless you go with me or the like of me.'

Our hero took the precaution to enquire if his guide might be trusted and was assured that the invitation would on no account have been given had there been the least danger, and that all he had to apprehend was a little fatigue. As Evan proposed he should pass a day at his chieftain's house, where he would be sure of an excellent welcome, there seemed nothing very formidable in the task he undertook. Rose, indeed, turned pale when she heard of it, but her father did not attempt to damp his young friend's curiosity by an alarm of danger which really did not exist. A knapsack with a few necessaries being bound on the shoulders of a deputy gamekeeper, our hero set forth with a fowling-piece in his hand, accompanied by his new friend Evan Dhu and followed by the gamekeeper and two wild Highlanders, one of whom had upon his shoulder a hatchet at the end of a pole called a Lochaber axe and the other a ducking gun. Evan gave Edward to understand that this martial escort was by no means necessary as a guard, but merely, as he said adjusting his plaid with an air of dignity, that he might appear decently at Tully Veolan, as Vich Ian Vohr's foster-brother ought to do. 'Ah, if you Saxon Duinhé-wassal (English gentleman) saw but the chief himself with his tail on!'

'With his tail on?' echoed Edward in some surprise.

'Yes – that is, with all his usual followers, when he visits those of the same rank. There is,' he continued, drawing himself proudly up while he counted upon his fingers the officers of his chief's retinue, 'there is his *hanchman*, or right-hand man, then his *bhaird*, or poet; then his *bladier*, or orator, to make harangues to the great folks whom he visits; then his *gilly-more*, or armour-bearer, to carry his sword and target and his gun; then his *gilly-casflue* who carries him on his back through the sikes and brooks; then his *gilly-constraine* to lead his horse by the bridle in steep and difficult paths; then his *gillie-trusharnish* to carry his knapsack; and the piper and the piper's man, and it may be a dozen young lads besides to follow the laird and do his honour's bidding.'

'And does your master regularly maintain all these men?'

'Aye, and many a fair head beside, that would not ken where to lay itself but for the mickle barn at Glennaquoich.'

With similar tales of the grandeur of the chief in peace and war, Evan Dhu beguiled the way till they approached more closely those huge mountains which Edward had seen at a distance. It was towards evening as they entered one of the tremendous passes between the high and low country. The path, extremely steep and rugged, wound up a chasm between two tremendous rocks following the passage which a foaming stream appeared to have worn in the course of ages. A few slanting beams of sun, now setting, reached the water in its darksome bed and showed it chafed by a hundred rocks and broken by a hundred falls. The descent from the path to the stream was a precipice, with here and there a projecting fragment of granite or a scathed tree which had warped its twisted roots into the fissures of the rock. On the right, the mountain rose above the path with almost equal inaccessibility, but the hill on the opposite side displayed a shroud of copsewood, with which some pines were intermingled.

'This, said Evan, 'is the pass of Bally Brough, which was kept in former times by ten of the clan Donnochie against a hundred Low Country carles. The graves of the slain are still to be seen in that little corrie on the opposite side of the burn – if your eyes are good you can see the green specks among the heather. See, there is an earn, which you southrons call an eagle. You have no such birds as that in England. He is going to fetch his supper from the laird of Bradwardine's braes, but I'll send a slug after him.'

He fired but missed the superb monarch of the feathered tribes who continued his majestic flight to the southward. A thousand birds of prey, hawks, kites, carrion crows and ravens, disturbed from the lodgings which they had just taken up for the evening, rose at the report of the gun, and mingled their hoarse and discordant notes with the echoes which replied to it and the roar of the mountain cataracts. Evan, disconcerted at having missed his mark when he meant to have displayed peculiar dexterity, covered his confusion by whistling part of a pibroch as he reloaded his piece, and proceeded in silence up the pass.

It issued in a narrow glen between two lofty mountains. They advanced up the mazes of the brook, crossing them occasionally. Edward rose in his guide's opinion by showing that he did not fear wetting his feet. Indeed, he was anxious to remove the opinion which Evan seemed to entertain of the effeminacy of the Lowlanders, and particularly of the English.

Through the gorge of this glen they found access to a black bog of tremendous extent, full of large pit-holes, which they traversed with great difficulty and some danger by tracks which no one but a Highlander could have followed. The path itself, on which the travellers half walked, half waded, was rough and quaggy. Sometimes the ground was so completely unsafe that it was necessary to spring from one hillock to another. This was an easy matter to the Highlanders, who wore thin-soled brogues fit for the purpose and moved with a peculiar springing step, but Edward began to find the exercise fatiguing. The lingering twilight served to show them through this bog, but deserted them almost totally at the bottom of a steep and stony hill. The night, however, was pleasant and not dark and Waverley, calling up mental energy to support personal fatigue, held on his march gallantly, though envying his Highland attendants, who continued without a symptom of abated vigour the rapid and swinging pace which, according to his computation, had already brought them fifteen miles upon their journey.

After crossing the mountain, Edward's baggage was shifted from the shoulders of the gamekeeper to that of one of the *gillies* and the former was sent off in a different direction. On asking the meaning of this separation, Waverley was told that the Lowlander must go to a hamlet about three miles off for the night, for Donald Bean Lean, the worthy person whom they supposed to be possessed of the cattle, did not much approve of strangers approaching his retreat. This seemed reasonable and silenced a qualm which came across Edward's mind. Evan immediately added, 'that indeed he himself had better get forward and announced their approach to Donald Bean Lean, as the arrival of a *sidier roy* (red soldier) might otherwise be a disagreeable surprise.' And without waiting for an answer he was out of sight in an instant.

Waverley was now left to his own meditations, for his attendant with the battle-axe spoke very little English. They were traversing a thick wood of pines and the path was altogether undiscernible in the murky darkness. The Highlander seemed to trace it by instinct, without hesitation, and Edward followed his footsteps as close as he could.

After journeying a considerable time in silence, he could not help asking, 'Was it far to the end of their journey?'

'Ta cove was tree, four mile, but as the Duinhé-wassal was a wee taiglit, Donald could, tat is, might – would – should send ta curragh.'

This conveyed no information. The *curragh* which was promised might be a man, a horse, a cart, or chaise, and no more could be got from the man with the battle-axe but a repetition of 'Aich aye! Ta curragh.'

Edward began to conceive his meaning when he found himself on the banks of a lake, where his conductor gave him to understand they must sit down for a while. The moon showed the expanse of water and the indistinct forms of mountains. The cool yet mild air of the summer night refreshed Waverley after his toilsome walk, and the perfume which it wafted from the birch trees was exquisitely fragrant.

He had now time to give himself up to the full romance of his situation. Here he sat on the banks of an unknown lake under the guidance of a wild native whose language was unknown to him, on the visit to the den of some renowned outlaw, at deep midnight, through scenes of difficulty and toil, separated from his attendant, left by his guide – what a fund of circumstances for the exercise of the romantic imagination, and all enhanced by the solemn feeling of uncertainty at least, if not of danger! The only circumstance which assorted ill with the rest was the cause of his journey – the Baron's milk cows! This degrading incident he kept in the background

His companion gently touched him and, pointing in a direction straight across the lake, said, 'Yon's ta cove'. A small point of light was seen to twinkle and, gradually increasing in size and lustre, seemed to flicker like a meteor upon the verge of the horizon. While Edward watched the distant dash of oars was heard. The measured splash arrived near and presently a loud whistle was heard. His friend with the battle-axe immediately whistled clear and shrill in reply, and a boat manned with four or five Highlanders pushed for a little inlet near which Edward was seated. He advanced to meet them with his attendant, was immediately assisted into the boat by two stout mountaineers, and had no sooner seated himself than they began to row across the lake with great rapidity.

chapter seventeen

The Hold of a Highland Robber

The party preserved silence, interrupted only by the monotonous chant of a Gaelic song sung by the steersman, and by the dash of oars which the notes seemed to regulate as they dipped them in cadence. The light assumed a redder and more irregular splendour. The red glaring orb of what appeared to be a large fire seemed to rest on the very surface of the lake. They approached nearer and the light of the fire sufficed to show that it was kindled at the bottom of a huge dark crag rising abruptly from the edge of the water. Its front, changed by the reflection to a dusky red, formed a strange and awful contrast to the banks around, which were from time to time faintly enlightened by pallid moonlight.

The boat neared the shore. The fire, amply supplied with branches of pinewood by two figures, who in the red reflection appeared like demons, was kindled in the jaws of a lofty cavern into which an inlet from the lake seemed to advance. Waverley conjectured that the fire had been kindled as a beacon to the boatmen. They rowed right for the mouth of the cave, then shipped their oars. The skiff passed the point of rock on which the fire was blazing and stopped where the cavern ascended from the water by five or six broad ledges of rock, as easy and regular as natural steps. At this moment water was suddenly flung upon the fire which sunk with a hissing noise, and with it disappeared the light it had afforded. Four or five active arms lifted Waverley out of the boat, placed him on his feet and almost carried him into the recesses of the cave. Guided in this manner towards a hum of voices which seemed to sound from the centre of the rock, at an acute turn Donald Bean Lean and his whole establishment were before his eyes.

The interior of the cave was illuminated by torches made of pine, which emitted a bright and bickering light assisted by the red glare of a large charcoal fire, round which were seated five or six armed Highlanders, while others were indistinctly seen couched on their plaids in the more remote recesses of the cavern. In one large aperture there hung by the heels the carcasses of a sheep and two cows, lately slaughtered. The principal inhabitant of this singular mansion, attended by Evan Dhu, came forward to meet his guest, totally different in appearance and manner from what Waverley's imagination had anticipated. The profession which he followed, the wilderness in which he dwelt, the wild warrior forms that surrounded him, were all calculated to inspire terror. Waverley prepared himself to meet a stern, gigantic, ferocious figure.

Donald Bean Lean was the very reverse of all these. He was thin in person and low in stature, with light sandy-coloured hair and small pale features, from which he derived his agnomen of *Bean*, or white, and although his form was well proportioned he appeared rather a diminutive and insignificant figure. He had served in some inferior capacity in the French army, and in order to receive his English visitor in great form, and probably meaning to pay him a compliment, he had laid aside the Highland dress to put on an old blue and red uniform and a feathered hat, in which he looked so incongruous that Waverley would have been tempted to laugh had laughter been either civil or safe. He received Captain Waverley with a profusion of French politeness and Scottish hospitality.

Being placed at a convenient distance from the fire, the heat of which the season rendered oppressive, a strapping Highland damsel placed before Waverley, Evan and Donald Bean three cogues, or wooden vessels, containing *imrigh*, a sort of strong soup made out of a particular part of the inside of the beeves. After this, steaks roasted on the coals were supplied in liberal abundance, and disappeared before Evan Dhu and their host with a promptitude that seemed like magic and astonished Waverley, who was much puzzled to reconcile their voracity with what he had heard of the abstemiousness of the Highlanders. He was ignorant that this abstinence was with the lower ranks only compulsory, and that, like some animals of prey, those who practice it were usually gifted with the power of indemnifying themselves to good purpose when chance threw plenty in their way. The whisky came forth in abundance to crown the cheer. The Highlanders drank it copiously and undiluted, but Edward, having mixed a little with water, did not find it so palatable as to invite him to repeat the draught. Their host bewailed himself exceedingly that he could offer him no wine. 'Had he but known four-and-twenty hours before, he would have had some had it been within the circle of forty miles round him.'

From this he passed on to the political and military state of the country, and Waverley was astonished, even alarmed, to find him so accurately acquainted with the strength of garrisons quartered north of the Tay. He even mentioned the exact number of recruits who had joined Waverley's troop from his uncle's estate, and observed that they were *pretty men*, meaning not handsome but stout warlike fellows. He put Waverley in mind of one or two minute circumstances which had happened at a general review of the regiment, which satisfied him that the robber had been an eye-witness. Evan Dhu having by this time retired from the conversation and wrapped himself up in his plaid to take some repose, Donald asked Edward in a very significant manner whether he had nothing in particular to say to him.

Waverley, somewhat startled, answered he had no motive in visiting him but curiosity to see his extraordinary place of residence. Donald Bean Lean looked him steadily in the face for an instant and then said, with a significant nod, 'You might as well have confided in me. I am as much worthy of trust as the Baron of Bradwardine or Vich Ian Vohr – but you are equally welcome to my house.'

Waverley felt an involuntary shudder creep over him at the mysterious language held by this lawless bandit, which deprived him of the power to ask the meaning of his insinuations. A heath pallet had been prepared for him in a recess of the cave and here, covered with such spare plaids as could be mustered, he lay for some time watching the motions of the other inhabitants of the cavern. Small parties of two or three entered or left without any other ceremony than a few words in Gaelic to the principal outlaw. Those who entered seemed to have returned from some excursion of which they reported the success, and went without further ceremony to the larder, where cutting with their dirks their rations from the carcasses, they proceeded to broil and eat them. The liquor was under stricter regulation, being served out either by Donald himself, his lieutenant, or the strapping Highland girl aforesaid, who was the only female that appeared. The allowance of whisky, however, would have appeared prodigal to any but Highlanders who, living entirely in the open air can consume great quantities of ardent spirits without the usual baneful effects either upon the brain or constitution.

At length the fluctuating groups began to swim before the eyes of our hero as they gradually closed, nor did he open them before the morning sun was high on the lake, though there was but a glimmering twilight in the recesses of Uaimh an Ri, or the King's cavern, as the abode of Donald Bean Lean was proudly denominated.

chapter eighteen

Waverley Proceeds on his Journey

Edward was surprised to observe the cavern totally deserted. If it had not been for the decayed fire, now sunk into grey ashes, and the remnants of the festival consisting of bones half burned and half gnawed and an empty keg or two, there remained no traces of Donald and his band. When Waverley sallied forth to the entrance of the cave, he perceived that the point of rock on which remained the mark of last night's beacon was accessible by a small path along the little inlet of water where the skiff which brought him there was still lying moored. When he reached the platform on which the beacon had been established he would have believed his farther progress by land impossible, only he soon observed one or two ledges of rock, and making use of them as a staircase he clambered around the projecting shoulder of the crag on which the cavern opened, and descending with some difficulty on the other side gained the precipitous shores of a Highland loch, about four miles in length and a mile and a half over, surrounded by savage mountains on the crests of which the morning mist was still sleeping.

Looking back to the place from which he came he could not help admiring a retreat of such seclusion and secrecy. The rock seemed a huge precipice which barred all farther passage by the edge of the lake in that direction. There could be no possibility of descrying the entrance of the narrow and low-browed cave from the other side, so that unless the retreat had been sought for with boats upon the lake or disclosed by treachery, it might be a safe and secret residence. Waverley looked around for Evan Dhu and his attendant who, he rightly judged, would be at no great distance. Accordingly, at a distance of about half a mile he beheld a Highlander angling in the lake, with another attending him whom he recognized for his friend with the battle-axe.

Much nearer to the cave he heard the notes of a lively Gaelic song, guided by which, in a sunny recess shaded by a glittering birch tree and carpeted with a bank of firm white sand, he found the damsel of the cavern busy arranging a repast of milk, eggs, barley bread, fresh butter and honeycomb. The poor girl had made a circuit of four miles in search of the eggs, the meal which baked her cakes and of the other materials of the breakfast, being all delicacies which she had to beg or borrow from distant cottagers. The followers of Donald Bean Lean used little food except the flesh of the animals which they drove away from the Lowlands. Bread itself was a delicacy seldom thought of because hard to obtain, and milk, poultry, butter etc were out of the question. Although Alice had occupied a part of the morning in providing for her guest, she had secured time also to arrange her own person in her best trim. Her finery was very simple. A short russet-coloured jacket and a petticoat were her whole dress, but these were clean and neatly arranged. A piece of scarlet embroidered cloth confined her hair, which fell over it in a profusion of rich dark curls. The scarlet plaid which formed part of her dress was laid aside that it might not impede her activity. Her proudest ornaments were a pair of gold ear-rings and a gold rosary which her father, Donald, had brought from France, the plunder probably of some battle.

Her form was well proportioned and had a natural and rustic grace. The smiles and the laughing eyes, with which in dumb show she gave Waverley that morning greeting which she wanted English words to express, might have been interpreted by a coxcomb or a young soldier conscious of a handsome person as meant to convey more than courtesy. Nor do I take it upon myself to say that the wild mountaineer would have welcomed any staid old gentleman with the cheerful pains she bestowed upon Edward. She seemed eager to place him by the meal which she had so sedulously arranged and to which she now added a few bunches of cranberries.

Evan and his attendant now returned along the beach, the latter bearing a large salmon-trout, while Evan strolled forward with an easy and self-satisfied gait towards the spot where Waverley was agreeably employed at the breakfast table. Evan said something in Gaelic to Alice which made her laugh yet colour up to the eyes through a complexion well embrowned by sun and wind. Evan intimated that the fish should be prepared for breakfast. A spark from the lock of his pistol produced a light, and a few fir branches were quickly in flame and as speedily reduced to hot embers on which the trout was broiled in large slices. To crown the repast, Evan produced from the pocket of his short jerkin a large scallop shell, and from under his plaid a ram's horn full of whisky. Of this he took a copious dram. He offered the same cordial to Alice and to Edward, which they both declined. With the bounteous air of a lord, Evan then proffered the scallop to Dugald Mahony, his attendant, who without waiting to be asked a second time drank it off with great gusto.

Evan then moved towards the boat, inviting Waverley to attend him. Alice, flinging her plaid around her, advanced up to Edward and with the utmost simplicity offered her cheek to his salute. Evan advanced as if to secure a similar favour, but Alice escaped up the rocky bank as fleetly as a deer, and turning round and laughing called something out to him in Gaelic which he answered in the same tone and language. Then, waving her hand to Edward, she was soon lost among the thickets, though they continued for some time to hear her lively carol as she proceeded gaily on her solitary journey.

They now entered the gorge of the cavern, and stepping into the boat the Highlander pushed off and hoisted a clumsy sail, while Evan assumed the helm. As they glided along the silver mirror Evan opened the conversation with a panegyric upon Alice, who, he said, was both *canny* and *fendy*, and was the best dancer of the strathspey in the whole strath. Edward assented, yet he could not help regretting that she was condemned to such a perilous and dismal life.

'Oich! For that,' said Evan, 'there is nothing in Perthshire that she need want, if she ask her father to fetch it, unless it is too hot or too heavy.'

'But to be the daughter of a cattle-stealer, a common thief.'

'Common thief! No such thing. Donald Bean Lean never *lifted* less than a drove in all his life.'

'Do you call him an uncommon thief then?'

'No – he that steals a cow from a poor widow or a stirk from a cottar is a thief. He that lifts a drove from a Sassenach laird is a gentleman-drover. And besides, to take a tree from the forest, a salmon from the river, a deer from the hill, or a cow from the Lowland strath, is what no Highlander need ever think shame upon.'

'But what can this end in, were he taken in such an appropriation?'

'To be sure, he would *die for the law*, as many a pretty man has done before him.'

'Die for the law!'

'Aye, that is, with the law, or by the law, be strapped up on the gallows of Crieff, where his father died, and his goodsire died, and where, I hope, he'll live to die himself, if he's not shot or slashed in a *creagh*.'

'You hope such a death for your friend, Evan?'

'That do I. Would you have me wish him to die on a bundle of wet straw in yon den of his? Like a mangy tyke?'

'But what becomes of Alice then?'

'If such an accident were to happen, as her father would not need her help any longer, I ken nought to hinder me to marry her myself.'

'Gallantly resolved,' said Edward, 'but in the meanwhile, Evan, what has your father-in-law (that shall be, if he have the good fortune not to be hanged) done with the Baron's cattle?'

'Oich,' answered Evan, 'they were all trudging before the sun blinked ower Ben Lawers this morning, and they'll be in the pass of Bally Brough by this time, in their way back to the parks of Tully Veolan.'

'And where are we going, Evan, if I may be so bold as to ask?' said Waverley.

'Where would ye be ganging, but to the laird's own house of Glennaquoich? Ye would not think to be in his country without going to see him. It would be as much as a man's life's worth.'

'And are we far from Glennaquoich?'

'But five bits of miles, and Vich Ian Vohr will meet us.'

In about half an hour they reached the upper end of the lake where, after landing Waverley, the two Highlanders drew the boat into a little creek among thick flags and reeds, where it lay perfectly concealed. The oars they put in another place of concealment.

The travellers pursued for some time a delightful opening into the hills down which a little brook found its way to the lake. Waverley renewed his questions about their host of the cavern.

'Does he always reside in that cave?'

'Out, no! It's past the skill of man to tell where he's to be found at all times. There's not a dern nook, or cove or corrie in the whole country that he's not acquainted with.'

'And do others beside your master shelter him?'

'My master? *My* master is in Heaven,' answered Evan haughtily, and then immediately assuming his usual civility of manner, 'but you mean my chief. No, he does not shelter Donald Bean Lean, nor any that are like him, he only allows him wood and water.'

'No great boon, I should think Evan, when both seem to be very plenty.'

'Ah, but ye don't see through it. When I say wood and water, I mean the loch and the land, and I fancy Donald would be put till't if the laird were to look for him wi' threescore men in the wood of Kailychat yonder, and if our boats, with a score or two more, were to come down the loch to Uaimh an Ri, headed by mysel.'

'But suppose a strong party came against him from the low country. Would not your chief defend him?'

'Na, he would not ware the spark of a flint for him if they came with the law.'

'And what must Donald do then?'

'He behoved to rid this country of himsell and fall back, it may be, over the mount upon Letter Scriven.'

'And if he were pursued to that place?'

'I'se warrant he would go to his cousin's at Rannoch.'

'Well, but if they followed him to Rannoch?'

'That,' quoth Evan, 'is beyond all belief, and indeed, to tell you the truth, there durst not a Lowlander in all Scotland follow the fray a gunshot beyond Bally Brough, unless he had the help of the *Sidier Dhu*.'

'Whom do ye call so?'

'The *Sidier Dhu*? The black soldier, that is the independent companies that were raised to keep peace in the Highlands. Vich Ian Vorh commanded one of them for five years, and I was a sergeant myself. They call them *Sidier Dhu* because they wear the tartans, as they call your men, King George's men, *Sidier Roy*, or red soldiers.'

'But when you were in King George's pay, Evan, you were surely King George's soldiers?'

'You must ask Vich Ian Vohr about that, for we are for his line and care not much which o' them it is. At any rate, nobody can say we are King George's men now, when we have not seen his pay this twelvemonth.'

And now the report of a gun was heard and a sportsman was seen, with his dogs and attendant, at the upper end of the glen.

'Shough,' said Dugald Mahony, 'tat's ta Chief.'

'It is not,' said Evan imperiously. 'Do you think he would come to meet a Sassenach duinhé-wassel (English gentleman) in such a way as this?'

But as they approached a little nearer, he said, with an appearance of mortification, 'And it is even he sure enough, and he has not his tail on after all. There is no living creature with him but Callum Beg.'

In fact, Fergus MacIvor had no idea of raising himself in the eyes of an English young man of fortune by appearing with a retinue of idle Highlanders disproportioned to the occasion. He was well aware that such an unnecessary attendance would seem to Edward rather ludicrous than respectable, and while few men were more attached to ideas of chieftainship and feudal power, he was cautious of exhibiting external marks of dignity unless at the time and in the manner when they were most likely to produce an imposing effect. Therefore, although had he been to receive a brother chieftain he would probably have been attended by all that retinue which Evan had described, he judged it more respectable to meet Waverley with a single attendant, a handsome Highland boy who carried his master's shooting-pouch and broadsword.

Waverley was struck with the chieftain's grace and dignity. Above the middle size and finely proportioned, the Highland dress which he wore in its simplest mode set off his person to great advantage. He wore the trews, or close trousers, made of tartan, checked scarlet and white. In other particulars his dress resembled Evan's, excepting that he had no weapon save a dirk, richly mounted with silver. His page carried the claymore, and the fowling-piece which he held in his hand seemed only designed for sport. He had shot some young wild ducks, as the broods of grouse were yet too young for the sportsman. His countenance was decidedly Scotch, with all the peculiarities of the northern physiognomy, but had yet so little of its harshness that it would have been pronounced in any country extremely handsome. The martial air of the bonnet with a single eagle's feather added to the manly appearance of his head, ornamented with a natural and graceful cluster of close black curls.

An air of affability increased the favourable impression derived from this handsome exterior. Yet a skilful physiognomist would have been less satisfied with the countenance on the second view. The eyebrow and upper lip bespoke a habit of peremptory command. Even his courtesy, though unconstrained, seemed to indicate a sense of personal importance, and upon any check a sudden though transient lour of the eye showed a haughty temper, not less to be dreaded because it seemed much under its owner's command.

It was not, however, upon their first meeting that Edward made these less favourable remarks. The chief received him with the utmost kindness, upbraided him gently for choosing so rude an abode as he had done the night before, and entered into a lively conversation with him about Donald Bean's housekeeping but without the least hint as to his predatory habits or the immediate occasion of Waverley's visit, a topic which our hero also avoided.

chapter nineteen

The Chief and his Mansion

The father of Fergus engaged heart and hand in the insurrection of 1715, and was forced to fly to France after the attempt in favour of the Stuarts had proved unsuccessful. More fortunate than other fugitives, he obtained employment in the French service and married a lady of rank in that kingdom, by whom he had two children, Fergus and Flora. The Scottish estate had been forfeited and exposed to sale, but was bought in at a small price in the name of the young proprietor, who came to reside upon his native domains.[1] It was soon perceived that he was a character of uncommon acuteness and ambition.

Fergus MacIvor applied himself with great earnestness to appease all the dissensions which frequently arose among other clans in his neighbourhood, so that he became an umpire in their quarrels. His own power he strengthened at every expense his fortune would permit, and indeed stretched his means to maintain the rude and plentiful hospitality which was the most valued attribute of a chieftain. He crowded his estate with a tenantry hardy and fit for the purposes of war, but greatly outnumbering what the soil could maintain. His allegiance was refused to none who were proper men of their hands and were willing to assume the name of MacIvor.

While in command of one of the independent companies raised by government to preserve peace in the Highlands, he acted with vigour and preserved great

---

[1] After the 1715 rising, convicted Jacobite leaders were deprived of their estates, though properties under entail, ie with a named inheritor as in the case of Tully Veolan, could pass to that inheritor.

order in the country under his charge.[1] In his campaigns against the banditti he exercised to the utmost the discretionary power conceived to belong to the military parties who were called in to support the law. He acted with suspicious lenity to those freebooters who made restitution on his summons and offered submission to himself, while he rigorously pursued and sacrificed to justice all such interlopers as dared to despise his admonitions. On the other hand, if any officers of justice, military parties or others, presumed to pursue thieves or marauders through his territories without his consent, nothing was more certain than that they would meet with some foil or defeat, upon which Fergus MacIvor was the first to condole with them, and after greatly blaming their rashness never failed to lament the lawless state of the country. These lamentations did not exclude suspicion, and matters were so represented to government that our chieftain was deprived of his military command.

Whatever he felt, he had the art of entirely suppressing every appearance of discontent, but in a short time the neighbouring country began to feel bad effects from his disgrace. Donald Bean Lean and others carried on their ravages with little opposition, as the Lowland gentry were chiefly Jacobites and disarmed. This forced many into contracts of blackmail with Fergus MacIvor, which not only established him their protector but moreover supplied funds for his feudal hospitality, which the discontinuance of his pay might have otherwise diminished.

In all this Fergus had a further object than merely ruling despotically over a small clan. From his infancy he had devoted himself to the cause of the exiled family, and had persuaded himself not only that their restoration to the crown of Britain would be speedy, but that those who assisted them would be raised to honour and rank. It was with this view that he laboured to reconcile the Highlanders among themselves, and augmented his own force to be prepared for the first favourable opportunity of rising. With this purpose also he conciliated the favour of such Lowland gentlemen in the vicinity as were friends to the good cause. For the same reason, having incautiously quarrelled with Mr Bradwardine, who was much respected in the country, he took advantage of the foray of Donald Bean Lean to solder up the dispute. Some indeed surmised that he caused the enterprise to be suggested to Donald to pave the way to reconciliation. This zeal in their behalf the house of Stuart repaid with a considerable share of their confidence, an occasional supply of louis-d'ors and a parchment with a huge seal purporting to be an earl's patent granted by no less a person that James the Third King of England and Eighth King of Scotland to his right trusty and well-beloved Fergus MacIvor of Glennaquoich in the county of Perth and kingdom of Scotland.

With this future coronet glittering before his eyes, Fergus plunged deeply into the plots of that unhappy period. Like all such active agents, he easily reconciled his conscience to going certain lengths in the service of his party, from which honour and pride would have deterred him had his sole object been the advancement of his own interest.

The Chief and his guest had by this time reached the house of Glennaquoich,

---

[1] The independent companies were formed in 1739 to become the British army's first Highland regiment of the line, known as the Black Watch.

which consisted of a high rude-looking square tower, with the addition of a house of two storeys. Around the house, which stood on an eminence in the midst of a narrow Highland valley, there appeared none of that attention to convenience, still less to ornament, which usually surrounds a gentleman's habitation. An enclosure or two, divided by dry stone walls, were the only part of the domain that was fenced. The narrow slips of level ground which lay by the side of the brook exhibited a scanty crop of barley, liable to constant depredations from the herds of wild ponies and black cattle that grazed upon the adjacent hills. These made incursions which were repelled by the dissonant shouts of half a dozen Highland swains, all running as if they had been mad and everyone hallooing a half-starved dog to the rescue of the forage. The hills were high and heathy but without any variety of surface, so that the whole view was wild and desolate rather than grand and solitary.

Before the gate were assembled about a hundred Highlanders in complete dress and arms, at sight of whom the chieftain apologized to Waverley in a negligent manner. 'He had forgot,' he said, 'that he had ordered a few of his clan out for the purpose of seeing that they were fit to protect the country and prevent such accidents as had befallen the Baron of Bradwardine. Before they were dismissed, perhaps Captain Waverley might choose to see them go through part of their exercise?

Edward assented, and the men executed with agility and precision some of the ordinary military movements. They then showed extraordinary dexterity in the management of the pistol and firelock. They took aim standing, sitting, leaning or lying prostrate, and always with effect upon the target. Next they paired off for the broadsword exercise, and having manifested their individual skill united in two bodies and exhibited a mock encounter in which the charge, the rally, the fight, the pursuit and all the current of a heady fight were exhibited to the sound of the great war bagpipe.

On a signal from the Chief the skirmish was ended. Matches were then made for running, wrestling, leaping, pitching the bar and other sports, in which this feudal militia displayed incredible swiftness, strength and agility, and accomplished the purpose which their chieftain had at heart by impressing on Waverley no light sense of their merit as soldiers and the power of him who commanded them.

'And what number of such gallant fellows have the happiness to call you leader?' asked Waverley.

'In a good cause and under a chieftain whom they loved, the race of Ivor have seldom taken the field under five hundred claymores. But you are aware, Captain Waverley, that the disarming act, passed about twenty years ago, prevents their being in the complete state of preparation as in former times. I keep no more of my clan under arms than may defend my own or my friends' property when the country is troubled with such men as your last night's landlord. Government, which has removed other means of defence, must connive at us protecting ourselves.

'But with your force you might soon put down such gangs as that of Donald Bean Lean.'

'Yes, doubtless, and my reward would be a summons to deliver up to General Blakeney at Stirling the few broadswords they have left us. But come, captain, the sound of the pipes informs me that dinner is prepared. Let me have the honour to show you into my rude mansion.'

chapter twenty

A Highland Feast

The hall in which the feast was prepared occupied all the first storey of the tower, and a huge oaken table extended through its whole length. The apparatus for dinner was simple and the company numerous. At the head of the table was the Chief himself, with Edward and two or three Highland visitors of neighbouring clans. The elders of the clan, wadsetters and tacksmen as they were called, who occupied portions of his estate as mortgagers or lessees, sat next in rank. Beneath them, their sons and nephews and foster-brethren, then the officers of the Chief's household according to their order, and lowest of all, the tenants who actually cultivated the ground. Even beyond this long perspective, Edward might see upon the green, to which a huge pair of folding doors opened, a multitude of Highlanders of a yet inferior description who nevertheless were considered as guests and had their share of the cheer of the day. In the distance was a changeful group of women, ragged boys and girls, beggars young and old, large greyhounds and terriers and pointers and curs of low degree, all of whom took some interest in the main action of the piece.

The hospitality, apparently unbounded, had yet its line of economy. Some pains had been bestowed on the dishes of fish, game etc at the upper end of the table and immediately under the eye of the English stranger. Lower down stood immense clumsy joints of mutton and beef. But the central dish was a yearling lamb, called 'a hog in harst', roasted whole. It was set upon its legs with a bunch of parsley in its mouth, probably exhibited in that form to gratify the pride of the cook, who piqued himself more on the plenty than the elegance of his master's table. The sides of this poor animal were fiercely attacked by the clansmen, some with dirks, others with knives usually in the same sheath with the dagger, so that it was soon rendered a mangled spectacle. Lower down still, the victuals seemed of yet coarser quality though sufficiently abundant. Broth, onions, cheese and the fragments of the feast regaled the sons of Ivor who feasted in the open air.

The liquor was supplied under similar regulations. Excellent claret and champagne were liberally distributed among the Chief's immediate neighbours. Whisky and strong-beer refreshed those who sat near the lower end. Nor did this inequality of distribution give the least offence. Everyone present understood that his taste was to be formed according to the rank which he held at table, and consequently the tacksmen and their dependants always professed the wine was too cold for their stomachs, and called for the liquor which was assigned to them from economy.

Three bagpipers screamed during the whole time of dinner a tremendous war tune, and the echoing of the vaulted roof and clang of the Celtic tongue produced such a Babel of noises that Waverley dreaded his ears would never recover. MacIvor apologized for the confusion occasioned by so large a party, and pleaded the necessity of his situation on which unlimited hospitality was a paramount duty. 'These stout idle kinsmen of mine,' he said, 'account my estate as held in trust for their support, and I must find them beef and ale while the rogues will do nothing for themselves but practise the broadsword or wander about the hills shooting, fishing, drinking and making love to the lasses of the strath. But what can I do, Captain Waverley? Every thing will keep after its kind, whether it be a hawk or a Highlander.' Edward made the expected answer, in a compliment upon his possessing so many bold followers.

The Chieftain made a signal for the pipes to cease and said, 'Where is the song hidden, my friends, that MacMurrough cannot find it?' MacMurrough, the family *bhairdh*, an aged man, immediately began to chant with low and rapid utterance a profusion of Celtic verses, which were received by the audience with enthusiasm. As he advanced his ardour seemed to increase. He had at first spoken with his eyes fixed on the ground. Now he cast them around as if commanding attention, and his tones rose into wild and impassioned notes accompanied with appropriate gesture. He seemed to Edward to recite many proper names, to lament the dead, to apostrophize the absent, to exhort and animate those who were present. Waverley thought he even discerned his own name, and was convinced he was right from the eyes of the company being at that moment turned towards him simultaneously. Their wild countenances assumed a fiercer expression. All bent towards the reciter, many sprang up and waved their arms in ecstacy, and some laid their hands on their swords, When the song ceased there was a deep pause, while the aroused feelings of the poet and the hearers gradually subsided. The Chieftain filled with claret a small silver cup which stood beside him. 'Give this,' he said to an attendant, 'to MacMurrough nan Fion (ie of the songs) and when he has drank the juice bid him keep, for the sake of Vich Ian Vohr, the gourd which contained it.' The gift was received by MacMurrough with profound gratitude. He drank the wine and, kissing the cup, shrouded it with reverence in the plaid which was folded on his bosom. He then burst forth into an extemporaneous effusion of thanks and praises of his chief. It was received with applause. It was obvious that the clan regarded the generosity of their chieftain with high approbation. Many Gaelic toasts were then proposed, of some of which the Chieftain gave his guest the following versions: 'To him that will not turn his back on friend or foe.' 'To him that never forsook a comrade.' 'To him that never bought or sold justice.' 'Hospitality to the exile, and broken bones to the tyrant.' 'Highlanders shoulder to shoulder.'

Edward was particularly solicitous to know the meaning of that song which appeared to produce such effect upon the company. 'As I observe,' said the Chieftain, 'that you have passed the bottle during the last three rounds, I was about to propose to you to retire to my sister's tea-table, who can explain these things to you better than I can.'

Edward readily assented to this proposal and the Chieftain left the table followed by Waverley. As the door closed behind them, Edward heard Vich Ian Vohr's health invoked with a wild cheer that expressed the satisfaction of the guests and the depth of their devotion to his service.

chapter twenty-one

The Chieftain's Sister

The drawing-room of Flora MacIvor was furnished in the plainest manner, for at Glennaquoich every other expenditure was retrenched for the purpose of maintaining the hospitality of the chieftain and multiplying the number of his dependants and adherents. But there was no appearance of parsimony in the dress of the lady herself, which was elegant and rich, and arranged in a manner which partook partly of the Parisian fashion and partly of the more simple dress of the Highlands. Her hair fell in jetty ringlets on her neck, confined only by a circlet richly set with diamonds. This peculiarity she adopted in compliance with the Highland prejudices, which could not endure that a woman's head should be covered before wedlock.

Flora MacIvor bore a striking resemblance to her brother. They had the same dark eyes and eyebrows, the same clearness of complexion, excepting that Fergus's was embrowned by exercise and Flora's possessed the utmost feminine delicacy. But the haughty and somewhat stern regularity of Fergus's features was beautifully softened in those of Flora. The eager glance of the keen black eye which in the Chieftain seemed impatient, had in his sister's acquired a gentle pensiveness. His looks seemed to seek glory, power, all that could exalt him above others, while those of his sister seemed to pity rather than envy those who were struggling for any other distinction. Early education had impressed upon her mind the most devoted attachment to the exiled family of Stuart. She believed it the duty of her brother, of his clan, of every man in Britain, at whatever personal hazard, to contribute to that restoration which the partisans of the Chevalier St George had not ceased to hope for.[1] For this she was prepared to do all, suffer all, sacrifice all. Ambitious by nature, Fergus's political faith was tinctured, if not tainted, by the interest and advancement so easily combined with it, and at the moment he should unsheathe his claymore it might be difficult to say whether it would be most with the view of making James Stuart a king or Fergus MacIvor an earl.

---

[1] Chevalier St George was the French title granted to James VIII and III, the 'Old Pretender'.

In Flora's bosom the zeal of loyalty burned pure and unmixed with any selfish feeling. She would have as soon have made religion the mask of ambitious views as have shrouded them under patriotism. Such instances of devotion were not uncommon among the followers of the unhappy race of Stuart. But peculiar attention on the part of the Chevalier de St George to Fergus and his sister when orphans had riveted their faith. Fergus, upon the death of his parents, had been for some time page of honour in the train of the Chevalier's lady and was treated by her with the utmost distinction. This was also extended to Flora, who was maintained at a convent at the princess's expense and then removed into her own family where she spent nearly two years. Both retained the most grateful sense of her kindness.

Flora was highly accomplished and acquired elegant manners, yet she had not learned to substitute the gloss of politeness for the reality of feeling. When settled in the lonely regions of Glennaquoich her resources in French, English and Italian literature were few and interrupted, and in order to fill her vacant time she bestowed a part of it upon the music and poetical traditions of the Highlanders. Her resolution was strengthened in these researches by the delight which her enquiries seemed to afford those to whom she resorted for information.

Her love of her clan was a more pure passion than that of her brother. He was too much a politician that we should term him the model of a Highland chieftain. Flora felt the same anxiety for cherishing and extending their patriarchal sway, but it was with the generous desire of vindicating from want and oppression those whom her brother was by birth entitled to govern. The savings of her small pension from the Princess Sobieski were dedicated to relieve the peasantry's absolute necessities when in sickness or extreme old age – at every other period they toiled to procure something which they might share with the Chief.[1] Flora was much beloved by them. Miss MacIvor's society was extremely limited. Her most intimate friend had been Rose Bradwardine, to whom she was much attached. Rose was so tenderly watched by her father and her wishes so limited that none arose but what he was willing to gratify and scarce any which did not come within the compass of his power. With Flora it was otherwise. While almost a girl she had undergone the most complete change of scene, from gaiety and splendour to solitude and comparative poverty. The ideas and wishes which she chiefly fostered respected great national events and changes not to be brought without hazard and bloodshed. She stood very high in the opinion of the old Baron.

It was generally believed that Flora's entreaties had no small share in allaying the wrath of Fergus upon occasion of their quarrel. She dwelt first upon the Baron's age and then represented the injury which the cause might sustain and the damage which might arise to his own character. Otherwise it is probable that it would have terminated in a duel. She had urged their reconciliation, which the Chieftain more readily agreed to, as it favoured some ulterior projects of his own.

---

[1]   Maria Clementina Sobieska was the wife of James VIII and III.

chapter twenty-two

Highland Minstrelsy

My dear Flora,' Fergus said to his sister, 'I must tell you that Captain Waverley is a worshipper of the Celtic muse, not the less so perhaps that he does not understand a word of her language. I have told him you are eminent as a translator of Highland poetry. Will you read or recite to our guest in English the extraordinary string of names which MacMurrough has tacked together in Gaelic? I know you are in the bard's councils and acquainted with his songs long before he rehearses them in the hall.'

'How can you say so Fergus! You know how little these verses can possibly interest an English stranger, even if I could translate them as you pretend.'

'No less than they interest me, lady fair. Today your joint composition, for I insist you had a share in it, has cost me the last silver cup in the castle. When the hand of the chief ceases to bestow, the breath of the bard is frozen in utterance. Well, I would it were ever so. There are three things that are useless to a modern Highlander – a sword which he must not draw, a bard to sing of deeds which he dare not imitate, and a large goatskin purse without a louis-d'or to put into it.'

'I assure you, Captain Waverley, that Fergus esteems MacMurrough a far greater poet than Homer, and would not give up his goatskin purse for all the louis-d'ors which it could contain.'

'Well pronounced, Flora. Now do you two talk of bards and poetry while I return to do the final honours to the senators of the tribe of Ivor.' So saying he left the room.

The conversation continued between Flora and Waverley, for her two young women companions took no share in it. Waverley was equally amused and surprised with the accounts which the lady gave him of Celtic poetry.

'The recitation,' she said, 'of poems recording the feats of heroes, the complaints of lovers and the wars of contending tribes forms the chief amusement of a winter fireside in the Highlands. Some of these are said to be very ancient, and if they are ever translated into any of the languages of civilized Europe cannot fail to produce a sensation.[1] Others are more modern, the compositions of family bards whom chieftains retain as poets and historians of their tribes. These possess various degrees of merit, but much evaporates in translation.'

'And your bard, is he reckoned among the favourite poets of the mountains?'

'His reputation is high among his countrymen and you must not expect me to depreciate it.'

'But the song seemed to awaken all these warriors young and old.'

'The song is little more than a catalogue of names of the Highland clans and an exhortation to them to emulate the actions of their forefathers.'

---

[1] James Macpherson's versions of heroic Celtic verse, *Fragments of Ancient Poetry, Collected in the Highlands of Scotland*, were published in 1760 and did indeed cause a sensation, which of course Scott knew.

'Am I wrong in conjecturing that there was some allusion to me in the verses?'

'You have a quick observation, Captain Waverley. The Gaelic language is well adapted for extemporaneous poetry, and a bard seldom fails to augment the effect of a song by throwing in any stanzas suggested by the circumstances attending the recitation.'

'I would give my best horse to know what the Highland bard could find to say of such an unworthy southern as myself.'

'It shall not even cost you a lock of his mane. Una, *mavourneen*! (She spoke a few words to one of the young girls, who instantly tripped out of the room.) I have sent Una to learn from the bard the expressions he used.'

Una returned and repeated to her mistress a few lines in Gaelic. Flora, slightly colouring, turned to Waverley. 'It is impossible to gratify your curiosity, Captain Waverley, without exposing my own presumption. If you will give me a few moments, I will endeavour to engraft the meaning of these lines upon a rude English translation which I have attempted of part of the original. As the evening is delightful, Una will show you the way to one of my favourite haunts, and Cathleen and I will join you there.'

Una conducted Waverley out. At a distance he heard the hall still resounding with the clang of bagpipes and applause. Having gained the open air, they walked a little way up the bleak and narrow valley in which the house was situated, following the course of the stream that wound through it. About a quarter of a mile from the castle, two brooks had their junction. The larger of the two came down the bare valley, but the other stream seemed to issue from a narrow and dark opening betwixt two large rocks, rapid and furious like a maniac from his confinement, all foam and uproar.

It was up the course of this last stream that Waverley was conducted. A small path led him through scenery very different from that which he had just quitted. Around the castle all was cold and bare yet tame even in desolation, but this narrow glen seemed to open into the land of romance. The rocks assumed a thousand peculiar forms. A crag of huge size presented its bulk as if to forbid further progress, and it was not until he approached its very base that Waverley discerned the acute turn by which the pathway wheeled its course around this formidable obstacle. In another spot, projecting rocks from opposite sides of the chasm approached so near to each other that two pine trees laid across and covered with turf formed a rustic bridge at the height of at least one hundred and fifty feet. It had no ledges and was barely three feet in breadth.

While gazing at this pass of peril, which crossed like a single black line the small portion of blue sky not intercepted by the projecting rocks, it was with horror that Waverley beheld Flora appear, propped in mid air upon this trembling structure. She stopped upon observing him below, and with an air of graceful ease which made him shudder waved her handkerchief to him. He was unable, from the dizziness which her situation conveyed, to return the salute, and was never more relieved than when the fair apparition passed on from the precarious eminence which she seemed to occupy with so much indifference.

Passing under the bridge, the path ascended rapidly from the edge of the brook and the glen widened into a sylvan amphitheatre, waving with birch, young oaks and hazels with here and there a yew tree. The rocks now receded, but still showed their shaggy crests. Still higher rose peaks, some bare, some clothed with wood, some round and purple with heath and others splintered into rocks and crags. At a short turning the path suddenly placed Waverley in front of a romantic waterfall. After a broken cataract of about twenty feet the stream was received in a natural basin filled to the brim with water which, where the bubbles of the fall subsided, was so clear that although of great depth the eye could discern each pebble at the bottom. Eddying round this reservoir, the brook formed a second fall which seemed to seek the very abyss. Then wheeling out from among the smooth dark rocks it wandered down the glen, forming the stream which Waverley had just ascended. The borders of this reservoir corresponded in beauty of a stern and commanding cast. Mossy banks of turf were interrupted by huge fragments of rock and decorated with trees and shrubs, some of which had been planted under the direction of Flora, but so cautiously that they added to the grace without diminishing the romantic wildness of the scene.

Here Waverley found Flora gazing on the waterfall. Farther back stood Cathleen holding a small Scottish harp. The sun now stooping in the west seemed to add more than human brilliancy to the full expressive darkness of Flora's eye and enhanced the grace of her form. Edward thought he had never, even in his wildest dreams, imagined a figure of such exquisite loveliness. The wild beauty of the retreat, bursting upon him as if by magic, augmented his delight and awe.

Flora, like every beautiful woman, was conscious of her own power and pleased with its effects. But as she possessed excellent sense, she gave the romance of the scene full weight in appreciating the feelings with which Waverley seemed obviously to be impressed. She quietly led the way to a spot at such a distance from the cascade that its sound should rather accompany than interrupt her voice and instrument, and sitting down upon a mossy fragment of rock she took the harp from Cathleen.

'I have given you the trouble of walking to this spot, Captain Waverley, both because I thought the scenery would interest you and because a Highland song would suffer still more from my imperfect translation were I to produce it without its own wild accompaniments. The seat of the Celtic Muse is in the mist of the secret and solitary hill and her voice in the murmur of the mountain stream. He who woos her must love the barren rock more than the fertile valley, and the solitude of the desert better than the festivity of the hall.'

Few could have heard this declaration without exclaiming that the muse whom she invoked could never find a more appropriate representative. But Waverley, though the thought rushed on his mind, found no courage to utter it. Indeed, the romantic delight with which he heard the first notes from her instrument amounted almost to pain. He would not for worlds have quitted her side, yet he almost longed for solitude, that he might examine at leisure his complication of emotions.

Flora had exchanged the measured recitative of the bard for an uncommon Highland air which had been a battle song in former ages. A few irregular strains introduced a wild tone which harmonized well with the distant waterfall and the soft evening breeze in the rustling leaves of an aspen. The following verses convey little idea of the feelings with which they were heard by Edward:

Mist darkens the mountain, night darkens the vale,
But more dark is the sleep of the sons of the Gael:
A stranger commanded – it sunk on the land,
It has frozen each heart, and benumb'd every hand!

The dirk and the target lie sordid with dust,
The bloodless claymore is but redden'd with rust;
On the hill or the glen if a gun should appear,
It is only to war with the heath-cock or deer.

The deeds of our sires if our bards should rehearse,
Let a blush or a blow be the meed of their verse!
Be mute every string, and be hush'd every tone,
That shall bid us remember the fame that is flown.

But the dark hours of night and of slumber are past,
The morn on our mountains is dawning at last;
Glenaladale's peaks are illumed with the rays,
And the streams of Glenfinnan leap bright in the blaze.

Ye sons of the strong, when the dawning shall break,
Need the harp of the aged remind you to wake?
That dawn never beam'd on your forefather's eye,
But it roused each high chieftain to vanquish or die.

O sprung from the Kings who in Islay kept state,
Proud chiefs of Clan Ranald, Glengarry, and Sleat!
Combine like three streams from one mountain of snow,
And resistless in union rush down on the foe!

True son of Sir Evan, undaunted Lochiel,
Place thy targe on thy shoulder and burnish thy steel!
Rough Keppoch, give breath to thy bugle's bold swell,
Till far Coryarrick resound to the knell![1]

Here a large greyhound, bounding up the glen, jumped upon Flora and interrupted her music by his importunate caresses. At a distant whistle he turned and shot down the path again. 'That is Fergus's faithful attendant, Captain Waverley, and that was his signal. He likes no poetry but what is humorous, and comes in

---

[1] By Scott.

good time to interrupt my catalogue of the tribes.' Waverley expressed his regret at the interruption.

'You cannot guess how much you have lost! The bard has addressed three long stanzas to Vich Ian Vohr, enumerating all his great properties. Besides, you should have heard an admonition to the fair-haired stranger who lives in the land where the grass is always green, the rider on the shining pampered steed whose hue is like the raven and whose neigh is like scream of the eagle. This valiant horseman is conjured to remember that his ancestors were distinguished by their loyalty as well as by their courage. All this you have lost.'

chapter twenty-three

Waverley Continues at Glennaquoich

As they returned to the castle the Chieftain pressed Waverley to stay for a week or two, in order to see a grand hunting party in which he and some other Highland gentlemen proposed to join. The charms of melody and beauty were too strongly impressed on Edward to permit his declining an invitation so pleasing. It was agreed that he should write a note to the Baron expressing his intention to stay a fortnight at Glennaquoich and requesting him to forward by the bearer any letters which may have arrived for him.

This turned the discourse upon the Baron, whom Fergus extolled as a gentleman and soldier. Flora observed he was the very model of old Scottish cavalier, with all his excellencies and peculiarities. The amiable Rose was next mentioned, with the warmest encomium on her person, manners and mind. 'Her very soul is in home,' said Flora, 'and in the discharge of all those quiet virtues of which home is the centre. Her husband will be the object of all her care and affection.'

Waverley soon prepared his dispatches for Tully Veolan. As he knew the Baron was punctilious in such matters, he was about to impress his billet with a seal on which his armorial bearings were engraved, but he did not find it. He mentioned his loss, borrowing the family seal of the Chieftain. He thought he must have left it at Tully Veolan.

'Surely,' said Miss MacIvor, 'Donald Bean Lean would not –'

'My life for him in such circumstances,' answered her brother.

'I am surprised you can countenance that man.'

'I countenance him? This sister of mine would persuade you, Captain Waverley, that I take a 'collop of the foray', or a portion of the robber's booty paid by him to the laird through whose grounds he drove his prey. Unless I find some way to charm Flora's tongue, General Blakeney will send a party from Stirling (this he said with haughty irony) to seize Vich Ian Vohr in his own castle.'

'Now Fergus, you have men enough to serve you without enlisting banditti. Why don't you send this Donald Bean Lean, whom I hate for his duplicity even more than for his rapine, out of your country at once? No cause should induce me to tolerate such a character.'

'No cause, Flora?' said the Chieftain significantly.

'No cause, Fergus! Not even that which is nearest to my heart. Spare it the omen of such evil supporters!'

'O but sister,' rejoined the Chief gaily, 'Evan Dhu is in love with Donald's daughter and you cannot expect me to disturb him in his amours. Why the whole clan would cry shame on me.'

'Well, Fergus, there is no disputing with you, but I would all this would end well.'

'Devoutly prayed, and the best way in the world to close a dubious argument. But hear ye not the pipes, Captain Waverley? Perhaps you would like better to dance in the hall than to be deafened with their harmony without taking part in the exercise they invite.'

Waverley took Flora's hand. The dance and merry-making proceeded and closed the day's entertainment at the castle of Vich Ian Vohr. Edward at length retired, his mind agitated by conflicting feelings which detained him from rest for some time in that state of mind in which fancy takes the helm and the soul drifts along with a confused tide of reflections. At a late hour he fell asleep and dreamed of Flora MacIvor.

volume II

chapter one

A Stag Hunt and its Consequences

The hunting was delayed for about three weeks. The interval was spent by Waverley with great satisfaction, for the impression which Flora had made grew daily stronger. Her manners, her language, her talents for poetry and music gave additional influence to her eminent personal charms. Waverley became daily more delighted with his hospitable landlord and more enamoured of his bewitching sister.

At length the period fixed for the hunting arrived, and Waverley and the Chieftain departed for the place of rendezvous, a day's journey north of Glennaquoich. Fergus was attended by about three hundred of his clan, well armed. Waverley complied so far with the custom of the country as to adopt the trews, brogues and bonnet, which less exposed him to be stared at as a stranger. They found on the spot appointed several distinguished Chiefs, to all of whom Waverley was presented and by all cordially received. Their clansmen appeared in such numbers as amounted to a small army. These assistants spread through the country, forming a circle which drove the deer towards the glen where the Chiefs and principal sportsmen lay in wait.

For many hours after sunrise the mountain ridges and passes retained silence and solitude, and the Chiefs with their followers amused themselves with various pastimes. At length signals of the approach of the game were descried and heard. Distant shouts resounded as the Highlanders climbing rocks, struggling through copses, wading brooks and traversing thickets, compelled the astonished deer into a narrower circuit. The report of muskets was heard, repeated by a thousand echoes. The baying of the dogs soon added to the chorus, which grew ever louder. The deer began to show themselves and as the stragglers came bounding down the pass two or three at a time, the Chiefs showed their skill by distinguishing the fattest deer, and their dexterity in bringing them down with their guns. Fergus exhibited remarkable address, and Edward was also so fortunate as to attract the notice and applause of the sportsmen.

Now the main body of the deer appeared at the head of the glen presenting the most formidable phalanx, their antlers appearing over the ridge of the steep pass like a leafless grove. Their number was very great, and from a desperate stand which they made, with the tallest of the red-deer stags in front in a sort of battle array, the more experienced sportsmen began to auger danger. The work of destruction, however, now commenced. Dogs and hunters were at work, and muskets and fusees resounded from every quarter. The deer made at length a fearful charge right upon the spot where the most distinguished sportsmen had taken their stand. The word was given in Gaelic to fling themselves upon their faces, but Waverley, upon whose English ears the signal was lost, had almost fallen a sacrifice to his ignorance. Fergus, observing his danger, sprang up and pulled him to the ground just as the whole herd broke down upon them. The tide being irresistible and wounds from a stag's horn highly dangerous, the Chieftain may be considered as having saved his guest's life. He detained him with a firm grasp until the whole herd had fairly run over them. Waverley then attempted to rise, but found that he had suffered several severe contusions, and had sprained his ankle violently.

This checked the mirth of the meeting, although the Highlanders, accustomed to such incidents, had suffered no harm themselves. Edward was deposited on a couch of heather. The surgeon, or he who assumed the office, was an old smoke-dried Highlander, wearing a venerable grey beard and having for his sole garment a tartan frock, the skirts of which descended to his knee and made the vestment serve at once for doublet and breeches. He observed great ceremony, and though our hero was writhing with pain, would not proceed to any operation which would assuage it until he had perambulated his couch three times, moving from east to west according to the course of the sun. Edward, whom pain rendered incapable of expostulation, submitted in silence.

After this ceremony the old Esculapius let Edward blood with a cupping-glass, and proceeded, muttering all the while to himself in Gaelic, to boil herbs with which he compounded an embrocation which had a speedy effect in alleviating the pain and swelling.[1] Edward was given to understand that not one of the ingredients had been gathered except during the full moon. The exhaustion of pain and fatigue threw him into a profound but feverish sleep, which he owed partly also to an opiate draught which the old Highlander had administered from some concoction of herbs.

Early next morning MacIvor had a litter prepared of birch and hazel, which was borne by his people with caution and dexterity. The various tribes assembled, each at the pibroch of his clan headed by their patriarchal ruler. Some were seen winding up the hills or descending the passes, the sound of their bagpipes dying away upon the ear. Others made a moving picture upon the narrow plain, their feathers and loose plaids waving in the morning breeze and their arms glittering in the rising sun. MacIvor commenced his march, but not towards the quarter from which they had come. He gave Waverley to understand that the greater part of his followers were bound upon a distant expedition and that when he had deposited Waverley in the house of a gentleman, who he was sure would pay him every attention, he himself would need to accompany them the greater part of the way.

Waverley was surprised that Fergus had not mentioned this ulterior destination when they set out. A few of the clansmen remained for the purpose of escorting

---

[1] Esculapius was the Greek and Roman god of medicine and a name applied to physicians.

the Chieftain, who walked by the side of Edward's litter. About noon, after a journey which his bruises and the roughness of the way rendered inexpressibly painful, Waverley was hospitably received in the house of a gentleman related to Fergus, an old man about seventy. He wore no dress but what his estate afforded. The cloth was the fleeces of his own sheep woven by his own servants and stained into tartan by the dyes from herbs and lichens. His linen was spun by his daughters and maid-servants from his own flax. Nor did his table offer an article but what was native produce.

This good old man would have received Waverley with kindness had he been the meanest Saxon peasant. But his attention to a friend of Vich Ian Vohr was unremitted. Other embrocations were applied to the injured limb and new spells were put in practice. At length Fergus took farewell of Waverley for a few days, and hoped by that time Waverley would be able to ride one of the Highland ponies of his host and return to Glennaquoich.

The next day Waverley learned that his friend had departed with dawn, leaving Callum Beg. On asking his host if he knew where the Chieftain was gone, the old man looked fixedly at him with something mysterious and sad in his smile, which was his only reply.

The sixth morning had arrived and he was able to walk about with a staff, when Fergus returned with about a score of his men. He seemed in the highest spirits, and finding that Waverley was able to sit upon horseback, proposed their immediate return to Glennaquoich. Waverley's bosom beat thick when they approached the old tower and could distinguish the fair form of its mistress advancing to meet them. Welcoming Waverley with much kindness, Flora expressed her regret for his accident and her surprise that her brother should not have taken better care to put a stranger on his guard against the perils of the sport. Edward readily exculpated the Chieftain, who indeed had probably saved his life.

Fergus said three of four words to his sister in Gaelic. The tears instantly sprung to her eyes, but they seemed to be tears of joy for she looked up to heaven and folded her hands as in an expression of prayer or gratitude. After the pause of a minute she presented to Edward some letters which had been forwarded from Tully Veolan, and delivered some to her brother. Edward speedily found that those which he had received contained matters of very deep interest.

chapter two

News from England

Waverley's father usually wrote to him with the pompous affectation of one who was too much oppressed by public affairs to attend to those of his own family. Latterly, the burthen of Mr Richard Waverley's epistles consisted in certain mysterious hints of greatness and influence which he was speedily to attain. Sir Everard's letters were of a different tenor, short but affectionate. Mr Pembroke wrote to our hero one letter, but it was of the bulk of six epistles, containing a précis of a supplementary manuscript in reference to the two tracts with which he had presented Waverley.

Richard Waverley had acquired a certain name in public life and even established the character of a profound politician. The weakest party were so satisfied with his sentiments and abilities as to propose that, in the case of a certain revolution in the ministry, he should take a place in the new order of things greatly higher in both emolument and influence than that which he now enjoyed. There was no resisting so tempting a proposal, notwithstanding that the Great Man by whose banner he had hitherto stood firm, was the principal object of the proposed attack by the new allies. Unfortunately, this scheme was blighted in the very bud by a premature movement. All the gentlemen concerned were informed that the king had no further occasion for their services and in Waverley's case, which the minister considered as aggravated by ingratitude, dismissal was accompanied by contempt. The public, and even the party of whom he shared the fall, sympathized little in the disappointment of this selfish statesman, and he retired to the country under the reflection that he had lost character, credit and what he at least equally deplored, emolument.

Richard Waverley's letter to his son was a masterpiece of its kind. An unjust monarch and an ungrateful country were the burthen of each paragraph. He spoke of long services and unrequited sacrifices, though nobody could guess in what the latter consisted unless it were in his deserting for the lucre of gain the tory principles of his family. He could not repress some threats of vengeance, however impotent, and finally acquainted his son that he should testify his sense of this ill treatment by throwing up his commission as soon as the letter reached him.

The next letter which Edward opened was from Sir Everard. His brother's disgrace seemed to have removed all recollection of their differences, and the good but credulous baronet at once set it down as a new instance of the injustice of the existing government. It was both the opinion of Richard Waverley and his own that Edward, the representative of the family of Waverley Honour, should not remain in a situation which subjected him to such treatment as that with which his father had been stigmatized. He requested his nephew therefore to transmit his resignation to the War Office. A letter from Aunt Rachael spoke out even more plainly. She considered the disgrace of Richard as the just reward of his forfeiting his allegiance to a lawful though exiled sovereign. She hoped her dear Edward would as speedily as possible get rid of the badge of servitude to the usurping family.

These letters highly excited Waverley's indignation. Of the real cause of his father's disgrace Edward was totally ignorant, nor had he investigated the politics of the period in which he lived or remarked the intrigues in which his father had been so actively engaged. Indeed, any impressions which he had accidentally adopted were rather unfavourable to the existing government and dynasty. He entered, therefore, without hesitation into the resentful feeling of the relations who had the best title to dictate his conduct. If he could have any doubt upon the subject it would have been decided by the following letter from his commanding officer:

Sir,

Having carried somewhat beyond the line of duty an indulgence towards errors which may arise from youth and inexperience, and that altogether without effect, I am reluctantly compelled to use the only remaining remedy which is in my power. You are, therefore hereby commanded to repair to Dundee, the headquarters of the regiment, within three days after the date of this letter. If you shall fail to do so, I must report you to the War Office as absent without leave, and also take other steps which will be disagreeable to you as well as to,

Sir,

Your obedient Servant,

J. Gardiner, Lieut. Co.

Commanding the — Regt. Dragoons

Edward's blood boiled as he read this letter. He had acquired habits which rendered the rules of military discipline as unpleasing to him. An idea that in his own case they would not be enforced in a very rigid manner had also obtained possession of his mind, and had been sanctioned by the indulgence of his lieutenant-colonel. Neither had anything occurred, to his knowledge, that should have induced his commanding officer so suddenly to assume a tone of dictatorial authority. He could not but suppose that it was designed to make him feel the same pressure which had been exercised in his father's case, and that the whole was a concerted scheme to degrade every member of the Waverley family.

Without a pause, therefore, Edward wrote a few cold lines, thanking his lieutenant-colonel for past civilities and expressing regret at his different tone towards him. The strain of his letter called upon him to lay down his commission, and he therefore inclosed the formal resignation, and requested Colonel Gardiner would have the goodness to forward it to the proper authorities.

Having finished this magnanimous epistle, he felt somewhat uncertain concerning the terms in which his resignation ought to be expressed, upon which subject he resolved to consult Fergus MacIvor. It was none of this Chieftain's faults to be indifferent to the wrongs of his friends, and for Edward he felt a sincere interest. The proceeding appeared as extraordinary to him as it had done to Edward. He indeed knew of more motives than Waverley for the peremptory order that he should join his regiment. But that the commanding officer should have proceeded in so harsh a manner was a mystery. He soothed our hero to the best of his power, and began to turn his thoughts on revenge for his insulted honour.

'I would have vengeance fall on the head, not on the hand, on the tyrannical and oppressive government which directed these reiterated insults, not on the tools of office employed in the execution of the injuries.'

'Upon the government!'

'Yes, upon the usurping house of Hanover, whom your grandfather would no more have served than he would have taken wages of red-hot gold from the great fiend of hell!'

'But since the time of my grandfather two generations of this dynasty have possessed the throne.'

'True, and because we have passively given them so long an opportunity of showing their character, because both you and I myself have lived in quiet submission, have truckled to the times so far as to accept commissions under them, are we not on that account to resent injuries which our fathers only apprehended but which we have actually sustained? Or is the cause of the unfortunate Stuart family become less just because their title has devolved upon an heir who is innocent of the charges of misgovernment brought against his father? Trust to me to show you an honourable road to a glorious revenge. Let us seek Flora, who has more news to tell us of what has occurred during our absence. She will rejoice to hear that you are relieved of your servitude. But first add a postscript, marking the time when you received this colonel's first summons, and express your regret that the harshness of his proceedings prevented your anticipating them by sending your resignation. Then let him blush for his injustice.'

chapter three

An Eclaircissement

The Chieftain observed with great satisfaction the growing attachment of Waverley to his sister, nor did he see any bar to their union excepting the situation which Waverley's father held in the ministry and Edward's commission in the army. These obstacles were now removed. In every other respect the match would be most eligible. The happiness and honourable provision of his sister, whom he dearly loved, appeared to be insured by the proposed union. And his heart swelled when he considered how his own interest would be exalted in the eyes of the ex-monarch by an alliance with one of those powerful English families of the ancient cavalier faith. Nor could Fergus perceive any obstacle to such a scheme. Waverley's attachment was evident, and as his person was handsome and his taste apparently coincided with her own, he anticipated no opposition on the part of Flora. Indeed, any opposition from his sister, dear as she was to him, would have been the last obstacle on which he would have calculated.

Influenced by these feelings, the Chief now led Waverley in quest of Miss MacIvor. They found Flora with her faithful attendants, Una and Cathleen, busied in preparing what appeared to Waverley to be white bridal favours. He asked for what joyful occasion Miss MacIvor made such ample preparation.

'It is for Fergus's bridal,' said she, smiling.

'Indeed! He has kept his secret well. I hope he will allow me to be his bride's-man.'

'That is a man's office, but not yours.'

'And who is the fair lady?'

'Did I not tell you long since that Fergus wooed no bride but Honour?'

'And am I then incapable of being his assistant in the pursuit of Honour, Miss MacIvor?' said our hero, colouring deeply. 'Do I rank so low in your opinion?'

'Far from it, Captain Waverley. I would to God you were of our determination!'

'Sister, you may wish Edward Waverley (no longer captain) joy of being freed from the slavery to the usurper.'

'Yes,' said Waverley, undoing the cockade from his hat, 'it has pleased the king who bestowed this badge to resume it in a manner which leaves little reason to regret his service.'

'Thank God for that!' cried the enthusiast.

'And now, sister, replace his cockade with one of a more lively colour. I think it was the fashion of the ladies of yore to send forth their knights to high achievement.'

'Not till the knight-adventurer had well weighed the justice and the danger of the cause, Fergus. Mr Waverley is just now too agitated by emotion for me to press him upon a resolution of consequence.'

Waverley felt half-alarmed at the thought of adopting the badge of what was esteemed rebellion by the majority of the kingdom, yet he could not disguise his chagrin at the coldness with which Flora parried her brother's hint. 'Miss MacIvor thinks the knight unworthy of her favour,' said he somewhat bitterly.

'Not so,' she replied with great sweetness. 'Why should I refuse my brother's valued friend a boon which I am distributing to his whole clan? But he has taken his measures with his eyes open. His life has been devoted to this cause from his cradle. With him the call is sacred, were it even a summons to the tomb. But how can I wish you, so far from every friend who might advise you, how can I wish you to plunge yourself into so desperate an enterprise?'

Fergus strode through the apartment biting his lip, and then with a constrained smile said, 'Well, sister, I leave you to act your new character of mediator between the Elector of Hanover and the subjects of your lawful sovereign and benefactor,' and left the room.

There was a painful pause, at length broken by Miss MacIvor. 'My brother is unjust because he can bear no interruption that seems to thwart his loyal zeal.'

'And do you not share his ardour?'

'God knows mine exceeds his, if that be possible. But I am not rapt by the bustle of military preparation beyond consideration of the grand principles of justice and truth, on which our enterprise is grounded, and these can only be furthered by measures in themselves true and just. To induce you to an irretrievable step of which you have not considered the justice or the danger is neither the one nor the other.'

'Incomparable Flora!' said Edward, taking her hand, 'how much do I need such a monitor! Durst I but hope that you would deign to be to me that affectionate friend who would strengthen me to redeem my errors, my future life –'

'Hush, my dear sir! You now carry your joy at escaping the hands of a jacobite recruiting officer to an unparalleled excess of gratitude.'

'Nay, dear Flora, you cannot mistake the meaning of these feelings which I have almost involuntarily expressed, and since I have broke the barrier of silence let me profit by my audacity. Or may I mention to your broth –'

'Not for the world, Mr Waverley.'

'What am I to understand? Is there any fatal bar –'

'None, sir, I owe it to myself to say that I never yet saw the person on whom I thought with reference to the present subject.'

'The shortness of our acquaintance perhaps –'

'I have not even that excuse. Captain Waverley's character is so open, of that nature that cannot be construed, either in its strength or its weakness.'

'And for that weakness you despise me?'

'Forgive me – and remember it is but within this half hour that there existed between us a barrier to me insurmountable. Permit me to arrange my ideas upon so unexpected a topic and in less than an hour I will give you reasons for the resolution I shall express.' So saying, Flora withdrew, leaving Waverley to meditate upon the manner in which she had received his addresses.

chapter four

Upon the Same Subject

Fergus MacIvor had too much tact to renew the subject. His head was so full of guns, broadswords, bonnets and tartan hose that Waverley could not draw his attention to any other topic.

'Are you to take the field so soon, Fergus, that you are making all these martial preparations?'

'When we have settled that you go with me you shall know all, but otherwise the knowledge might be prejudicial to you.'

'But are you serious in your purpose, with such inferior forces to rise against an established government? It is mere frenzy.'

'I shall take good care of myself. I will not slip my dog before the game's a-foot. But once more, will you join with us and you shall know all?'

'How can I? I who have so lately held that commission now posting back to those who gave it. My accepting it implied a promise of fidelity.'

'A rash promise is not a steel handcuff. It may be shaken off, especially when it was given under deception and has been repaid by insult. But if you cannot immediately make up your mind to a glorious revenge, go to England and ere you cross the Tweed you will hear tidings that will make the world ring.'

'But your sister, Fergus? I feel that my happiness must depend upon the answer which Miss MacIvor shall make to what I ventured to tell her this morning.'

'And is this your sober earnest, or are we in the land of romance and fiction?'

'My earnest, undoubtedly. How could you suppose me jesting on such a subject?'

'Then in sober earnest I am very glad to hear of it – you are the only man in England for whom I would say so much. But your own family, will they approve your connecting yourself with the sister of a high-born Highland beggar?'

'My uncle's situation, his opinions and his indulgence entitle me to say that birth and personal qualities are all he would look to. And where can I find both united in such excellence as in your sister?'

'O nowhere! But your father will expect to be consulted.'

'Surely, but his late breach with the ruling powers removes all apprehension of objection on his part. Do not think of my friends, dear Fergus. Let me rather have your influence with your lovely sister.'

'My lovely sister is very apt to have a decisive will of her own. But you shall not want my interest. I think I saw Flora go towards the waterfall – follow, man, follow. Seek Flora out, and learn her decision as soon as you can.'

Waverley ascended the glen with an anxious heart. Love, with all its romantic train of hopes and fears, was mingled with other feelings less easily defined. Sunrise had seen him possessed of an esteemed rank in the honourable profession of arms, his father rising in the favour of his sovereign. All this had passed away like a dream. He himself was dishonoured, his father disgraced, and he had become involuntarily the confidant if not the accomplice of plans dark and dangerous, which must infer either the subversion of the government he had so lately served or the destruction of all who had participated in them. How could he make the selfish request that Flora should leave Fergus and, retiring with him to England wait as a distant spectator the success of her brother's undertaking, or the ruin of all his hopes and fortunes? Or to engage himself in the dangerous councils of the Chieftain, to be whirled along by him, renouncing almost all the power of deciding upon the rectitude or prudence of his actions? What other conclusion remained saving rejection by Flora, an alternative not to be thought of with anything short of mental agony. Pondering the doubtful and dangerous prospect before him, he at length arrived near the cascade, where he found Flora.

She was quite alone. Edward attempted to say something, but found himself unequal to the task. Flora seemed at first equally embarrassed, but recovered herself more speedily and was the first to speak. 'It is too important, Mr Waverley, to permit me to leave you in any doubt upon my sentiments. I should incur my own heavy censure did I delay expressing my sincere conviction that I can never regard you otherwise than as a valued friend. I see I distress you, and I grieve for it, but better now than later.'

She sat down upon a fragment of rock. 'I dare hardly tell you my feelings, they are so different from those usually ascribed to young women at my period of life. From my infancy I have had but one wish – the restoration of my royal benefactors to their rightful throne. It is impossible to express to you the devotion of my feelings on this subject, which excludes every thought respecting what is called my settlement in life. Let me but live to see the day of that happy restoration, and a highland cottage, a French convent or an English palace will be alike indifferent to me.'

'But, dearest Flora, how is your enthusiastic zeal for the exiled family inconsistent with my happiness?'

'Because you seek a heart whose principal delight should be in augmenting your domestic felicity and returning your affection even to the height of romance. To a man of less keen sensibility Flora MacIvor might give content if not happiness.'

'And why should you think yourself a more valuable treasure to one who is capable of loving than to me?'

'Because the tone of our affections would be more in unison, and because his more blunted sensibility would not require the return of enthusiasm which I have not to bestow. But you would for ever refer to the idea of domestic happiness which your imagination is capable of painting, and whatever fell short would be construed into coldness and indifference.'

'In other words, Miss MacIvor, you cannot love me.'

'I could esteem you as much, if not more, than any man I have ever seen, but I cannot love you as you ought to be loved. O do not, for your own sake, desire so hazardous an experiment. The woman whom you marry ought to have affections and opinions moulded upon yours. Her wishes, her feelings, her hopes, her fears, should all mingle with yours. She should enhance your pleasures and share your sorrows.'

'And why will not you be the person you describe?'

'Have I not told you that my mind is bent exclusively towards an event upon which I have no power but those of my earnest prayers?'

'And might not the granting of the suit I solicit even advance the interest to which you have devoted yourself? My family is wealthy and powerful, inclined to the Stuart race, and should a favourable opportunity…'

'A favourable opportunity! Inclined! Can such lukewarm adherence be gratifying to your lawful sovereign? Think what I should suffer as a member of a family where the rights which I hold most sacred are only deemed worthy of support when they appear on the point of triumphing without it!'

'Your doubts are unjust. The cause that I shall assert I dare support through every danger, as undauntedly as the boldest who draws sword in it.'

'Of that I cannot doubt for a moment. But consult your own good sense and reason. Let your part in this perilous drama rest upon conviction and not upon a hurried and probably temporary feeling.'

Waverley attempted to reply but words failed him. Every sentiment that Flora had uttered vindicated the strength of his attachment, for even his loyalty, though wildly enthusiastic, was generous and noble and disdained to avail itself of any indirect means of supporting the cause to which she was devoted.

After walking a little way in silence, Flora resumed the conversation. 'Fergus is anxious that you should join him in his present enterprise. But do not consent to this. You could not further his success and you would inevitably share his fall, if it be God's pleasure that fall he must. Your character would also suffer irretrievably. Let me beg you will return to your own country, and having publicly freed yourself from every tie to the usurping government, find opportunity to serve your injured sovereign and stand forth at the head of your natural followers, a worthy representative of the house of Waverley.'

'And should I be so happy as thus to distinguish myself, might I then hope –'

'I can but explain with candour the feelings which I now entertain. How they might be altered by events too favourable perhaps to be hoped for, it were in vain even to conjecture. Only be assured, Mr Waverley, that after my brother's honour and happiness there is none which I shall more sincerely pray for than for yours.'

With these words she parted from him. Waverley reached the castle amidst a medley of conflicting passions. He avoided Fergus, as he did not feel able either to encounter his raillery or reply to his solicitations. The wild revelry of the feast, for MacIvor kept open table for his clan, served to stun reflection. In his own apartment, Edward endeavoured to sum up the day. That the repulse from Flora would be persisted in for the present there was no doubt. But could he hope for ultimate success in case circumstances permitted the renewal of his suit? Could he hope that interest might be improved into a warmer attachment? He taxed his memory to recall every word she had used, and ended by finding himself in the same state of uncertainty. It was very late before sleep brought relief after the most painful and agitating day which he had ever passed.

chapter five

A Letter from Tully Veolan

In the morning there came music to Waverley's dreams. He imagined himself transported back to Tully Veolan and that he heard David Gellatly singing in the court. The notes waxed louder until Edward awoke in earnest. The illusion did not seem entirely dispelled. It was the voice of Davie Gellatly:

My heart's in the Highlands, my heart is not here,
My heart's in the Highlands a-chasing the deer;
A-chasing the wild deer and following the roe,
My heart's in the Highlands wherever I go.[1]

Edward began to dress himself in all haste, during which the minstrelsy of Davie changed its tune more than once:

There's nought in the Highlands but syboes and leeks,
And lang-leggit callans gaun wanting the breeks;
Wanting the breeks and without hose and shoon,
But we'll a' win the breeks when King Jamie comes hame.[2]

By the time Waverley had issued forth, David had associated himself with two or three of the Highland loungers who always graced the gates of the castle, and was capering full merrily in a foursome reel to the music of his own whistling. He continued until an idle piper obeyed the unanimous call of *Seid suas* (blow up). Young and old then mingled in the dance. The appearance of Waverley did not interrupt David's exercise, though he contrived by grinning and nodding to convey to our hero symptoms of recognition. Then, while whooping and snapping his fingers over his head, he of a sudden prolonged his sidestep until it brought him to Edward and still keeping time to the music he thrust a letter into his hand. Edward, who perceived Rose's handwriting, retired to peruse it.

I fear I am using an improper freedom, yet I cannot trust to anyone else to let you know some things which have happened here. My dear father is gone, and when he can return God only knows. You have probably heard that in consequence of troublesome news from the Highlands warrants were sent out for apprehending several gentlemen in these parts, among others my dear father. In spite of all my entreaties, he joined with some others and they have all gone northward. I am not so much anxious concerning his immediate safety as about what may follow afterwards, for these troubles are only beginning. I thought you would be glad to learn that my father had escaped, in case you happen to have heard that he was in danger.

The day after my father went off there came a party of soldiers to Tully Veolan. The officer was very civil to me, only said his duty obliged him to search for arms and papers. My father had taken away all the arms except the old useless things which hung in the hall and he had put all his papers out of the way. But Mr Waverley, they made strict enquiry after you and asked where you now were. The officer is gone back, but a non-commissioned officer and four men remain as a sort of garrison in the house. They have behaved very well but these soldiers have hinted as

---

[1]   Robert Burns's version of a traditional song.
[2]   According to Scott, lines traditionally sung to the tune of 'We'll never have peace until Jamie [ie James VIII and III] comes hame'.

if you would be in great danger. I cannot write what wicked falsehoods they said, but you will best judge what you ought to do. The party that returned carried off your servant prisoner, with your two horses and everything you left at Tully Veolan. I hope you will get safe home to England, where you used to tell me there was no military violence nor fighting among clans permitted. I hope you will exert your indulgence as to my boldness in writing to you, where it seems to me that your safety and honour are concerned. Farewell, Captain Waverley, I shall probably never see you more, but I will always remember with gratitude your kindness, and your attentions to my dear father. I remain your obliged servant, Rose Comyne Bradwardine.

'P.S. I hope you will send a line by David Gellatly to say you have received this and will take care of yourself. My compliments to my dear Flora and to Glennaquoich. Is she not as handsome and accomplished as I described her?

That the Baron should fall under the suspicion of government seemed only the natural consequence of his political predilections, but how *he* should have been involved in such suspicions, conscious that until yesterday he had been free from harbouring a thought against the reigning family, seemed inexplicable. Still, he was aware that unless he meant at once to embrace the proposal of Fergus MacIvor it would deeply concern him to leave this suspicious neighbourhood without delay. Upon this he determined as Flora's advice favoured him doing so and because he felt inexpressible repugnance at the idea of being accessory to the plague of civil war. Whatever the original rights of the Stuarts, since that period four monarchs had reigned in peace and glory over Britain, sustaining the character of the nation abroad and its liberties at home. Was it worth while to disturb a government so long settled and to plunge a kingdom into all the miseries of civil war to replace upon the throne the descendants of a monarch by whom it had been wilfully forfeited? If his own final conviction of the goodness of their cause should recommend allegiance to the Stuarts, still it was necessary to clear his own character by showing that he had taken no step to this purpose during his holding the commission of the reigning monarch.

He instantly wrote to thank Rose for her anxiety on his account and to express his earnest good wishes for her welfare and that of her father. The feelings which this task excited were speedily lost in the necessity of bidding farewell to Flora MacIvor. The pang attending this reflection was inexpressible, but time pressed, calumny was busy with his fame, and every hour's delay increased the power to injure it.

He sought out Fergus and communicated the contents of Rose's letter, with his own resolution instantly to go.

'You run your head into the lion's mouth,' answered MacIvor. 'I shall have to deliver you from some dungeon in Stirling or Edinburgh Castle. Once more, will you take the plaid and stay among the mists and the crows in the bravest cause ever sword was drawn in?'

'For many reasons, my dear Fergus, you must hold me excused. I must run my hazard.'

'You are determined then?'

'I am.'

'Wilful will do't. But you cannot go on foot – you shall have brown Dermid.'

'If you will sell him, I shall certainly be much obliged.'

'If your proud English heart cannot be obliged by a gift or loan, I will not refuse money at the entrance of a campaign. His price is twenty guineas. I will ride with you as far as Bally Brough. Callum Beg, see that our horses are ready, with a pony for yourself to attend and carry Mr Waverley's baggage. Put on Lowland dress, Callum, and see you keep your tongue close, if you would not have me cut it out.'

chapter six

Waverley's Reception in the Lowlands after his Highland Tour

It was noon when the two friends stood at the top of the pass of Bally Brough. 'I must go no further,' said Fergus.

'Adieu, Fergus. Do not permit your sister to forget me.'

'And adieu, Waverley. You may soon hear of her with a prouder title. Get home and make friends as fast as you can. There will speedily be unexpected guests on the coast of Suffolk, or my news from France has deceived me.'

Thus parted the friends, Fergus returning to his castle while Edward followed by Callum Beg, the latter transformed into a low-country groom, proceeded to the little town of — .

Edward paced on under the painful feelings which separation and uncertainty produce in the mind of a youthful lover. He forgot Flora MacIvor's prejudices in her magnanimity, and almost pardoned her indifference when he recollected the grand object which seemed to fill her soul. What would be her feelings in favour of the happy individual who should be so fortunate as to awaken them? Then came the question, whether he might not be that happy man. All that was common-place was melted away and obliterated in these dreams, which only remembered the points of grace and dignity that distinguished Flora. Edward was in the fair way of creating a goddess out of a high-spirited and beautiful young woman, and time was wasted in castle-building, until at the descent of a steep hill he saw beneath him the market town of — .

Callum pressed closer to his side and hoped, 'when they cam to the public, his honour wad not say nothing about Vich Ian Vohr, for its people were bitter whigs, deil burst tem.'

Waverley assured the prudent page he would be cautious. Upon alighting at the sign of the Seven-branched Golden Candlestick they were received by mine host, a tall thin puritanical figure, who seemed to debate within himself whether he ought to give shelter to those who travelled on a Sunday.[1] Reflecting, however, that he possessed the power of mulcting them for this irregularity, Mr Ebeneezer Cruickshanks condescended to admit them.

To this sanctified person Waverley addressed his request, that he would procure him a guide, with a saddle-horse to carry his portmanteau to Edinburgh.

'And where may ye be coming from?' demanded mine host of the Candlestick.

'I have told you where I wish to go. I do not conceive any further information necessary.'

'Ahem!' returned the Candlestick, somewhat disconcerted at this rebuff. 'It's the sabbath, sir, and I cannot enter into ony carnal transactions on sic a day, when the people should be humbled and the backsliders should return, and moreover when the land was mourning for covenants burnt, broken and buried.'[2]

'My good friend, if you cannot let me have a horse and a guide, my servant shall seek them elsewhere.'

'A weel! Your servant? And what for gangs he not forward wi you himsel?'

'Look ye, sir, I came here for my own accommodation and not to answer impertinent questions. Either say you can or cannot get me what I want.'

Mr Ebeneezer Cruickshanks left the room with some indistinct muttering, but whether negative or acquiescent Edward could not distinguish. The hostess, a civil, quiet drudge, came to take his orders for dinner, but declined to answer upon the subject of the horse and guide.

From a window which overlooked the narrow court in which Callum Beg dressed the horses, Waverley heard the following dialogue betwixt the subtle foot-page of Vich Ian Vohr and his landlord:

'Ye'll be frae the north, young man?' began the latter.

'And you may say that.'

'And ye'll hae ridden a lang way today, it may weel be?'

'Sae lang I could weel tak a dram.'

'Gudewife, bring the gill stoup.'

My host of the Golden Candlestick, having as he thought opened his guest's heart by this hospitable propitiation, resumed his scrutiny.

'Ye're a Highlandman by your tongue.'

'I am but just Aberdeen-a-way.'

---

[1]   In the Book of Revelation the seven golden candlesticks represent the seven Churches of the New Testament, and an inn of that name suggests the devout character of the inn-keeper.

[2]   The National Covenant, 1638, was a pledge to establish the Presbyterian Church in Scotland. The Solemn League and Covenant, 1643, was an agreement between Scottish Presbyterians and English Parliamentarians which many Covenanters believed would bring Presbyterianism to the whole of Britain. The failure of this to happen intensified factionalism among Scottish Presbyterians.

'And did your master come from Aberdeen wi' you?'

'Ay, that's when I left it myself,' answered the impenetrable Callum Beg.

'And what kind of gentleman is he?'

'I believe he is ane o' King George's state officers. At least he's aye for ganging on to the south, and he has a hantle silver and never grudges ony thing till a poor body.'

'He wants a guide and a horse to Edinburgh?'

'Ay, and ye maun find it him forthwith.'

'Ahem! It will be chargeable.'

'He cares not for that a boddle.'

Mr Cruickshanks, though not satisfied either with the reserve of the master or the readiness of the man, was contented to lay a tax upon the reckoning and horsehire that might compound for his ungratified curiosity. The charge did not amount to much more than double what in fairness it should have been.

Callum Beg announced the ratification of the treaty, adding, 'Ta auld devil was ganging to ride wi' the Duinhé-wassal herself.'

'That will not be very pleasant, Callum, nor altogether safe, but a traveller must submit to these inconveniences. Meanwhile, my good lad, here is a trifle for to drink Vich Ian Vohr's health.'

The hawk's eye of Callum flashed delight upon a golden guinea. Then he gathered close up to Edward with an expression peculiarly knowing and spoke in an undertone, 'If his honour thought ta auld devil was a bit dangerous, she could easily provide for him. And teil ane ta wiser.'

'How, and in what manner?'

'Her ain sel could wait for him, a wee bit frae the toun, and kittle his quarters wi' her *skene-occle*.'

'Skene-occle? What's that?'

Callum unbuttoned his coat, raised his left arm and pointed to the hilt of a small dirk snugly deposited in the lining of his jacket. Waverley discovered in Callum's handsome features just the degree of roguish malice with which a lad of the same age in England would have brought forward a plan for robbing an orchard.

'Good God, Callum, would you take a man's life?'

'Indeed, and I think he has had just a lang enough lease o't, when he's betraying honest folk that come to spend silver at his public.'

Edward saw nothing was to be gained by argument, and enjoined Callum to lay aside all practices against the person of Ebenezer Cruickshanks, to which the page seemed to acquiesce with an air of great indifference.

At length the ungainly figure and ungracious visage of Ebenezer presented themselves. The upper part of his form was shrouded in a large belted greatcoat crested with a huge cowl which when drawn over the head and hat, completely overshadowed both. His hand grasped a huge whip, garnished with brass mounting. His thin legs tenanted a pair of gambadoes fastened with rusty clasps. Thus accoutred, he stalked into the apartment and announced his errand. 'Your horses are ready.'

'You go with me yourself then, landlord?'

'I do, as far as Perth, where ye may be supplied with a guide to Embro'.'

He placed under Waverley's eye the bill, and at the same time, self-invited, filled a glass of wine and drank devoutly to a blessing on their journey. Waverley stared at the man's impudence, but as their connection was to be short made no observation upon it. Having paid his reckoning, he mounted Dermid and sallied forth from the Golden Candlestick followed by the puritanical figure after he had, at the expense of some time and difficulty, elevated his person to the back of a raw-boned phantom of a broken-down blood-horse, on which Waverley's portmanteau was deposited. Our hero could hardly help laughing at the appearance of his new squire.

Edward's mirth did not escape mine host of the Candlestick who infused a double portion of souring into his countenance and resolved internally that the young *Englisher* should pay early for such contempt. Callum also enjoyed with undissembled glee the ridiculous figure of Mr Cruickshanks. As Waverley passed him he pulled off his hat respectfully and, approaching his stirrup, bade him 'Tak heed the auld whig played him nae cantrap.'

Waverley bade him farewell, and then rode briskly onward, not sorry to be out of hearing of the shouts of the children as they beheld old Ebenezer rise and sink in his stirrups to avoid the concussions of a hard trot upon a half-paved street.

chapter seven

Shows that the Loss of a Horse's Shoe May Be a Serious Inconvenience

The travellers journeyed in silence until it was interrupted by the annunciation that Mr Cruickshanks' 'naig had lost a fore-foot shoe'. He assured Waverley that Cairnvreckan, a village they were about to enter, had an excellent blacksmith, 'but as he was a professor, he would drive a nail for no man on the Sabbath, unless it were a case of absolute necessity, for which he always charged sixpence each shoe'. This made slight impression on the hearer, who only wondered what college this professor belonged to, not aware that the word was used to denote any person who pretended to uncommon sanctity of faith and manner.

As they entered the village they speedily distinguished the smith's house, which betokened none of the Sabbatical silence which Ebenezer had augured. On the contrary, hammer clashed, anvil rang and the bellows groaned. Nor was the labour of a rural and pacific nature. The master smith, John Mucklewrath, with two assistants, toiled busily in repairing old muskets, pistols and swords which lay scattered around his workshop. The open shed containing the forge was crowded with persons who came and went as if receiving and communicating important news, and a single glance at the people who traversed the street or assembled in groups announced that some extraordinary intelligence was agitating the public mind of Cairnvreckan. 'There is some news,' said mine host of the Candlestick, pushing his lanthorn-jawed visage and bare-boned nag rudely forward, 'there is some news, and if it please my Creator I will forthwith obtain speerings thereof.'

Waverley dismounted and gave his horse to a boy who stood idling near. While he looked about the buzz around saved him the trouble of interrogatories. The names of Lochiel, Clanranald, Glengary and other distinguished Highland Chiefs, among whom Vich Ian Vohr was repeatedly mentioned, were as familiar in men's mouths as household words, and from the alarm generally expressed he conceived that their descent into the Lowlands had either already taken place or was instantly apprehended.

A large-boned hard-featured woman, dressed as if her clothes had been flung on with a pitchfork, her cheeks flushed where they were not smutted with soot, jostled through the crowd and, brandishing high a child of two years old which she danced in her arms without regard to its screams of terror, sang forth,

> 'Charlie is my darling, my darling, my darling,
> Charlie is my darling,
> The young Chevalier.[1]

D'ye hear what's come ower ye now, ye whingeing whig carles? D'ye hear wha's coming to cow yere cracks?

> Little wot ye wha's coming,
> Little wot ye wha's coming,
> A' the wild Macraws are coming.'[2]

The Vulcan of Cairnvreckan, who acknowledged his Venus, regarded her with a grim countenance, while some of the senators of the village hastened to interpose.[3] 'Whist, gudewife, is this a time to be singing your ranting fule-sangs in? A day when the land should give testimony against popery and prelacy, and independency and supremacy and a' the errors of the church.'

'And that's a' your whiggery,' re-echoed the virago, 'and your presbytery, ye cut-lugged graning carles. What d'ye think the lads wi' the kilts will care for yere synods and yere presbyteries and yere stool of repentance? Vengeance on the black face o't!'

Here John Mucklewrath interposed his matrimonial authority. 'Gae hame, and be damned and put on the sowens for supper.'

'And you, ye doiled dotard,' replied his gentle helpmate, 'ye stand there hammering dog-heads for fules that will never snap them at a Highlandman, instead of earning bread for your family and shoeing this young gentleman's horse that's just come frae the north. Ise warrant him nane of your whingeing King George folk, but a gallant Gordon, at the least o' him.'

The eyes of the assembly were now turned upon Waverley, who begged the

---

[1]   Song lyric by Robert Burns. There was a later version by Carolina Oliphant, Lady Nairn.

[2]   From 'The Chevalier's Muster Roll', probably dating from the 1715 Jacobite Rising.

[3]   Vulcan, the Roman god of fire; blacksmith.

smith to shoe his guide's horse with all speed, as he wished to proceed on his journey, for he had heard enough to make him sensible that there would be danger in delaying. The smith's eyes rested on him with suspicion, not lessened by the eagerness with which his wife enforced Waverley's mandate.

'And what may your name be, sir?' quoth Mucklewarth.

'It is of no consequence to you, my friend, provided I pay your labour.'

'But it may be of consequence to the state sir,' replied an old farmer smelling strongly of whisky and peat-smoke, 'and I doubt we maun delay your journey till you have seen the laird.'

'You certainly,' said Waverley haughtily, 'will find it both difficult and dangerous to detain me, unless you can produce some proper authority.'

There was a whisper among the crowd – 'may be the Chevalier himsel' – and an increasing disposition to resist Waverley's departure. He attempted to argue, but Mrs Mucklewrath drowned his expostulations. 'Ye'll stop ony gentleman that is the Prince's friend?' for she too had adopted the opinion respecting Waverley. 'I dare ye to touch him,' spreading her long fingers garnished with sable claws which a vulture might have envied. 'I'll set my ten commandments in the face o' the first loon that lays a finger on him.'[1]

'Deil be in me but I put this het gad down her throat,' cried Mucklewrath in a rhapsody of wrath, snatching a bar from the forge, and he might have executed his threat had he not been withheld by a part of the mob, while the rest endeavoured to force the termagant out of his presence.

Waverley meditated a retreat in the confusion, but his horse was nowhere to be seen. Ebenezer had withdrawn both horses from the press and, mounted on the one and holding the other, answered the repeated call of Waverley for his horse, 'Na, na! If ye are nae friend to kirk and the king, ye maun answer to honest men for breach o'contract and I maun keep the nag and the walise for damage and expense, in respect my horse and mysell will lose tomorrow's day's-wark.' Edward, hemmed in and hustled by the rabble, and every moment expecting personal violence, at length drew a pocket-pistol, threatening on the one hand to shoot whomsoever dared to stop him and on the other menacing Ebenezer with a similar doom if he stirred a foot with the horses. One man with a pistol is equal to a hundred unarmed because though he can shoot but one, no one knows but that he himself may be that luckless individual. Ebenezer, whose natural paleness had waxed three shades more cadaverous, would probably not have ventured dispute had not the Vulcan of the village rushed at Waverley with the red-hot bar of iron with such determination as made the discharge of his pistol an act of self-defence. The unfortunate man fell, and while Edward thrilled with a natural horror at the incident had not the presence of mind to unsheathe his sword, the populace threw themselves upon him, disarmed him and were about to use him with great violence when the appearance of a venerable clergyman, the pastor of the parish, put a curb upon their fury.

The worthy man had been alarmed by the discharge of the pistol and the

---

[1] Ten commandments, ie fingernails.

increasing hubbub around the smithy. Mr Morton's first attention was turned to the body of Mucklewrath over which his wife was howling and tearing her elf locks in a state little short of distraction. Upon raising up the smith, the first discovery was that he was alive, and the next that he was likely to live. The bullet had grazed his head and stunned him for a moment or two. He now arose to demand vengeance, and with difficulty acquiesced in the proposal of Mr Morton that Waverley should be carried before the laird, as a justice of the peace. The rest of the assistants unanimously agreed to the measure recommended.

All controversy being thus laid aside, Waverley, escorted by the whole village who were not bedridden, was conducted to the house of Cairnvreckan, about half a mile distant.

chapter eight

An Examination

Major Melville of Cairnvreckan, an elderly gentleman who had spent his youth in military service, received Mr Morton with kindness and our hero with civility. The matter of the smith's hurt was enquired into, and as the injury was trifling and the circumstances rendered the infliction an act of self-defence, the Major conceived he might dismiss the matter on Waverley's depositing a small sum for the benefit of the wounded person.

'I would wish, sir,' continued the Major, 'that my duty terminated here, but it is necessary that we should have some further enquiry into the cause of your journey through the country at this distracted time.'

Ebenezer Cruickshanks now communicated all he knew or suspected from the reserve of Waverley and the evasions of Callum Beg. The horse upon which Edward rode he knew to belong to Vich Ian Vohr, though he dared not tax Edward's former attendant with the fact lest he should have his house burnt over his head by that godless gang, the MacIvors. He concluded by exaggerating his own services to kirk and state of attaching this suspicious and formidable delinquent. He intimated hopes of future reward and of instant reimbursement for loss of time, and even of character, by travelling in the state business upon the Sabbath.

Major Melville answered that so far from claiming any merit in this affair, Mr Cruickshanks ought to deprecate the imposition of a heavy fine for neglecting to lodge an account with the nearest magistrate of any stranger who came to his inn. But he would not impute this conduct to disaffection, but only suppose that his zeal for kirk and state had been lulled asleep by the opportunity of charging double horse-hire.

Major Melville then commanded the villagers to return to their homes. The apartment was thus cleared of every person but Mr Morton and Waverley himself. There ensued a painful and embarrassed pause, till Major Melville, looking upon Waverley with much compassion and consulting a paper in his hand, requested to know his name.

'Edward Waverley.'

'I thought so, late of – dragoons and nephew of Sir Everard Waverley of Waverley Honour?'

'The same.'

'Permit me to ask you how your time has been disposed of since you obtained leave of absence from your regiment?'

'My reply must be guided by the nature of the charge. I request to know what that charge is, and upon what authority I am detained to reply to it?'

'The charge, Mr Waverley, is of a very high nature, and affects your character both as a soldier and a subject. You are charged with spreading mutiny and rebellion among the men you commanded, and setting them an example of desertion by prolonging your absence from the regiment contrary to the express orders of your commanding-officer. The civil crime of which you stand accused is that of high treason and levying war against the king, the highest delinquency of which a subject can be guilty.'

He handed Waverley a warrant from the supreme criminal court of Scotland, for apprehending the person of Edward Waverley, Esq suspected of treasonable practices and other high crimes.

The astonishment which Waverley expressed at this communication was imputed by Major Melville to conscious guilt, while Mr Morton was disposed to construe it into the surprise of innocence unjustly suspected. There was something true in both conjectures, for although Edward's mind acquitted him of the crimes with which he was charged, yet a hasty review of his own conduct convinced him he might have great difficulty in establishing his innocence.

'It is a very painful part of this painful business,' said Mr Melville, 'that I must request to see such papers as you have on your person.'

'You shall, sir, without reserve,' said Edward, throwing his pocketbook upon the table.

'Did Mr Waverley know one Humphry Houghton, a non-commissioned officer in Gardiner's dragoons?'

'Certainly. He was sergeant of my troop, and son of a tenant of my uncle.'

'Exactly – and had a share of your confidence and an influence among his comrades?'

'I had never occasion to repose confidence in a person of his description. I favoured Sergeant Houghton as a clever, active young fellow, and I believe his fellow soldiers respected him accordingly.'

'But you used through this man to communicate with such of your troop as were recruited upon Waverley Honour?'

'Certainly. The poor fellows, finding themselves in a regiment chiefly composed of Scotch or Irish, looked up to me in any of their little distresses and naturally made their sergeant their spokesman.'

'His influence, then, extended particularly over those soldiers from your uncle's estate?'

'Surely – but what is that to the present purpose?'

'To that I am just coming. Have you, since leaving the regiment, had any correspondence with Sergeant Houghton?'

'I hold correspondence with a man of his rank and situation! How, or for what purpose?'

'That you are to explain, but did you not send to him for some books?'

'A trifling commission which I gave him because my servant could not read. I bade him by letter to select some books and send them to me at Tully Veolan.'

'And of what description were those books?'

'They related almost entirely to elegant literature. They were designed for a lady.'

'Were there not treasonable tracts and pamphlets among them?'

'There were some political treastises, into which I hardly looked. They had been sent to me by a friend whose heart is more to be esteemed than his prudence or political sagacity. They seemed to be dull compositions.'

'That friend was a Mr Pembroke, a non-juring clergyman, the author of two treasonable works of which the manuscripts were found among your baggage?'[1]

'But of which I never read six pages.'

'Do you know a person that passes by the name of Wily Will or Will Ruthven?'

'I never heard of such a name till this moment.'

'Did you not through such a person communicate with Sergeant Houghton, instigating him to desert with as many of his comrades as he could seduce to join him, and unite with the Highlanders under the command of the young Pretender?'

'I assure you I am not only entirely guiltless of the plot you have laid to my charge, but I detest it from the bottom of my soul, nor would I be guilty of such a treachery to gain a throne, either for myself or any other man alive.'

'But if I am rightly informed, your time was spent between the house of this Highland Chieftan and that of Mr Bradwardine of Bradwardine, also in arms for this unfortunate cause.'

'I do not mean to disguise it, but I do deny being privy to any of their designs against the government.'

'You do not however, deny that you attended your host Glennaquoich to a rendezvous, where under pretence of a hunting match most of the accomplices of his treason were assembled to concert measures for taking arms?'

'I acknowledge having been at such a meeting, but I neither heard nor saw anything which could give it that character.'

'From thence you proceeded, with Glennaquoich and a part of his clan, to join the army of the young Pretender, and returned after having paid your homage to him to arm the remainder and unite them to his bands on their way southward?'

---

[1] Non-juring described a clergyman who refused to swear allegiance to the crown.

'I never went with Glennaquoich on such an errand. I never so much as heard that the person you mention was in the country.'

He then detailed the history of his misfortune at the hunting match, and added that on his return he found himself suddenly deprived of his commission, and did not deny that he then, for the first time, observed a disposition in the Highlanders to take arms but added that having no inclination to join their cause and no longer any reason to remain in Scotland he was now on his return to his native country to which he had been summoned, as Major Melville would perceive from the letters on the table.

Major Melville perused the letters of Richard Waverley, Sir Everard and Aunt Rachael, but the inferences he drew were different from what Waverley expected. They held the language of discontent, threw out hints of revenge, and that of Aunt Rachael, which plainly asserted the justice of the Stuart cause, was held to contain the open avowal of what the others only intimated.

'Did you not receive repeated letters from your commanding officer commanding you to return to your post and acquainting you with the use made of your name to spread discontent through your soldiers?'

'I never did, Major Melville. One letter I received from him, containing a civil intimation that I would employ my leave otherwise than in constant residence of Bradwardine, as to which I thought he was not called upon to interfere. And finally I had, on the same day I observed myself superseded in the Gazette, a second letter from Colonel Gardiner commanding me to join the regiment, an order which I received too late to obey. If there were any intermediate letters, and certainly from Colonel Gardiner's high character I think it probable, they have never reached me.'

Beset on every hand by accusations, alone and in a strange land, Waverley almost gave up his life and honour for lost and, leaning his head upon his hand, resolutely refused to answer any further questions.

Without expressing surprise at the change in Waverley's manner Major Melville proceeded composedly to put several other queries to him. 'What does it avail me to answer you?' said Edward sullenly. 'You appear convinced of my guilt, and wrest every reply I have made to support your own preconceived opinion. If I am capable of the cowardice and treachery your charge burdens me with, I am not worthy to be believed in any reply. I do not see why I should lend my accusers arms against my innocence.' And he resumed his posture of sullen silence.

'Allow me,' said the magistrate, 'to remind you of one reason that may suggest the propriety of a candid confession. The inexperience of youth lays it open to the more designing and artful, and one of your friends at least ranks high in the latter class. From your ingenuousness and unacquaintance with the manners of the Highlands I should be disposed to place you among the former. In such a case an error like yours may be attoned for, and I would willingly act as intercessor. But as you must be acquainted with the strength of the individuals who assumed arms, I must expect you will merit this mediation by a frank avowal of all that has come to your knowledge. In which case I think I can promise that a very short restraint will be the only ill consequence.'

Waverley listened with great composure until the end of this exhortation when, springing from his seat, he replied, 'Major Melville, I have hitherto answered your questions with candour, or declined them with temper, because their import concerned myself alone. But as you esteem me mean enough to commence informer against others, who received me as a guest and friend, I declare that I consider your questions an insult infinitely more offensive than your suspicions. You should sooner have my heart out of my bosom, than a single syllable of information upon subjects which I could only have become acquainted with in the full confidence of unsuspecting hospitality.'

'Mr Waverley,' said the Major, 'I am afraid I must sign a warrant for detaining you in custody, but this house shall for the present be your prison.'

Our hero bowed and withdrew under guard to a handsome bedroom where, declining all offers of food or wine he flung himself on the bed and, stupefied by the harassing events and mental fatigue of this miserable day, sunk into a deep and heavy slumber.

chapter nine

A Conference, and the Consequence

When Waverley retired, the Laird and Clergyman of Cairnvreckan sat down in silence to their evening meal. While the servants were in attendance neither chose to say anything. Both were men of ready and acute talent. Major Melville had been versed in camps and cities. He was vigilant by profession and cautious from experience, had met with much evil in the world and therefore his opinions of others were sometimes unjustly severe. Mr Morton had passed from the literary pursuits of a college to the ease and simplicity of his present charge, where his opportunities of witnessing evil were few, and where the love and respect of his parishioners repaid his affectionate zeal in their behalf by endeavouring to disguise from him their own occasional transgressions.

When the servants had withdrawn, the silence continued until Major Melville, filling his glass and pushing the bottle to Mr Morton, commenced.

'A distressing affair this. I fear this youngster has brought himself within the compass of a halter.'

'God forbid!' answered the clergyman.

'I fear even your merciful logic will hardly deny the conclusion.'

'Surely, Major, I should hope it might be averted, for aught we have heard tonight.'

'Indeed! But my good parson, you are one of those who would communicate to every criminal the benefit of clergy.'

'Unquestionably I would. Mercy and long-suffering are the grounds of the doctrine I am called to teach.'

'True, but mercy to a criminal may be gross injustice to the community.'

'But I cannot see that this youth's guilt is at all established to my satisfaction.'

'Because your good nature blinds your good sense. This young man, descended of a family of hereditary Jacobites, goes to Tully Veolan – the principles of the Baron are well known. He engages there in a brawl in which he is said to have disgraced the commission he bore. Colonel Gardiner writes to him, first mildly, then more sharply. The mess invite him to explain the quarrel. He neither replies to his commander nor his comrades. In the meanwhile his soldiers become mutinous and at length, while the rumour of this unhappy rebellion becomes general, Sergeant Houghton and another fellow are detected in correspondence with a French emissary. Captain Waverley urges him to desert with the troop and join their captain who was with Prince Charles. In the meanwhile this trusty captain is residing at Glennaquoich with the most desperate Jacobite in Scotland. He goes with him at least as far as their famous hunting rendezvous. Two other summonses are sent him ordering him to repair to the regiment. He returns an absolute refusal and throws up his commission.'

'He had already been deprived of it.'

'But he regrets that the measure had anticipated his resignation. His baggage is seized and is found to contain enough jacobital pamphlets to poison a whole country. Then when news arrives of the approach of the rebels he sets out in a sort of disguise, refusing to tell his name and attended by a very suspicious character, and mounted on a horse known to have belonged to Glennaquoich, and bearing letters from his family expressing high rancour against the house of Brunswick.'

Mr Morton prudently abstained from argument, which he perceived would only harden the magistrate in his opinion, and asked him how he intended to dispose of the prisoner?

'It is a question of some difficulty, considering the state of the country.'

'Could you not detain him here till this storm blows over?'

'My good friend, neither your house nor mine will be long out of harm's way. I have just learned that the commander-in-chief has declined giving the insurgents battle at Corryerick, and marched northwards, leaving the road to the low country undefended.'

'Good God! Is the man a coward or an idiot?'

'He has the courage of a common soldier, does what he is commanded, but is as fit to act for himself in circumstances of importance as I, my dear parson, to occupy your pulpit.'

This intelligence diverted the discourse from Waverley for some time. At length, however, the subject was resumed.

'I believe,' said Major Melville, 'that I must give this young man in charge to the armed volunteers lately sent out to overawe the disaffected districts. They are now recalled towards Stirling, and a small body comes this way tomorrow, commanded by the westland man Gilfillan.'

'The Cameronian.[1] I wish the young gentleman may be safe with him. Strange things are done in the heat of minds in so agitating a crisis, and I fear Gilfillan is of a sect which has suffered persecution without learning mercy.'

'He has only to lodge Mr Waverley in Stirling Castle. I will give strict instructions to treat him well.'

'You will have no objection to my seeing him tomorrow in private?'

'None, certainly. But with what view do you make the request?'

'Simply to make the experiment whether he may not be brought to communicate some circumstances which may be useful to alleviate, if not to exculpate, his conduct.'

The friends now retired to rest, each filled with the most anxious reflections on the state of the country.

chapter ten

A Confidant

Waverley awoke from troubled dreams to a full consciousness of the horrors of his situation. He might be delivered up to military law which, in the midst of civil war, was not likely to be scrupulous in the choice of victims or the quality of evidence. Nor did he feel much more comfortable at the thought of a trial before a Scottish court of justice, where he knew the forms differed from those of England, and had been taught to believe, however erroneously, that the rights of the subject were less carefully protected. Bitterness rose in his mind against the government and he cursed his rejection of MacIvor's invitation to accompany him to the field. 'Had I yielded to the first impulse of indignation how different had been my present situation! I had then been free and in arms, fighting, like my forefathers, for love, for loyalty and for fame. And now I am here, at the disposal of a cold-hearted man, perhaps to be turned over to a dungeon or the infamy of a public execution.'

While Edward was ruminating on these painful subjects, Mr Morton availed himself of Major Melville's permission to pay him an early visit.

'I believe, sir,' said the unfortunate young man, 'that in any other circumstances I should have much gratitude to express to you, but such is the present tumult of my mind that I can hardly offer you thanks.'

---

[1]   Follower of Richard Cameron, a leader of the Reformed Presbyterian Church; soldier in the Cameronian Regiment raised in 1689 in support of William of Orange.

Mr Morton replied that far from making any claim upon his good opinion, his only wish was to find out the means of deserving it. 'I do not intrude myself on your confidence for the purpose of learning circumstances which can be prejudicial to yourself or to others. My earnest wish is that you would intrust me with any particulars that could lead to your exculpation.'

'I know that I am innocent, but I hardly see how I can hope to prove myself so.'

'It is for that very reason that I venture to solicit your confidence. Your situation will, I fear, preclude your taking steps for recovering intelligence which I would willingly undertake on your behalf, and if you are not benefited by my exertions at least they cannot be prejudicial to you.'

Waverley, after a few minutes reflection, was convinced that reposing confidence in Mr Morton could hurt neither Mr Bradwardine nor Fergus MacIvor, and that it might possibly be of some service to himself. He therefore ran briefly over the events, neither mentioning Flora nor Rose Bradwardine in the course of his narrative.

Mr Morton seemed particularly struck with Waverley's visit to Donald Bean Lean. 'I am glad you did not mention this to the Major. It is capable of great misconstruction on the part of those who do not consider the power of curiosity and of romance as motives of youthful conduct. There are men in the world who do not believe that danger is often incurred without adequate cause, and who are sometimes led to assign motives entirely foreign to the truth. Bean Lean is renowned as a sort of Robin Hood, and the stories which are told of his enterprise are the common tales of the winter fireside. Being neither destitute of ambition nor encumbered with scruples, he will probably attempt to distinguish himself during these unhappy commotions.'

The confidence which this good man appeared to repose in his innocence had the natural effect of softening Edward's heart. He shook Mr Morton warmly by the hand and, assuring him that his kindness had relieved his mind of a heavy load, told him that whatever might be his own fate, he belonged to a family who had both gratitude and the power of displaying it. The worthy clergyman was doubly interested in the cause for which he had volunteered his services, observing the genuine feelings of his young friend.

Edward now enquired if Mr Morton knew what was likely to be his destination.

'Stirling Castle, and I am pleased for your sake, for the governor is a man of honour and humanity. But I am more doubtful of your treatment upon the road. Major Melville is obliged to intrust the custody of your person to another.'

'I am glad of it. I detest that cold-blooded Scotch magistrate. He had no sympathy, and the petrifying accuracy with which he attended to every form of civility while he tortured me by his questions and his suspicions was as tormenting as the racks of the Inquisition.[1] Who is to have charge of so important a state prisoner as I am?'

'I believe a person called Gilfillan, one of the sect who are termed Cameronians. They claim to represent the more severe Presbyterians, who in Charles Second's

---

[1]   Roman Catholic Church tribunal set up in the thirteenth century to punish heretics.

and James Second's days refused to profit by the toleration which was extended to others of that religion. They held conventicles in the open fields, and being treated with great cruelty by the Scottish government more than once took arms. They take their name from their leader, Richard Cameron. This person, whom they call Gifted Gilfillan, has long been a leader among them, and now heads a small party under whose escort Major Melville proposes you shall travel. And now, farewell my young friend. I must not weary the Major's indulgence.'

chapter eleven

Things Mend a Little

About noon Mr Morton returned and brought an invitation to dinner from Major Melville. Mr Morton's favourable report had somewhat staggered the preconceptions of the old soldier. In the state of the country the mere suspicion of disaffection might infer criminality indeed, but certainly not dishonour. Besides, according to intelligence, the Highlanders had withdrawn from the Lowland frontier with the purpose of following the army in their march to Inverness. This news put him in such good humour that he readily acquiesced in Mr Morton's proposal to pay some hospitable attention to his unfortunate guest, and added he hoped the whole affair would prove a youthful escapade which might be easily atoned by a short confinement.

The kind mediator had some trouble to prevail on Waverley to accept the invitation. He pleaded that the invitation argued the Major's disbelief of any part of the accusation, which was inconsistent with Waverley's conduct as a soldier and a man of honour, and that to decline his courtesy might be interpreted into a consciousness that it was unmerited. He so far satisfied Edward that the proper course was to meet the Major on easy terms that Waverley agreed to be guided by his new friend

The meeting was stiff and formal enough. But Edward, soothed and relieved by the kindness of Morton, held himself bound to behave with ease, though he could not affect cordiality. The Major's wine was excellent. He told his old campaign stories and displayed much knowledge of men and manners, and Mr Morton had a fund of placid gaiety. Waverley, whose life was a dream, became the most lively of the party. He had remarkable natural powers of conversation, though easily silenced by discouragement. His spirits were abundantly elastic. The trio were engaged in a lively discourse, apparently delighted with each other, and the kind host was pressing a third bottle of Burgundy, when the sound of a drum was heard at some distance. The Major cursed with a muttered military oath the circumstances which recalled him to his official functions.

chapter twelve

A Volunteer Sixty Years Since

Upon hearing the unwelcome sound of the drum, Major Melville hastily opened a door, and stepped out upon a terrace which divided his house from the highroad. Waverley and his new friend followed him. They soon recognized in solemn march first, the performer upon the drum, secondly, a large flag on which was inscribed the words COVENANT, KIRK, KING, KINGDOMS. The commander of the party was a thin, rigid-looking man about sixty years old. Spiritual pride was, in this man's face, elevated and yet darkened by fanaticism. It was impossible to behold him without the imagination placing him in some crisis where religious zeal was the ruling principle. A martyr at the stake, a soldier in the field, a banished wanderer consoled by the supposed purity of his faith under every earthly privation, perhaps a persecuting inquisitor as terrific in power as unyielding in adversity – any of these seemed congenial characters to this personage. There was something in the affected precision and solemnity of his deportment and discourse that bordered upon the ludicrous, so that one might have feared, admired or laughed at him. His dress was that of a west-country peasant, in no respect affecting either the mode of the age or of the Scottish gentry at any period. His arms were a broadsword and pistols, which might have seen the rout of Pentland or Bothwell Brigg.[1]

As he came up to meet Major Melville he touched solemnly his huge blue bonnet. The group of about thirty armed men who followed was of a motley description. They were in ordinary Lowland dress which, contrasted with the arms which they bore, gave them a mobbish appearance, so much is the eye accustomed to connect uniformity of dress with the military character. A few apparently partook of their leader's enthusiasm, men obviously to be feared in a combat where their natural courage was exalted by religious zeal. Others puffed and strutted, filled with the importance of conveying arms and the novelty of their situation, while the rest dragged their limbs listlessly along or straggled from their companions to procure such refreshments as the cottages and alehouse afforded.

Greeting Mr Gilfillan civilly, the Major requested to know if he had received the letter he sent to him, and could undertake the charge of the state-prisoner mentioned as far as Stirling Castle. 'Yea,' was the concise reply.

'But your escort, Mr Gilfillan, is not so strong as I expected.

'Some of the people hungered by the way and tarried until their poor souls were refreshed with the word.'

'I am sorry, sir, you did not trust to refreshing your men at Cairnvreckan. Whatever my house contains is at the command of persons employed in the service.'

'It was not of creature comforts I spake,' answered the Covenanter, regarding

---

[1] Government victories over the Covenanters at Rullion Green in the Pentland Hills in 1666, and at Bothwell Brig in 1679.

Major Melville with something like contempt, 'howbeit, I thank you. The people remained waiting upon the precious Mr Jabesh Rentowel for the outpouring of the afternoon exhortation.'

'And have you, when the rebels are about to spread themselves through this country, actually left a great part of your command at a field-preaching?'

Gilfillan smiled scornfully as he made this indirect answer. 'Even thus are the children of this world wiser in their generation than the children of light.'

'However, sir, as you are to take charge of this gentleman to Stirling, I beseech you to observe military discipline upon your march. I would advise you to keep your men more closely together instead of straggling like geese upon a common. And for fear of surprise I recommend a small advance party, so that when you approach a village or wood – but as I don't observe you listen to me, Mr Gilfillan, I suppose I need not give myself the trouble to say more. But one thing I would have you well aware of, that you are to treat your prisoner with no incivility, and are to subject him to no other restraint than is necessary for his security.'

'I have looked into my commission,' said Mr Gilfillan, 'subscribed by a worthy nobleman, William Earl of Glencairn, nor do I find therein that I am to receive any commands from Major William Melville.'[1]

Major Meville reddened to the very ears, the more so as he observed Mr Morton smile at the same moment. 'Mr Gilfillan,' he answered with some asperity. 'I beg ten thousand pardons for interfering with a person of your importance. I thought, however, that as you have been bred a grazier, there might be occasion to remind you of the difference between Highland men and Highland cattle, and if you should happen to meet with any gentleman who has seen service I should imagine that listening to him would do you no sort of harm. But I have done, and have only once more to recommend this gentleman to your civility as well as to your custody. Mr Waverley, I am truly sorry we should part in this way.'

He shook our hero by the hand. Morton also took an affectionate farewell, and Waverley, having mounted his horse with a file upon each side to prevent his escape, set forward with Gilfillan and his party. Through the village they were accompanied with the shouts of children, who cried out, 'Eh, see the Southland gentleman that's gaun to be hanged for shooting lang John Mucklewrath.'

chapter thirteen

An Incident

It was about four o'clock in the afternoon that Mr Gilfillan commenced his march in hopes, although Stirling was eighteen miles distant, he might be able

---

[1]   The Earl of Glencairn was governor of Dumbarton Castle.

to reach it that evening. He marched stoutly along at the head of his followers, eyeing our hero from time to time as if he longed to enter into controversy with him. At length, he slackened his pace till he was alongside his prisoner's horse, and after marching a few steps in silence he suddenly asked, 'Can ye say what the carle was wi' the black coat wha was wi' the Laird of Cairnvreckan?'

'A Presbyterian clergyman,' answered Waverley.

'Presbyterian! Ane of these dumb dogs that cannot bark; they tell ower a clash of terror and a clatter of comfort in their sermons, without ony sense or life. Ye've been fed in siccan a fauld, belike?'

'No, I am of the Church of England.'

'And they're just neighbour-like, and nae wonder they gree sae weel. Wha wad hae thought the goodly structure of the Kirk of Scotland wad hae been defaced by carnal ends and the corruptions of the time! I trow, gin ye were na blinded wi' the graces and favours and enjoyments and employments and inheritances of this wicked world, I could prove to you in what a filthy rag you put your trust, and that your surplices and vestments are but cast-off garments of the muckle harlot that sitteth upon seven hills and drinketh of the cup of abomination.'[1]

This military theologian's matter was copious and his voice powerful, so that there was little chance of his ending his exhortation till the party reached Stirling, had not his attention been attracted by a pedlar who had joined the march from a cross-road and who sighed with great regularity at all fitting passages of his homily.

'And what may ye be, friend?' said Gilfillan.

'A puir pedlar, that's bound for Stirling and craves the protection of your honour in these kittle times. Ah, your honour has a notable faculty in explaining the causes of the backslidings of the land, aye, your honour touches the root of the matter.'

'Friend,' said Gilfillan with a more complacent voice than he had hitherto used, 'honour not me. I do not go out to steadings and to market towns to have cotters and burghers pull off their bonnets to me as they do to Major Melville o' Cairn-vreckan, and call me laird or captain or honour. No, my sma' means have had the blessing of increase, but the pride of my heart has not increased with them, nor do I delight to be called captain, though I have the commission of that gospel-searching nobleman, the Earl of Glencairn. While I live, I am and will be called Habakkuk Gilfillan, who will stand up for the standards of doctrine agreed to by the ance-famous Kirk of Scotland, while he has a plack in his purse or a drap o' bluid in his body.'

'Ah,' said the pedlar, 'I have seen your land about Mauchlin – a fertile spot.[2] Siccan a breed o' cattle is not on ony laird's land in Scotland.'

'Ye say right,' retorted Gilfillan eagerly, for he was not inaccessible to flattery. 'There's no the like o' them even at the Mains of Kilmaurs.'[3] The leader returned to his theological discussions, while the pedlar contented himself with groaning and expressing his edification at suitable intervals.

---

[1]   The whore of Babylon, Revelation 17:4, was for some Protestants a metaphor for the Church of Rome.

[2]   Mauchline, a village near Kilmarnock, Ayrshire. Robert Burns farmed there.

[3]   Kilmaurs Place in Ayrshire was the estate of the earls of Glencairn.

The rays of the sun were lingering on the very verge of the horizon as the party ascended a steep path which led to the summit of rising ground. The country was unenclosed, being part of a very extensive heath, which exhibited in many places hollows filled with furze and broom; in others, little dingles of stunted brushwood. A thicket crowned the hill up which the party ascended. The foremost, being the stoutest and most active, had pushed on and having surmounted the ascent were out of ken. Gilfillan, with the pedlar and the small party who were Waverley's immediate guard, were near the top of the ascent, and the remainder straggled after them.

The pedlar missing, as he said, a little doggie that belonged to him, began to whistle for the animal. The signal gave offence to his companion, because it appeared to indicate inattention to the treasures of theological knowledge which he was pouring out. He therefore signified gruffly that he could not waste his time in waiting for a useless cur.

'But your honour will consider the case of Tobit...'[1]

'Tobit!' exclaimed Gilfillan with great heat. 'Tobit and his dog both are altogether heathenish and none but a prelatist or a papist would draw them into question. I doubt I hae been mista'en in you, friend.'

'Very likely,' answered the pedlar with great composure, 'but ne'ertheless I shall take leave to whistle again upon poor Bawty.'

This last signal was answered in an unexpected manner, for six or eight stout Highlanders, who lurked among the brushwood, sprung into the hollow and began to lay about them with their claymores. Gilfillan, unappalled at this apparition, cried out manfully, 'The sword of the Lord and of Gideon!' and drawing his broadsword would probably have done as much credit to the good old cause as any of its doughty champions at Drumclog when the pedlar, snatching a musket from the person next to him, bestowed the butt of it with such emphasis on the head of his late instructor in the Cameronian creed that he was levelled to the ground.[2] In the confusion, the horse which bore our hero was shot by one of Gilfillan's party. Waverley sustained some severe contusions, but he was almost instantly extricated from the fallen steed by two Highlanders, who hurried him away from the scuffle. They ran with great speed, half supporting and half dragging our hero, who could distinguish a few shots fired about the spot which he had left. This proceeded from Gilfillan's party, who had now assembled, the stragglers in front and rear having joined the others. At their approach the Highlanders drew off, but not before they had grievously wounded Gilfillan and two of his people. A few shots were exchanged, but the westlanders, now without a commander and apprehensive of a second ambush, did not make any serious effort to recover their prisoner.

---

[1]   In the Book of Tobit, part of the Apocrypha, Tobit's son Tobias is accompanied by a dog. Protestants rejected the Apocrychpa's legitimacy.

[2]   'Sword of the Lord and of Gideon' was the war cry of the Old Testament hero Gideon who fought the Midianites. The Covenanters defeated government troops under John Graham of Claverhouse at Drumclog in 1679.

chapter fourteen

Waverley is Still in Distress

The velocity with which Waverley was hurried along nearly deprived him of sensation, for the injury he had received from his fall prevented him from aiding himself. When this was perceived by his conductors, they called to their aid two or three others, and swathing our hero in one of their plaids divided his weight among them and transported him at the same rapid rate as before. They did not slacken their pace till they had run nearly two miles, when they continued still to walk very fast.

The twilight had given place to moonshine when the party halted upon the brink of a precipitous glen, which seemed full of trees and tangled brushwood. At the bottom of a narrow and abrupt descent the party stopped before a rudely-constructed hovel. The door was open and the inside appeared as uncomfortable as its exterior foreboded. There was no floor of any kind, the roof seemed rent in several places, the walls were composed of loose stones and turf and the thatch of branches. The fire was in the centre and filled the whole wigwam with smoke. An old withered Highland sybil appeared busy in the preparation of some food. By the light which the fire afforded Waverley could discover that his attendants were not of the clan of Ivor, for Fergus was strict in requiring that they should wear the tartan striped in the mode peculiar to their race.

Edward glanced around the interior of the cabin. The only furniture, excepting a washing tub and a wooden press sorely decayed, was a large wooden bed, planked all round and opening by a sliding panel. In this recess the Highlanders deposited Waverley, after he had by signs declined any refreshment. His slumbers were broken. Strange visions passed before his eyes. Shivering, violent headache and shooting pain in his limbs succeeded these symptoms, and in the morning it was evident that Waverley was quite unfit to travel.

After a long consultation six of the party left the hut, leaving behind an old and a young man. The former undressed Waverley and bathed his contusions, which swelling and livid colour now made conspicuous. His own portmanteau, which the Highlanders had not failed to bring off, supplied him with linen. The bedding of his couch seemed clean and comfortable, and his aged attendant closed the door of the bed after a few words of Gaelic, from which Waverley gathered that he exhorted him to repose.

The fever which accompanied the injuries did not abate till the third day, when it gave way to the care of his attendants and the strength of his constitution. He could now raise himself in his bed, though not without pain. He observed that there was a great disinclination to permit the door of the bed to be left open, and at length, after Waverley had repeatedly drawn open and the old woman and the elderly Highlander had as frequently shut the hatchway to his cage, the old gentleman put an end to the contest by securing it on the outside.

While musing upon the cause of this contradictory spirit in persons who appeared to consult his welfare, it occurred to him that during the worst crisis of his illness a feminine figure, younger than his Highland nurse, had appeared to flit around his couch. Of this he had a very indistinct recollection, but his suspicions were confirmed when he often heard the voice of another female conversing in whispers with his attendant. Who could it be? And why should she desire concealment? Fancy turned to Flora MacIvor, but Waverley was compelled to conclude his conjecture altogether improbable, since to suppose that she had left her comparatively safe situation at Glennaquoich to descend into the low country, now the seat of war, and to inhabit such a lurking place as this, was a thing hardly to be imagined. Yet his heart bounded as he sometimes could distinctly hear a light female step or the suppressed sounds of a female voice of softness and delicacy.

Having nothing else to amuse his solitude, he employed himself in contriving to gratify his curiosity. At length, the infirm state of his wooden prison-house supplied the means, for out of a spot which was somewhat decayed he was able to extract a nail. Through this minute aperture he could perceive a female form wrapped in a plaid. The form was not that of Flora, nor was the face visible, and to crown his disappointment, while he laboured with the nail to enlarge the hole a slight noise betrayed his purpose and the object of his curiosity instantly disappeared, nor, so far as he could observe, did she again revisit the cottage.

All precautions to blockade his view were from that time abandoned, and he was assisted to rise and quit his couch. But he was not allowed to leave the hut. Waverley, who had not yet recovered strength enough to attempt his departure in spite of opposition, was under the necessity of remaining patient. His fare was better than he could have conceived, for poultry and even wine were no strangers to his table, and the Highlanders treated him with great respect. His sole amusement was gazing from the shapeless aperture which was meant to answer the purpose of a window, upon a rough brook which raged and foamed through a rocky channel canopied with trees and bushes.

Upon the sixth day of his confinement Waverley found himself so well that he began to meditate his escape from this miserable prisonhouse, thinking any risk preferable to the stupefying uniformity. Two schemes seemed practicable, yet both attended with danger. One was to go back to Glennaquoich and join Fergus MacIvor, by whom he was sure to be kindly received, and in his present state of mind the rigour with which he had been treated fully absolved him in his own eyes from his allegiance to the existing government. The other project was to endeavour to attain a Scottish seaport and take shipping for England. His mind wavered between these plans.

Upon the evening of the seventh day the door of the hut suddenly opened and two Highlanders entered, whom Waverley recognized as having been part of his original escort. They conversed with the old man and his companion, and then made Waverley understand that he was to prepare to accompany them. This was a joyful annunciation. His romantic spirit was now wearied with inaction and with a throbbing mixture of hope and anxiety, Waverley watched as those who were just arrived snatched a hasty meal, and the others assumed their arms and made preparations for their departure.

As he sat in the smoky hut he felt a gentle pressure upon his arm. He looked round – it was Alice, the daughter of Donald Bean Lean. She showed him a packet of papers in such a manner that the motion was remarked by no one else, put her finger for a second to her lips, and passed on to assist in packing Waverley's clothes. It was obviously her wish that he should not seem to recognize her, yet she repeatedly looked back at him, and when she saw that he remarked what she did, she folded the packet with great speed in one of his shirts, which she deposited in the portmanteau.

Was Alice his unknown warden who had watched his bed during his sickness? Was he in the hands of her father? And if so, what was his purpose? Spoil, his usual object, seemed in this case neglected, for not only Waverley's property was restored but his purse. All this perhaps the packet might explain, but it was plain from Alice's manner that she desired he should consult it in secret. She shortly afterwards left the hut, and it was only as she tripped out from the door that she gave Waverley a parting smile and nod of significance ere she vanished in the dark glen.

At length the whole party arose and made signs to our hero to accompany them. Before his departure, however, he shook hands with old Janet, who had been so sedulous in his behalf, and added substantial marks of his gratitude for her attendance.

'God bless you! God prosper you, Captain Waverley!' said Janet in good Lowland Scotch, though he had never hitherto heard her utter a syllable save in Gaelic.

chapter fifteen

A Nocturnal Adventure

The Highlander who assumed command by whispers and signs imposed the strictest silence. He delivered to Edward a sword and pistol, and laid his hand on the hilt of his own claymore, as if to make him sensible that they might have occasion to use force. He then placed himself at the head of the party, who moved up the pathway in Indian file, Waverley being placed nearest to their leader. He moved with great precaution, as if to avoid giving any alarm, and halted as soon as he came to the verge of the ascent. Waverley heard at no great distance an English sentinel call out 'All's well'. The heavy sound sunk on the night wind down the woody glen and was answered by the echoes in its banks. A second, third and fourth time the signal was repeated fainter and fainter, as if at a greater and greater distance. It was obvious a party of soldiers were near and upon their guard, though not sufficiently so to detect men skilful in every art of predatory warfare, like those with whom he now watched their ineffectual precautions.

When these sounds had died upon the silence of the night, the Highlanders began their march with the most cautious silence. Waverley could only discern that they passed at some distance from a large building. A little farther on, the leading Highlander snuffed the wind like a setting spaniel and then made a signal again to halt. He stooped down, wrapped up in his plaid so as to be scarce distinguishable from the heathy ground, and advanced to reconnoitre. In a short time he returned and dismissed his attendants excepting one, and intimating to Waverley that he must imitate his cautious mode of proceeding, all three crept forward.

The smell of smoke proceeded from a ruinous sheepfold made of loose stones. Close by a low wall the Highlander intimated to Waverley that he might peep into the sheepfold. Waverley did so, and beheld an outpost of four or five soldiers lying by their watch-fire. They were all asleep except the sentinel, who paced backwards and forwards with his firelock on his shoulder, which glanced red in the light of the fire, casting his eye frequently to the moon obscured by mist.

A sudden breeze arose and swept the clouds before it, and the night planet poured her full effulgence upon a blighted heath skirted with stunted trees in the quarter from which they had come, but open to the observation of the sentinel in that to which their course tended. The wall of the sheepfold concealed them, but any advance beyond its shelter seemed impossible.

The Highlander looked anxiously around for a few minutes, then leaving his attendant with Waverley, he retreated in the same manner as they had advanced. Edward could perceive him crawling with the dexterity of an Indian, availing himself of every bush to escape observation, and never passing over the more exposed parts until the sentinel's back was turned. At length he reached the thickets which partly covered the moor in that direction. The Highlander disappeared, but only for a few minutes, for he suddenly issued forth, and advancing boldly upon the open heath he fired at the sentinel. A wound in the arm proved a disagreeable interruption to the poor fellow's meteorological observations, as well as to the tune he was whistling. He returned the fire ineffectually and his comrades, starting up in alarm, advanced towards the spot from which the first shot had issued. The Highlander, after giving them a full view of his person, dived among the thickets.

While the soldiers pursued the cause of their disturbance in one direction, Waverley, adopting the hint of his remaining attendant, made the best of his speed in that which his guide originally intended, now unobserved and unguarded. When they had run about a quarter of a mile the brow of a rising ground concealed them from observation. They still heard the shouts of the soldiers and the distant roll of a drum beating to arms, but these hostile sounds were now far in their rear, and died upon the breezes as they rapidly proceeded.

When they had walked about half an hour they came to the stump of an ancient oak. In an adjacent hollow they found several Highlanders, with a horse or two. They had not joined them above a few minutes when the cause of their delay, Duncan Duroch, appeared, out of breath and with all the symptoms of having run for his life, but laughing and in high spirits at the success of the stratagem by which he had baffled his pursuers. The alarm which he excited seemed still to continue, for shots were heard at a great distance, which served as an addition to the mirth of Duncan and his comrades.

Waverley was then mounted upon one of the horses, a change which the fatigue of the night and his recent illness rendered exceedingly acceptable. His portmanteau was placed on another pony, Duncan mounted a third, and they set forward at a round pace accompanied by their escort. At the dawn of the morning they attained the banks of a rapid river. The country around was at once fertile and romantic. Steep banks of wood were broken by corn fields, which presented an abundant harvest already in great measure cut down.

On the opposite bank of the river stood a massive castle, the half-ruined turrets of which were already glittering in the first rays of the sun. Upon one of these a sentinel watched, whose bonnet and plaid streaming in the wind declared him to be a Highlander, as a white ensign which floated from another tower announced that the garrison was held by the insurgent adherents of the house of Stuart.

Passing hastily through a small and mean town, the party crossed a narrow bridge, and turning up an avenue of huge old sycamores, Waverley found himself in front of the gloomy yet picturesque structure which he had admired at a distance. A huge iron-grated door was already thrown back, and a second studded thickly with iron nails admitted them into the interior courtyard. A gentleman dressed in Highland garb and having a white cockade in his bonnet, assisted Waverley to dismount from his horse and with much courtesy bid him welcome to the castle.

The governor, having conducted Waverley to a half-ruinous apartment, where there was a camp-bed, and having offered him refreshment, was about to leave him.

'Will you not add to your civilities,' said Waverley, 'by having the kindness to inform me where I am, and whether I am to consider myself a prisoner?'

'I am not at liberty to be so explicit upon this subject as I could wish. Briefly, however, you are in the Castle of Doune in the district of Menteith, and in no danger whatever.'[1]

'And how am I to be assured of that?'

'By the honour of Donald Stuart, governor of the garrison, and lieutenant-colonel in the service of his Royal Highness Prince Charles Edward.' So saying he hastily left the apartment, as if to avoid further discussion.

Our hero, exhausted by the fatigues of the night, now threw himself upon the bed, and was in a few minutes fast asleep.

---

[1]   Doune Castle, near Stirling.

chapter sixteen

The Journey Is Continued

B efore Waverley awakened, the day was far advanced. A copious breakfast was soon supplied, but Colonel Stuart did not again present himself. As he contemplated the strangeness of his fortune, which seemed to delight in placing him at the disposal of others without the power of directing his own motions, Edward's eye suddenly rested upon his portmanteau. The mysterious appearance of Alice immediately rushed upon his mind, and he was about to secure the packet which she had deposited when the servant of Colonel Stuart made his appearance, and took up the portmanteau upon his shoulders.

'May I not take out a change of linen, my friend?'

'Your honour sall get ane o' the Colonel's ain ruffled sarks, but this maun gang in the baggage-cart.'

And so saying he coolly carried off the portmanteau, leaving our hero in a state where disappointment and indignation struggled for mastery. He heard a cart rumble out of the courtyard, and made no doubt that he was now dispossessed of the only documents which seemed to promise some light upon the dubious events which had of late influenced his destiny. With such melancholy thoughts he beguiled four or five hours of solitude.

When this was elapsed, the trampling of horse was heard, and Colonel Stuart appeared to request his guest to take some farther refreshment before his departure. The offer was accepted, for a late breakfast had not left our hero incapable of doing honour to dinner. His host cautiously avoided any reference to the military operations or politics of the time, and to Waverley's enquiries concerning these points replied that he was not at liberty to converse upon such topics.

When dinner was finished the governor arose and, wishing Edward a good journey, disappeared. A servant acquainted Waverley that his horse was ready. He descended into the courtyard and found a trooper holding a saddled horse, on which he mounted and sallied from the portal of Doune Castle, attended by a score of armed men on horseback. Their uniform was incomplete, and sat awkwardly upon those who wore it. Waverley's eye, accustomed to looking at a well-disciplined regiment, could easily discover that the motions and habits of his escort were not those of trained soldiers, and that although expert in the management of their horses, their skill was that of huntsmen rather than of troopers. The men, however, were hardy-looking fellows and might be individually formidable as irregular cavalry. The commander was mounted upon an excellent hunter, and although dressed in uniform, his change of apparel did not prevent Waverley from recognizing his old acquaintance, Mr Falconer of Balmawhapple.

Although the terms upon which Edward had met with this gentleman were not of the most friendly, he would have sacrificed every recollection of their foolish quarrel for the pleasure of enjoying once more the social intercourse from which he had been so long excluded. But apparently the remembrance of his defeat by the Baron of Bradwardine still rankled in the mind of the proud laird. He carefully avoided giving the least sign of recognition, riding doggedly at the head of his men, preceded by a trumpet, which was sounded from time to time, and a standard.

In about two hours time the party were near Stirling Castle, over whose battlements the union flag was brightening in the evening sun. To shorten his journey, Balmawhapple took his route through the royal park, which reaches up to and surrounds the rock upon which the fortress is situated. With a mind more at ease, Waverley could not have failed to admire the mixture of romance and beauty – the field which had been the scene of tournaments of old – the rock from which the ladies beheld the contest – the towers of the Gothic church – and, surmounting all, the fortress itself, at once a castle and a palace, where valour received the prize from royalty, and knights and dames closed the evening among the revelry of the dance, the song and the feast.

But Waverley had other subjects of meditation, and an incident soon occurred of a nature to disturb meditation of any kind. Balmawhapple, as he wheeled his little body of cavalry around the base of the castle, commanded his trumpet to sound a flourish and his standard to be displayed. This insult produced a flash of fire from one of the embrasures upon the rock, and ere the report could be heard, the rushing sound of a cannonball passed over Balmawhapple's head, and the bullet burying itself in the ground at a few yards distance covered him with earth. The cavaliers retreated with more speed than regularity. Balmawhapple, however, answered the fire of the castle by discharging one of his horse-pistols at the battlements, although the distance being nearly half a mile I could never learn that this retaliation was attended with any particular effect.

The travellers now passed the memorable battlefield of Bannockburn.[1] At Falkirk, Balmawhapple proposed to repose for the evening. Sentinels were deemed unnecessary, and the only vigils performed were those of such as could procure liquor. A few resolute men might easily have cut off the party, but of the inhabitants some were favourable, many indifferent and the rest overawed. So nothing memorable occurred, excepting that Waverley's rest was sorely interrupted by the revellers hallooing forth their Jacobite songs.

Early in the morning they were again on the road to Edinburgh. As they approached the metropolis of Scotland, the sounds of war began to be heard. The distant report of heavy cannon apprized Waverley that the work of destruction was going forward. Even Balmawhapple seemed moved to take some precautions, by sending an advanced party in front of his troop. They speedily reached an eminence from which they could view Edinburgh stretching along the ridgy hill which slopes eastward from the Castle. The latter, being in a state of blockade by the northern insurgents, who had already occupied the town for two or three

---

[1]   Bannockburn, about 4km southeast of Stirling, was where in 1314 Robert the Bruce defeated the forces of English king Edward II.

days, fired at intervals upon such Highlanders as exposed themselves. The morning being calm and fair, the effect of this was to invest the Castle in wreaths of smoke, the edges of which dissipated slowly in the air, while the central veil was darkened by fresh clouds poured forth from the battlements, the whole giving an appearance of grandeur and gloom. Waverley reflected that each explosion might ring some brave man's knell.

Balmawhapple left the direct road, and sweeping to the southward so as to keep out of range of the cannon approached the ancient palace of Holyrood without having entered the walls of the city. He delivered Waverley into the custody of a guard of Highlanders, whose officer conducted him into the interior of the building.

A long gallery served as a vestibule to the apartments which the adventurous Charles Edward now occupied in the palace of his ancestors. Officers, both in the Highland and Lowland garb, passed and re-passed in haste, or loitered in the hall as if waiting for orders. Secretaries were engaged in making out passes, musters and returns. All seemed earnestly intent upon something of importance, but Waverley was suffered to remain seated unnoticed in the recess of a window, in anxious reflection upon the crisis of his fate, which seemed now rapidly approaching.

chapter seventeen

An Old and a New Acquaintance

While he was deep sunk in his reverie a friendly arm clasped his shoulders. Waverley turned and was warmly embraced by Fergus MacIvor. 'A thousand welcomes to Holyrood, once more possessed by her legitimate sovereign! Did I not say we should prosper?'

'Dear Fergus, it is long since I have heard a friend's voice. Where is Flora?'

'Safe, and a triumphant spectator of our success.'

'In this place?'

'Ay, in this city at least and you shall see her. But first you must meet a friend who has been frequent in his enquiries after you.'

He dragged Waverley by the arm, and ere he knew where he was conducted Edward found himself in a presence-room fitted up with some attempt at royal state. A young man, distinguished by his dignity and the notable expression of his well-formed and regular features, advanced out of a circle of military gentlemen and Highland chiefs. In his easy and graceful manners Waverley afterwards thought he should have discovered his high birth and rank, although the star on his breast and the embroidered garter at his knee had not appeared an indication.

'Let me present to your Royal Highness,' said Fergus, bowing profoundly –

'The descendant of one of the most ancient and loyal families in England,' said the young Chevalier. 'I beg your pardon for interrupting you, my dear MacIvor, but no master of ceremonies is necessary to present a Waverley to a Stuart.'

He extended his hand to Edward with the utmost courtesy, who could not have avoided rendering him the homage which seemed due to his rank, and was certainly the right of his birth. 'I am so sorry to understand, Mr Waverley, that you have suffered some restraint among my followers in Perthshire, but we are in such a situation that we hardly know our friends, and I am uncertain whether I can have the pleasure of considering Mr Waverley among mine.' He took out a paper and proceeded. 'I should indeed have no doubts upon this subject if I could trust to this proclamation set forth by the friends of the Elector of Hanover, in which they rank Mr Waverley among the nobility and gentry who are menaced with high treason for loyalty to their legitimate sovereign. But I desire to gain no adherents save from affection and conviction, and if Mr Waverley inclines to prosecute his journey to the south or join the forces of the Elector, he shall have my free permission to do so. But if Mr Waverley should determine to embrace a cause which has little to recommend it but its justice, and follow a prince who throws himself upon the affections of his people to recover the throne of his ancestors, I can only say he will follow a master who may be unfortunate, but I trust will never be ungrateful.'

Charles Edward's words penetrated the heart of our hero and easily out-weighed all prudential motives. To be thus personally solicited by a prince answered his ideas of romance. To be courted by him in the ancient halls of his paternal palace, recovered by the sword which he was already bending towards other conquests, gave Edward dignity and importance. Rejected and slandered upon the one side, he was irresistibly attracted to the cause which the political principles of his family had already recommended as the most just. These thoughts rushed through his mind like a torrent – and Waverley, kneeling to Charles Edward, devoted his heart and sword to the vindication of his rights!

The prince raised Waverley, and embraced him with an expression of thanks too warm not to be genuine. He presented Waverley to the various noblemen, chieftains and officers who were about his person, as a young man of the highest prospects, in whose enthusiastic avowal of his cause they might see evidence of the sentiments of the English families of rank. As a well-founded disbelief in the co-operation of the English Jacobites kept many Scottish men from his standard, nothing could be more seasonable for the Chevalier that the declaration in his favour of a representative of the house of Waverley Honour. This Fergus had foreseen. He loved Waverley, and rejoiced that they were engaged in the same cause, but he also exulted in beholding secured to his party a partisan of such consequence. He was far from insensible to the importance which he acquired with the prince, from having assisted in making the acquisition.

Charles Edward seemed eager to show the value which he attached to his new adherent. 'You have heard of my landing in remote Moidart, with only seven attendants, and the chiefs and clans whose loyal enthusiasm at once placed a solitary adventurer at the head of a gallant army.[1] You must also have learned that the commander-in-chief of the Elector marched into the Highlands with the intention of giving us battle, but that his courage failed him.[2] He marched north to Aberdeen, leaving the low country undefended. Not to lose so favourable an opportunity, I marched on to this metropolis, and while discussions were carrying forward upon the citizens, whether they should defend themselves or surrender, my good friend Lochiel saved them the trouble for farther deliberation by entering the gates with five hundred Camerons.[3] In the meanwhile, this doughty general has taken shipping for Dunbar and landed there yesterday. His purpose must be to recover possession of the capital. Now there are two opinions in my council of war, one that it will be safest to fall back towards the mountains and there protract the war until fresh succours arrive from France, and the whole body of the Highland clans shall have taken arms in our favour. The opposite opinion maintains that a retrograde movement is certain to throw discredit on our under-taking, and far from gaining new partisans will be the means of disheartening those who have joined our standard. Will Mr Waverley favour us with his opinion?'

Waverley coloured betwixt pleasure and modesty at the distinction implied in this question, and answered that the counsel would be far more acceptable to him which should first afford him an opportunity to evince his zeal in his Royal Highness's service.

'Spoken like a Waverley,' answered Charles Edward. 'Allow me, instead of the captain's commission which you have lost, to offer you the rank of major in my service, acting as one of my aides-de-camp until you can be attached to a regiment.'

'Your Royal Highness will forgive me,' answered Waverley, 'if I decline accepting any rank until the time and place where I may raise a sufficient body of men to make my command useful. In the meanwhile, I hope for your permis-sion to serve as a volunteer under my friend Fergus MacIvor.'

'At least,' said the Prince, obviously pleased with this proposal, 'allow me the pleasure of arming you after the Highland fashion.' He unbuckled the broad-sword which he wore, the steel basket-hilt of which was richly inlaid. 'This blade is a genuine Andrea Ferrara, an heirloom in our family, but I am convinced I put it into better hands than my own, and will add pistols of the same workmanship.[4] Colonel MacIvor, you must have much to say to your friend. I will detain you no longer.'

Thus licensed, the Chief and Waverley left the presence-chamber.

---

[1]   Prince Charles landed first on the Isle of Eriskay in July 1745 and then at Arisaig on the mainland, from where he continued with his small entourage to Glenfinnan via Borrodale in Moidart. He raised his standard in Glenfinnan, at the head of Loch Shiel, on 19 August.

[2]   The Elector of Hanover, ie George II. The commander-in-chief was General John Cope.

[3]   Donald Cameron of Lochiel was one of the first chieftains to join Prince Charles at the start of the 1745 campaign. He and his men entered Edinburgh unopposed thanks to the accidental opening of the Netherbow Port.

[4]   Andrea de Ferrara was an expert sixteenth-century Italian swordsmith, though in Scotland most swords marked with his name were not genuine.

chapter eighteen

The Mystery Begins to Be Cleared up

How do you like him?' was Fergus's first question, as they descended the large stone staircase.

'A prince to live and die under,' was Waverley's enthusiastic answer.

'I knew you would think so. Yet he has his foibles, or rather he has difficult cards to play. But let me hear the full story of your adventures, for they have reached us in a very mutilated manner.'

Waverley then detailed the circumstances. They reached the door of Fergus's quarters, the house of a buxom widow of forty who seemed to smile very graciously upon the handsome young Chief. Here Callum Beg received them. 'Callum,' said the Chief, 'get a plaid of MacIvor tartan and sash and a blue bonnet of the Prince's pattern. My green coat with silver lace will fit him exactly, and I have never worn it. Tell Ensign Maccombich to pick out a handsome target from among mine. The Prince has given Mr Waverley broadsword and pistols, I will furnish him with a dirk and purse. Add but a pair of low-heeled shoes and then, my dear Edward, you will be a complete son of Ivor.'

The Chieftain resumed the subject of Waverley's adventures. 'It is plain you have been in the custody of Donald Bean Lean. When I marched away to join the Prince, I laid my injunctions on him that he was to join me with all the force he could muster. But instead, the gentleman thought it better to make war on his own account, plundering both friend and foe. I will be tempted to hang that fellow. I recognize his hand particularly in the mode of your rescue from Gilfillan, but how he should not have plundered you passes my judgment.'

'How did you hear of my confinement?'

'The Prince himself told me. I recommended that you should be brought here as a prisoner, because I did not wish to prejudice you farther with the English government.'

'Now, my dear Fergus,' said Waverley, 'you may find time to tell me something of Flora.'

'She is well and residing with a relation in this city. Since our success a good many ladies of rank attend our military court, and there is a consequence annexed to the relatives of such a person as Flora MacIvor, and where there is such a jostling of claims and requests a man must use every fair means to enhance his importance.'

There was something in this last sentence which grated on Waverley's feelings. He could not bear that Flora should be considered as conducing her brother's preferment by the admiration which she must unquestionably attract, and it shocked him as unworthy of his sister's high mind and his own independent pride. Fergus, to whom such manoeuvres were familiar, did not observe the unfavourable impression he had made on his friend.

While thus conversing, Waverley heard in the court a well-known voice. 'I aver to you,' said the speaker, 'that a prisoner of war is on no account to be coerced with fetters.'

The growling voice of Balmawhapple was heard taking leave in displeasure, but he had disappeared before Waverley had reached the court in order to greet the worthy Baron. The uniform in which he was attired seemed to have added fresh rigidity to his perpendicular figure, and the consciousness of military authority had increased the self-importance of his demeanour. He received Waverley with his usual kindness, and expressed anxiety to hear of the circumstances attending the loss of his commission.

Fergus MacIvor, who now joined them, went hastily over Waverley's story and concluded with the flattering reception he had met from the young Chevalier. The Baron listened in silence, and shook Waverley heartily by the hand and congratulated him upon entering the service of his lawful Prince. Waverley made enquiry after Miss Bradwardine, and was informed she had come to Edinburgh with Flora MacIvor, under guard of a party of the Chieftain's men. This step was necessary, Tully Veolan having become a very unpleasant and even dangerous place of residence for an unprotected young lady, on account of its vicinity to the Highlands. One or two large villages had declared themselves on the side of the government and formed irregular bodies of partisans who had frequent skirmishes with the mountaineers and sometimes attacked the houses of the Jacobite gentry.

'I would propose to you,' continued the Baron, 'to walk as far as my quarters in the Luckenbooths, and to admire the High Street, whilk is, beyond a shadow of dubitation, finer than any street in London or Paris. But Rose, poor thing, is sorely discomposed with the firing of the Castle, though I have proved to her that it is impossible a bullet can reach these buildings. But I stand here talking to you two youngsters when I should be in the King's Park.'[1]

'But you will dine with Waverley and me on your return?' said Fergus.

'Well, I have some business in the town too. But I'll join you at three.' So saying, the Baron took leave of his friends.

chapter nineteen

A Soldier's Dinner

When our hero assumed the garb well calculated to give an appearance of strength to a figure which, though tall and well-made, was rather elegant than robust, he looked at himself in the mirror more than once and could not help acknowledging that the reflection seemed that of a very handsome fellow. His light brown hair became the bonnet which surrounded it. His person promised

---

[1] Holyrood Park, southeast of Holyrood Palace.

firmness and agility, to which the ample folds of the tartan added an air of dignity. His blue eye seemed of that kind 'which melted in love and kindled in war', and an air of bashfulness gave interest to his features without injuring their grace or intelligence.[1] 'He's a very pratty man,' said Evan Dhu (now Ensign Maccombich) to Fergus's buxom landlady.

'He's vera weel,' said the Widow Flockhart, 'but naething so well-far'd as your colonel.'

'I wasna comparing them,' quoth Evan, 'nor was I speaking about his being well-favoured, but only that Mr Waverley looks clean-made, and like a proper lad o' his quarters will not cry barley in a brulzie.'

'Will ye fight wi' Sir John Cope the morn, Ensign Maccombich?'

'Troth I'se ensure him, an' he'll bide us, Mrs Flockhart.'

'And will ye face these tearing chields the dragoons, Ensign Maccombich?'

'Claw for claw, Mrs Flockhart, and the devil tak the shortest nails.'

'And will the Colonel venture on the bagganets himsell?'

'Ye may swear it, Mrs Flockhart. The very first man will he be.'

'Merciful goodness! And if he's killed amang the red coats?'

'If it should sae befall, I ken ane that will na be living to weep for him. But we maun a' live the day and have our dinner. And there's Vich Ian Vohr has packed his dorlach, and Mr Waverley's wearied wi' majoring afore the muckle pier-glass, and that grey auld carle the Baron of Bradwardine, he's coming down the close wi' the droghling, coghling Baillie body they ca' Macwhupple trindling ahint him, like a turnspit after a French cook, and I am as hungry as a gled, my bonny dow. Sae bid Kate set on the broo', and do ye put on you pinners, for ye ken Vich Ian Vohr winna sit down till ye be at the head o' the table – and dinna forget the pint bottle o' brandy.'

Their fare was excellent, time, place and circumstances considered, and Fergus's spirits were extravagantly high. Indifferent to danger, he saw in imagination all his prospects crowned with success, and was totally indifferent to the probable alternative of a soldier's grave.

The Baron apologized for bringing Macwheeble. They had been providing for the expenses of the campaign. 'I had evermore,' said the old man, 'found the sinews of war more difficult to come by than either its flesh, blood or bones.'

'What, have you raised our only efficient body of cavalry and got ye none of the louis d'ors to help you?'

'No, Glennaquoich, cleverer fellows have been before me.'

'That's a scandal, but you will share what is left of my subsidy. It will save you an anxious thought tonight, and be all one tomorrow, for we shall be provided for one way or other before the sun sets.' Waverley pressed the same request. 'I thank you both,' said the Baron, 'but I will not infringe upon you. Baillie Macwheeble has provided the sum which is necessary.'

After fidgeting a while the Baillie addressed Glennaquoich, and told him if his honour had mair ready siller than was sufficient for his occasions he could

---

[1] From Thomas Cambell's poem 'The Wounded Hussar', 1799.

put it in safe hands and a great profit. At this proposal Fergus laughed heartily and answered, 'Many thanks, Baillie, but you must know it is a general custom among us soldiers to make our landlady our banker. Here, Mrs Flockhart,' said he, taking four or five pieces out of a well-filled purse and tossing the purse itself into her apron, 'be my banker if I live and my executor if I die, but take care to give something to the Highland cailliachs that shall cry the coronach loudest for the last Vich Ian Vohr.'

The soft heart of Mrs Flockhart melted within her at this speech. She set up a lamentable blubbering and positively refused to touch the bequest, which Fergus was obliged to resume. 'Well,' said the Chief, 'if I fall it will go to the grenadier that knocks my brains out.'

Where cash was concerned, Baillie Macwheeble did not willingly remain silent. 'Perhaps he had better carry the goud to Miss MacIvor, in case of accidents of war.'

'The young lady,' said Fergus, 'should such an event happen, will have other matters to think of than these wretched louis d'ors.'

'True – there's nae doubt o' that, but your honour kens that a full sorrow –'

'Is endurable by most folks more easily than a hungry one. True, Baillie, and I believe there may even be some who would be consoled by such a reflection for the loss of a whole generation. But there is a sorrow that knows neither hunger nor thirst.' He paused, and the whole company sympathized in his emotion. The Baron's thoughts naturally reverted to his daughter. 'If I fall, Macwheeble, you have all my papers and know all my affairs. Be just to Rose.' Some kindly feelings the Baillie had, especially where the Baron or his young mistress were concerned. He set up a lamentable howl. 'If this doleful day should come, while Duncan Macwheeble had a boddle it should be Miss Rose's.' Here he had recourse to the end of his long cravat to wipe his eyes.

'Come, Baillie,' said the Chief, 'be not cast down. Drink your wine with a joyous heart. The Baron shall return safe and victorious to Tully Veolan, and I shall take care of myself too.'

chapter twenty

The Ball

Waverley, the Baron and the Chieftain proceeded to Holyrood House. Many gentlemen of rank and education took a concern in the desperate under-taking of 1745. The ladies also of Scotland generally espoused the cause of the gallant young Prince, who threw himself upon the mercy of his countrymen rather like a hero of romance than a calculating politician. It is not therefore to be wondered that Edward should have been dazzled at the liveliness and elegance of the scene now exhibited in the long-deserted halls of the Scottish palace.

It was not long before the lover's eye discovered the object of his attachment. Flora MacIvor was returning to her seat with Rose Bradwardine by her side. Among much elegance and beauty they had attracted public attention, being certainly two of the handsomest women present. The Prince took much notice of both, particularly of Flora, with whom he danced.

Edward almost intuitively followed Fergus to the place where Miss MacIvor was seated. The sensation of hope with which he had nursed his affection seemed to vanish in her presence, and, like one striving to recover a forgotten dream, he would have given the world to have recollected the grounds on which he had founded expectations which now seemed so delusive. He accompanied Fergus with the sensation of a criminal who, while he moves through the crowds assembled to behold his execution, receives no clear sensation from the tumult on which he casts his wandering look.

Flora seemed a little discomposed at his approach. 'I bring you an adopted son of Ivor,' said Fergus.

'And I receive him as a second brother,' replied Flora.

There was a slight emphasis on the word which would have escaped every ear but one. It was however distinctly marked, and combined with her manner plainly intimated, 'I will never think of Mr Waverley as a more intimate connection.' Edward bowed and looked at Fergus, who bit his lip, a movement of anger which proved that he also put a sinister interpretation on the reception. 'This is an end of my day-dream!' Such was Waverley's first thought, so painful as to banish from his cheek every drop of blood.

'Good God!' said Rose Bradwardine, 'he is not yet recovered!'

These words were overheard by the Chevalier himself, who stepped hastily forward, enquired after Waverley's health and added that he wished to speak with him. By a strong effort Waverley recovered himself so far as to follow the Chevalier in silence to a recess in the apartment.

Here the Prince asked various questions about the great tory and catholic families of England, their connections, and the state of the affections towards the house of Stuart. Edward could not at any time have given more than general answers, and in the present state of his feelings his responses were indistinct. The Chevalier smiled once or twice at the incongruity of his replies, but continued the same style of conversation until he perceived that Waverley had recovered his presence of mind. It is probable that this audience was partly meant to further the idea that Waverley was a character of political influence, but it appeared that he had a different motive, personal to our hero. 'I cannot resist the temptation,' he said, 'of boasting of my own discretion as a lady's confidant. You see, Mr Waverley, that I know all, and I assure you I am deeply interested in the affair. But you must put a more severe restraint upon your feelings. There are many here whose eyes can see as clearly as mine, but the prudence of whose tongues may not be equally trusted.'

He turned easily away, leaving Waverley to meditate upon his parting expression. Making an effort to show himself worthy of the interest which his new master had expressed, he walked up to where Flora and Miss Bradwardine were still seated and succeeded, even beyond his own expectations, in entering into conversation upon general topics.

Distinguished by the favour of a Prince, destined, he had room to hope, to play a conspicuous part in the revolution which awaited a mighty kingdom, and equaling at least in personal accomplishments most of the noble persons with whom he now ranked, young, wealthy and high born, ought he to droop beneath the frown of a capricious beauty? Waverley determined upon convincing Flora that he was not to be depressed by rejection. There was a tone of encouragement also in the Chevalier's words, though he feared they only referred to the wishes of Fergus in favour of a union between him and his sister. But the whole circumstances of time and place combined to awaken his imagination, and to call upon him for manly and decisive conduct. Should he appear to be the only one disheartened on the eve of battle, how greedily would the tale be commented upon by the slander which had been already too busy with his fame.

Cheered at times by a smile of approbation from the Prince, Waverley exerted his powers of intelligence and eloquence, and attracted the admiration of the company. The conversation gradually assumed the tone best qualified for the display of his talents. The gaiety of the evening was exalted by the approaching dangers of tomorrow. All nerves were strung and prepared to enjoy the present. Waverley touched more than once the higher notes of feeling, and was supported by kindred spirits who felt the same impulse of mood. Many ladies declined the dance and joined the party to which the 'handsome young Englishman' seemed to have attached himself. His manners, free from the bashful restraint by which they were usually clouded, gave universal delight.

Flora MacIvor appeared to be the only female present who regarded him with a degree of coldness, yet even she could not suppress a sort of wonder at talents which she had never seen displayed with equal brilliancy. If a passing wish occurred that Waverley could have rendered himself uniformly thus amiable and attractive, its influence was momentary, for circumstances had arisen which rendered the resolution she had formed respecting his addresses irrevocable. With opposite feelings Rose Bradwardine bent her whole soul to listen. She felt a secret triumph at the public tribute paid to one whose merit she had learned to prize too early and too fondly. Without a thought of jealousy, without a feeling of fear or doubt, she resigned herself to the pleasure of observing the murmur of applause. When Waverley spoke, her ear was exclusively filled with his voice.

'Baron,' said the Chevalier, 'I would not trust my mistress in the company of your young friend. He is one of the most fascinating young men I have ever seen.'

'And by my honour, sir,' said the Baron, 'the lad can sometimes be as dowff as a sexagenary like myself. If your Royal Highness had seen him dreaming and dozing about the banks of Tully Veolan you would wonder where he hath sae suddenly acquired all this fine festivity and jocularity.'

'Truly,' said Fergus MacIvor, 'I think it can only be the inspiration of the tartans, for though Waverley has always been a man of sense, I have hitherto often found him a very inattentive companion.'

'We are the more obliged to him,' said the Chevalier, 'for having reserved for this evening qualities which such intimate friends had not discovered. But come, gentleman, the night advances, and the business of tomorrow must be early thought upon.'

chapter twenty-one

The March

Waverley was dreaming of Glennaquoich. The pibroch was distinctly heard, and this was no delusion, for the piper of the 'chlain MacIvor' was perambulating before the door of the Chieftain's quarters, and as Mrs Flockhart was pleased to observe, 'garring the very stane and lime wa's dinnle wi' his screeching'. It soon became too powerful for Waverley's dream, with which it had at first harmonized.

The sound of Callum's brogues in his apartment was the next note. 'Vich Ian Vohr and ta Prince are awa' to the lang green glen they ca' King's Park, and mony ane's on his ain shanks the day that will be carried on ither folks' ere night.'

Waverley sprang up, and with Callum's assistance adjusted his tartans in proper costume. Having declined Mrs Flockhart's compliment of a *morning*, ie a matutinal dram, being probably the only man in the Chevalier's army by whom such a courtesy would have been rejected, he departed with Callum.

Upon extricating themselves from the mean and dirty suburbs of the metropolis and emerging into the open air, Waverley felt a renewal both of health and spirits. When he had surmounted a small craggy eminence called St Leonard's Hill, the King's Park, the hollow between Arthur's Seat and the rising ground upon which the southern part of Edinburgh is now built, lay beneath him. It was occupied by the army of the Highlanders preparing for their march. The rocks in the background and the very sky itself rang with the clang of the bagpipers summoning, each with his appropriate pibroch, his chieftain and his clan. The mountaineers seemed to possess all the pliability of movement fitted to execute military manoeuvres. Their motions appeared spontaneous and confused, but the result was order and regularity, so that a general must have praised the conclusion though a martinet might have ridiculed the method by which it was attained.

The complicated medley created by the clans under their respective banners was a lively spectacle. They had no tents to strike, having slept upon the open field, although the autumn was waning and the nights beginning to be frosty.

There was exhibited a fluctuating and confused appearance of waving tartans and floating plumes, and banners displaying the signal words and emblems of chieftains and clans.

At length the wavering multitude arranged themselves into a dusky column of great length, stretching through the whole extent of the valley. In the front of the column the standard of the Chevalier was displayed, bearing a red cross upon a white ground with the motto *Tandem Triumphans*.[1] The few cavalry formed the advanced guard, and their standards were seen waving upon the extreme verge of the horizon. Many members of this body added to the liveliness by galloping their horses forward to join their proper station in the van. The confusion occasioned by those who endeavoured to press to the front through the crowd of Highlanders, maugre their oaths and opposition, added to the picturesque wildness of the scene.

While Waverley gazed upon this remarkable spectacle, rendered yet more impressive by the occasional discharge of cannon shot from the Castle, Callum reminded him that Vich Ian Vohr's folk were nearly at the head of the column. Waverley walked briskly forward. The leading men of each clan were well armed with broadsword, target and fusee, to which all added the dirk and most the pistol. These consisted of relations of the chief, however distant, who had title to his countenance and protection. Finer men than these could not have been selected out of any army in Christendom, and the independent habits which each possessed and the peculiar mode of discipline adopted in Highland warfare, rendered them equally formidable by their courage and spirit, and from their conviction of the necessity of acting in unison, giving their mode of attack the fullest opportunity of success.

But in an inferior rank were found individuals of an inferior description, the peasantry who bore the livery of penury, being indifferently accoutred, half naked, stinted in growth and miserable in aspect. These Helots, though forced into the field by the arbitrary authority of the chieftains under whom they hewed wood and drew water, were in general very sparingly fed, ill dressed and worse armed. The latter circumstance was owing chiefly to the disarming act, which had been carried into effect ostensibly through the whole Highlands, although most of the chieftains contrived to elude its influence by retaining the weapons of their own immediate clansmen and delivering up those of less value which they collected from their inferior satellites. It followed that many of these poor fellows were brought to the field in a very wretched condition.

From this it happened that the rear resembled banditti. Here was a pole-axe, there a sword without a scabbard; here a gun without a lock, there a scythe set straight upon a pole. Some had only their dirks, and bludgeons or stakes pulled out of hedges. The grim and wild appearance of these men created surprise in the Lowlands, but it also created terror. So little was the condition of the Highlands known that the character of their population conveyed to the Lowlanders as much surprise as if an invasion of African Negroes or Esquimaux Indians had

---

[1]　There are conflicting accounts of the nature of Charles Edward's standard. The Latin motto means 'triumphant at last.'

issued forth from the northern mountains of their own native country. It cannot be wondered if Waverley, who had hitherto judged of the Highlanders from the samples which the policy of Fergus had exhibited, should have felt astonished at the daring attempt of a body not exceeding four thousand men, and of those not above half well armed, to change the fate and alter the dynasty of the British kingdom.

As he moved along the column, the only piece of artillery possessed by the army which meditated so important a revolution was fired as the signal of march. No sooner was its voice heard than the whole line was in motion. A wild cry of joy from the advancing battalions rent the air and was then lost in the shrill clangour of the bagpipes, as the sound of these, in their turn, was partially drowned by the heavy tread of so many men put at once into motion. The banners glittered and shook as they moved forward, and the horse hastened to occupy their station as the advanced guard. They vanished from Waverley's eye as they wheeled round the base of Arthur's Seat under the ridge of basaltic rocks which front the little lake of Duddingston.

The infantry followed. It cost Edward some exertion to attain the place which Fergus's followers occupied in the line of march.

chapter twenty-two

An Incident Gives Rise to Unavailing Reflections

When Waverley reached the clan MacIvor they received him with a triumphant flourish upon the bagpipes and a loud shout. 'You shout,' said a Highlander of a neighbouring clan to Evan Dhu, 'as if the Chieftain were just come to your head.'

'*Mar e Bran is e brathait*, If it be not Bran, it is Bran's brother,' was the proverbial reply of Maccombich. Fergus advanced to embrace the volunteer.

The route pursued by the Highland army was the post-road betwixt Edinburgh and Haddington, until they crossed the Esk at Musselburgh, when they turned more inland and occupied the brow of Carberry Hill, a place already distinguished in Scottish history as the spot where the lovely Mary surrendered to her insurgent subjects.[1] The army of the government had quartered the night before to the west of Haddington with the intention of approaching Edinburgh by the lower coast road. By keeping the height which overhung the road it was hoped the Highlanders might find an opportunity of attacking them to advantage. The army halted upon the ridge of Carberry Hill. While they remained in this position a messenger came in haste to desire MacIvor to come to the Prince, and added

---

[1]   Haddington in East Lothian is east of Edinburgh. The River Esk flows into the Firth of Forth at Musselburgh. Mary Queen of Scots in 1567 surrendered to the Protestants lords at nearby Carberry Hill.

that their advanced post had had a skirmish with some of the enemy's cavalry, and that the Baron of Bradwardine had sent in a few prisoners.

Waverley soon observed five or six troopers who, covered with dust, had galloped in to announce that the enemy was in full march westward along the coast. Passing farther on, he was struck with a groan which issued from a hovel, and heard a voice in the English of his native country. He entered the hovel, and in its obscurity could discern a red bundle, for those who had stripped the wounded man of his arms and part of his clothes had left him the dragoon cloak in which he was enveloped.

'For the sake of God,' said the wounded man, 'give me a drop of water.'

'You shall have it,' answered Waverley, raising him in his arms and giving him some drink from his flask.

'I should know that voice,' answered the man, looking on Edward's dress with a bewildered look, 'no, this is not the young squire.'

The sound thrilled Edward with a thousand recollections of the well-known accents of his native country. 'Houghton!' he said, gazing on the ghastly features which death was fast disfiguring, 'can this be you?'

'I never thought to hear an English voice again,' said the wounded man. 'They left me to live or die here. But how could you stay away from us so long, and let us be tempted by that fiend Ruffen? We would have followed you through flood and fire.'

'Ruffen! I assure you, Houghton, you have been vilely imposed upon.'

'I often thought so' said Houghton, 'though they showed us your very seal, and so Tims was shot and I was reduced to the ranks.'

'I will get you a surgeon,' said Edward.

He saw MacIvor approaching. 'Brave news!' shouted the chief. 'The Prince has put himself at the head of the advance, and as he drew his sword called out, "My friends, I have thrown away the scabbard." Come, Waverley, we move instantly.'

'A moment, a moment, this poor prisoner is dying. Where shall I find a surgeon? The man will bleed to death.'

'Poor fellow! But it will be a thousand men's fate before night, so come along.'

'I cannot. I tell you he is son of a tenant of my uncle's.'

'O, if he is a follower of yours, he must be looked to. I'll send Callum to you.'

Waverley rather gained than lost in his opinion of the Highlanders by Callum's anxiety about the wounded man. They would not have understood Waverley's general philanthropy, but apprehending that the sufferer was one of his following, they unanimously allowed that Waverley's conduct was that of a kind and considerate chieftain. In about a quarter of an hour poor Humphry breathed his last, conjuring him not to fight with these wild petticoat-men against old England. Waverley beheld with sincere sorrow and no slight tinge of remorse the final agonies of mortality, now witnessed for the first time.

This melancholy interview with his late sergeant forced many painful reflections upon Waverley's mind. It was clear that Colonel Gardiner's proceedings had been strictly warranted, and even rendered indispensable, by the steps taken in Edward's name to induce his troop to mutiny. He now recollected that he had lost the seal in the cavern of Bean Lean. That the artful villain had used it as the means of carrying on an intrigue in the regiment for his own purposes was evident, and Edward had little doubt that in the packet placed in his portmanteau by his daughter he should find farther light upon his proceedings. In the meanwhile, the expostulation of Houghton – 'Why did you leave us?' rang like a knell in his ears.

'Yes, I have indeed acted towards you with thoughtless cruelty. I brought you from the protection of a generous and kind landlord, and when I had subjected you to all the rigour of military discipline I shunned to bear my own share of the burden and wandered from the duties I had undertaken. O, indolence and indecision of mind, to how much misery do you frequently prepare the way!'

chapter twenty-three

The Eve of Battle

The sun was declining when the Highlanders arrived upon those high grounds which command an extensive plain stretching northwards to the sea. The low coast-road to Edinburgh passed through this plain, and by this way the English general had chosen to approach the metropolis, being probably of the opinion that he would meet in front with the Highlanders advancing from Edinburgh. In this he was mistaken, for the sound judgment of the Chevalier left the direct passage free, but occupied the strong ground by which it was overlooked.

When the Highlanders reached the heights commanding the plain, they were immediately formed in array of battle along the brow of the hill. Almost at the same instant, the English van appeared with the purpose of occupying the plain between the high ground and the sea. Waverley could see the squadrons of dragoons followed by a train of field-pieces, which were brought into line and pointed against the heights. The march was continued by three or four regiments of infantry, their fixed bayonets showing like successive hedges of steel and their arms glancing like lightning as they wheeled into line and were placed in direct opposition to the Highlanders. A second train of artillery with another regiment of horse closed the long march and formed on the left flank of the infantry.

The Highlanders showed equal promptitude and zeal for battle. As fast as the clans came upon the ridge they were formed into line, so that both armies got into order of battle at the same moment. The Highlanders set up a tremendous yell, re-echoed by the heights behind them. The regulars returned a loud shout of defiance, and fired one or two of their cannon.

The Highlanders displayed great earnestness instantly to attack, but the ground through which they must have descended was not only marshy but intersected with walls of dry stone and traversed by a broad and deep ditch. The commanders therefore interposed to curb the Highlanders. The two armies, so different in aspect and discipline, yet each admirably trained, upon whose conflict the temporary fate at least of Scotland appeared to depend, now faced each other like two gladiators, each meditating upon the mode of attack. The leading officers of each army could be distinguished in front of their lines, busied with their spy-glasses and dispatching orders and receiving intelligence conveyed by the aides-de-camp, galloping in different directions. The space between the armies was at times occupied by the irregular contest of individual sharp-shooters, and a hat or bonnet was occasionally seen to fall, or a wounded man borne off by his comrades. From the neighbouring hamlets the peasantry cautiously showed themselves as if watching the issue of the expected engagement, and in the bay were two square-rigged vessels bearing the English flag, whose tops and yards were crowded with less timid spectators.

Fergus received orders to detach his clan towards the village of Preston, to threaten the right flank of Cope's army. The Chief occupied the churchyard of Tranent, a commanding situation and a convenient place, as Evan Dhu remarked, for any gentleman who might have the misfortune to be killed and chanced to be curious about Christian burial.[1] To dislodge this party, the English general sent two guns escorted by a party of cavalry. They approached so near that Waverley could recognise the standard of the troop he had formerly commanded, and hear the trumpets and kettledrums sound the advance. He could hear, too, the word given in the English dialect by the well-distinguished voice of the commanding officer for whom he had once felt so much respect. It was at that instant that he saw the wild appearance of his Highland associates, heard their whispers in an uncouth language, looked upon his own dress, and wished to awake from what seemed a dream, strange and horrible. 'Good God,' he thought, 'am I then a traitor to my own country, a renegade to my standard, and a foe to my native England!'

The daylight was nearly consumed, and both armies prepared to rest upon their arms for the night in the lines which they occupied.

'There will be nothing done tonight,' said Fergus. 'Ere we wrap ourselves in our plaids, let us go see what the Baron is about.'

They found the good old careful officer, after having sent out his night patrols and posted his sentinels, engaged in reading the Evening Service of the Episcopal Church to the remainder of his troop.[2] His voice was sonorous, and though his spectacles upon his nose and the appearance of Saunders Saunderson in military array had something ludicrous, yet the danger in which they stood, the military costume and their horses saddled and picketed behind them, gave an impressive and solemn effect to the office of devotion.

'I am not so strict a catholic as to refuse to join in this good man's prayer,' whispered Fergus. Edward assented, and they remained till the Baron had concluded the service.

---

[1]   Preston, close to Prestonpans, east of Musselburgh. Tranent is inland, southeast of Preston.
[2]   In 1690 the Epsicopal Church was replaced in Scotland by Presbyterianism.

'Now lads,' said he, 'have at them in the morning with heavy hands and light consciences.' He then kindly greeted MacIvor and Waverley. 'Credit me, gentlemen, yon man is not his craft's master. He damps the spirits of the poor lads he commands by keeping them on the defensive, whilk implies inferiority or fear. Now they will lie on their arms yonder as anxious as a toad under a harrow, while our men will be quite fresh and blithe for action in the morning.'

'Hark!' answered Fergus, 'the English are setting their watch.'

The roll of drums and shrill accompaniment of fifes swelled up the hill – died away – resumed its thunder – and was at length hushed. The trumpets and kettledrums of the cavalry were next heard to perform the beautiful and wild points of war as signal for that piece of nocturnal duty, and then finally sunk upon the wind with a shrill and mournful cadence.

The friends looked round them ere they lay down to rest. The western sky twinkled with stars, but a mist rising from the ocean covered the eastern horizon and rolled in white wreaths along the plain where the adverse army lay couched upon their arms. Their advanced posts had kindled large fires, gleaming with obscure and hazy lustre through the heavy fog which appeared to encircle them with a doubtful halo.

The Highlanders lay stretched upon the ridge of the hill, buried (excepting their sentinels) in the most profound repose. 'How many of these brave fellows will sleep more soundly before tomorrow night, Fergus!'

'You must not think of that. You must think only of your sword, and by whom it was given. All other reflections are now TOO LATE.'

With the opiate contained in this remark, Edward endeavoured to lull his conflicting feelings. The Chieftain and he combining their plaids made a comfortable and warm couch. Callum, sitting down at their head, began a mournful song in Gaelic, to a low and uniform tune, which, like the sound of the wind at a distance, soon lulled them to sleep.

chapter twenty-four

The Conflict

When they had slept for a few hours they were awakened and summoned to the Prince. The village clock was heard to toll three as they hastened to where he was already surrounded by his principal officers and chiefs of clans. As Fergus reached the circle the consultation had broken up. 'Courage, my brave friends!' said the Chevalier, 'and each one put himself instantly at the head of his command. A faithful friend has offered to guide us through the morass to gain the firm plain upon which the enemy are lying. This difficulty surmounted, Heaven and your good swords must do the rest.'

The proposal spread unanimous joy, and each leader hastened to get his men into order with as little noise as possible. The army entered the path through the morass, conducting their march with astonishing silence and great rapidity. The mist had not risen to the higher grounds, so for some they had the advantage of star-light. But this was lost as the stars faded and the marching column, continuing its descent, plunged into the heaving ocean of fog which rolled its white waves over the whole plain. Some difficulties were now encountered, a narrow and marshy path, and the necessity of preserving union in the march. However, they continued a steady and swift movement.

As the clan of Ivor approached the firm ground, the challenge of a patrol was heard through the mist. 'Who goes there?' The patrol fired his carbine, and the report was instantly followed by the clang of his horse's feet as he galloped off. 'That loon will give the alarm,' said the Baron of Bradwardine.'

The clan of Fergus now gained the firm plain, the expanse unbroken by tree, bush or interruption of any kind. The rest of the army was following fast when they heard the drums of the enemy. They were not disconcerted. It only hastened their dispositions for the combat.

The Highland army was drawn up in two lines, extending from the morass towards the sea. The first was destined to charge the enemy, the second to act as a reserve. The few horse, headed by the Prince, remained between the two lines. The Adventurer had intimated a resolution to charge in person at the head of his first line, but his purpose was deprecated by all around him, and he was induced to abandon it.

Both lines were now moving forward. The clans formed each a separate phalanx, the best armed placed in front of each of these subdivisions. The others in the rear shouldered forward the front, and by their pressure added both physical impulse and additional ardour to those who were first to encounter the danger.

'Down with your plaid, Waverley,' cried Fergus, throwing off his own. The clansmen on either side stripped their plaids, prepared their arms, and there was an awful pause of about three minutes, during which the men, pulling off their bonnets, raised their faces to heaven and uttered a short prayer. Waverley felt his heart throb as it would have burst. It was not fear, it was not ardour, it was a compound of both, a new and deeply energetic impulse that chilled and astounded, then fevered and maddened his mind. The sounds around him combined to exalt his enthusiasm. The pipes played and the clans rushed forward, each in its own dark column. As they advanced they mended their pace, and the muttering sounds of the men to each other began to swell into a wild cry.

At this moment the sun, now above the horizon, dispelled the mist. The vapours rose like a curtain and showed the two armies in the act of closing. The line of the regulars glittered with the appointments of a complete army, flanked by cavalry and artillery. But the sight impressed no terror on the assailants. 'Forward, sons of Ivor,' cried their Chief, 'or the Camerons will draw the first blood.' They rushed on with a tremendous yell.

The horse, commanded to charge the advancing Highlanders, received a fire from their fusees as they ran on, and seized with a disgraceful panic wavered, halted and galloped from the field. The artillerymen, deserted by the cavalry, fled after discharging their pieces, and the Highlanders drew their broadswords and rushed with headlong fury against the infantry.

At this moment of confusion and terror, Waverley remarked an English officer standing alone by a field-piece which he had himself discharged against the clan MacIvor. Struck with his martial figure and eager to save him from inevitable destruction Waverley outstripped even the speediest of the warriors and called to him to surrender. The officer replied by a thrust with his sword, which Waverley received in his target and in turning it aside the Englishman's weapon broke. At the same time the battle-axe of Dugald Mahony was in the act of descending upon the officer's head. Waverley prevented the blow, and the officer, perceiving further resistance unavailing, resigned the fragment of his sword, and was committed by Waverley to Dugald with strict charge to use him well.

The battle still raged fierce and thick. The English infantry stood their ground with great courage, but their extended files were broken in many places by the close masses of the clans, and in the personal struggle which ensued the Highlanders' arms and their extraordinary fierceness gave them a decided superiority. Waverley observed Colonel Gardiner, deserted by his own soldiers, yet spurring his horse through the field to take command of a small body of infantry who continued a desperate and unavailing resistance. He had already received many wounds, his clothes and saddle marked with blood. To save this good and brave man became the instant object of Edward's exertions, but he could only witness his fall. Ere Waverley could make his way among the Highlanders, furious and eager for spoil, he saw his former commander brought from his horse by the blow of a scythe and receive more wounds than would have let out twenty lives. The dying warrior seemed to recognize Edward, for he fixed his eye upon him with an upbraiding yet sorrowful look. Then folding his hands as if in devotion he gave up his soul to his Creator. The look with which he regarded Waverley in his dying moments did not strike him so deeply at that crisis of confusion as when it recurred at the distance of some time.

Loud shouts of triumph now echoed over the whole field. The battle was fought and won, and the whole baggage, artillery and military stores of the regular army remained in possession of the victors. Scarce any escaped from the battle, excepting the cavalry who had left it at the onset. The loss of the victors was trifling. We have only to relate the fate of Balmawhapple who, mounted on a horse as headstrong and stiff-necked as her rider, pursued the dragoons above four miles, when some dozen of the fugitives turned round and cleaving his skull with their broadswords satisfied the world that the unfortunate gentleman had actually brains, thus giving proof of a fact greatly doubted during its progress. His death was lamented by few. His friend Lieutenant Jinker exculpated his favourite mare from any share in the catastrophe. 'He had tauld the laird a thousand times,' he said, 'that it was a burning shame to pit a martingale upon the puir thing, when he would ride her wi' a curb of half a yard lang, and that he could na but bring himself to some mischief by bringing her down. Whereas if he had had a wee bit running ring on the snaffle she wada rein'd as cannily as a cadger's pony.'

Such was the elegy of the Laird of Balmawhapple.

volume III

chapter one

An Unexpected Embarrassment

When the battle was over the Baron of Bradwardine sought the Chieftain of Glennaquoich and his friend Edward Waverley. He found the former determining disputes among his clansmen about precedence and deeds of valour, besides sundry questions concerning plunder. The Baron descended from his reeking charger. 'Weel my good young friends, a glorious and decisive victory,' said he, 'but these loons of troopers fled over soon. Well, I have fought once more in this old quarrel. But, Glennaquoich, and you, Mr Waverley, I pray ye to give me your best advice on a matter of mickle weight and which deeply affects the honour of the house of Bradwardine. I doubt na, lads, but that ye understand the true nature of the feudal tenures?'

Fergus, afraid of an endless dissertation, answered, 'Intimately, Baron.'

'And you are aware that the holding of the Barony of Bradwardine is of a nature honourable and peculiar, being *pro servitio detrahendi, seu exuendi, caligas regis post battalliam.*'[1]

Here Fergus turned his falcon eye upon Edward with an almost imperceptible rise of his eyebrow. 'Now, two points of dubitation. First, whether this service be due to the person of the Prince, and I pray your opinion anent that particular before we proceed farther.'

'Why, he is Prince Regent,' answered MacIvor with laudable composure, 'and in the court of France all honours are rendered to the person of Regent which are due to that of the King.'

'Far be it from me to diminish the lustre of his authority by withholding this act of homage, for I question if the Emperor of Germany himself hath his boots taken off by a free baron of the empire. But here lieth the second difficulty – the Prince wears no boots, but simply brogues and trews.'

This last dilemma had almost disturbed Fergus's gravity.

'Why,' said he, 'you know, Baron, the proverb tells us, 'It's ill taking the breeks off a Highlandman' – and the boots are here in the same predicament.'

'The word *caligae*, however,' continued the Baron, 'means rather sandals. The words of the charter are also alternative, *exuere sea detrahere*, that is to *undo*, as in the case of sandals or brogues, and to *pull off*, concerning boots. I deem it safest to place myself in the way of rendering the Prince this service, and to proffer performance thereof. And I shall cause Baillie Macwheeble to attend with a schedule intimating that if his Royal Highness shall accept of other assistance in

---

[1]   Latin, the service of removing the king's boots after battle.

pulling off his boots or brogues save that of the said Baron of Bradwardine, it shall in no wise prejudice the right of the said Cosmo Comyne Bradwardine to perform the said service in future.'

Fergus highly applauded this arrangement, and the Baron took a friendly leave of them with a smile of contented importance upon his visage.

'Long live our dear friend the Baron!' exclaimed the Chief, 'for the most absurd original that exists north of the Tweed.'

'How can you take pleasure in making a man of his worth so ridiculous?'

'Begging pardon, my dear Waverley, you are as ridiculous as he. Do you not see that the man's whole mind was wrapped up in this ceremony? He has thought of it since infancy as the most august privilege in the world, and I doubt not but the expected pleasure of performing it was a principle motive with him for taking up arms. But I must go to headquarters, to prepare the Prince for this extraordinary scene. So, *au revoir*, my dear Waverley.'

chapter two

The English Prisoner

The first occupation of Waverley was in quest of the officer whose life he had saved. He was guarded along with his companions in misfortune in a gentleman's house near the field of battle.

Upon entering the room where they stood crowded together, Waverley easily recognized him, not only by the dignity of his appearance, but by the appendage of Dugald Mahony, who had stuck to him from the moment of his captivity as if he had been skewered to his side. This close attendance was, perhaps, for the purpose of securing his promised reward from Edward, but it also operated to save the gentleman from being plundered in the general confusion. He hastened to assure Waverley that he had 'keepit ta *sidier roy* haill, and that he was na a plack the waur since the moment when his honour forbad her to gie him a bit clamhewit wi' her Lochaber axe.'

Waverley assured Dugald of a liberal recompence, and approaching the English officer expressed his anxiety to do anything which might contribute to his convenience.

'I am not so inexperienced a soldier, sir,' answered the Englishman, 'as to complain of the fortune of war. I am only grieved to see those scenes acted in our own island, which I have often witnessed elsewhere with comparative indifference.'

'Another such day as this,' said Waverley, 'and I trust the cause of your regrets will be removed, and all will again return to peace and order.'

The officer smiled and shook his head. 'I must not forget my situation so far as to attempt a confutation of that opinion, but notwithstanding your success and the valour which won it, you have undertaken a task to which your strength appears wholly inadequate.'

At this moment Fergus pushed into the press.

'Come, Waverley, the Prince has gone to Pinkie House for the night, and we must follow.'[1]

'Waverley!' said the English officer with great emotion, 'the nephew of Sir Everard Waverley.'

'The same, sir,' replied our hero, surprised.

'I am at once happy and grieved,' said the prisoner, 'to have met with you.'

'I am ignorant, sir, how I have deserved so much interest.'

'Did your uncle never mention a friend called Talbot?'

'I have heard him talk with great regard of such a gentleman – a colonel I believe in the army.'

'Yes, Mr Waverley, I am that Colonel Talbot, and I am proud to acknowledge that I owe my professional rank and my domestic happiness to your generous relative. Good God, that I should find his nephew in such a dress and engaged in such a cause!'

'Sir,' said Fergus haughtily, 'the dress and cause are those of men of birth and honour.'

'My situation forbids me to dispute your assertion, otherwise it were no difficult matter to show that neither courage nor pride can gild a bad cause. But with Mr Waverley's permission, and yours, sir, I would willingly speak a few words with him on affairs connected with his family.'

'Mr Waverley regulates his own motions. You will follow me, I suppose, to Pinkie,' said Fergus turning to Edward, 'when you have finished your discourse with this new acquaintance?' So saying the Chief adjusted his plaid with more than his usual air of haughty assumption, and left the apartment.

Waverley readily procured the freedom of adjourning to a large garden belonging to Colonel Talbot's place of confinement. They walked a few paces in silence. At length the Colonel addressed Edward.

'Mr Waverley, you have this day saved my life, and yet I would to God that I had lost it ere I found you wearing the uniform and cockade of these men.'

'I forgive your reproach, Colonel. It is well meant. But there is nothing extraordinary in finding a man, whose honour has been unjustly assailed, in the situation which promised to afford him satisfaction on his calumniators.'

'I should rather say, in the situation most likely to confirm the reports which they have circulated,' said Colonel Talbot, 'by following the very line of conduct ascribed to you. Are you aware of the infinite distress and even danger which your present conduct has occasioned to your nearest relatives?'

'Danger!'

'Yes, sir, danger. When I left England, your uncle and father had been obliged to

---

[1]   Pinkie House near Musselburgh was the seat of the Marquis of Tweeddale, then Secretary of State for Scotland.

find bail, to answer a charge of treason. I came to Scotland with the sole purpose of rescuing you from the gulf into which you have precipitated yourself, nor can I estimate the consequences to your family of your having openly joined the rebellion. Most deeply do I regret that I did not meet you before this last and fatal error.'

'I am really ignorant why Colonel Talbot should have taken so much trouble on my account.'

'Mr Waverley, I am indebted to your uncle for benefits greater than those which a son owes a father, and as I know there is no manner in which I can requite his kindness so well as by serving you, I will serve you, if possible, whether you will permit me or no. The personal obligation which you have this day laid me under adds nothing to my zeal in your behalf, nor can it be abated by any coldness with which you receive it.'

'Your intentions may be kind, sir, but your language is peremptory.'

'On my return to England after long absence, I found your uncle in the custody of a king's messenger. He is my oldest friend, my best benefactor! He never uttered a word that benevolence itself might not have spoken. I found this man in confinement, rendered harsher to him by his habits of life and – forgive me, Mr Waverley – by the cause through which this calamity had come upon him. Having, by my family interest, succeeded in obtaining Sir Everard's release, I set out for Scotland. I saw Colonel Gardiner and found that from a re-examination of the persons engaged in the mutiny and from his original good opinion of your character he was much softened towards you, and I doubted not that all might yet have been well. But this rebellion has ruined all.

'I have for the first time in a long military life seen Britons disgrace themselves by a panic flight, and that before a foe without either arms or discipline. I now find the heir of my dearest friend sharing a triumph for which he ought to have blushed.'

There was so much dignity in Colonel Talbot's manner, such a mixture of military pride and manly sorrow, that Edward stood mortified and distressed. He was not sorry when Fergus interrupted their conference a second time.

'His Royal Highness commanded Mr Waverley's attendance.' Colonel Talbot threw upon Edward a reproachful glance which did not escape the quick eye of the Chief. 'His *immediate* attendance.' Waverley turned towards the Colonel.

'We shall meet again. In the meanwhile, every possible accommodation – '

'I desire none,' said the Colonel. 'Let me fare like the meanest of those brave men who have preferred wounds and captivity to flight. I would almost exchange places with one of the fallen to know that my words have made a suitable impression on your mind.'

'Let Colonel Talbot be carefully secured,' said Fergus to the officer who commanded the guard. 'It is the Prince's particular command.'

'But let him want no accommodation suitable to his rank,' said Waverley.

'Consistent always with secure custody,' reiterated Fergus. The officer signified acquiescence to both these commands, and Edward followed Fergus to where Callum Beg, with three saddle-horses, awaited them.

chapter three

Rather Unimportant

I suppose you know,' said Fergus to Edward, 'the value of Colonel Talbot. He is held one of the best officers among the redcoats, a special friend and favourite of the Elector himself, and of that dreadful hero the Duke of Cumberland.[1] But what the Devil makes you look so dejected? I cannot tell what to make of you. You are blown about by every wind of doctrine. Here we have gained a victory and your behaviour is praised to the skies, and the Prince is eager to thank you in person, and all our beauties are pulling caps for you, and you are looking as black as a funeral.'

'I am sorry for Colonel Gardiner's death, he was once very kind to me.'

'Why, then, be sorry for five minutes, and then be glad again. His chance today may be ours tomorrow, and what does it signify? The next best thing to victory is honourable death.'

'But Colonel Talbot has informed me that my father and uncle are both imprisoned on my account.'

'We'll put in bail. Old Andrew Ferrara shall lodge his security.'

'Nay, they are already at liberty upon bail of a more civic description.'

'Then why is thy noble spirit cast down, Edward? You need not be apprehensive on their account, and we will find some means of conveying to them assurances of your safety.'

Edward was silenced but not satisfied. He had been more than once shocked at the small degree of sympathy which Fergus exhibited even for those whom he loved, and more especially if they thwarted him in a favourite pursuit. Fergus sometimes observed that he had offended Waverley, but was never sufficiently aware of the extent of his displeasure, so that the reiteration of these offences somewhat cooled the volunteer's attachment to his officer.

The Chevalier paid Waverley many compliments on his distinguished bravery. He then made enquiries concerning Colonel Talbot, and when he had received all the information which Edward was able to give, he proceeded, 'I cannot but think, Mr Waverley, that since this gentleman is so particularly connected with our excellent friend Sir Everard Waverley, the colonel's own private sentiments cannot be unfavourable to us, whatever mask he may have assumed.'

'I am under the necessity of differing widely from your Royal Highness.'

'Well, it is worth making a trial. I therefore entrust you with the charge of Colonel Talbot, and I trust you will find means of ascertaining what are his real dispositions.'

'I am convinced,' said Waverley, bowing, 'that if Colonel Talbot chooses to grant his parole, it may be depended upon, but if he refuses it, I trust your Royal

---

[1] William Augustus, Duke of Cumberland (1721–65), third son of George II, was commander of the government forces pursuing the Jacobite army. He already had a reputation for ruthlessness, which was greatly increased by his actions after the battle of Culloden in 1746.

Highness will devolve on some other person the task of laying him under restraint.'

'I will trust him with no person but you,' said the Prince smiling. 'It is of importance that there should appear to be good intelligence between you, even if you are unable to gain his confidence. You will therefore receive him into your quarters, and in case he declines giving his parole you must apply for a proper guard.'

When Waverley rejoined Colonel Talbot, he found he had recovered his natural manner, which was that of the English gentleman and soldier, manly and generous, and not unsusceptible of prejudice against those of a different country or who opposed him in political tenets. When Waverley acquainted Colonel Talbot with the Chevalier's purpose to commit him to his charge, 'I did not think to have owed so much obligation to that young gentleman,' he said. 'I can at least willingly join in the prayer of the presbyterian clergyman, that as he has come among us seeking an earthly crown, his labours may speedily be rewarded with a heavenly one. I will willingly give my parole not to attempt an escape without your knowledge, since it was to meet you that I came to Scotland, and I am glad it has happened even under this predicament. But I suppose we shall be but a short time together. Your Chevalier with his plaids and blue caps will, I presume, be continuing his crusade southward?'

'Not as I hear. I believe the army makes some stay in Edinburgh.'

'And besiege the Castle?' said Talbot, smiling sarcastically. 'Well, unless my old commander General Guest turn false metal, or the castle sink into the North Loch, events which I deem equally probable, I think we shall have some time to make up our acquaintance.[1] I have a guess that this gallant Chevalier has a design that I should become your proselyte, and as I wish you to be mine there cannot be a more fair proposal.'

chapter four

Intrigues of Love and Politics

Waverley and Colonel Talbot journeyed to Edinburgh together, and for some time they conversed upon ordinary topics. When Waverley again entered upon the subject which he had most at heart, the situation of his father and uncle, Colonel Talbot seemed desirous to alleviate than to aggravate his anxiety. This appeared particularly to be the case when he had heard Waverley's history. 'And so,' said the Colonel, 'you have been trepanned into the service of this Italian knight-errant by a few civil speeches from him and one or two of his Highland recruiting sergeants. It is sadly foolish to be sure, but not nearly so bad as I was

---

[1]   General Joshua Guest (1660–1747) was commander-in-chief of the Edinburgh district. The North Loch was to the north of Edinburgh Castle. Its drainage, completed in 1819, allowed the formation of Princes Street Gardens.

led to expect. However, you cannot desert at the present moment, that seems impossible. But I have little doubt that in the dissensions incident to this mass of wild and desperate men some opportunity may arise by which you may extricate yourself honourably from your rash engagement before the bubble bursts. If this can be managed, I would have you go to a place of safety in Flanders. And I think I can secure your pardon from government.'

'I cannot permit you to speak of any plan which turns on my deserting an enterprise in which I may have engaged hastily but certainly voluntarily.'

'Well,' said Colonel Talbot, smiling, 'leave me my hopes at least at liberty, if not my speech. But have you never examined your mysterious packet?'

'It is in my baggage. We shall find it in Edinburgh.'

Waverley's quarters had been assigned to him in a handsome lodging where there was accommodation for Colonel Talbot. His first business was to examine his portmanteau, and after a short search out tumbled the expected packet. Waverley opened it eagerly. He found a number of open letters, two from Colonel Gardiner addressed to himself. The earliest was a gentle remonstrance for neglect of the writer's advice respecting his leave of absence, which would speedily expire. 'There is great danger both of foreign invasion and insurrection among the disaffected at home. I therefore entreat you will repair to the head-quarters of the regiment. I am concerned to add that there is some discontent in your troop.'

The second letter, dated eight days later, reminded Waverley of his duty as an officer and a Briton, took notice of the increasing dissatisfaction of his men, and that some had been heard to hint that their Captain encouraged their mutinous behaviour. Finally, the writer expressed surprise that he had not obeyed his commands by repairing to headquarters, and conjured him, in a style in which paternal remonstrance was mingled with military authority, to redeem his error by immediately joining his regiment. 'That I may be certain that this reaches you, I dispatch it by Corporal Tims, with orders to deliver it into your own hand.'

As Colonel Gardiner must have had every reason to conclude that the letters had come safely to hand, less could not follow, in their being neglected, than that third and final summons which Waverley actually received. And his being superseded in consequence of his apparent neglect of this last command, was so far from being a harsh proceeding that it was plainly inevitable.

'What do you think of all this?' said Colonel Talbot, to whom Waverley silently handed the letters.

'Think! It renders thought impossible. It is enough to drive me mad.'

'Be calm, my young friend, let us see what are these dirty scrawls that follow.'

The first was addressed, 'For Master W. Ruffen': 'Dear sur, sum of our yong gulpins wul not bite, thof I tuold them you shoed me the Squoire's own seel. But Tims will deliver you the letters as desired. Yours, deer Sur, H.H.'

'This Ruffen, I suppose, is your Donald of the Cavern who has interrupted your letters and carried on a correspondence with the poor devil Houghton as if under your authority.'

The other letters were to the same purpose, and they soon received yet more complete light upon Donald Bean's machinations.

From one of Waverley's servants who had been taken at Preston, they learned that a pedlar called Ruthven or Ruffen had made frequent visits. He sold his commodities very cheap, seemed always willing to treat his friends at the ale-house, and easily ingratiated himself with many of Waverley's troop, particularly Sergeant Houghton and Tims. To these he unfolded in Waverley's name a plan for joining him in the Highlands, where report said the clans had already taken arms in great numbers. The men, educated as Jacobites so far as they had any opinions at all, easily fell into the snare. That Waverley was at a distance in the Highlands was sufficient excuse for transmitting his letters through the pedlar, and the sight of his well-known seal seemed to authenticate the negotiations in his name. When the Gazette appeared in which Waverley was superseded, a great part of his troop broke out into actual mutiny, but were disarmed by the rest of the regiment. Houghton and Tims were condemned to be shot, but afterwards permitted to cast lots for life. Houghton, the survivor, showed much penitence. He became also convinced that the instigator had acted without authority from Edward, saying 'if it was dishonourable and against Old England, the squire could know nought about it. He never did anything dishonourable, and in that belief he would live and die that Ruffen had done it all of his own head.'

Donald Bean Lean's motives were these. Of an intriguing spirit he had been long employed as a spy by those in the confidence of the Chevalier, to an extent beyond what was expected even by Fergus MacIvor, whom he regarded with fear and dislike. He was particularly employed in learning the strength of the regiments in Scotland, and had long had his eye upon Waverley's troop as open to temptation. Donald even believed that Waverley himself was at bottom in the Stuart interest. When he came to his cave with one of Glennaquoich's attendants, the robber was so sanguine as to hope that his talents were to be employed in some intrigue under the auspices of this wealthy young Englishman. Nor was he undeceived by Waverley's neglecting all hints afforded for explanation. His conduct passed for prudent reserve, and Donald Bean, supposing himself left out of a secret, determined to have his share in the drama. For this purpose he possessed himself of Waverley's seal. His first journey to the town where the regiment was quartered opened a new field of action. He knew there would be no service so well rewarded by the friends of the Chevalier as seducing a part of the regular army to his standard.

Waverley wrote a short state of what had happened to his uncle and his father, cautioning them not to attempt to answer his letter. The Colonel added long dispatches as well as letters to his own family. Talbot then gave Waverley's servant a letter to the commander of one of the English vessels cruising in the firth requesting him to put the bearer ashore at Berwick. The man was then furnished with money and directed to get on board the ship by means of bribing a fishing boat,

Tired of the attendance of Callum Beg who, he thought, had some disposition to act as a spy, Waverley hired as a servant a simple Edinburgh swain, who had mounted the white cockade in a fit of jealousy, because Jenny Jop had danced a whole night with Corporal Bullock of the Fusiliers.

chapter five

Intrigues of Society and Love

Colonel Talbot became more kindly towards Waverley after the confidence he had reposed in him, and the character of the Colonel rose in Waverley's estimation. The habit of authority had given his manners some peremptory hardness, notwithstanding the polish which they had received from his intimate acquaintance with the higher circles. The soldiership of the Baron of Bradwardine was marked by pedantry, that of Major Melville by a martinet attention to the minutiae of discipline. The military spirit of Fergus was so much blended with his plans and political views that it was that of a petty sovereign rather than of a soldier. But Colonel Talbot was in every point the English soldier. His whole soul was devoted to king and country. He was a man of extended knowledge and cultivated taste, although strongly tinged with those prejudices which are peculiarly English.

The character of Colonel Talbot dawned on Edward by degrees, for the delay of the Highlanders in the fruitless siege of Edinburgh Castle occupied several weeks. He would willingly have persuaded his new friend to become acquainted with some of his former intimates. But the Colonel, after one or two visits, declined further experiment. He characterized the Baron as the most intolerable pedant he had ever had the misfortune to meet, and the Chief as a Frenchified Scotchman possessing all the cunning and plausibility of the nation where he was educated with the proud, turbulent humour of that of his birth. 'If the devil,' he said, 'had sought out an agent expressly for the purpose of embroiling this miserable country, he could not have found a better than such a fellow, whose temper seems equally supple and mischievous, and who is followed by a gang of such cut-throats as you are pleased to admire so much.'

The ladies did not escape his censure. He allowed that Flora MacIvor was a fine woman and Rose Bradwardine a pretty girl. But he alleged that the former destroyed the effect of her beauty by an affectation of the grand airs which she had probably seen practised in the mock court of St Germains.[1] As for Rose, he said it was impossible for any mortal to admire such an uninformed thing, whose small education was as ill adapted to her sex or youth as if she had appeared in one of her father's old campaign coats. Now all this was mere prejudice in the excellent Colonel, with whom the white cockade, the white rose and Mac at the beginning of a name would have made a devil out of an angel.

---

[1] After James VII and II fled in 1688, the exiled Stuarts were based at Saint-Germains-en-Laye, near Paris.

Waverley looked upon these young ladies with very different eyes. He paid them almost daily visits, although he observed with deep regret that his suit made as little progress in the affections of the former as the arms of the Chevalier in subduing the fortress. Neither the dejection of Waverley nor the anger which Fergus scarcely suppressed could extend Flora's attention to Edward beyond that of ordinary politeness. On the other hand, as Rose's extreme timidity wore off her manners assumed a higher character. The agitating circumstances of the stormy time seemed to call forth a certain dignity of expression, and she omitted no opportunity to extend her knowledge and refine her taste.

To Waverley, Rose Bradwardine possessed an attraction which few men can resist, from the marked interest she took in everything which affected him. She was too inexperienced to estimate the full force of the attention which she paid to him. Her father was too abstracted in military discussions to observe her partiality, and Flora did not alarm her by remonstrance. Rose had revealed the state of her mind to that acute friend, although she was not herself aware of it. Flora was not only determined upon the final rejection of Waverley's addresses, but became anxious that they should be transferred to her friend. The real disposition of Waverley, notwithstanding his dreams of tented fields and military honour, seemed exclusively domestic. He asked no share in the busy scenes which were constantly passing around him, and was rather annoyed than interested in discussion of contending claims and interests. All this pointed him out as the person formed to make happy a spirit like that of Rose, which corresponded with his own.

Flora remarked this point in Waverley's character one day. 'His genius and elegant taste,' answered Rose, 'cannot be interested in such trifling discussions. Would you have him peace-maker general between all the gunpowder Highlanders in the army? Can you think these fierce, furious spirits are at all to be compared to Waverley?'

'I do not compare him with those uneducated men, my dear Rose. I only lament that he does not assume that place in society for which his talents eminently fit him, and that he does not lend their full impulse to that noble cause in which he has enlisted. I often believe his zeal is frozen by that cold-blooded Englishman whom he now lives with.'

'Colonel Talbot is very disagreeable, to be sure. He looks as if he thought no Scottish woman worth the trouble of handing her a cup of tea. But Waverley is so gentle, so well informed. Besides, you know how he fought.'

'For mere fighting,' answered Flora, 'I believe all men are pretty much alike. There is generally more courage required to run away. They have, besides, a certain instinct for strife, as we see in other male animals. But high and perilous enterprise is not Waverley's forte. I will tell you where he will be at home, my dear, and in his place – in the quiet circle of domestic happiness, lettered indolence and elegant enjoyments of Waverley Honour. He will refit the old library, and he will draw plans and landscapes and write verses and rear temples and dig grottoes. And he will stand in a clear summer night in the colonnade before the hall and gaze on the deer as they stray in the moonlight or lie shadowed by the huge old oaks. And he will repeat verses to his beautiful wife who shall hang upon his arm – and he will be a happy man.'

'And she will be a happy woman,' thought poor Rose.

chapter six

Fergus, a Suitor

Waverley had, as he looked closer at the Chevalier's court, less reason to be satisfied with it. Every person of importance had some separate object which he pursued with a fury altogether disproportioned. Almost all had their causes of discontent.

Waverley went to Fergus's lodgings to await his return from an audience at Holyrood House. 'You must meet me,' Fergus had said, 'to wish me joy of the success which I anticipate.'

In the Chief's apartment he found Ensign Maccombich waiting to make a report of his turn of duty. In a short time the Chief's voice was heard on the stair in a tone of impatient fury. He entered the room with all the marks of a man agitated by a towering passion. The veins of his forehead swelled, his nostril became dilated, his cheek and eye inflamed. These appearances of half-suppressed rage were the more frightful because they were obviously caused by a strong effort to temper an almost ungovernable paroxysm, and resulted from an internal conflict of the most dreadful kind.

As he entered the apartment he unbuckled his broadsword and threw it down with such violence that it rolled to the other end of the room. 'I know not what,' he exclaimed, 'witholds me from taking a solemn oath that I will never more draw it in this cause. Load my pistols, Callum, and bring them hither instantly – instantly!' Callum, whom nothing ever disconcerted, obeyed very coolly. Evan Dhu swelled in sullen silence, awaiting to hear where or upon whom vengeance was to descend.

'So, Waverley,' said the Chief after a moment's recollection. 'Yes, I remember I asked you to share my triumph and you have come to witness my – disappointment.' Evan now presented the written report he had in his hand, which Fergus threw from him with great passion. 'I wish to God,' he said, 'the old den would tumble down upon the heads of the fools who attack and the knaves who defend it. I see, Waverley, you think I am mad. Leave us, Evan, but be within call.'

When his officer left the room, the Chieftain gradually reassumed some degree of composure. 'I know, Waverley, that Colonel Talbot has persuaded you to curse ten times a day your engagement with us – nay, never deny it, for I am at this moment tempted to curse my own. Would you believe it, I made this morning two suits to the Prince, and he has rejected them both. What do you think of it?'

'What can I think till I know what your requests were?'

'Why, what signifies what they were, man? I tell you it was I that made them, to whom he owes more than to any three that have joined the standard, for I negotiated the whole business and brought in all the Perthshire men. I am not likely to ask anything very unreasonable, and if I did they might have stretched a point. You remember my earl's patent, dated some years back for services rendered. Now sir, I value that bauble of a coronet as little as you, for I hold that the chief of such a clan as the Sliochd nan Ivor is superior in rank to any earl in Scotland. But I had a particular reason for assuming this cursed title at this time. I learned that the Prince has been pressing that foolish Baron of Bradwardine to disinherit his male heir who has taken a command in the Elector of Hanover's militia and to settle his estate upon your pretty little friend Rose. And this the old man seems well reconciled to. As Rose Bradwardine would always have made a suitable match for me but for this predilection of her father for the heir-male, it occurred to me there now remained no obstacle.'

'But Fergus,' said Waverley, 'I had no idea that you had any affection for Miss Bradwardine, and you are always sneering at her father.'

'I have as much affection for Miss Bradwardine, my good friend, as I think it necessary to have for the future mistress of my family and the mother of my children. She is a very pretty intelligent girl, and with a little of Flora's instruction will make a very good figure. As to her father, he is an original it is true, and an absurd one, but he has given such severe lessons to that dear defunct Laird of Balmawhapple and others that nobody dare laugh at him. I tell you there could have been no earthly objection. I had settled the thing entirely in my own mind.'

'But had you asked the Baron's consent, or Rose's?'

'To what purpose? To have spoke to the Baron before I had assumed my title would only have provoked an irritating discussion on the subject of the change of name. And as to Rose, I don't see what objection she could have made, if her father were satisfied.'

'Perhaps the same that your sister makes to me, you being satisfied.'

Fergus gave a broad stare at the comparison, but cautiously suppressed the answer which rose to his tongue. 'So, sir, I craved a private interview, and I asked you to meet me here, thinking like a fool that I should want your countenance as bride's-man. Well, I state my pretensions – they are acknowledged. I propose to assume the rank which the patent bestowed. And then he dares to tell me that my patent must be suppressed for the present, for fear of disgusting that rascally coward (naming the chief rival of his own clan) who has no better title to be chieftain that I to be the Emperor of China, and who is pleased to shelter his reluctance to come out under a pretended jealousy of the Prince's partiality to me. The Prince asks it as a personal favour not to press my just and seasonable request at this moment. After this put your faith in princes!'

'And did your audience end here?'

'End? O, no. I stated the particular reasons I had for wishing that his Royal Highness would impose upon me any other mode of exhibiting my devotion, as what would at any other time have been a mere trifle was, at this crisis, a severe sacrifice. And then I explained my full plan.'

'And what did the Prince answer?'

'Answer? Why, he answered that he was glad I had made him my confidant to prevent more grievous disappointment, for he could assure me that Miss Brad-wardine's affections were engaged, and he was under a particular promise to favour them. "So, my dear Fergus," said he with his most gracious smile, "as the marriage is out of the question, there need be no hurry about the earldom." And so he glided off.'

'And what did you do?'

'I'll tell you what I *could* have done – sold myself to the devil or the elector, which ever offered the dearest revenge. However, I am now cool. I know he intends to marry her to some of his rascally Frenchmen or his Irish officers, but I will watch them close, and let the man that would supplant me look well to himself.'

chapter seven

'To one thing constant never.'[1]

I am the very child of caprice,' said Waverley to himself as he bolted the door of his apartment and paced it with hasty steps. 'What is it to me that Fergus MacIvor should wish to marry Rose Bradwardine? I love her not. I might have been loved by her perhaps – but I rejected her simple and natural attachment instead of cherishing it into tenderness. The Baron, too – I would not have cared about his estate. The devil might have taken the barren moors for what I would have minded. But framed as she is for domestic affection and tenderness, for giving and receiving all those quiet attentions which sweeten life, she is sought by Fergus MacIvor. He will not use her ill – of that he is incapable – but he will neglect her after the first month. He will be too intent on subduing some rival chieftain, on gaining some heathy-hill and adding to his bands some new troop of caterans, to enquire what she does. And such a catastrophe of the most gentle creature on earth might have been prevented if Mr Edward Waverley had had his eyes! I cannot understand how I thought Flora so very much handsomer than Rose. She is taller indeed, and her manner more formed, but many people think Miss Bradwardine's more natural. I will look at them particularly this evening.'

With this resolution Waverley went to drink tea at the house of a lady of

---

1   Shakespeare, *Much Ado About Nothing*, Act II, scene 3

quality where he found both the ladies. All rose as he entered, but Flora immediately resumed the conversation in which she was engaged. Rose, on the contrary, almost imperceptibly made a little way in the crowded circle for the corner of a chair. 'Her manner is most engaging,' thought Waverley.

Waverley was invited to read Shakespeare, and *Romeo and Juliet* was selected. Edward read with great taste and spirit several scenes from the play. All the company applauded with their hands and many with their tears. Flora was among the former, Rose belonged to the latter class of admirers. 'She has more feeling too,' said Waverley internally.

The conversation turning upon the play and the characters. Fergus declared that the only one worth naming as a man of spirit was Mercutio. The ladies, of course, declared loudly in favour of Romeo, but this opinion did not go undisputed. Several ladies severely reprobated the levity with which the hero transfers his affection from Rosalind to Juliet. Flora remained silent until her opinion was requested, and then answered, she thought the circumstance objected to such as in the highest degree evinced the art of the poet. 'Romeo is described as a young man particularly susceptible to the softer passions. His love is at first fixed upon a woman who could afford it no return. Now, as it was impossible that Romeo's love could not continue without hope, the poet has, with great art, seized the moment when he was reduced to despair to throw in his way an object more accomplished than her by whom he had been rejected, and who is disposed to repay his attachment.'

'Miss MacIvor,' said a young lady, 'will you persuade us love cannot subsist without hope, or that the lover must become fickle if the lady is cruel? I did not expect such an unsentimental conclusion.'

'A lover may persevere under very discouraging circumstances. Affection can withstand severe storms of rigour, but not a long polar frost of indifference. Love will subsist on wonderfully little hope, but not altogether without it.'

Shortly afterwards the party broke up and Edward returned home, musing on what Flora had said. 'I will love my Rosalind no more,' said he. 'I will speak to her brother and resign my suit. But for a Juliet – would it be handsome to interfere with Fergus's pretensions? Though it is impossible they can ever succeed, and should they miscarry, what then?'

chapter eight

A Brave Man in Sorrow

There were whole days in which Waverley thought neither of Flora nor of Rose, but which were spent in melancholy conjectures upon the state of matters at Waverley Honour and the dubious issue of the civil contest in which he was engaged. Colonel Talbot often engaged him in discussions upon the justice of the cause he had espoused. 'I wish you to be aware that the right is not with you, and that you ought, as an Englishman and a patriot, to take the first opportunity to leave this unhappy expedition before the snowball melt.'

Waverley had little to say when the Colonel urged him to compare the strength by which his party had undertaken to overthrow the government with that which was now assembling for its support. To this Waverley had but one answer. 'If the cause I have undertaken be perilous, there would be the greater disgrace in abandoning it.'

One night when our hero had retired to bed he was awakened about midnight by a suppressed groan from the apartment of Colonel Talbot. Waverley distinctly heard one or two deep-drawn sighs. The Colonel must have been taken suddenly ill. He opened the door very gently and perceived the Colonel seated by a table on which lay a letter and picture. He raised his head hastily as Edward stood uncertain whether to advance or retire. His cheeks were stained with tears.

As if ashamed at being found giving way to such emotion, Colonel Talbot rose with apparent displeasure. 'I think, Mr Waverley, my own apartment and the hour might have secured even a prisoner against –'

'Do not say *intrusion*, Colonel Talbot. I heard you breathe hard and feared you were ill. That alone could have induced me to break in upon you.'

'I am perfectly well,' said the Colonel.

'But you are distressed. Is there anything can be done?'

'Nothing, Mr Waverley. I was only thinking of home, and some unpleasant occurrences there.'

'Good God, my uncle!'

'No, it is a grief entirely my own. I am ashamed you should have seen it disarm me. I would have kept it secret from you, for I think it will grieve you and yet you can administer no consolation. I see you are surprised, and I hate mystery. Read that letter.

The letter was from Colonel Talbot's sister:

> The news of the unhappy affair at Preston came upon us with the dreadful addition that you were among the fallen. You know Lady Emily's state of health. She was much harassed with the sad accounts from Scotland, but kept up her spirits for the sake of the future heir, so long hoped for. Alas, my dear brother, these hopes are now ended! Notwithstanding all my care, this unhappy rumour reached her without preparation. She was taken ill immediately, and the poor infant scarce survived its birth. Although the contradiction of the horrible report by your own letter has greatly revived her spirits, Dr — apprehends serious, even dangerous, consequences to her health, especially from uncertainty aggravated by ideas she has formed of the ferocity of those with whom you are prisoner. Do therefore, my dear brother, endeavour to gain your

release by parole, by ransom or any way that is practicable. I do not exaggerate Lady Emily's state of health, but I dare not suppress the truth. Your most affectionate sister,

LUCY TALBOT

Edward stood motionless, for the conclusion was inevitable that by the Colonel's journey in quest of him he had incurred this heavy calamity. Colonel Talbot and Lady Emily, long without a family, had fondly exulted in the hopes which were now blasted. But this disappointment was nothing to the extent of the threatened evil, and Edward with horror regarded himself as the cause of both.

Ere he could collect himself sufficiently to speak, Colonel Talbot had recovered his usual composure of manner, though his troubled eye denoted his mental agony.

'She is a woman who may justify even a soldier's tears.' He reached him the miniature. 'And yet what you see of her there is the least of the charms she possesses – possessed I should perhaps say – but God's will be done.'

'You must fly instantly to her relief. It is not – it shall not be too late.'

'Fly? How is it possible? I am a prisoner, upon parole.'

'I am your keeper – I restore your parole – I am to answer for you.'

'You cannot do so consistently with your duty, nor can I accept a discharge from you. You would be made responsible.'

'I will answer it with my head, if necessary. I have been the unhappy cause of the loss of your child, make me not the murderer of your wife.'

'No, my dear Edward,' said Talbot, taking him by the hand, 'you are in no respect to blame. You hardly knew of my existence when I left England in quest of you. It is a responsibility sufficiently heavy that we must answer for the foreseen and direct result of our actions. For their indirect operation the great and good Being who alone can foresee the dependence of events on each other hath not pronounced his frail creatures liable.'

'But that you should have left Lady Emily in the situation the most interesting to a husband to seek a –'

'I only did my duty, and I do not regret it. If the path of honour were always smooth there would be little merit in following it, but it moves often in contradiction to our interest, and sometimes to our better affections. These are the trials of life. But we can talk of this tomorrow. Strive to forget it for a few hours. It will dawn, I think, by six and it is now past two. Good night.'

Edward retired, without trusting his voice with a reply.

chapter nine

Exertion

The morning was well advanced before Waverley appeared, out of breath but with an air of joy that astonished Colonel Talbot.

'There,' said he, throwing a paper on the table, 'there is my morning's work. Alick, pack up the Colonel's clothes. Make haste, make haste.' The Colonel examined the paper with astonishment. It was a pass from the Chevalier to Colonel Talbot, to repair to Leith and there embark for England, he only giving his parole of honour not to bear arms against the house of Stuart for the space of a twelvemonth.

'In the name of God,' said the Colonel, his eyes sparkling with eagerness, 'how did you obtain this?'

'I was at the Chevalier's levee as soon as he usually rises – but will tell you not a word more unless I see you begin to pack.'

'Before I know whether I can avail myself of this passport, or how it was obtained?'

'Now I see you busy I will go on. When I first mentioned your name his eyes sparkled almost as bright as yours did two minutes since. "Had you," he earnestly asked, "shown any sentiments favourable to his cause?" "Not in the least, nor was there any hope you would do so." His countenance fell. I requested your freedom. "Impossible," he said. I told him my own story and yours. He has a heart and a kind one, Colonel Talbot, you may say what you please. He wrote the pass with his own hand. "I will not trust myself with my council," he said, "they will argue me out of what is right. I will not endure that a friend should be loaded with the painful reflections which must afflict you in case of further misfortune in Colonel Talbot's family, nor will I keep a brave enemy a prisoner under such circumstances. Besides, there is the good effect such lenity will produce on the minds of the great English families with whom Colonel Talbot is connected."'

'There the politician peeped out.'

'Well, at least he concluded like a king's son: "Take the passport. I come here to war with men, but not to distress or endanger women."'

'I never thought to have been so much indebted to the Pretend –'

'To the Prince,' said Waverley, smiling.

'To the Chevalier. It is a good travelling name which we may both freely use. Well, dear Waverley, this is more than kind and shall not be forgotten. I cannot hesitate upon giving my parole. And now, how am I to get off?'

'All that is settled. My horses wait and a boat has been engaged to put you on board the *Fox* frigate. I sent a messenger down to Leith on purpose.'

'That will do excellently well. You must entrust me with the packet of papers which you recovered by means of your Miss Bean Lean. I may have an opportunity of using them to your advantage. But I see your Highland friend. See how he walks as if the world were his own, with his bonnet on one side of his head and his plaid puffed out across his breast.'

'For shame, Colonel Talbot, you swell at sight of the tartan as the bull is said to do at scarlet. You and MacIvor have some points not much unlike, so far as national prejudice is concerned. You judge too harshly of the Highlanders.'

'Not a whit. Let them stay in their own barren mountains, and puff and swell and hang their bonnets on the horns of the moon if they have a mind, but what business have they to come where people wear breeches and speak an intelligible language. I could pity the Pre – I mean the Chevalier himself for having so many desperadoes about him.'

'A fine character you'll give of Scotland upon your return.'

In a short time they arrived at the seaport.

'Farewell Colonel, may you find all as you would wish it. Perhaps we may meet sooner than you expect. They talk of an immediate route to England.'

'Tell me nothing of that,' said Talbot, 'I wish to carry no news of your motions.'

'Simply then, adieu. Say, with a thousand greetings, all that is dutiful and affectionate to Sir Everard and Aunt Rachael. Think of me as kindly as you can.'

'And adieu, my dear Waverley. Many, many thanks for your kindness. Unplaid yourself at the first opportunity. I shall ever think of you with gratitude.'

And thus they parted.

chapter ten

The March

About the beginning of November the young Chevalier, at the head of about six thousand men, resolved to penetrate the centre of England. They set forward on this crusade in weather which would have rendered any other troops incapable of marching, but which gave these active mountaineers advantages over a less hardy enemy. In defiance of a superior army, they took Carlisle, and soon afterwards prosecuted their daring march to the southward.

As Colonel MacIvor's regiment marched in the van, he and Waverley, who now equalled any Highlander in endurance, were perpetually at its head. They marked the progress of the army, however, with very different eyes. Fergus, all air and fire and confident against the world, measured nothing but that every step was a yard nearer London. He neither asked nor desired any aid, except that of the clans, to place the Stuarts once more on the throne, and when a few adherents joined the standard he always considered them in the light of new claimants upon the favours of the future monarch, who must therefore subtract so much of the bounty which ought to be shared among his Highland followers.

Edward's views were very different. In those towns in which they proclaimed James the Third, the mob stared, heartless and dull. The Jacobites had been taught to believe that the north-western counties abounded with wealthy squires and hardy yeomen devoted to the cause of the White Rose. But of the wealthier Tories they saw little. Some fled from their houses, some feigned themselves sick, some surrendered themselves to the government as suspected persons. Of such as remained, the ignorant gazed with astonishment and aversion at the wild appearance and unknown language of the Scottish clans. Their scanty numbers, apparent deficiency in discipline and poverty of equipment seemed certain tokens of the calamitous termination of their rash undertaking.

Fergus admired the luxuriant beauty of the country and the situation of many of the seats which they passed. 'Is your uncle's park as fine as that, Edward?'

'It is three times as extensive.'

'Flora will be a happy woman.'

'I hope Miss MacIvor will have much happiness unconnected with Waverley Honour.'

'I hope so too, but to be mistress of such a place will be a pretty addition to the sum total.'

'An addition the want of which, I trust, will be amply supplied by some other means.'

'How,' said Fergus, stopping short, 'how am I to understand that, Mr Waverley? Am I to understand that you no longer desire my alliance and my sister's hand?'

'Your sister has refused mine, both directly and by all the means by which ladies repress undesired attentions.'

'I have no idea of a lady dismissing or a gentleman withdrawing his suit after it has been approved by her legal guardian without giving him an opportunity of talking the matter over. You did not, I suppose, expect my sister to drop into your mouth like a ripe plum?'

'As to the lady's title to dismiss her lover, Colonel, you must argue with her as I am ignorant of the customs of the Highlands in that particular. But as to my title to acquiesce in a rejection from her, I will tell you plainly that I would not take the hand of an angel with an empire for her dowry if her consent did not flow from her own free inclination.'

'An angel with the dowry of an empire,' repeated Fergus in a tone of bitter irony, 'is not likely to be pressed upon a —shire squire. But sir, if Flora MacIvor have not the dowry of an empire, she is *my* sister, and that is sufficient to secure her against being treated with anything approaching levity.'

'She is Flora MacIvor, sir, which to me, were I capable of treating any woman with levity, would be a more effectual protection.'

The brow of the Chieftain was now fully clouded, but Edward felt too indignant to avert the storm by the least concession. They both stood still, and Fergus seemed half disposed to say something more violent, but by a strong effort suppressed his passion and walked sullenly on. Waverley pursued his course silently in the same direction, determined to let the Chief take his own time in recovering the good humour he had so unreasonably discarded.

After they had marched on in this sullen manner for about a mile, Fergus resumed the discourse in a different tone. 'I believe I was warm, my dear Edward, but you provoke me with your want of knowledge of the world. You have taken a pet at Flora's high-flying notions of loyalty, and now like a child you quarrel with the plaything you have been crying for and beat me because my arm cannot reach to Edinburgh to hand it to you. I shall write to Edinburgh and put all to rights, that is, if you desire I should do so. I cannot suppose that your good opinion of Flora can be at once laid aside.'

'Colonel MacIvor,' said Edward, 'I am fully sensible of the value of your good offices, but Miss MacIvor has made her election freely, and as my attentions in Edinburgh were received with more than coldness I cannot consent that she should again be harassed upon this topic. You saw the footing upon which we stood and must have understood it. Had I thought otherwise, I would have earlier spoken.'

'Very well, Mr Waverley, the thing is at an end. I shall make due enquiry, however, and learn what my sister thinks of all this. We will then see whether it is to end here.'

'It is impossible Miss MacIvor can change her mind, and it is certain I will not change mine.'

MacIvor's eye flashed fire, and he measured Edward as if to choose where he might best plant a mortal wound. But no one knew better than Fergus that there must be some decent pretext for a mortal duel, so that he was compelled to stomach this supposed affront until the whirligig of time should bring about an opportunity of revenge.

Waverley's servant always led a saddle-horse for him, though his master seldom rode him. But now, incensed at the domineering conduct of his late friend, he mounted his horse, resolving to seek the Baron of Bradwardine and request permission to volunteer in his troop.

'I am well free of this superb specimen of pride and self-opinion. Were Flora an angel she would bring with her a second Lucifer of ambition and wrath for a brother-in-law.'[1]

The Baron joyfully embraced the opportunity of Waverley's offering his services. The good-natured gentleman, however, laboured to effect a reconciliation between the two quondam friends. Fergus turned a cold ear to his remonstrances, and Waverley saw no reason why he should be the first in courting a renewal of the intimacy which the chieftain had so unreasonably disturbed.

---

[1]   Lucifer, one of the many names for Satan.

chapter eleven

The Confusion of King Agramant's Camp[1]

Waverley had ridden a little off from the main body when Ensign Maccombich approached, pronounced the single word 'Beware!' and then walked swiftly on. Waverley's servant Alick Polwarth rode up close to his master.

'The ne'er be in me, sir, if I think you're safe amang these Highland runthereouts.'

'What do you mean, Alick?'

'The MacIvors, sir, have gotten it into their heads that ye hae affronted Miss Flora, and I hae heard mae nor ane say they wadna tak muckle to mak a black cock o' ye.'

Coupling this with the hint of Evan, Waverley judged it most prudent to set spurs to his horse and ride briskly back to his squadron. A ball whistled past him, and the report of a pistol was heard.

'It was that deevil's buckie, Callum Beg,' said Alick. 'I saw him whisk away.'

Edward, justly incensed, observed the battalion of MacIvor at some distance, and an individual running fast to join the party. This he concluded was the intended assassin. Unable to contain himself he commanded Alick to go to the Baron of Bradwardine about half a mile in front and acquaint him with what had happened. He himself immediately rode up to Fergus's regiment. The Chief was on horseback, and on perceiving Edward approaching he put his horse in motion towards him.

'Colonel MacIvor,' said Waverley, 'I have to inform you that one of your people has this instant fired at me.'

'As that is a pleasure which I presently propose to myself, I should be glad to know which of my clansmen dared to anticipate me.'

'The gentleman who took your office himself is Callum Beg.'

'Stand forth from the ranks, Callum! Did you fire at Mr Waverley?'

'No,' answered the unblushing Callum.

'You did,' said Alick Polwarth, already returned at full gallop. 'You did. I saw you plainly.'

'You lie,' replied Callum with his usual impenetrable obstinacy. Fergus demanded Callum's pistol. The pan and muzzle were black with smoke – it had been that instant fired.

'Take that,' said Fergus, striking the boy upon the head with the pistol butt with his whole force. 'Take that for acting without orders and lying to disguise it.' Callum received the blow without appearing to flinch and fell without sign of life. 'Stand still upon your lives,' said Fergus to the rest of the clan. 'I blow out the brains of the first man who interferes between Mr Waverley and me.' They stood motionless. Callum lay on the ground bleeding copiously, but no one ventured to give him any assistance.

---

[1] In Ariosto's *Orlando Furioso*, Bk 14, Agramant is a Moorish king who besieges Paris. God commands the Archangel Michael to spread confusion in his camp.

'And now for you, Mr Waverley, please to turn your horse twenty yards with me.' Waverley complied, and Fergus said with great coolness, 'I could not but wonder, sir, at the fickleness of taste which you expressed the other day. But it was not an angel who had charms for you, unless she brought an empire for her fortune. I have now an excellent commentary upon that obscure text.'

'I am at a loss even to guess at your meaning.'

'Your affected ignorance shall not serve you, sir. The Prince himself has acquainted me with your manoeuvres. I little thought that your engagements with Miss Bradwardine were the reason of your breaking off your intended match with my sister.'

'Did the Prince tell you I was engaged to Miss Bradwardine? Impossible.'

'He did, sir, so either draw and defend yourself, or resign your pretensions to the lady.'

'This is absolute madness, or some strange mistake.'

'O, no evasion! Draw your sword,' said the infuriated Chieftain, his own already unsheathed.

'Must I fight in a madman's quarrel?'

'Then give up now and for ever all pretensions to Miss Bradwardine's hand.'

'What title have you,' cried Waverley, 'or any man living to dictate such terms to me?' And he also drew his sword.

At this moment, the Baron of Bradwardine and several of his troop came up upon the spur. The clan, seeing them approach, put themselves in motion to support their Chieftain and a scene of confusion commenced which seemed likely to terminate in bloodshed. The Baron lectured, the Chieftain stormed, the Highlanders screamed in Gaelic, the horsemen swore in Lowland Scotch. At length the Baron threatened to charge the MacIvors unless they resumed their ranks, and many of them presented their firearms at him and the troopers when a cry arose of 'Make way! *Place a Monseigneur!*' This announced the approach of the Prince and his body guard. His arrival produced some degree of order. The Highlanders resumed their ranks, the cavalry fell in, and the Baron and Chieftain were silent.

The Prince, having heard the original cause of the quarrel through the villainy of Callum Beg, ordered him into custody for immediate execution. Fergus, however, requested he might be left to his disposal and promised his punishment should be exemplary. To deny this might have seemed to encroach on the authority of the Chieftains and they were not persons to be disobliged. Callum was therefore left to the justice of his own tribe.

The Prince next demanded to know the new cause of quarrel between Colonel MacIvor and Waverley. There was a pause.

'If I owed less to your disinterested friendship, I could be most seriously angry with both of you for this very extraordinary broil at the moment when my father's service demands the most perfect unanimity. But the worst is that my very best friends hold they have liberty to ruin themselves as well as the cause they are engaged in.' Both the men protested their resolution to submit every difference to his arbitration. 'Indeed,' said Edward, 'I hardly know of what I am accused. I am ignorant of the cause for which Colonel MacIvor is disposed to fasten a quarrel upon me.'

'If there is an error,' said the Chieftain, 'it arises from a conversation which I held this morning with his Royal Highness himself.'

'With me?' said the Chevalier. 'How can Colonel MacIvor have so far misunderstood me?'

He then led Fergus aside and after five minutes earnest conversation spurred his horse towards Edward. 'Is it possible, Mr Waverley, that I am mistaken in supposing that you are an accepted lover of Miss Bradwardine, a fact of which I was so much convinced that I alleged it to Vich Ian Vohr as a reason why you might not continue to be ambitious of an alliance which holds too many charms to be lightly laid aside?'

'Your Royal Highness,' said Waverley, 'must have founded on circumstances altogether unknown to me when you supposed me an accepted lover of Miss Bradwardine. For the rest, my confidence is too slight to admit of my hoping for success after positive rejection.'

The Chevalier was silent for a moment, looking steadily at them both, and then said, 'Gentlemen, allow me to be umpire in this matter, not as Prince Regent but as Charles Stuart, a brother adventurer in the same gallant cause. Consider your own honour and how far it is becoming to give our enemies the advantage and our friends the scandal of showing that we are not united. And forgive me if I add that the ladies who have been mentioned crave more respect than to be made themes of discord.'

He took Fergus apart and spoke to him earnestly for two or three minutes, and then returning to Waverley said, 'I believe I have satisfied Colonel MacIvor that his resentment was founded upon a misconception, and I trust Mr Waverley is too generous to harbour any recollection of what is passed. You must state this matter properly to your clan, Vich Ian Vohr, to prevent a recurrence of their violence. And now, gentlemen, let me have the pleasure to see you shake hands.'

They advanced coldly, each apparently reluctant to appear more forward in concession. They did, however, shake hands, and parted, taking a respectful leave of the Chevalier.

chapter twelve

A Skirmish

After a council of war held at Derby on 5 December, the Highlanders relinquished their desperate attempt to penetrate farther into England and, greatly to the dissatisfaction of their daring leader, determined to return northward. They commenced their retreat, and by their extreme celerity outstripped the Duke of Cumberland, who now pursued them with a large body of cavalry.

This retreat was virtual resignation of their towering hopes. None had been so sanguine as Fergus MacIvor, none so cruelly mortified at the change of measures. He remonstrated with the utmost vehemence at the council of war, and when his opinion was rejected shed tears of indignation. From that moment his whole manner was so much altered that he could scarcely have been recognized for the same ardent spirit for whom the earth seemed too narrow but a week before. The retreat had continued for several days when Edward, to his surprise, received a visit from the Chieftain in a hamlet about half way between Shap and Penrith.

Edward awaited with some anxiety an explanation of this unexpected visit, nor could he help being shocked with the change in his appearance. His eye had lost much of its fire, his cheek was hollow, even his gait seemed less elastic. And his dress, to which he used to be attentive, was carelessly flung about him. He invited Edward to walk out with him by a little river. 'Our fine adventure is now totally ruined, Waverley, and I wish to know what you intend to do. I received a packet from my sister yesterday, and had I got the information sooner it would have prevented a quarrel. In a letter I acquainted her with the cause of our dispute, and she now replies that she never had any purpose of giving you encouragement. So it seems I have acted like a madman. Poor Flora! She writes in high spirits, what a change will the news of this unhappy retreat make.'

Waverley, much affected by the deep tone of melancholy, affectionately entreated Fergus to banish from his remembrance any unkindness which had arisen between them. They once more shook hands, but now with sincere cordiality. 'Had you not better leave this luckless army,' said Fergus, 'and get down before us into Scotland and embark for the continent? Your friends will easily negotiate your pardon, and to tell you the truth I wish you would carry Rose Bradwardine with you as your wife, and take Flora also under your joint protection.'

'How,' answered Edward, 'can you advise me to desert the expedition in which we all embarked?'

'Embarked? The vessel is going to pieces, and it is full time for all who can to get into the long-boat to leave her.'

'Why did the Highland chiefs consent to this retreat if it is so ruinous?'

'O they think that, as on former occasions, the heading and hanging will chiefly fall to the lot of the Lowland gentry, that they will be left secure in their poverty and their fastnesses, to listen, according to the proverb, "to the wind upon the hill till the waters abate".[1] But they will be disappointed. They have been too often troublesome to be so repeatedly passed over, and this time John Bull has been too heartily frightened. The Hanoverian ministers always deserve to be hanged for rascals, but now they will deserve the gallows as fools if they leave a single clan in the Highlands in a situation to be again troublesome to government. Ay, they will make root and branch work, I warrant them.'

'And while you recommend flight to me, a counsel which I will rather die than embrace, what are your own views?'

---

[1]   Traditional proverb.

'O my fate is settled. Dead or captive I must be before tomorrow.'

'What do you mean by that? The enemy is still a day's march in our rear, and we are still strong enough to keep him in check.'

'What I tell you is true.'

'Upon what authority can you found so melancholy a prediction?'

'On one which never failed a person of my house. I have seen the Bodach Glas.'[1]

'Bodach Glas?'

'Have you been so long at Glennaquoich and never heard of the Grey Spectre?'

'No, never.'

'If that hill were Benmore and that long blue lake Loch Tay or my own Loch an Ri, the tale would be better suited with the scenery. However, even Saddleback and Ulswater will suit what I have to say better than English hedgerows and farm-houses. When my ancestor Ian nan Chaistel wasted Northumberland there was with him a captain of a band of Lowlanders. In their return through the Cheviots they quarrelled about the division of the booty, and came from words to blows. The Lowlanders were cut off to a man and their chief fell the last by the sword of my ancestor. Since then, his spirit has crossed the Vich Ian Vohr of the day when any great disaster was impending, especially before approaching death. My father saw him twice, before he was made prisoner at Sherriff Muir and on the morning of the day on which he died.'

'How can you, my dear Fergus, tell such nonsense with a grave face?'

'I tell you the truth, ascertained by three hundred years' experience, and last night by my own eyes. Since this unhappy retreat commenced I have scarce been able to sleep for thinking of my clan and this poor Prince, whom they are leading back like a dog in a string. Last night I felt so feverish that I left my quarters and walked out. I crossed a foot-bridge and kept walking back and forwards, when I observed by the clear moonlight a tall figure in a grey plaid, which kept about four yards before me.'

'You saw a Cumberland peasant in his ordinary dress, probably.'

'I thought so at first, and was astonished at the man's audacity in daring to dog me. I called to him, but received no answer. I felt an anxious throbbing of my heart, and stood still and turned myself to the four points of the compass. By heaven, Edward, turn as I would the figure was instantly before my eyes. I was then convinced it was the Bodach Glas. My hair bristled and knees shook. I determined to return to my quarters. My ghastly visitant glided before me until he reached the foot-bridge. There he stopped and turned full round. A desperate courage made me resolve to make my way in spite of him. I made the sign of the cross, drew my sword and uttered, "In the name of God, Evil Spirit, give place!" "Vich Ian Vohr," it said in a voice that made my blood curdle, "beware of tomorrow!" The words were no sooner spoken than it was gone. I got home and threw myself on my bed, and this morning I took my horse and rode forward to make up matters with you. I would not willingly fall until I am in charity with a wronged friend.'

---

[1] Bodach Glas, *Gaelic*, Grey Spectre or old man. The bodach glas, a spectre shrouded in a grey cloak, is frequently evoked in Celtic tradition as a harbinger of disaster and as bogy man.

Edward had little doubt that this phantom was the operation of an exhausted frame and depressed spirits working upon the belief common to all Highlanders in such superstitions. He did not the less pity Fergus, for whom he felt all his former regard revive. With the view of diverting his mind from these gloomy images he offered to remain in his quarters till Fergus's corps should come up. The Chief seemed much pleased, yet hesitated. 'We are, you know, in the rear – the post of danger in a retreat.'

'And therefore the post of honour.'

'Well, let Alick have your horse in readiness in case we should be overmatched, and I shall be delighted to have your company.'

When Waverley joined the clan MacIvor all the resentment they had entertained against him seemed blown off at once. Even Dhu received him with a grin of congratulation, and even Callum, who was running about as active as ever with a great patch upon his head, appeared delighted.

They were now in full march, every caution being taken to prevent surprise. MacIvor's people and a fine clan-regiment commanded by Cluny MacPherson had the rear. They had passed an open moor and were entering a small village called Clifton. The winter sun had set, and Edward began to rally Fergus upon the false predictions of the Grey Spirit. 'The ides of March are not past,' said MacIvor with a smile, when suddenly a large body of cavalry was seen to hover upon the moor's dark surface.[1] To line the road by which the enemy must move upon the village was the work of a short time. Night sunk down, dark and gloomy, though the moon was at full. Sometimes, however, she gleamed a dubious light upon the scene.

Favoured by the night, a large body of dismounted dragoons attempted to penetrate the high-road. They were received by such heavy fire as checked their progress. Unsatisfied with the advantage thus gained Fergus, to whose ardent spirit danger seemed to restore all elasticity, drawing his sword and calling out 'Claymore!' encouraged his clan to rush down upon the enemy. Mingling with the dismounted dragoons they forced them at sword point to fly to the open moor, where a considerable number were cut to pieces. But the moon, which suddenly shone out, showed to the English the small number of assailants disordered by their own success. Two squadrons of horse moved to support their companions. Several of the Highlanders, amongst others their brave Chieftain, were cut off and surrounded. Waverley, looking eagerly for Fergus, from whom he had been separated in the darkness and tumult, saw him with Evan Dhu and Callum defending themselves desperately against a dozen horsemen. The moon was again at the moment totally overclouded and Edward could neither bring aid to his friends nor discover which way lay his own road to rejoin the rear-guard. After narrowly escaping being slain or made prisoner by parties of the cavalry he encountered in the darkness he at length reached an enclosure, and clambering over it concluded himself on the way to the Highland forces whose pipes he heard. For Fergus hardly a hope remained, unless that he might be made prisoner. Revolving his fate with sorrow and anxiety, the Bodach Glas recurred to Edward's recollection, and he said to himself with surprise, 'What, can the devil speak truth?'

---

[1] Ides of March, 15 March, was the day which Julius Caesar was warned of and on which he was assassinated.

chapter thirteen

Chapter of Accidents

Edward was in a most dangerous situation. He soon lost the sound of the bag-pipes, and when he at length approached the high road, he learned from the noise of kettledrums and trumpets that the English cavalry now occupied it, and were between him and the Highlanders. He resolved to avoid the English military and endeavour to join his friends by making a circuit to the left on a beaten path. The path was muddy and the night dark and cold, but these were hardly felt among the apprehensions which falling into the hands of the King's forces excited.

After about three miles he reached a hamlet. Conscious that the common people were in general unfavourable to the cause he espoused, yet anxious to procure a horse and guide to Penrith, where he hoped to find the Chevalier's army, he approached the alehouse of the place. There was a great noise within. An English oath or two and a campaign song convinced him the hamlet was occupied by the Duke of Cumberland's soldiers. Endeavouring to retire as softly as possible, Waverley groped his way along a small paling. As he reached a gate his out-stretched hand was grasped by that of a female, whose voice at the same time uttered, 'Edward, is't thou, man?'

'Here is some unlucky mistake,' thought Edward, struggling to disengage himself.

'Nean o' thy foun, now, man, or the redcoats will hear thee. Come into feyther's or they'll do ho a mischief.'

'A good hint,' thought Edward, following the girl through a little garden into a kitchen, where she kindled a match at an expiring fire and to light a candle. She had no sooner looked on Edward then she dropped the light with a shrill scream of, 'O feyther, feyther!'

The father speedily appeared, a sturdy old farmer in leather breeches and boots brandishing a poker.

'What hast ho here, wench?'

'O!' cried the poor girl almost in hysterics, 'I thought it was Ned Williams and it is one of the plaid-men.'

'And what was thee ganging to do wi' Ned Williams at this time o' neete?' To this the damsel made no reply, but continued sobbing and wringing her hands.

'And thee, lad, doest ho know that the dragoons be a town? They'll sliver thee loike a turnip, mon.'

'I know my life is in great danger,' said Waverley, 'but if you can assist me I will reward you handsomely. I am no Scotchman, but an unfortunate English gentleman.'

'Be ho Scot or no,' said the honest farmer, 'I wish thou hadst kept the other side of the hallan, but since thou art here, Jacob Jopson will betray no man's blood, and the plaids did not do so much mischief when they were here yesterday.' Accordingly, he set about sheltering our hero for the night. The yeoman cut a rasher of bacon, which Cicely soon broiled, and her father added a tankard of his best ale. It was settled that Edward should remain there till the troops marched in the morning, then hire or buy a horse from the farmer and endeavour to overtake his friends. A clean though coarse bed received him.

With the morning came the news that the Highlanders had evacuated Penrith and marched off towards Carlisle, and that detachments of the Duke of Cumberland's army covered the roads in every direction. Ned Williams (the right Edward) was now called to council by Cicely and her father. Ned, who perhaps did not care that his handsome namesake should remain too long in the house of his sweetheart, proposed that Edward, exchanging his uniform for the dress of the country, should go with him to his father's farm near Ullswater and remain until the military movements had ceased. A price was agreed at which the stranger might board with Farmer Williams till he could depart with safety.

By following bye-paths known to the young farmer they hoped to escape any unpleasant rencontre. Edward with his guide traversed those fields which the night before had been the scene of action. A brief gleam of December's sun shone sadly on the broad heath, which exhibited the dead bodies of men and horses and a number of carrion crows, hawks and ravens.

'And this, then, was thy last field,' thought Waverley, his eye filling at the recollection of the many splendid points of Fergus's character, all his imperfections forgotten. 'Here fell the last Vich Ian Vohr. On a nameless heath and in an obscure night skirmish was quenched that ardent spirit who thought it little to cut a way for his master to the British throne! The sole support of a sister, whose spirit was even more exalted than thine own. Here ended all thy hopes for Flora and the long line which it was thy boast to raise yet more highly by thy adventurous valour.'

Waverley resolved to search for the body of his friend. The timorous young man who accompanied him remonstrated, but Edward was determined. The followers of the camp had already stripped the dead of all they could carry away, but the country people, unused to scenes of blood, had not yet approached. About sixty or seventy dragoons lay slain. Of the Highlanders, not above a dozen had fallen. He could not find Fergus. On a little knoll lay the carcases of three English dragoons, two horses and Callum Beg, whose hard skull a trooper's broadsword had at length cloven. It was possible his clan had carried off the body of Fergus, but it was also possible he had escaped, especially as Evan Dhu was not found among the dead. Or he might be prisoner. The approach of a party sent for the purpose of compelling the country people to bury the dead now compelled Edward to rejoin his guide, who awaited him in great anxiety.

At the house of Farmer Williams Edward passed for a young kinsman, a clergyman residing there till the tumults permitted him to pass through the country. This accounted sufficiently for the grave manners and retired habits of their guest. A tremendous fall of snow rendered his departure impossible for more than ten days. They received news of the retreat of the Chevalier into Scotland, then that he had retired upon Glasgow, and that the Duke of Cumberland had besieged Carlisle, barring all possibility of Waverley's escaping into Scotland. On the eastern border, Marshal Wade was advancing upon Edinburgh, and all along the frontier, militia and volunteers were in arms to suppress insurrection. The surrender of Carlisle, and the severity with which the rebel garrison were threatened, soon formed an additional reason against venturing upon a solitary journey through hostile country.

In this secluded situation the arguments of Colonel Talbot often recurred to our hero. A still more anxious recollection haunted him, the dying look of Colonel Gardiner. Most devoutly did he hope that it might never again be his lot to draw his sword in civil conflict. Then his mind turned to the supposed death of Fergus, to the desolate situation of Flora, and with yet more tender recollection to that of Rose Bradwardine. In many a winter walk by the shores of Ulswater he acquired a more complete mastery of a spirit tamed by adversity than his former experience had given him. He felt that the romance of his life was ended and that its real history had now commenced.

chapter fourteen

A Journey to London

The family at Fasthwaite were soon attached to Edward. He had that gentleness and urbanity which attracts corresponding kindness, and to their simple ideas his learning gave him consequence and his sorrows interest. The last he ascribed to the loss of a brother in the skirmish near Clifton.

In the end of January Edward found in an old newspaper a piece of intelligence that rendered him deaf to the news from the north, and the prospect of the Duke's speedily overtaking and crushing the rebels.

'Died at his house in Berkeley Square upon 10 inst Richard Waverley, Esq, second son to Sir Giles Waverley of Waverley Honour. He died of a lingering disorder, augmented by an impending accusation of high treason. An accusation of the same grave crime hangs over his elder brother, Sir Everard Waverley. We understand that the day of his trial will be fixed early in the next month, unless Edward Waverley, son of Richard, shall surrender himself to justice. In that case, we are assured it is his Majesty's gracious purpose to drop further proceedings. This unfortunate gentleman has been in arms in the Pretender's service, but he has not been heard of since the skirmish at Clifton.'

'Good God! Am I then a parricide? My father, who never showed the affection of a father while he lived, cannot have been so much affected by my supposed

death as to hasten his own. No, I will not believe it. But it were worse than parricide to suffer any danger to hang over my noble and generous uncle, if such an
evil can be averted by any sacrifice on my part.'

Waverley immediately explained that he was under the necessity of going to
London with as little delay as possible. The best course seemed to get into the
great north road about Boroughbridge and there take the Northern Diligence,
which completed the journey from Edinburgh to London in three weeks.[1]

Our hero took an affectionate farewell of his Cumberland friends, whose
kindness he tacitly hoped one day to acknowledge by substantial proofs of gratitude. After some vexatious delays he found himself in the vehicle *vis-à-vis* to the
lady of Lieutenant Nosebag, adjutant of the — dragoons, a jolly woman of about
fifty. She had just returned from the north, and informed Edward how nearly her
regiment had cut the petticoat people into ribbons at Falkirk. 'You, sir, have
served in the dragoons?' Waverley was so much at unawares that he acquiesced.

'O, I knew it at once. I saw you were military from your air, and I was sure
you could be none of the foot-wobblers. What regiment pray?' Waverley justly
concluded that this good lady had the whole army-list by heart, and answered,
Gardiner's dragoons, ma'am, but I have retired some time.'

'O, those as won the race at the battle of Preston. Pray, sir, were you there?'

'I was so unfortunate, madam, as to witness that engagement.'

'And that was a misfortune that few of Gardiner's stayed to witness – ha! ha!
I beg your pardon, but a soldier's wife loves a joke.'

Fortunately the good lady did not stick long to one subject. 'We are coming
to Ferrybridge now,' she said, 'where a party of *ours* was left to support the
constables that are examining papers and stopping rebels.' In the inn she dragged
Waverley to the window. 'Yonder comes Corporal Bridoon of our poor dear
troop. Come Mr – pray what's your name, sir?'

'Butler, Madam' said Waverley, resolved rather to make free with the name of
a fellow-officer than run the risk of detection by inventing one not to be found
in the regiment.

In every town where they stopped she wished to examine the corps de garde, if
there was one, and once very narrowly missed introducing Waverley to a recruiting sergeant of his own regiment. Never was he more rejoiced at the termination
of a journey than when the arrival of the coach in London freed him from the
attentions of Madam Nosebag.

---

[1] Waverley's circumstances meant he could not afford to hire a post-chaise but had to travel
     by stage coach.

chapter fifteen

What's To Be Done Next?

It was twilight when they arrived, and Edward took a hackney coach to Colonel Talbot's house in one of the principal squares at the west end. When Waverley knocked at his door he found it at first difficult to procure admittance, but at length was shown into an apartment where the Colonel was at table. Lady Emily, still pallid from indisposition, sat opposite him. The instant he heard Waverley's voice he started up and embraced him. 'Frank Stanley, my dear boy, how d'ye do? Emily, my love, this is young Stanley.'

The blood started to the lady's cheek as she received Waverley with courtesy mingled with kindness, while her trembling hand showed how much she was discomposed. 'I wonder you have come here, Frank,' said the Colonel. 'The doctors tell me the air of London is very bad for your complaints. But we are delighted to see you, though I fear we must not reckon upon your staying long.'

'Some particular business brought me up.'

'I sha'nt allow you to stay long. Spontoon,' to a military looking servant, 'don't let anyone disturb us – my nephew and I have business to talk of.'

When the servants had retired, 'In the name of God, Waverley, what has brought you here? It may be as much as your life is worth.'

'Dear Mr Waverley,' said Lady Emily, 'to whom I owe so much, how could you be so rash?'

'My father – my uncle – this paragraph,' he handed the paper to Colonel Talbot.

'No wonder they are obliged to invent lies to find sale for their journals. It is true however, my dear Edward, that you have lost your father, but as to his situation having hurt his health, the truth is that Mr Richard Waverley through this whole business showed great want of sensibility, both to your situation and that of your uncle. The last time I saw him he told me with great glee that as I was so good as to take charge of your interests he had thought it best to patch up a separate negotiation for himself through some channels which former connections left open to him.'

'And my dear uncle?'

'Is in no danger whatsoever. Sir Everard has gone down to Waverley Honour freed from all uneasiness, unless upon your account. But you are in peril yourself, warrants are out to apprehend you. How did you come here?'

Edward told his story.

'Edward, I wish you had never stirred from Cumberland, for there is an embargo in all the sea-ports and a strict search for adherents of the Pretender, and the tongue of that confounded woman will wag like the clack of a mill.'

'Do you know anything of my fellow traveller?'

'Her husband was my sergeant major for six years. I must send Spontoon to see what she is about. Tomorrow you must keep your room from fatigue. Lady Emily is to be your nurse and Spontoon and I your attendants.'

In the morning the Colonel visited his guest. 'I have some good news. Your reputation is cleared of neglect of duty and accession to the mutiny. I have had a correspondence on this subject with your Scotch parson, Morton. You must know that Donald of the Cave has been made prisoner. He confessed before a magistrate, one Major Melville, his full intrigue with Houghton, explaining how it was carried on and fully acquitting you. These are particulars which cannot but tell in your favour.'

'What is become of him?'

'Oh, he was hanged at Stirling after the rebels raised the siege.'

'Well, I have little cause either to regret or rejoice at his death. He has done me both good and harm to a very considerable extent.'

'His confession wipes from your character all those suspicions which gave the accusation against you a complexion different from that which so many unfortunate gentlemen in arms against their government may be justly charged. Their treason is an action arising from mistaken virtue, and cannot be classed as a disgrace though it be criminal. Where the guilty are numerous, clemency must be extended to far the greater number, and I have little doubt in obtaining a remission for you.'

Spontoon traced Madame Nosebag and found her full of ire at discovery of an imposter who had travelled with her. The accuracy of her description might probably lead to the discovery that Waverley was the pretended Captain Butler, an identification fraught with danger to Edward, perhaps to his uncle, and even to Colonel Talbot. Which way to direct his course was now the question.

'To Scotland,' said Waverley.

'With what purpose?' said the Colonel. 'Not to engage again with the rebels I hope.'

'No. I consider my campaign ended when I could not rejoin them. Now they are gone to make a winter campaign in the Highlands, where I would rather be burdensome than useful. And, to confess the truth, I am heartily tired of the trade of war. The plumed troops used to enchant me in poetry, but the night marches, couches under the winter sky and such accompaniments of the glorious trade are not at all to my taste in practice. I had my fill of fighting at Clifton. I am quite satisfied with my military experience and shall be in no hurry to take it up again.'

'I am very glad you are of that mind – but then what would you do in the north?'

'There are some seaports on the eastern coast still in the hands of the Chevalier's friends, where I can embark for the continent. And there is a person in Scotland upon whom my happiness depends more than I was always aware, and about whom I am very anxious.'

'Then Emily was right and there is a love affair in the case after all. And which of these two pretty Scotchwomen is the distinguished fair? Not Miss Glen — I hope.'

'No.'

'Well, I don't discourage you. I think it will please Sir Everard, only I hope that intolerable papa with his snuff and his long stories will find it necessary to be an inhabitant of foreign parts. The Baronet has a great opinion of the family and he wishes much to see you settled. But I will bring you his mind upon the subject since you are debarred correspondence for the present, for I think you will not be long in Scotland before me.'

'What can induce you to return to Scotland? No longings towards the land of mountains and floods, I am afraid.'

'None, on my word, but Emily's health is now, thank God, re-established and I have little hopes of concluding the business which I have at present most at heart until I can have a personal word with the Commander-in-Chief. I am now going out to arrange matters for your departure.'

In about two hours Colonel Talbot returned. 'Now, there is little time to lose. Edward Waverley must continue to pass as Francis Stanley, my nephew. He shall set out tomorrow with Spontoon, well known on the road as my servant which will check enquiry. At Huntingdon you will meet the real Frank Stanley. A while ago, doubtful if Emily's health would permit me to go north myself, I procured for him a passport to go in my stead. As he went chiefly to look after you, his journey is now unnecessary. He knows your story.'

Travelling in the manner projected, Waverley met with Frank Stanley at Huntingdon. The two young men were acquainted in a minute.

'I can read my uncle's riddle,' said Stanley. 'The cautious old soldier did not care to hint that I might hand over to you this passport. You are therefore to be Francis Stanley.'

chapter sixteen

Desolation

Waverley reached the borders of Scotland without any adventure. Here he heard of the decisive battle of Culloden. It was no more than he had expected, yet it came upon him like a shock, by which he was for a time altogether unmanned. The generous, the noble-minded Adventurer was a fugitive with a price upon his head. His adherents, so brave, so faithful, were dead, imprisoned or exiled. Where now was the high-souled Fergus, if indeed he had survived Clifton? Where the pure-hearted Baron of Bradwardine, whose foibles seemed foils to set off the goodness of his heart and unshaken courage? Where were Rose and Flora? Of Flora he thought with the regard of a brother for a sister. Of Rose with a sensation yet more deep and tender.

When he arrived at Edinburgh he felt the full difficulty of his situation. Many had seen and known him as Edward Waverley. How then could he avail himself of a passport as Francis Stanley? He resolved, therefore, to move northward as soon as possible. He was, however, obliged to wait a day or two in expectation of a letter from Colonel Talbot. On the street in the dusk he carefully shunned observation, but one of the first persons he met at once recognized him. It was Mrs Flockhart, Fergus MacIvor's landlady.

'Mr Waverley, is this you? Na, you need na be feared for me. I wad betray nae gentleman in your circumstance. How merry Colonel MacIvor and you used to be in our house!' And the good-natured widow shed a few tears. 'As it is nigh darkening, sir, wad ye just step in bye to our house and tak a dish of tea? And if ye like to sleep in the little room I wad tak care ye are no disturbed.'

Waverley accepted her invitation, satisfied he would be safer in her house than anywhere else. When he entered the parlour his heart swelled to see Fergus's bonnet with the white cockade hanging beside the little mirror.

'Ay,' said Mrs Flockhart, 'the poor Colonel bought a new ane just the day before the march and I winna let them tak that ane doon. The neighbours ca' me a Jacobite – but they may say their say. He was as kind-hearted a gentleman as ever lived. Oh, d'ye ken, sir, when he is to suffer?'

'Suffer! Why, where is he?'

'Eh, Lord's sake, de'ye no ken? The Chief and Ensign Maccombich were ta'en somewhere beside the English border, when it was sae dark that his folk never missed him till it was ower late and they were like to gang clean daft. Now the word is the Colonel is to be tried wi' them that were ta'en at Carlisle. The Lady Flora is away to Carlisle to him.'

'And Miss Bradwardine, where is she?'

'Wha kens where ony o' them is now? Puir things, they're sair ta'en down for their white cockades and white roses. But she gaed north to her father's in Perthshire, when the government troops cam back to Edinbro'.'

'Do you know what's become of Miss Bradwardine's father?'

'The auld laird? Na, naebody kens that but they say he fought very hard in that bluidy battle at Inverness.'

Such conversation was enough to determine Edward, at all hazards, to proceed instantly to Tully Veolan. As he advanced northward, the traces of war became visible. Broken carriages, dead horses, unroofed cottages, bridges destroyed, all indicated the movements of hostile armies. In those places where the gentry were attached to the Stuart cause their houses seemed dismantled or deserted, and the inhabitants were gliding about with fear and dejection in their faces.

It was evening when he approached Tully Veolan, with feelings how different from those which attended his first entrance. Then, a disagreeable day was one of the greatest misfortunes which his imagination anticipated. Now, how changed, yet how elevated was his character! Danger and misfortune are rapid though severe teachers. 'A sadder and a wiser man,' he felt, in internal confidence and dignity, a compensation for the dreams which experience had so rapidly dissolved.

As he approached the village he saw with anxiety that a party of soldiers were quartered near it. To avoid the risk of being stopped and questioned, he fetched a large circuit avoiding the hamlet and approaching the upper gate of the avenue by a bye-path. Great changes had taken place. One leaf of the gate, broken down and split for fire wood, lay in piles. The other swung uselessly upon its loosened hinges. The battlements above the gate were thrown down and the carved Bears hurled from their posts. Several large trees were felled, and the cattle of the villagers and the hoofs of dragoon horses had poached into black mud the verdant turf which Waverley had so much admired.

Upon entering the courtyard, Edward saw the place had been sacked by the King's troops, who in wanton mischief had attempted to burn it. Though the thickness of the walls had resisted the fire, the stables and outhouses were totally consumed. The towers of the main building were scorched and blackened, the pavement of the court shattered, the doors torn down or hanging by a single hinge, the windows demolished and the court strewn with broken furniture. The fountain was demolished. The whole tribe of Bears, large and small, which seemed to have served as targets for the soldiers, lay on the ground in tatters. With an aching heart Edward viewed these wrecks of a mansion so respected. His anxiety to learn the fate of the proprietors increased with every step. On the terrace new scenes of desolation were visible. The walks were destroyed, the borders overgrown with weeds and the fruit trees cut down. Two immense chestnut trees, of which the Baron was particularly vain, the spoilers had mined and placed gunpowder in the cavity. One had been shivered to pieces by the explosion. About one fourth of the trunk of the other was torn from the mass which, mutilated on one side, still spread its ample boughs.

Viewing the front of the building, wasted and defaced, Waverley's eyes sought the little balcony which belonged to Rose's apartment. Beneath it lay the flowers and shrubs which had been hurled from the bartizan. Several of her books were mingled with broken flower pots. Among these Waverley distinguished one of his own, a small copy of Ariosto, and gathered it as a treasure, though wasted by the wind and rain.[1]

While plunged in sad reflections he heard a voice singing in well-remembered accents an old Scottish song:

They came upon us in the night
And brake my bower and slew my knight;
My servants a' for life did flee
And left us in extremitie.[2]

He called first low, then louder, 'Davie, Davie Gellatly.' The poor simpleton showed himself among the ruins of a greenhouse, but at first sight of a stranger retreated as if in terror. Waverley began to whistle a tune which Davie had expressed great pleasure in listening to. Davie again stole from his lurking place.

---

[1] Ludovico Arisoto (1474–1533), Italian author of *Orlando Furioso*.
[2] From the ballad 'The Lament of the Border Widow', in Scott's *Minstrelsy of the Scottish Border*, 1803, vol iii.

'It's his ghaist,' muttered Davie, yet coming nearer he seemed to acknowledge his living acquaintance. The poor fool himself seemed the ghost of what he was. His peculiar dress showed only miserable rags of its finery, the lack of which was supplied by the remnants of tapestried hangings and window curtains. The poor creature looked hollow-eyed and meagre to a pitiable degree. He at length approached Waverley, looked him sadly in the face, and said, 'A' dead and gane – a' dead and gane.'

'Who are dead?' said Waverley.

'Baron and Baillie and Saunders Saunderson and Lady Rose that sang sae sweet – a' dead and gane.'

With these words he made a sign to Waverley to follow him and walked rapidly towards the bottom of the garden. Edward, over whom an involuntary shuddering stole, followed him in hope of an explanation.

Davie scrambled over the ruins of the wall that had once divided the garden from the wooded glen. He jumped into the bed of the stream and proceeded at a great pace, climbing over fragments of rock. Waverley followed with difficulty, for the twilight began to fail. A twinkling light among the tangled bushes seemed a surer guide. He soon pursued an uncouth path, and at length reached the door of a wretched hut. A fierce barking of dogs was heard, but it stilled at his approach. A voice sounded from within.

'Wha hast thou brought here?' said an old woman, in great indignation. Davie had no hestitation to knock at the door. There was a dead silence, except the deep growling of the dogs, and he next heard the mistress of the hut approach the door, not probably to undo the latch but to fasten a bolt. To prevent this, Waverley lifted the latch himself.

In front was an old wretched-looking woman, exclaiming, 'Wha comes into folks' houses in this gait at this time o' the night?' Two grim and half-starved greyhounds laid aside their ferocity and appeared to recognize him. Half-concealed by the opened door, with a cocked pistol in his right-hand and his left in the act of drawing another from his belt, stood a tall gaunt figure in the remnants of a faded uniform and a beard of three weeks' growth.

It was the Baron of Bradwardine, who threw aside his weapon and greeted Waverley with a hearty embrace.

chapter seventeen

Comparing of Notes

The Baron related how after all was lost at Culloden, he had returned home under the idea of more easily finding shelter among his own tenants than elsewhere. Soldiers had been sent to lay waste his property, but their proceedings were checked by an order from the civil court. The estate might not be forfeited to the crown to the prejudice of Malcolm Bradwardine, the heir-male. The new laird speedily showed that he intended utterly to exclude his predecessor from all benefit in the estate. This was the more ungenerous as all the country knew that from a romantic idea of not prejudicing this man's right as heir-male the Baron had refrained from settling his estate on his daughter. 'When my kinsman came to the village wi' the new factor to lift the rents, some wanchancy person fired a shot at him in the gloaming, whereby he was so affrighted that he fled to Stirling. And now he has advertised the estate for sale. And if I were to grieve about sic matters, this would grieve me mair than its passing from my immediate possession, for now it passes from the lineage that should have possessed it. And now they have sent soldiers here to abide on the estate and hunt me like a partridge upon the mountains. I thought when I heard you at the door they had driven the auld deer to his den at last. But Janet, canna ye gie us something for supper?'

'Ou ay, sir, I'll brander a moor-fowl, and ye see puir Davie's roasting the black hen's eggs. Davie's no sae silly as folks tak him for, Mr Wauverley, he wadna hae brought you here unless he kend ye was a friend to his honour – indeed the very dogs kend ye, for ye was aye kind to beast and body. His Honour lies a' day and whiles a' night in the cove in the dern hag, yet when the country's quiet and the night very cauld his Honour whiles creeps down here to get a warm at the ingle and a sleep amang the blankets and gangs awa in the morning. How can we do enough for his Honour when we and ours have lived on his ground this twa hundred years, and when he keepit my puir Jamie at school and college, and when he saved me frae being ta'en to Perth as a witch.'

Waverley at length found an opportunity to interrupt Janet by an enquiry after Miss Bradwardine.

'She's weel and safe, thank God, at the Duchran,' answered the Baron. 'The laird's distantly related to us, and though he be of Whig principles yet he is not forgetful of auld friendship at this time. The Baillie's doing what he can to save something out of the wreck for puir Rose, but I doubt I shall never see her again, for I maun lay my banes in some far country.'

'Hout na, your Honour, ye were just as ill aff in the feifteen and gat the bonnie baronie back.[1] And now the eggs is ready and the muir-cock's brandered and there's the heel o' the loaf that cam from the Baillie's and plenty of brandy that Lucky Macleary sent down.'

They then began to talk of future prospects. The Baron's plan was to escape to France, where he hoped to get some military employment. He invited Waverley to go with him, in which he acquiesced should Colonel Talbot fail in procuring his pardon. It was now wearing late. Davie had been long asleep between the dogs. Their ferocity, with the old woman's reputation of being a witch, contributed a good deal to keep people from the glen. Baillie Macwheeble supplied Janet underhand with meal for their maintenance.

The Baron occupied his usual couch and Waverley reclined in an easy chair

[1] Feifteen, ie the Jacobite Rising of 1715.

of tattered velvet which had once garnished the state bedroom of Tully Veolan, and went to sleep as comfortably as in a bed of down.

chapter eighteen

More Explanation

With the first dawn of day Janet was scuttling about the house to wake the Baron.

'I must go back,' he said to Waverley, 'to my cove. Will you walk down the glen wi' me?'

They followed an entangled footpath by the side of the stream. The Baron explained to Waverley that he would be under no danger in remaining a day or two at Tully Veolan, if he pretended to be looking at the estate as agent for an English gentleman who designed to be purchaser. He recommended him to visit the Baillie, who still lived at the factor's house. Stanley's passport would be an answer to the officer who commanded the military, and as to any of the country people who might recognize Waverley, the Baron assured him he was in no danger of being betrayed by them.

'I believe,' said the old man, 'half the people of the barony know the auld laird is somewhere hereabout. I often find bits of things in my way, that the poor bodies leave because they think they may be useful to me. I hope they will get a wiser master and as kind a one as I was.'

The quiet equanimity with which the Baron endured his misfortunes had something in it venerable and even sublime. There was no fruitless repining, no turbid melancholy. He bore his hardships with a good-humoured though serious composure.

'It grieves me sometimes to look upon these blackened walls of the house of my ancestors, but doubtless officers cannot always keep the soldiers' hand from depredation.'

They were standing beneath a steep rock which the Baron began to ascend, striding with the help of his hands from one precarious footstep to another till he got about half way up, where bushes concealed the mouth of a hole into which he insinuated first his head and shoulders and then the rest of his long body, his legs and feet finally disappearing coiled up like a huge snake entering his retreat. Waverley had the curiosity to clamber up and look in upon him in his den. He looked not unlike that ingenious puzzle called *a reel in a bottle*, the marvel of children who can neither comprehend the mystery how it has got in or how it is to be taken out. The cave was very narrow, too low to admit almost of his sitting. His sole amusement was the perusal of his old friend Titus Livius, varied by occasionally scratching Latin proverbs and texts of Scripture with his knife on the roof and walls.[1] As the cave was dry and filled with clean straw and withered fern, 'it made,' as he said, coiling himself up with an air of snugness which contrasted strangely with his situation, 'unless when the wind was due north a very passable *gite* for an old soldier.' Neither was he without sentries, as Davie and Janet were constantly on the watch.

With Janet, Edward now sought an interview. He had recognized her as the old woman who had nursed him during his sickness after his delivery from Gifted Gilfillan, and the hut was certainly the place of his confinement. His first question was, 'Who was the young lady who visited the hut during his illness?' Janet paused for a little, then said, 'It was just a leddy that has na her equal in the world – Miss Rose Bradwardine!'

'Then Miss Rose was probably also the author of my deliverance,' inferred Waverley.

'That was she e'en, but sair affronted wad she hae been if she had thought ye had been ever to ken a word about the matter, for she gard me speak aye Gaelic when ye was in hearing to make ye trow we were in the Hielands.'

A few more questions brought out the whole mystery respecting Waverley's deliverance. When Waverley communicated to Fergus Rose's account of Tully Veolan being occupied by soldiers, the Chieftain was eager to prevent their establishing a garrison so near him. He resolved to send some of his people to drive out the redcoats and bring Rose to Glennaquoich. But the news of Cope's march into the Highlands to disperse the forces of the Chevalier obliged him to join the standard with his whole forces.

He issued orders to Donald Bean Lean to drive the soldiers from Tully Veolan and to take his abode near it for the protection of the Baron's family. Donald proposed to interpret this charge in the way most advantageous to himself, and resolved to make hay while the sun shone. He achieved without difficulty the task of driving the soldiers from Tully Veolan, but then set about to raise exactions upon the tenantry and otherwise to turn the war to his own advantage. Meanwhile he waited upon Rose with a pretext of great devotion for the service in which her father was engaged. Rose learned that Waverley had killed the smith at Cairnvreckan and was to be executed by martial law. In the agony which these tidings excited she proposed to Donald Bean the rescue of the prisoner. He had the art, pleading all the while duty and discipline, to hold off until poor Rose offered to bribe him with some valuable jewels which had been her mother's.

Donald Bean swore secrecy upon his drawn dirk. He was especially moved to this act of good faith by some attentions that Miss Bradwardine had showed to his daughter Alice, which highly gratified the pride of her father. Alice was very communicative in return for Rose's kindness, readily confided to her the papers respecting the intrigue with Gardiner's regiment, and as readily undertook to restore them to Waverley without her father's knowledge.

While Donald Bean was lying in wait for Gilfillan, a strong party was sent to

---

[1]   Titus Livius, or Livy (*c*.59BC–AD17), was the author of a *History of Rome*.

drive back the insurgents and encamp at Tully Veolan. This unwelcome news reached Donald as he was returning to Tully Veolan. He resolved to deposit his prisoner in Janet's cottage, the very existence of which could hardly be suspected. This effected he claimed his reward and left the neighbourhood with his people to seek more free course for his adventures elsewhere.

New and fearful doubts started in Rose's mind, and she took the daring resolution to explain to the Prince himself the danger in which Mr Waverley stood, judging that Charles Edward would interest himself to prevent his falling into the hands of the opposite party. Her letter reached Charles Edward on his descent to the low country, and aware of the political importance of having it supposed that he was in correspondence with English Jacobites, he ordered the transmission of Waverley to the governor of Doune Castle. Donald Bean durst not disobey, for the army of the Prince was now so near him that punishment might have followed. The governor was directed to send Waverley to Edinburgh as a prisoner because the Prince was apprehensive that he might have resumed his purpose of going to England.

Although Rose's letter was couched in the most cautious terms, she expressed so anxious a wish that she should not be known to have interfered that the Chevalier suspected the deep interest which she took in Waverley's safety. This conjecture led to false inferences, for the emotion Edward displayed on approaching Flora and Rose at the ball of Holyrood was placed by the Chevalier to the account of the latter. Common fame, it is true, frequently gave Waverley to Miss MacIvor, but the Prince knew that common fame is very prodigal in such gifts, and watching attentively the behaviour of the ladies towards Waverley, he had no doubt that the young Englishman was beloved by Rose Bradwardine.

To Rose Bradwardine, then, Waverley owed the life which he now thought he could willingly have laid down to serve her. A little reflection convinced him, however, that to live for her sake was more agreeable. The pleasure of being allied to a man of the Baron's high worth was also an agreeable consideration. His absurdities seemed in the sunset of his fortune to add peculiarity without exciting ridicule. His mind occupied with such projects of future happiness, Edward sought Mr Duncan Macwheeble.

chapter nineteen

'Now is Cupid a child of conscience – he makes restitution.'[1]

E dward found Duncan Macwheeble in his office immersed among papers and accounts. Before him was an immense bicker of porridge and a horn spoon.

---

[1]   Shakespeare, *The Merry Wives of Windsor*, Act V, scene 5.

Eagerly running his eye over a voluminous law paper, he from time to time shovelled an immense spoonful of these nutritive viands into his capacious mouth. His nightcap and morning gown had whilome been of tartan, but the honest Baillie had got them dyed black lest their original ill-omened colour might remind his visitors of his unlucky excursion to Derby. His face was daubed with snuff up to the eyes and his fingers with ink up to the knuckles. He looked dubiously at Waverley. Nothing could give the Baillie more annoyance than the idea of acquaintance being claimed by any of the unfortunate gentlemen who were now so much more likely to need assistance than to afford profit. But this was the rich young Englishman, the Baron's friend too. What was to be done?

While these reflections gave an air of absurd perplexity to the poor man's visage, Waverley could not help laughing. As Mr Macwheeble had no idea of any person laughing heartily who was either encircled by peril or oppressed by poverty, Edward's countenance greatly relieved the embarrassment of his own, and giving him a tolerably hearty welcome he asked what he would choose for breakfast. His visitor had, first, something for his private ear and begged leave to bolt the door. This precaution savoured of danger, but Duncan could not now draw back.

Edward communicated his present situation and future schemes. The wily agent listened with apprehension when he found Waverley was still in a state of proscription – was somewhat comforted by learning that he had a passport – rubbed his hand with glee when he mentioned the amount of his present fortune – opened huge eyes when he heard the brilliancy of his future expectations – but when he expressed his intention to share them with Miss Rose Bradwardine, he started from his stool, flung his best wig out of the window, chucked his cap to the ceiling, danced a Highland jig with inimitable grace and agility, and then threw himself exhausted into a chair exclaiming, 'Lady Wauverley! – ten thousand a year! – Lord preserve my poor understanding!'

'Now, Mr Macwheeble,' said Waverley, 'let us proceed to business.' This word had somewhat a sedative effect. However, he prepared to make what he called a 'sma' minute to prevent parties from resiling'. With some difficulty Waverley made him comprehend that he was going a little too fast. He explained that he wanted first to make his residence safe by writing to the officer at Tully Veolan that Mr Stanley was upon a visit of business at Mr Macwheeble's, and had sent his passport for Captain Foster's inspection. This produced a polite answer from the officer.

Waverley's next request was that Mr Macwheeble would dispatch a man to the post-town at which Colonel Talbot was to address him, with directions to wait there until the post should bring a letter for Mr Stanley.

Edward enquired if Macwheeble had heard anything lately of the Chieftain of Glennaquoich.

'Not one word, but that he was still in Carlisle Castle. I dinna wish the young gentleman ill, but I hope they that hae got him will keep him and no let him back to this Hieland border to plague us wi' blackmail and a' manner of violent spoliation. For my part I never wish to see a kilt in the country again, nor a redcoat, nor a gun for that matter, unless it were to shoot a paitrick. They're a' tarred wi' ae stick and when they've done ye wrang they have na a plack to pay you.'

Cockyleeky and Scotch collops soon reeked in the Baillie's parlour. His corkscrew was just introduced into the muzzle of a bottle of claret when the sight of the grey pony passing the window induced the Baillie to place it aside. Enter Jock Scriever, his apprentice, with a packet for Mr Stanley. It is Colonel Talbot's seal. Edward's fingers tremble as he undoes it. Two official papers, sealed in all formality, drop out. They are hastily picked up by the Baillie, whose eyes, or rather spectacles, are greeted with 'Protection by his Royal Highness to the person of Cosmo Comyne Bradwardine, Esq of that ilk, forfeited for his accession to the late rebellion', the other a protection in favour of Edward Waverley, Esq. Colonel Talbot's letter was in these words:

My dear Edward

I waited upon his Royal Highness immediately upon my arrival, and found him in no very good humour. 'Would you think it,' he said, 'there have been half a dozen of the most respectable gentlemen and best friends to government north of the Forth, who have fairly wrung from me the promise of a pardon for that stubborn old rebel the Baron of Bradwardine. They allege that his high personal character and the clemency which he showed to such of our people as fell into the rebels' hands should weigh in his favour, especially as the loss of his estate is likely to be severe enough punishment. It's a little hard to be forced in a manner to pardon such a mortal enemy to the House of Brunswick.' I said I was rejoiced to learn that his Royal Highness was in the course of granting such requests, as it emboldened me to present one of a like nature in my own name. He was very angry but I persisted. I touched modestly on my services abroad and his own expressions of friendship and goodwill. He was embarrassed but obstinate. I hinted at the policy of detaching the heir of such a fortune as your uncle's from the machinations of the disaffected, but I made no impression. I mentioned the obligations I lay under to Sir Everard and to you personally. I perceived that he still meditated a refusal, and taking my commission from my pockets I said as a last resource that as his Royal Highness did not think me worthy of a favour which he had not scrupled to grant to other gentlemen, I must beg my leave to deposit, with all humility, my commission in his Royal Highness's hands and to retire from the service. He was not prepared for this. He told me to take up my commission, said some very handsome things of my services, and granted my request. You are therefore once more a free man, and I have promised that you will be a good boy in future and remember what you owe to the lenity of government. Thus you see *my* prince can be as generous as *yours*. If you can find the Baron you will have the pleasure in being the first to communicate the joyful intelligence. I give you leave to escort him to Duchran and to stay a week there, as I understand a certain fair lady is in that quarter. And I have the pleasure to tell you that whatever progress you can make in her good graces will be highly agreeable to Sir Everard and Mrs Rachael. Make good use of your time, for when your week is expired it will be necessary that you go to London to plead your pardon in the law court. Ever, dear Waverley, your's most truly,

PHILIP TALBOT

chapter twenty

Happy's the wooing
That's not long a-doing[1]

Waverley proposed to acquaint the Baron with these tidings, but the cautious Baillie observed that if the Baron were to appear instantly in public, the villagers might become riotous in expressing their joy and give offence to the 'powers that be'. He proposed that Waverley should go to Janet's and bring the Baron to the Baillie's under cloud of night. He himself would go to Captain Foster and show him the Baron's protection, and obtain his countenance for harbouring him. He would have horses ready on the morrow to set him on his way to the Duchran along with Mr Stanley.

When it was near sunset Waverley hastened to the hut. Poor old Janet, bent double with age and bleared with peat smoke, was tottering about the hut with a birch broom, muttering to herself as she endeavoured to make her floor a little clean for the reception of her guests. Waverley's step made her fall a-trembling, so much had her nerves been on the rack for her patron's safety. With difficulty Waverley made her comprehend that the Baron was now safe. It was equally hard to make her believe that he was not to enter again upon possession of his estate. 'It behoved to be,' she said, 'he wad get it back again. Naebody wad be sae grippal as to tak his geer after they had gi'en him a pardon.' Waverley gave her some money and promised that her fidelity should be rewarded. 'How can I be rewarded, sir, sae weel as just to see my auld master and Miss Rose come back and bruick their ain?'

Waverley now took leave of Janet and soon stood beneath the Baron's cave. At a low whistle he observed the Baron peeping out to reconnoitre like an old badger with his head out of his hole. 'Ye hae come rather early, my good lad,' said he descending. 'I question if the redcoats hae beat the tattoo yet, and we're not safe till then.'

---

[1] Proverb similar to one included in James Kelly, *A Complete Collection of Scottish Proverbs*, 1721.

'Good news cannot be told too soon,' said Waverley, and communicated to him the happy tidings. The old man stood for a moment in silent devotion, then exclaimed, 'Praise be to God – I shall see my bairn again.'

'And never, I hope, to part with her more,' said Waverley.

'I trust in God, not, unless it be to win the means of supporting her, for my things are but in a bruckle state.'

'And if,' said Waverley timidly, 'there were a situation in life which would put Miss Bradwardine beyond uncertainty, would you object, my dear Baron, because it would make one of your friends the happiest man in the world?' The Baron looked at him in with great earnestness. 'I shall not,' continued Edward, 'consider my sentence of banishment repealed unless you will give me permission to accompany you to the Duchran and – '

The Baron seemed collecting all his dignity to make a suitable reply to what, at another time, he would have treated as propounding a treaty of alliance between the houses of Bradwardine and Waverley, but his efforts were in vain. In joyful surprise he gave way to his feelings, threw his arms around Waverley's neck and sobbed, 'My son, my son! If I had searched the world I would have made my choice here.' Edward returned the embrace and for a short while they both kept silence. At length it was broken by Edward. 'But Miss Bradwardine?'

'She never had a will but her old father's, and in my proudest days I could not have wished a mair eligible espousal for her than the nephew of my excellent old friend. But I hope, young man, ye deal not rashly in this matter. I hope ye hae secured the approbation of your ain friends, particularly of your uncle.' Edward assured him that it had Sir Everard's entire approbation.

'I now wish,' said the Baron, 'that I could have left Rose the auld hurley-house and the riggs belonging to it. And yet,' he said more cheerfully, 'it's maybe as weel as it is, for as Baron of Bradwardine I might have thought it my duty to insist upon certain compliances respecting name and bearings, whilk now, as a landless laird wi' a tocherless daughter no one can blame me for departing from.'

Edward, with all the ardour of a young lover, assured the Baron that he sought for his happiness only in Rose's heart and hand, and thought himself as happy in her father's simple approbation as if he had settled an earldom upon his daughter.

When they reached the Baillie's house the goose was smoking on the table. A joyous greeting took place between the Baillie and his patron. Auld Janet was established in the kitchen's ingle-nook, and even the dogs, in the liberality of Macwheeble's joy, had been stuffed with food and now lay snoring on the floor.

The next day conducted the Baron and Waverley to the Duchran. We will not attempt to describe the meeting of father and daughter, loving each other so affectionately and separated under such perilous circumstances, still less attempt to analyse the deep blush of Rose at the compliments of Waverley. The next morning the Baron took upon himself the task of announcing the proposal of Waverley to Rose, which she heard with a proper degree of maidenly timidity. Waverley had, the evening before, found five minutes to apprize her of what was coming.

Waverley was now considered as a received lover. He was made to sit next to Miss Bradwardine at dinner, to be her partner at cards, and if he came into the room the seat nearest to her was vacated for his occupation. There were giggles and jests, and a provoking air of intelligence seemed to pervade the whole family, but Rose and Edward endured these little vexations as other folks have done before and since. They are not supposed to have been particularly unhappy during Waverley's six days stay at the Duchran.

Edward was to go to Waverley Honour to make arrangements for his marriage, thence to London to take the proper measures for pleading his pardon, and return as soon as possible to claim the hand of his plighted bride. He also intended to visit Colonel Talbot. But above all, it was his most important object to learn the fate of the unfortunate Chief of Glennaquoich, to visit him at Carlisle and to try whether anything could be done for procuring an alleviation of the punishment to which he was almost certain to be condemned. In case of the worst he intended to offer to Flora an asylum with Rose, or otherwise assist her in any mode which might seem possible.

The Colonel was still in Edinburgh, where Edward met him. He wished him joy in the kindest manner on his approaching happiness, but on the subject of Fergus he was inexorable. 'Justice, which demanded some penalty of those who had wrapped the whole nation in fear and mourning, could not perhaps have selected a fitter victim. He came to the field with the fullest light upon the nature of his attempt. That he was brave, generous and possessed many good qualities only rendered him more dangerous. That he was enlightened and accomplished made his crime less excusable. That he was an enthusiast in a wrong cause only made him more fit to be its martyr. Above all, he had been the means of bringing many hundreds of men into the field who without him would never have broke the peace of the country.

'I repeat,' said the Colonel, 'that this young gentleman has fully understood the desperate game which he has played. He threw for life or death, a coronet or a coffin, and he cannot now be permitted to draw stakes because the dice have gone against him.'

Such was the reasoning of these times, held even by brave and humane men towards a vanquished enemy. Let us devoutly hope that we shall never again see such scenes or hold such sentiments.

chapter twenty-one

'Tomorrow? O that's sudden! – Spare him, spare him.'[1]

Edward reached Carlisle with the most distant hope of saving Fergus. He had furnished funds for the defence of the prisoners as soon as he heard that the day of the trial was fixed. Edward pressed into the court, which was extremely crowded, but by his extreme agitation it was supposed he was a relation of the prisoners and people made way for him. There were two men at the bar. The verdict of GUILTY was already pronounced. There was no mistaking the stately form and noble features of Fergus MacIvor, although his dress was squalid and his countenance tinged with the sickly yellow hue of long imprisonment. By his side was Evan Maccombich. Edward felt sick and dizzy as he gazed on them. The Clerk of Arraigns pronounced: 'Fergus MacIvor of Glennaquoich and Evan Maccombich in the Dhu of Tarrascleugh, you and each of you stand attainted of high treason. What have you to say for yourselves why the court should not pronounce judgment against you, that you die according to the law?'

Fergus, as the judge was putting on the fatal cap of judgment, placed his own bonnet upon his head, regarded him with a steadfast look and replied in a firm voice, 'I cannot let this audience suppose that to such an appeal I have no answer. But what I have to say you would not bear to hear, for my defence would be your condemnation. Proceed then, in the name of God, to do what is permitted to you. Yesterday and the day before you have condemned loyal and honourable blood to be poured forth like water. Spare not mine. Were that of all my ancestors in my veins I would have periled it in this quarrel.'

Evan Maccombich seemed anxious to speak, but the confusion of the court and the perplexity arising from thinking in a language different from that in which he was used to express himself, kept him silent. There was a murmur of compassion among the spectators, from the idea that the poor fellow intended to plead the influence of his superior as an excuse for his crime. The judge commanded silence and encouraged Evan to proceed.

'I was only ganging to say, my lord,' said Evan, 'that if your excellent honour would let Vich Ian Vohr go free, and let gae back to France and no to trouble King George's government again, that ony six o' the very best of his clan will be willing to be justified in his stead, and if you'll just let me gae down to Glennaquoich I'll fetch them up to ye mysell, to head or hang, and you may begin wi' me the very first man.'

A sort of laugh was heard at the extraordinary nature of the proposal. The judge checked this indecency and Evan, looking sternly around, said, 'If the Saxon gentlemen are laughing because a poor man such as me thinks my life, or the life of six of my degree, is worth that of Vich Ian Vohr it's like enough they may be right. But if they laugh because they think I would not keep my word and come

---

1   Shakespeare, *Measure for Measure*, Act II, scene 2.

back to redeem him, I can tell them that they ken neither the heart of a Hieland-man nor the honour of a gentleman.'

There was no further inclination to laugh among the audience, and a dead silence ensued.

The judge then pronounced upon the prisoners the sentence of the law of high treason, with all its horrible accompaniments. The execution was appointed for the ensuing day. 'For you, Fergus MacIvor,' continued the judge, 'I can hold out no hope of mercy. You must prepare against tomorrow for your last sufferings here and your great audit hereafter.'

'I desire nothing else, my lord,' answered Fergus in the same manly and firm tone.

The hard eyes of Evan, perpetually bent on his Chief, were moistened. 'For you, poor ignorant man, who following the ideas in which you have been educated have this day given us a striking example how the loyalty due to the king and state alone are, from your unhappy ideas of clanship, transferred to some ambitious individual, who ends by making you the tool of his crimes – for you I feel so much compassion that if you can make up your mind to petition for grace I will endeavour to procure it for you. Otherwise –'

'Grace me no grace,' said Evan. 'Since you are to shed Vich Ian Vohr's blood the only favour I would accept from you is to bid them loose my hands and gie me my claymore, and bide you just a minute sitting where you are.'

'Remove the prisoners,' said the judge. 'His blood be upon his own head.'

Almost stupefied with his feelings, Edward found that the rush of the crowd had conveyed him out into the street. His immediate wish was to speak with Fergus once more. He applied at the castle where his friend was confined but was refused admittance. None should be admitted to see the prisoner excepting his confessor and his sister.

'And where was Miss MacIvor?' They gave him the direction.

Repulsed from the gate of the castle he had recourse to Fergus's solicitor, who told him that it was thought the public were in danger of being debauched by the account of the last moments of these persons and that all who were not near kindred were to be excluded from attending upon them. Yet he promised to get him an order for admittance to the prisoner before his irons were knocked off for execution.

'Is it of Fergus MacIvor they speak thus?' thought Waverley. 'Of Fergus, the bold, the chivalrous. The lofty chieftain of a tribe devoted to him? The brave, the active, the noble, the love of ladies and the theme of song? Is it he who is to be dragged on a hurdle to the common gallows, to die a lingering and cruel death and to be mangled by the hand of the most outcast of wretches?'

Returning to the inn Edward wrote a scarce intelligible note to Flora, intimat-ing his purpose to wait upon her. When he reached Miss MacIvor's place of abode he was instantly admitted. In a large and gloomy tapestried apartment Flora was seated by a window, sewing a garment of white flannel. She rose to receive him, but neither ventured to attempt speech. Her person was considerably emaciated, and her face and hands, as white as the purest marble, formed a strong contrast with her sable dress and jet-black hair. Yet there was nothing negligent about her dress. The first words she uttered were, 'Have you seen him?'

'Alas no, I have been refused admittance.'

'Shall you obtain leave, do you suppose?'

'For – for – tomorrow?' said Waverley, but muttering the last word so faintly that it was almost unintelligible.

'Aye, then or never,' said Flora. 'But I hope you will see him while the earth yet bears him. He always loved you. How often have I pictured to myself the possibility of this horrid issue and tasked myself to consider how I could support my part, and yet how far has all my anticipation fallen short of the unimaginable bitterness of this hour.'

'Dear Flora, if your strength of mind –'

'Ay,' she answered somewhat wildly, 'there is a busy devil at my heart that whispers – but it were madness to listen to it – that the strength of mind on which Flora prided herself has – murdered her brother!'

'Good God! How can you give utterance to a thought so shocking?'

'It haunts me like a phantom. I know it is unsubstantial, but it *will* intrude its horrors on my mind, will whisper that it was I taught my brother to gage all on this desperate cast. O that I had but once said, "He that striketh with the sword shall die by the sword." But O, Mr Waverley, I spurred his fiery temper and half of his ruin at least lies with his sister!'

The horrid idea Edward endeavoured to combat by every incoherent argument that occurred to him.

'The attempt did not always seem so desperate and hazardous as it was, and it would have been chosen by the bold spirit of Fergus whether you had approved it or no. Your counsels only served to dignify but not to precipitate his resolution.'

'Do you remember,' Flora said, looking up from her needlework with a ghastly smile, 'you once found me making Fergus's bride-favours, and now I am sewing his bridal-garment. Our friends here are to give hallowed earth in their chapel to the bloody relics of the last Vich Ian Vohr. But they will not all rest together, no – his head! I shall not have the last miserable satisfaction of kissing the cold lips of my dear, dear Fergus!'

Flora, after one or two hysterical sobs, fainted in her chair. An attendant entered hastily from an anti-room and begged Edward to leave the room, but not the house. When he was recalled after the space of nearly half an hour, he found that by a strong effort Miss MacIvor had greatly composed herself. He ventured to urge Miss Bradwardine's claim to be considered an adopted sister.

'I have had a letter from my dear Rose,' she replied, 'to the same purpose. Sorrow is selfish, or I would have written to express that I feel a gleam of pleasure at learning her happy prospects, and that the good old Baron has escaped the general wreck. Give this to my dearest Rose. It is my only ornament of value, and it was the gift of a princess.' She put into his hands a case containing the chain of diamonds with which she used to decorate her hair. 'The kindness of my friends has secured me a retreat in a convent of the Scottish Benedictine nuns at Paris. Tomorrow, if I can survive tomorrow, I set forward on my journey, And now, Mr Waverley, adieu. May you be as happy with Rose as you deserve, and think sometimes on the friends you have lost. Do not attempt to see me again. It would be a mistaken kindness.'

She gave her hand, on which Edward shed a torrent of tears, and with a faltering step withdrew and returned to Carlisle.

chapter twenty-two

'A darker departure is near
The death-drum is muffled. And sable the bier.'[1]

After a sleepless night, dawn found Waverley in front of the old Gothic gate of Carlisle Castle. But he paced it long in every direction before the gates were opened and the drawbridge lowered. He produced his order to the sergeant of the guard and was admitted. The place of Fergus's confinement was a gloomy apartment in a huge old tower surrounded by outworks. The grating of the bars and bolts was answered by the clash of chains as the Chieftain, heavily fettered, shuffled along the stone floor to fling himself into his friend's arms.

'My dear Edward,' he said in a firm and even cheerful voice, 'this is truly kind. I heard of your approaching happiness with the highest pleasure. And how does Rose, and how is our old whimsical friend the Baron?'

'How, my dear Fergus, can you talk of such things at such a moment?'

'Why, we have entered Carlisle with happier auspices, to be sure. But I am no boy to sit down and weep because the luck has gone against me. I knew the stake which I risked. We played the game boldly and the forfeit shall be paid manfully. And now – the Prince, has he escaped the bloodhounds?'

'He has, and is in safety!'

'Praised be God for that! Tell me the particulars of his escape.'

Waverley communicated that remarkable history to which Fergus listened with deep interest.[2] He then asked after several other friends and made many enquiries concerning the fate of his own clansmen. They had suffered less than other tribes, for having dispersed and returned home after the captivity of their Chieftain, as was the custom among the Highlanders, they were not in arms when

---

1 Thomas Campbell, 'Lochiel's Warning', in *Gertrude of Wyoming…And Other Poems*, 1809.
2 Charles Edward Stuart escaped after the defeat at Culloden and spent several months as a fugitive assisted by loyal followers. On 20 September 1746 he embarked for France from Loch nan Uamh, near where he had first set foot on mainland Scotland.

the insurrection was finally suppressed and were treated with less rigour. This Fergus heard with great satisfaction.

'You are rich,' he said, 'and you are generous. When you hear of these poor MacIvors being distressed by some harsh overseer or agent of government, remember you have worn their tartan and are an adopted son of their race. Will you promise this to the last Vich Ian Vohr?'

Edward pledged his word, which he afterwards so amply redeemed that his memory still lives in these glens as the Friend of the Sons of Ivor.

'Would to God I could bequeath to you my rights to the love and obedience of this primitive and brave race, or at least persuade poor Evan to accept of his life upon their terms, and be to you what he has been to me, the kindest – the bravest – most devoted –'

The tears which his own fate could not draw forth fell fast for that of his foster-brother.

'But that cannot be. You cannot be to them Vich Ian Vohr, and poor Evan must attend his foster-brother in death as he has done throughout his whole life.'

'And I am sure,' said Maccombich, raising himself from the floor, on which, for fear of interrupting, he had lain so still that in the obscurity of the apartment Edward was not aware of his presence, 'I am sure Evan never desired nor deserved a better end than just to die with his chieftain.'

'And now,' said Fergus, 'what think you of the Bodach Glas? I saw him again last night. He stood in the slip of moonshine which fell from that narrow window. Why should I fear him, I thought. Tomorrow I shall be as immaterial as he. "False spirit," I said, "art thou come to enjoy thy triumph in the fall of the last descendant of thine enemy?" The spectre seemed to beckon and smile as he faded from my sight. What do you think of it? I asked the same question at the priest, who admitted that the church allowed that such apparitions were possible, but urged me not to dwell upon it as imagination plays us such strange tricks. What do you think of it?'

'Much as your confessor,' said Waverley. A tap at the door announced that good man, and Edward retired while he administered to both prisoners the last rites in the mode which the church of Rome prescribes.

Soon after he was re-admitted, a file of soldiers entered with a blacksmith, who struck the fetters from the legs of the prisoners.

'You see the compliment they pay to our Highland strength. We have lain chained here like wild beasts, and when they free us they send six soldiers with loaded muskets to prevent our taking the castle by storm.'

The drums of the garrison beat to arms. 'That is the last turn-out,' said Fergus, 'that I shall hear and obey. And now, my dear, dear Edward, let us speak of Flora.'

'We part not *here*!' said Waverley.

'O yes, we do, you must come no farther. Not that I fear what is to follow for myself,' he said proudly, 'But what a dying man can suffer firmly may kill a living friend to look upon. This same law of high treason,' he continued with astonishing composure, 'is one of the blessings with which your free country has accommodated poor old Scotland.[1] Her own jurisprudence was much milder. But I suppose one day – when there are no longer any wild Highlanders to benefit by its tender mercies – they will blot it from their record, as levelling them with a nation of cannibals. The mummery, too, of exposing the senseless head. I hope they will set it on the Scotch gate, that I may look, even after death, to the blue hills of my own country that I love so dearly.'

The sound of wheels and horses' feet was now heard in the courtyard of the castle. 'As I have told you why you must not follow me and my time flies fast, tell me how you found poor Flora?'

Waverley, with a voice interrupted by suffocating sensations, gave some account of the state of her mind.

'Poor Flora, she could have borne her own death, but not mine. Waverley, you can never know the purity of feeling which combines two orphans like Flora and me, left alone in the world and being all in all to each other. But her strong sense of duty and loyalty will give new nerve to her after the acute sensation of this parting has passed. She will then think of Fergus as of the heroes of our race upon whose deeds she loved to dwell.'

'Shall she not see you then? She seemed to expect it.'

'A necessary deceit will spare her the last dreadful parting. I could not part from her without tears, and I cannot bear that these men should think they have the power to extort them. She was made to believe she would see me at a later hour, and this letter will apprise her that all is over.'

An officer appeared and intimated that the High Sheriff waited before the gate to claim the bodies of Fergus MacIvor and Evan Maccombich. Supporting Edward by the arm and followed by Evan Dhu and the priest, Fergus moved down the stairs of the tower, the soldiers bringing up the rear. The court was occupied by a squadron of dragoons and a battalion of infantry. Within their ranks was the sledge on which the prisoners were to be drawn to the place of execution, about a mile distant from Carlisle. It was painted black and drawn by a white horse. At one end sat the Executioner, a horrid looking fellow with the broad axe in his hand. At the other was an empty seat for two persons. Through the dark Gothic archway were seen on horseback the High Sheriff and his attendants. 'This is well GOT UP for a closing scene,' said Fergus, smiling disdainfully as he gazed around. Evan Dhu exclaimed, 'These are the very chields that galloped off at Gladsmuir ere we could kill a dozen of them. They look bold enough now.'

Fergus embraced Waverley, kissed him on each side of his face, and stepped nimbly into his place. Evan sat down by his side. As Fergus waved his hand to Edward the ranks closed around the sledge, and the whole procession began to move forward. There was a momentary stop at the gateway, while the governor of the castle handed over the criminals to the civil power. 'God save King George!' said the High Sheriff. When the formality concluded Fergus stood erect in the sledge and with a steady voice, replied, 'God save King *James*!' These were the last words which Waverley heard him speak.

---

[1] Although Scotland preserved its own legal system after the 1707 Act of Union, in 1708 the British parliament introduced the English law of treason into Scotland along with more severe punishment, including live disembowelling.

The procession resumed. The dead march was instantly heard and its melancholy sounds were mingled with a muffled peal tolled from the neighbouring cathedral. The sound of the military music died away as the procession moved on. The sullen clang of the bells was soon heard to sound alone.

Waverley stood in the empty courtyard as if stupefied, his eyes fixed upon the dark pass where he had seen the last glimpse of his friend. At length, he pulled his hat over his eyes, and walked as swiftly as he could through the empty streets till he regained his inn, then threw himself into an apartment and bolted the door.

In about an hour and a half, the sound of the drums and fifes performing a lively air, and the confused murmur of the crowd which now filled the streets, apprised him that all was over.

In the evening the priest visited and informed him that he did so by directions of his deceased friend, to assure him that Fergus MacIvor had died as he had lived and remembered his friendship to the last. He added he had seen Flora, who seemed more composed since all was over. Waverley forced on this good man a ring of some value and a sum of money to be employed in the services of the Catholic Church for the memory of his friend.

The next morning ere daylight he took leave of Carlisle, promising to himself never again to enter its walls. He dared hardly to look back towards the battlements of the gate under which he passed. 'They're no there,' said Alick Polwarth, who guessed the cause of the dubious look which Waverley cast backward. 'The heads are ower the Scotch yate. It's a great pity of Evan Dhu, who was a very weel-meaning good-natured man, to be a Hielandman, and indeed so was the Laird o' Glennaquoich for that matter, when he was na in ane o' his tirrivies.'

chapter twenty-three

Dulce Domum

The horror with which Waverley left Carlisle softened by degrees into melancholy, accelerated by the painful yet soothing task of writing to Rose, and endeavouring to place it in a light which might grieve her without shocking her imagination. The picture which he drew for her benefit he gradually familiarised to his own mind, and his next letters were more cheerful. When he reached his native country he began to experience that pleasure which almost all feel who return to a verdant, highly populated country from scenes of waste desolation or of melancholy grandeur. But how were those feelings enhanced when he recognised the old oaks of Waverley Chase, thought with what delight he should introduce Rose to all his favourite haunts, beheld the towers of the venerable hall arise above the woods, and finally threw himself into the arms of his venerable relations.

The happiness of their meeting was not tarnished by a single word of reproach. Whatever pain Sir Everard and Rachael had felt during Waverley's perilous engagement with the Chevalier, it assorted too well with their principles to incur censure. Colonel Talbot had smoothed the way for Edward's favourable reception by dwelling upon his bravery and generosity at Preston until the imagination of the Baronet and his sister ranked the exploits of Edward with those of the vaunted heroes of their line.

The appearance of Waverley, dignified by military discipline, had acquired an athletic and hardy character which delighted all the inhabitants of Waverley Honour. They crowded to see him and sing his praises. All was now in a bustle to prepare for the nuptials. The match seemed to the Baronet and Mrs Rachael in the highest degree eligible, having every recommendation but wealth, of which they themselves had more than enough.

It was more than two months ere Waverley alighted once more at the mansion of the Laird of Duchran to claim the hand of his plighted bride. The day of the marriage was fixed for the sixth after his arrival. The Baron of Bradwardine felt a little hurt that including the family of the Duchran and all the immediate vicinity who had title to be present, there could not have been above thirty persons collected. 'When he was married,' he observed, 'three hundred horse of gentlemen born, besides servants and some score or two of Highland lairds were present on the occasion.' But his pride found some consolation in reflecting that it might give fear and offence to the ruling powers if they were to collect together kith, kin and allies of their houses.

The marriage took place on the appointed day. The Reverend Mr Rubrick, chaplain to the Baron, had the satisfaction to unite their hands, and Frank Stanley acted as bridesman. Lady Emily and Colonel Talbot had proposed being present, but her health was found inadequate to the journey. In amends, it was arranged that Edward Waverley and his lady should in their way to Waverley Honour spend a few days at an estate which Colonel Talbot had been tempted to purchase in Scotland as a very great bargain.

chapter twenty-four

This is no mine ain house, I ken by the bigging o't.

OLD SONG[1]

The nuptial house travelled in great style. There was a coach and six upon the newest pattern which Sir Everard had presented to his nephew, and the family coach of Mr Rubrick, both crowded with ladies. There were gentlemen

---

[1] Traditional. A Jacobite version is included in James Hogg, *The Jacobite Relics of Scotland*, 1819.

on horseback, with their servants, to the number of a score. Baillie Macwheeble met them on the road to entreat that they would pass by his house. The Baron stared and said his son and he would certainly pay their compliments to the Baillie, but could not think of bringing with them the 'hail matrimonial procession'. He added that as he had understood the Barony had been sold, he was glad to see his old friend Duncan had regained his situation under the new proprietor. The Baillie ducked and fidgeted, and then again insisted upon his invitation until the Baron could not refuse to consent, without making evident sensations which he was anxious to conceal.

He fell into a deep study as they approached the top of the avenue, and was only startled from it by observing that the battlements were replaced, the ruins cleared away and that the two great stone Bears had resumed their posts over the gateway. 'Now this new proprietor,' he said to Edward, 'has shown mair gusto, as the Italians call it, in the short time he has had this domain than that hound Malcolm – and now I talk of hounds, is not yon Ban and Buscar come scouping up the avenue with Davie Gellatly?'

'And I vote we go to meet them, sir, for I believe the present master of the house is Colonel Talbot, who will expect to see us. We hesitated to mention to you that he had purchased your ancient patrimonial property, and if you do not incline to visit him we can pass on to the Baillie's.'

The Baron drew a long breath, took a long snuff, and observed since they had brought him so far, he could not pass the Colonel's gate, and would be happy to see the new master of his old tenants. He alighted and gave his arm to his daughter.

Not only had the felled trees been removed but their stumps had been grubbed up and the earth round them sown with grass. The marks of devastation were already totally obliterated. There was a similar reformation in David Gellatly, who met them now and then stopping to admire the new suit which graced his person, in the same colours as formerly but bedizened fine enough to have served Touchstone himself.[1] He danced up first to the Baron and then to Rose, passing his hands over his clothes crying, 'Bra', bra' Davie' and scarce able to sing a bar for the breathless extravagance of his joy. The dogs acknowledged their old master with a thousand gambols. 'Upon my conscience, Rose, the gratitude o' thae dumb brutes and of that puir innocent brings tears into my auld een. I'm obliged to Colonel Talbot for putting my hounds into such good condition, and likewise for puir Davie.'

As he spoke, Lady Emily and her husband met the party at the lower gate with a thousand welcomes. She apologised for having used a little art to wile them back to a place which might awaken painful reflections – 'But as it was to change masters, we were very desirous that the Baron –'

'Mr Bradwardine, madam, if you please,' said the old gentleman.

'Mr Bradwardine, then, and Mrs Waverley should see and approve of what we have done towards restoring the mansion to its former state.'

When the Baron entered the court all seemed as much as possible restored to

---

[1] Jester in Shakespeare's *As You Like It*.

the state in which he had left it some months before. The pigeon-house was replenished, the fountain played, and all the Bears were replaced and repaired with so much care that they bore no tokens of the violence which had descended upon them. The house itself had been thoroughly repaired, as well as the gardens. The Baron gazed in silent wonder. At length he addressed Colonel Talbot.

'While I acknowledge my obligation to you for the restoration of these bears, I cannot but marvel that you have nowhere established your own crest, Colonel Talbot.' He took another long pinch of snuff. The Colonel, the Baron, Rose, Lady Emily with young Stanley and the Baillie entered the house, while Edward and the rest of the party remained on the terrace to examine a new green-house stocked with the finest plants. 'What I mean to say, Colonel Talbot' said the Baron, 'is that yours is an ancient descent, and since you have lawfully acquired the estate for you and yours, which I have lost for me and mine, I wish it may remain in your name as many centuries as it has done in that of the late proprietors.'

'That is very handsome, Mr Bradwardine.'

'And yet I cannot but marvel that you, Colonel, should have chosen to establish your household gods in a manner to expatriate yourself.'

'Why really, sir, I do not see why, to keep the secret of these foolish boys, Waverley and Stanley, and my wife, one old soldier should impose upon another. You must know that I have so much prejudice in favour of my native country that the sum of money which I advanced to the seller of this extensive barony has only purchased for me a box in –shire called Brerewood Lodge, the chief merit of which is that it is a very few miles of Waverley Honour.'

'Who then, in the name of Heaven, has bought this property?'

'That,' said the Colonel, 'it is this gentleman's profession to explain.'

The Baillie had all this while shifted from one foot to another with great impatience, 'like a hen upon a het girdle', and chuckling like the said hen in all the glory of laying an egg, he now drew from his pocket a formidable budget of papers and untied the red tape with a hand trembling with eagerness. 'Here is the disposition and assignation by Malcolm Bradwardine of Inch Grabbit, signed and tested in terms of the statute, whereby for a certain sum of sterling paid to him he has disponed, alienated and conveyed the whole estate and barony of Bradwardine, Tully Veolan and others, with the fortalice and manor-place –'

'For God's sake to the point, sir. I have all that by heart,' said the Colonel.

'To Cosmo Comyne Bradwardine, Esq' pursued the Baillie, 'his heirs and assignees, simply and irredeemably –'

'Pray read short, sir.'

'I read as short as is consistent with style – Under the burden and reservation always –'

'Mr Macwheeble, this would outlast a Russian winter. In short, Mr Bradwardine, your family estate is your own once more in full property, only burdened with the sum advanced to re-purchase it, which I understand is utterly disproportioned to its value. Which sum being advanced by Mr Edward Waverley, chiefly from the price of his father's property which I bought from him, is secured to his lady your daughter and her family by this marriage.'

'It is a Catholic security,' shouted the Baillie, 'to Rose Comyne Bradwardine, alias Waverley, in liferent, and the children of the said marriage in fee, and I made up a wee bit minute of an ante-nuptial contract so it cannot be subject to reduction after.'

It is difficult to say whether the worthy Baron was most delighted with the restitution of his property or with the generosity that left him unfettered to dispose of it after his death. When his first joy and astonishment were over, his thoughts turned to the unworthy heir male who, he pronounced, 'has sold his birth-right for a mess o' pottage.'

'But wha cookit the parridge for him?' exclaimed the Baillie. 'Wha but your honour's to command, Duncan Macwheeble? I circumvented them, I played at bogle about the bush wi' them, I cajoled them. I have gien Inch Grabbit and Jamie Howie a bonnie begunk. I scared them wi' our wild tenantry and the MacIvors that are but ill-settled yet, till they durst na gang ower the doorstane after gloaming. I beflum'd them wi' Colonel Talbot – wad they offer to keep up the price again the Duke's friend?'

The Baron was now summoned to do the honours of Tully Veolan to new guests. These were Major Melville and the Reverend Mr Morton. The shouts of the villagers were also heard beneath in the courtyard, for Saunders Saunderson, who had kept the secret for several days with laudable prudence, had unloosed his tongue.

While Edward received Major Melville with politeness, and the clergyman with the most grateful kindness, his father-in-law looked a little uncertain as to how he should answer the claims of hospitality to his guests. Lady Emily relieved him by intimating that she hoped the Baron would approve of the entertainment she had ordered in expectation of so many guests, and that they would find such accommodations provided as might support the ancient hospitality of Tully Veolan. It is impossible to describe the pleasure which this assurance gave the Baron, who with an air of gallantry offered his arm to the fair speaker and led the way, in something between a stride and a minuet step, into a large dining parlour, followed by all the rest of the good company.

All here, as well as in the other apartments, had been disposed as much as possible according to the old arrangement. There was one addition to this fine old apartment, however, which drew tears into the Baron's eyes. It was a huge and spirited painting representing Fergus MacIvor and Waverley in Highland dress, the scene a wild and mountainous pass, down which the clan were descending in the background. The ardent and impetuous character of the unfortunate Chief of Glennaquoich was finely contrasted with the contemplative expression of his happier friend. Beside this painting hung the arms which Waverley had borne in the unfortunate civil war.

The dinner was excellent. Saunderson attended in full costume with all the former servants who had been collected, excepting one or two who had not been heard of since the affair of Culloden. The wine was pronounced to be superb, and it had been contrived that the Bear of the fountain in the courtyard should play excellent brandy punch for the benefit of the lower orders.

When the dinner was over, the Baron, about to propose a toast, cast a sorrowful look upon the sideboard. 'Those must be thankful who have saved life and lands,' he said, 'yet I cannot but regret an old heirloom –'

Here the Baron's elbow was gently touched by his Major Domo and turning round he beheld in his hands the celebrated Blessed Bear of Bradwardine. I question if the recovery of his estate afforded him more rapture. A tear mingled with the wine which the Baron filled, as he proposed a cup of gratitude to Colonel Talbot and 'The prosperity of the united houses of Waverley Honour and Bradwardine!'

chapter twenty-five

A Postscript, Which Should Have Been a Preface

Our journey is now finished, gentle reader, yet, like the driver who has received his full hire, I still linger near you and make with becoming diffidence a trifling additional claim upon your good nature.

There is no European nation which, within the course of half a century or little more, has undergone so complete a change as this kingdom of Scotland. The effects of the insurrection of 1745, the destruction of the patriarchal power of the Highland chiefs, the abolition of the heritable jurisdictions of the Lowland nobility and barons, and the total eradication of the Jacobite party, which long continued to pride themselves upon maintaining ancient Scottish manners and customs, commenced this innovation. The general influx of wealth and extension of commerce have since rendered the present people of Scotland a class of beings as different from their grandfathers as the existing English are from those of Queen Elizabeth's time. The change, though steadily and rapidly progressive, has nevertheless been gradual, and like those who drift down a deep and smooth river, we are not aware of progress until we fix our eye on the now distant point from which we set out. Those who still cherished a lingering though hopeless attachment to the house of Stuart have now almost entirely vanished, and with them, doubtless, much absurd political prejudice, but also many living examples of disinterested attachment to the principles of loyalty which they received from their fathers, and of old Scottish faith, hospitality, worth and honour.

It was my accidental lot, though not born a Highlander, to reside during my childhood and youth among persons of the above description, and now I have embodied in imaginary scenes and ascribed to fictitious characters a part of the incidents which I then received from those who were actors in them. The exchange of mutual protection between a Highland gentleman and an officer of rank in the king's service, together with the spirited manner in which the latter asserted his right to return the favour he had received, is literally true. Scarce a gentleman who was 'in hiding' after the battle of Culloden, but could tell a tale of strange concealments, and of wild escapes as extraordinary as any which I have ascribed to my heroes. Of this the escape of Charles Edward himself is the most striking example. The accounts of the battle of Preston and the skirmish at Clifton are taken from intelligent eye-witnesses and corrected from the History of the Rebellion by the late author of *Douglas*.[1] The Lowland Scottish gentlemen and the subordinate characters are drawn from the general habits of the period, of which I witnessed some remnants in my younger days, and partly gathered from tradition. It has been my object to describe these persons by their habits, manners and feelings.

I feel no confidence, however, in the manner in which I have executed my purpose. Indeed, so little was I satisfied with my production that I laid it aside, and only found it again by mere accident, after it had been mislaid for several years. I would willingly persuade myself that the preceding work will not be found altogether uninteresting. To elder persons it will recall scenes and characters familiar to their youth, and to the rising generation the tale may present some idea of the manners of their forefathers.

As I have inverted the usual arrangements, placing these remarks at the end of the work to which they refer, I will venture on a second violation of form, by closing the whole with a Dedication:

These volumes

being respectfully inscribed

to

our Scottish Addison

Henry Mackenzie

by

an unknown admirer

of

his genius

The End

---

[1] John Home (1722–1808), best known for his tragedy *Douglas*, wrote *The History of the Rebellion in the Year 1745*, 1802.

Glossary of Scots, Gaelic, dialect and unusual words

Words explained in the text or footnotes are not included

Accolade embrace

Ahint behind

Aide-de-camp military aid to a general

Ain own

Ane one

Anent concerning, about

Apotheosis deification

Architrave moulding round an arch or door

Auld old

Bagganet bayonet

Bag-wig wig with the hair at the back confined in a bag.

Bairn child

Baron-baillie baron's deputy

Bartizan parapet or projecting gallery

Bean Gaelic *bàn* fair-haired, white

Beflum deceive through persuasive language

Beg Gaelic *beag* small

Begunk trick

Bhaird Gaelic *bàrd* bard

Bicker bowl

Bickering gleaming, sparkling

Bide stay

Biggin building

Bluid blood

Bluidy bloody

Boddle coin worth two pence Scots, ie something of little value

Bogle about the bush game of hide-and-seek

Box small country house

Bra fine

Brake broke

Brander grill, broil

Breeks breeches, trousers

Brogue shoe made from untanned hide

Bruckle brittle

Bruick enjoy possession of

Cadger travelling merchant, carter

Cailliach Gaelic *cailleach* old woman

Cam came

Canny cautious, shrewd

Cantrap trip

Carl or **carle** man, fellow

Cateran Highland raider, marauder

Chield fellow, young man

Chlain Gaelic *clann*, clan, literally children

Clamhewit blow, beating

Claymore Gaelic *claidheamh-mór* great sword, Highland broadsword

Cockyleeky chicken and leek soup

Coghling coughing

Collop slice of meat; **Scotch collops**

slices of veal cooked with an egg and lemon sauce

Coronach Gaelic *corranach* lament, funeral song

Corps de garde French, body of soldiers on guard duty

Corrie Gaelic *coire*, cauldron or place resembling one, a hollow in a mountainside or between mountains

Cow yere cracks stop the gossip, cut the cackle

Creagh Gaelic *creach* raid

Cry barley in a brulzie call for a truce in a quarrel

Curragh coracle, boat made from hide stretched over a wicker frame

Cut-lugged crop-eared

Deevil's buckie obstinate person

Deil Devil

Dern secret, dark

Dhu Gaelic *dubh* black, dark

Dinnle shake, vibrate

Dispone make over, legally convey

Doch and dorroch Gaelic *deoch an dorais* stirrup cup

Doiled confused, crazy

Doon down

Doorstane doorstep, threshold

Dorlach bundle, pack

Dow dove, sweetheart

Dowff dull, melancholy

Drap drop

Droghling walking unsteadily

Duinhé-Wassell Gaelic *duin' uasal* gentleman

Dulce domum Latin, sweet home

Een eyes

Embro Edinburgh

Evite avoid, escape

Far ben on close terms

Fauld fold, pen

Fendy able to fend for oneself, resourceful

Fiat command

Flemit chased, put to flight

Foun Cumbrian, fun

Frae from

Fule fool

Fusee light musket

Gae go

Gaid went

Gait, gate way

Gambado boot, gaiter

Gaun going

Gane gone

Gang go

Gar make

Gare! gare! Place à Monseigneur French, Look out! Look out! Make way for his royal highness

Gear possessions

Ghaist ghost

Gien given

Gill quarter pint

Gillie-wet-foot Gaelic *gille-cas-fliuch* boy or servant with wet feet from carrying his chieftain across a stream.

Gin if

Gite French, lodging

Gled kite, or other bird of prey

Goud gold

Grace cup cup signifying the last drink at the end of a meal

Graning groaning

Gree agree

Grippal greedy, mean

Guid good

Gulpin simpleton, credulous person

Hag section of a wood marked for felling

Hail whole, sound

Hallan inner wall, partition

Hantle large number, a great deal

Harst harvest

Helots serfs of the Spartans

Heritor landowner

Het hot

Ho Cumbrian, you

Hurley-house ruinous house

In loco parentis Latin, in the position of a parent

Ither other

Ken know

Kittle tickle; tricky

Lang long

Lealand unploughed land

Levee morning reception

Loike Cumbrian, like

Loon fellow, scoundrel

Louis d'ors French gold coin, roughly the value of a guinea

Mains estate's home farm

Mae more

Mair more

Mart cow or ox fattened for slaughter

Maugre in spite of

Maun must

Mavourneen Gaelic *Mo mhuirnean* my darling

Meal-ark meal chest

Merry-bout drinking session

Mickle large, great deal of

Mon man

Mony many

Naig nag

Nean Cumbrian, none

Neete Cumbrian, night

Of that ilk of that place or name

Ony any

Orra occasional, odd

Ower over

Paitrick partridge

Palinode a poem of retraction or recantation

Parridge porridge

Pibroch bagpipe music

Pier-glass large mirror

Pinners flaps on a woman's headdress

Pit put

Plack Scottish coin worth a third of an English penny

Presbytery church court

Press cupboard

Pretty fine, gallant

Public public house, tavern

Puir poor

Quondam Latin, former

Ranting noisy, boisterous

Reel in a bottle cylinder in a bottle

Resiling withdrawing

Rigg strip of land

Route fashionable social gathering

Runthereout vagabond, rover

Sae so

Sair sore

Sans tache French, without stain, spotless

Sark shirt, shift

Sassenach Gaelic *sasunnach* Englishman, speaker of English

Scathed damaged, harmed

Scouping bounding, skipping

Scutcheon in heraldry, a shield bearing a coat of arms

Sectory member of a dissenting sect

Sel self

Shanks legs

Sic, siccan such

Sidier dhu Gaelic *saighdear dhub* black soldier, soldier of an independent Highland company

Sidier roy Gaelic *saighdear rhuadh* red soldier, 'redcoat'

Sike rivulet

Siller silver

Sliochd Gaelic, offspring, tribe

Sma' small

Sowens oat husks and meal soaked in water and then fermented

Speering asking, inquiring

Stane stone

Strathspey slow reel

Sybil ancient prophetess

Tacksman leaseholder, in the Highlands usually holding a large lease from the clan chief which was sublet

Taiglit tired

Tak take

Tappit hen lidded jug, usually pewter, with a knob in the shape of a hen's crest

Target shield

Tauld told

Tearing reckless

Teil devil

Till to

Tirrivie tantrum

Tocherless without a dowry

Trepanned trapped, ensnared

Trindling trundling

Trow trust, believe

Truckle submit

Twa two

Untill to

Ursa Major Latin, Great Bear

Usquebaugh Gaelic *uisge beatha* water of life ie whisky

Wa' wall

Wad would

Wada would have

Wadsetter holder of a wadset or mortgage

Walise valise, bag for attaching to a saddle

Wanchancy dangerous, risky

Ware waste

Waur worse

Weel well

Wha who

Whilk which

Whilome once, formerly

Winna won't

Wot know

Wrang wrong

Yer your

Ivanhoe

Sir Walter Scott
Newly adapted for the modern reader
by David Purdie
ISBN 978-1-908373-58-8 HBK £19.99
ISBN 978-1-908373-26-7 PBK £9.99

Fight on, brave knights. Man dies, but glory lives!

Ivanhoe has been cut down to size in this modern retelling of Scott's classic novel: the original text has been slashed from an epic 194,000 words to a more manageable 95,000.

Banished from his father's court, Wilfred of Ivanhoe returns from Richard the Lionheart's Crusades to claim love, justice and glory. Tyrannical Norman knights, indolent Saxon nobles and the usurper Prince John stand in his way. A saga of tournaments and melees, chivalry and love, nobility and merry men, Ivanhoe's own quest soon becomes a battle for the English throne itself…

This is exactly what's needed in order to rescue Sir Walter Scott.
ALEXANDER McCALL SMITH

Knights getting shorter… [Ivanhoe] has been brought up to date by Professor David Purdie who is president of the Sir Walter Scott Society and should know the ropes.
THE HERALD

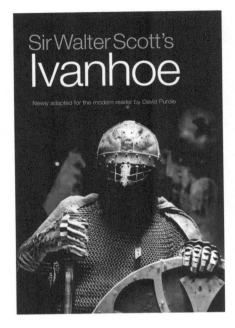

I applaud this new, shorter version of Ivanhoe which makes this wonderful novel, once so popular, accessible to a new generation of readers who will be able to enjoy its classic blend of history and romance.
PROFESSOR GRAHAM TULLOCH, Editor of the Edinburgh Edition of the Waverley novels